PRAISE F

MW01092944

"Crackling with tension from the very start, Reay's latest is a twisty, smart read infused with the heady atmosphere of the 1970s London art world. The novel deftly explores the nature of artistic genius, the ethics of deception, and the cost of speaking up for what is true. A gem of a read!"

—Fiona Davis, *New York Times* bestselling author of *The Stolen Queen*

"Art . . . London . . . seventies glam . . . Yes, please. *The English Masterpiece* by Katherine Reay has *all* the goodies—especially for historical fiction lovers and art aficionados. One young woman, an art curator's assistant at a famed national gallery, is in *way* over her head as she races to expose the truth behind a Picasso masterpiece: Is it a forgery? Will she jeopardize her budding career and take down those around her in the process? Buckle your seatbelt as all hell breaks loose. Readers will relish Reay's stylish prose and rich, unforgettable characters amid a propulsive cat-and-mouse chase into the opulent and obsessive world of multimillion-dollar art and deception."

—Lisa Barr, *New York Times* bestselling author of *The Goddess of Warsaw*

"A taut and thrilling game of cat and mouse ensues in Katherine Reay's *The English Masterpiece*, a story of reality, illusion, and imposters set in the winding streets of seventies London. Reay is a master at the top of her game!"

—Bryn Turnbull, author of *The Berlin Apartment*

"An exhibit honoring the recently deceased Picasso and an alleged forgery at the Tate sets the stage for this historical page-turner. Just when you think the stakes couldn't get any higher Reay ratchets up the tension even more. With an eye for the telling details, this author transports the reader back to London in the 1970s. Art lovers and historical fiction fans alike will find this book impossible to put down."

—Renee Rosen, *USA TODAY* bestselling
author of *Let's Call Her Barbie*

"Like a true Picasso, Katherine Reay's *The English Masterpiece* is layered, compelling, imaginative, and filled with intrigue."

—Jenni Walsh, *USA TODAY* bestselling
author of *Unsinkable* and *Ace, Marvel, Spy*

"An exhilarating tale that will keep readers spellbound until the very last page, *The English Masterpiece* is a fresh and thought-provoking read. In a story that explores what it means to live and create authentically, Katherine Reay has given us an underdog heroine to root for as she navigates London's prestigious, and increasingly dangerous, art scene, unraveling a mystery where nothing is what it seems. I could not put this book down."

—Kristin Beck, author of *The Winter Orphans*

"*The English Masterpiece* is a stylish mystery that plunges the reader into the glamorous world of million-dollar art and the inner workings of a famed national gallery. A single sentence dooms the career of the young woman who utters it. As Lily Summers tries to clear her name, she discovers pieces of a puzzle that attract more danger. A thoroughly enjoyable, inventive plot that will keep you up all night."

—Janie Chang, author of *The Phoenix Crown*

"*The English Masterpiece* is a showstopper of a book. All the elements needed for a spectacular story: the drama and intrigue of the Tate Modern and the London art scene, a forged Picasso, and two women's careers caught in the balance. Reay has deftly crafted a fast-paced escapade that will propel readers from the gripping first pages through the satisfying conclusion. Not to be missed!"

—Aimie K. Runyan, internationally
bestselling author of *The Wandering
Season* and *Mademoiselle Eiffel*

"Both deeply moving and edge-of-your-seat suspenseful, *The Berlin Letters* is an eloquent reminder of the brutal totalitarianism of Soviet Communism and the unsung heroes who fought to tear down the Iron Curtain and free Eastern Europe."

—Beatriz Williams, *New York Times*
bestselling author of *The Summer Wives*

"*The Berlin Letters* is a thrilling read that has it all: secret codes, espionage, and a fascinating glimpse into the world behind the Berlin Wall. Katherine Reay always delivers well-researched historical fiction with a perfect blend of heartwarming characters and fast-paced action. Fans of historical spy novels are going to love this enthralling read!"

—Madeline Martin, *New York Times* bestselling
author of *The Keeper of Hidden Books*

"Surrounding the Cold War and the fall of the Berlin Wall, Reay's action-packed novel is told in dual-narrative form between a daughter with a rebellious streak and her father's buried secrets. A story of hope and resilience, *The Berlin Letters* is a thrilling story full of intrigue, espionage, code-breaking, and at its core, loyalty and humanity. You won't be able to put it down!"

—Eliza Knight, *USA TODAY* and international
bestselling author of *Starring Adele Astaire*

"Both a gripping tale of espionage and a moving portrait of a family ripped apart, *The Berlin Letters* offers readers a fascinating glimpse at a fraught period of all-too-recent history and the people caught in the crosshairs of geopolitics who chose, each in their own way, to fight back."

—Jennifer Thorne and Lee Kelly,
co-authors of *The Antiquity Affair*

"In her nail-biting latest . . . Reay builds an immersive world behind the Iron Curtain, full of competing loyalties and a constant, chilling sense of paranoia. Readers will be enthralled."

—*Publishers Weekly* for *A Shadow in Moscow*

"This book is a consummately rendered and captivating espionage account of the Cold War, told from the perspective of two sympathetic and admirable women . . . Filled with surprise twists and turns, and ultimately uplifting and inspiring, I found this superlative novel an enduring gem. Five stars!"

—Historical Novel Society for *A Shadow in Moscow*

"Rich with fascinating historical detail and unforgettable characters, *A Shadow in Moscow* deftly explores two female spies who will risk everything to change the world. Katherine Reay eloquently portrays the incredible contributions of women in history, the extraordinary depths of love, and, perhaps most important of all, the true cost of freedom in her latest stunning page-turner. A story that will leave readers examining what they hold most dear and positively brimming with hope, this is an important, timely tour de force—and a must-read for anyone who has ever wondered if just one person can make a difference."

—Kristy Woodson Harvey, *New York Times*
bestselling author of *The Wedding Veil*

"Katherine Reay's latest has it all—intrigue, twists and turns, acts of bravery and sacrificial love, and an unforgettable Cold War setting with clever, daring women at the helm. An expertly delivered page-turner by a true master of the craft!"

—Susan Meissner, *USA TODAY* bestselling author
of *The Nature of Fragile Things*, for *A Shadow in Moscow*

"This riveting story of two female spies operating in Moscow during different eras has everything you could ever want in a novel—suspense, intrigue, compelling characters, exotic settings, deep insight, and gasp-inducing plot twists. A word of advice: Clear your calendar before opening *A Shadow in Moscow*. Once you start, you won't be able to stop until you regretfully reach the last page of Katherine Reay's masterfully written novel."

—Marie Bostwick, *New York Times* bestselling author of *Esme Cahill Fails Spectacularly*

"Spellbinding. Reay's fast-paced foray into the past cleverly reveals a family's secrets and how a pivotal moment shaped future generations. Readers who enjoy engrossing family mystery should take note."

—*Publishers Weekly* for *The London House*

"*The London House* is a tantalizing tale of deeply held secrets, heartbreak, redemption, and the enduring way that family can both hurt and heal us."

—Kristin Harmel, *New York Times* bestselling author of *The Forest of Vanishing Stars*

"*The London House* is a thrilling excavation of long-held family secrets that proves sometimes the darkest corners of our pasts are balanced with slivers of light. Arresting historical fiction destined to thrill fans of Erica Roebuck and Pam Jenoff."

—Rachel McMillan, author of *The London Restoration*

"Expertly researched and perfectly paced, *The London House* is a remarkable novel about love and loss and the way history—and secrets—can impact a family and ultimately change its future."

—Syrie James, bestselling author of *The Lost Memoirs of Jane Austen*

"The town of Winsome reminds me of Jan Karon's Mitford, with its endearing characters, complex lives, and surprises where you don't expect them. You'll root for these characters and will be sad to leave this charming town."

—Lauren K. Denton, bestselling author
of *The Hideaway*, for *Of Literature and Lattes*

"In her ode to small towns and second chances, Katherine Reay writes with affection and insight about the finer things in life."

—Karen Dukess, author of *The Last Book Party*,
for *Of Literature and Lattes*

"Reay understands the heartbeat of a bookstore."

—Baker Book House for *The Printed Letter Bookshop*

"*The Printed Letter Bookshop* is both a powerful story and a dazzling experience. I want to give this book to every woman I know—I adored falling into Reay's world, words, and bookstore."

—Patti Callahan Henry, bestselling author

THE ENGLISH MASTERPIECE

ALSO BY KATHERINE REAY

Dear Mr. Knightley

Lizzy & Jane

The Brontë Plot

A Portrait of Emily Price

The Austen Escape

The Printed Letter Bookshop

Of Literature & Lattes

The London House

A Shadow in Moscow

The Berlin Letters

NONFICTION

Awful Beautiful Life with Becky Powell

THE ENGLISH MASTERPIECE

A NOVEL

KATHERINE REAY

HARPER MUSE

The English Masterpiece

Copyright © 2025 by Katherine Reay

Published by Harper Muse, an imprint of HarperCollins Focus LLC.

This book is a work of fiction. The characters, incidents, and dialogue are drawn from the author's imagination and are not to be construed as real. Any resemblance to actual events or persons, living or dead, is entirely coincidental.

Any internet addresses (websites, blogs, etc.) in this book are offered as a resource. They are not intended in any way to be or imply an endorsement by HarperCollins Focus LLC, nor does HarperCollins Focus LLC vouch for the content of these sites for the life of this book.

Library of Congress Cataloging-in-Publication Data

Names: Reay, Katherine, 1970- author.
Title: The English masterpiece: a novel / Katherine Reay.
Description: Nashville: Harper Muse, 2025. | Summary: "Set in the art world of 1970s London, The English Masterpiece is a fast-paced read to the end, full of glamour and secrets, tensions and lies, as one young woman races against the clock to uncover the truth about a Picasso masterpiece. Perfect for fans of Kate Quinn and Ariel Lawhon" --Provided by publisher.
Identifiers: LCCN 2024056805 (print) | LCCN 2024056806 (ebook) | ISBN 9781400347278 (trade paperback) | ISBN 9781400347285 (epub) | ISBN 9781400347292
Subjects: LCGFT: Novels.
Classification: LCC PS3618.E23 E54 2025 (print) | LCC PS3618.E23 (ebook) | DDC 813/.6--dc23/eng/20241127
LC record available at https://lccn.loc.gov/2024056805
LC ebook record available at https://lccn.loc.gov/2024056806

Printed in the United States of America

25 26 27 28 29 LBC 5 4 3 2 1

TO MOM AND DAD,
HAPPY 60TH ANNIVERSARY!
ALL MY LOVE,
KATHERINE

Art is a lie that makes us realize the truth.
—Pablo Picasso

Everything is expressed through relationships.
—Piet Mondrian

CHAPTER 1

Lily

come see me as soon as you arrive

After sliding my boss's note into my top desk drawer, I walk down the corridor and tap on Diana's door and, as usual, pause for a second or two before I open it. I used to wait until she called me in, but over the last couple of years—as we've come to work more closely together—it feels natural and efficient to simply signal my entrance rather than ask permission. After all, many times she's on the telephone. My discreetly stepping in feels more respectful than interrupting her.

As usual, this morning she's on the telephone, nodding and murmuring her agreement to something said across the line. Her face is dour, stern. Her slender shoulders curl in as if she's protecting herself. What's gone wrong so early on a Monday? I settle myself in the chair across from her desk, lay my notepad in my lap, and, pressing my pencil atop it, sit ready to take notes.

The call stretches on and my thoughts and eyes start to wander. Diana is the Tate Gallery's keeper of the Modern Collections—the first female keeper in the United Kingdom at any major institution—and her office reflects her stature and her tastes. It's a beautiful space. My focus first settles upon her desk. Despite sitting across from it hundreds of times, I never tire of taking it in. It's massive, imperious, and simply stunning. It's not fluted or curved, as George IV designs aren't frilly, but its formidable bulk, wood inlays, and detailing convey delicacy nonetheless. Power too. A dichotomy held in perfect balance by both this impressive desk and the woman who owns it—because she must own it. Otherwise such a valuable antique, if from the Gallery's collection, would certainly grace Director Browning's office rather than hers.

We've all heard the rumors. Family money. Old European roots. Hohenberg ties and generational estates sprinkled from east to west along the Danube. Diana has let a little of her history slip out over our five years together, but just a little. The rest I've picked up from gossip around the Gallery. A wisp from those who like and respect her; most from those who want her to fail. But it's not her history so much as her reticence in sharing it that impresses me most. Her example has taught me that if you have status, money, and power, you don't need to talk about it. Rather you wear it lightly, effortlessly, like an Egyptian cotton shift on a warm summer day.

When I started working for Diana, I thought I'd won the golden ticket, a secretarial job that fit my skills in a world that means everything to me. But it's become so much more—a career beyond my wildest dreams. Not only has Diana succeeded in an industry—because make no mistake, art *is* an industry—where most women flounder, but she opened the way for me to succeed as well, promoting me to assistant keeper of the Modern Collections last December—an unheard-of promotion that sent shock waves through the London museum scene.

Her belief in me has definitely engendered my loyalty to her, and I lean forward, offering my silent support for whatever has upset her so.

She nods in understanding, and my gaze again shifts, this time from her face to the crystal dish that sits to her left, as with delicate fingers, nails varnished a demure shade of pink, she reaches for the gold key she keeps there. She disappears behind the desk to open one of the file drawers that make up its two sides.

Diana emerges again and sets the folder she's retrieved in front of her and ends the call with, *"Nosotras hablaremos pronto. Gracias."*

Spanish. I think of the Prado and the Museo de Bellas Artes de Sevilla. I think of Gaudi, Dalí, Picasso, and Miro. I think of—

"Lily?"

"Yes?" I blink.

"Pablo Picasso died yesterday."

I glance to the edge of her desk. *The Times* the security guard delivers every morning sits crumpled. I haven't read the paper yet and chastise myself for being unprepared. I had heard the great artist was ill, but I didn't expect this news. Did anyone? The gods are immortal, after all, aren't they? "I'm sorry."

She offers a slight shrug. The motion accentuates the hollows beneath her collarbone. Her lithe frame always reminds me of Twiggy, not that she'd appreciate the comparison.

"That was Antonia at the Sofia. She's pulling together an exhibit to honor him in Madrid this summer."

I lift my pen, suspecting we'll do the same.

But rather than race into the day as Diana usually does in our morning meetings, she sits back, and her face, always chiseled and in motion, falls slack. "Do you remember the doves?"

I laugh and drift into the memory. In my third year here, Picasso reached his ninetieth birthday and towns and museums all over the world conjured outlandish ways to celebrate, both to honor and to curry favor with him. Director Browning invited eighty-nine schoolchildren to line the Tate's massive front stone steps and gave each a dove to hold in homage to the great artist's *Child with a Dove.* All the children laughed and twittered, trying to control their birds with small hands, which gripped the poor creatures much too tightly. Then Richard, holding the ninetieth dove himself, called upon the children to lift their birds high and cued the press to ready their cameras. At the count of three, ninety birds were launched into the air.

Happy Birthday, Picasso!

Chaos ensued. Children laughed, screamed, and ducked. Cameras clicked. And the Tate Gallery's massive stone steps were covered in so much bird poop that it took Maintenance a full day to hand scrub it away. But it was also the best day ever! And to commemorate it, everyone in attendance was gifted a beautiful print of the painting. Mine still rests atop my desk.

"We, too, must do something." Diana pulls herself straight. "We've got a problem and this might be our solution."

I cringe. We don't have *a* problem—we have several. First of all, last week I handed my boss the expenditures and projections for the American New Realism Exhibition she installed at the Tate's Serpentine Gallery in Kensington Gardens three months ago. It's out of money—with four months left to go.

It's not Diana's fault, though she's being blamed for it. Nor is there anything wrong with the exhibit. It's bold, cutting-edge, and it's the Serpentine Gallery's first international exhibition. The initial press was stunning. But labor strikes, inflation, and mounting economic fears have people tightening their belts in all sorts of ways. Donations are down, as is attendance—the exhibit has only achieved a tenth of our conservative estimations, and enthusiasm for the arts in general is waning as well. I guess such a mindset doesn't readily welcome the new, the bold, or the American.

To counter that problem, only yesterday Diana devised an add-on for the exhibit's final month. She hopes to lessen the American influence by promoting a British one. The British Emerging Artists Exhibition. New works and new names that will shift the focus from the Yanks and put it back here at home, with the added benefit of garnering government funds and encouraging more local support. I love her idea. I have plans for her idea. I hope to be part of it—I push away the thought.

The next problem of late is that one of our major donors, Ian Campbell, the eleventh Duke of Argyll, passed away as well. His death, just this past Saturday—I did read about that one—has put our year-end fiscal plans in jeopardy, not to mention our entire 1974 budget. Anticipating it, Diana has been devising ways to bring in new donors, but it's proving a tough problem as some are calling the tensions and wariness of this time as dire as the days preceding the Second World War.

"Let's use the far north gallery room and install a small Picasso exhibition. Intimate. Exclusive. Not the showstoppers. Well, some of the showstoppers. An exhibit that will focus on *his* favorites. Personal pieces with meaning."

I start scribbling notes. "When?"

"Two weeks?" Her voice lifts in question. Part of me suspects she's asking herself, pondering the feasibility of pulling off something of this magnitude so soon, but another part believes she's asking my opinion as well.

I straighten in my chair. "It's tight, but . . ." My voice drifts away because I don't have a good answer. We need to be realistic. The logistics of such a show, even a small and intimate one, are astounding. But I also believe we can do it. Together Diana and I can do anything.

I lift my brows as I mentally list all we would need to accomplish for what she envisions to become reality within fourteen short days. "Are you wanting paintings from the Continent?"

"A few. There are a couple at the Louvre I'll request and one or two from Spain."

"You'll need *Woman in an Armchair* and at least a few of the engraved plates from the *Vollard Suite*."

"Of course." Her face regains a touch of its usual animation. "My favorites. I also want *The Old Guitarist* from the Art Institute in Chicago. It shouldn't be too hard, not for something like this. The Yanks always want to be the center of things."

I feel my nose scrunch as I murmur my agreement. But I don't truly agree. Her confidence of obtaining one of Picasso's most famous paintings from Chicago is overly optimistic. Our recent requests for loans from MoMA and the Met have been summarily—even rudely—turned down. I can't imagine Chicago's Art Institute will be more obliging, especially as it, too, will want to honor the world's greatest artist.

Pencil to paper, I mark out the days. "Shipping from America will take over a week with a rush on it. Then there's the paper-work, installation, press—"

Diana cuts me off with a wave of her hand, gold bracelets tinkling with the quick motion. "We can't let any of that stall us. This exhibition must make an impact, and that is as much about art as it is about timing." She claps her hands together and leaves them in midair, palm pressing palm. "There's a lot on the line here, Lily. For both of us."

I swallow down all my objections. She's right. Many would like to see her fail. She's also right; my star rises only as hers continues to shine.

"I'll make a few telephone calls. Return in half an hour and I'll let you know how far I've gotten."

I stand, impressed with her boldness—as always.

"Also, request catering menus from the café for an opening champagne luncheon. We'll hold it in the room next to the north gallery. Tell Jeffrey I want him to clear his landscapes for a minimum of three days for setup, then he can reinstall on the twenty-fifth."

I bite my lip, hoping she isn't serious about me telling the keeper of the British Collections to "clear his landscapes." He's one who would love to see Diana fail.

She writes a quick note and hands it to me.

picasso exhibition, 1960

"Pass that to Lucy in Archives. I want everything we have on that exhibition." She points her Montblanc pen to the note card in my hand. "That was the 'blockbuster' one, first of its kind, and it changed the art world completely. We want this one to hearken to that moment in history and remind people of the Tate's pivotal role within our nation's and the world's relationship with Picasso."

I glance at the card and an incongruent thought comes to me. "Why don't you use capital letters?"

Diana blinks. "Excuse me?"

I wave the thick card stock. "Your notes. You never use capitalization."

"I . . ." Her voice fades away. "I didn't realize I still did that."

"When did you start?" I drop into the bucket chair across from her desk again. Though infrequent, these are my favorite moments with my boss. She rarely lets anything personal escape, but when she does it's always interesting.

"When I painted." She sighs. "I wanted a signature with style so I signed my first pieces with no capitals, and I suppose I carried it on from there."

"Diana Gilden." I say her name slowly and imagine each letter in my mind. "The *d* going up, in contrast to the dipping *g*, would have been a unique look."

"Yes. No." She shakes her head as if waking. "I mean, it was a long time ago."

"Do you still paint?"

"Never." The single word is short, sharp, and tastes bitter floating between us. Its afternotes carry a hint of regret.

The office's atmosphere, which felt amicable though somber seconds ago, strikes me with prickly, sharp edges now. I tap my pencil against my notepad to draw us back to work. "I'll start my list immediately and call Catering."

"Yes. Do." She sets her pen on her desk and straightens it so it lies perfectly parallel with her leather blotter. Her hand trembles. I stand and turn away before she can see I notice.

"Call Richard's secretary and ask when he's available."

I look back and watch as she blows a soft sigh through pursed lips. "If this is going to work, somehow I'll have to convince him this is his idea."

After closing the door quietly, I rush back to my desk to call the director's secretary. Diana is right—again. If Richard says no, there is no point in going one step further. But if he says yes, we've got mountains to move in two weeks' time . . .

CHAPTER 2

Diana

Diana opens the front door of her Mayfair home and steps into the marble foyer, noting as she always does the chessboard squares of black and white. This flooring always brightens her mood. The high mirrored shine of the black. The almost translucent pureness of the white. Only the finest marbles possess that water-like luminosity. The elegance. The contrast. The game.

She drops her keys into the Royal Delft bowl centered on the Louis XV table and lays her Hermès bag next to it. She then proceeds into the kitchen to the left and there she finds, lit by a single candle, her dinner. Her stomach growls as she takes in their butler's thoughtfulness, just as she smiled with pleasure the day before at the large and opulent vase of fresh-cut flowers Branford arranged in the center of the dining room table.

This evening the small plate of cheeses, grapes, apple slices, and crackers set upon the kitchen countertop, warm and welcoming, is just what she needs. It is the type of meal that can be an appetizer or a preparation for a glorious main dish. A meal that hints at more to come. And tomorrow more will come. The main dish will arrive. After a fortnight of meticulous planning and nonstop work, the Picasso Commemorative Exhibition is ready and she anticipates luxuriating in every aspect of her success. It will be glorious. It will be world-class. It will be all hers.

Diana picks up a piece of white cheddar and savors the dry

crumbling cube as it dissolves on her tongue with a sharp tang. She follows it with a bite of cold apple and notes the interplay between sharp and sweet, soft and crisp. She runs her finger over the gold scalloped edge of the Spode plate, delighting in its candlelight burnish.

She stills, noting a coolness in the house. It feels too empty, too quiet. Where might her husband be? A quick circle of the entire floor confirms Heinrich isn't present. Not in the kitchen or the dining room. Not in his library reading. Not in the living room, sitting in his favorite wing chair by the fire enjoying a glass of sherry or port.

Diana slowly climbs the stairs to the first floor. From the landing she scans the openings to each of the three bedrooms before she steps towards her own and pauses in the doorway. The evening light shifted during her short time in the kitchen and her walk up the stairs, and orange turns to gold as the setting sun illuminates the room's deep yellow velvet draperies, making them stand out in sharp relief against the reds, umbers, and browns of the ridiculously expensive Aubusson rug Heinrich purchased last year. Initially annoyed by his extravagance, she again concedes her husband has impeccable taste. While there is nothing of her taste within their house, as Heinrich makes every decision and sees to each minute detail, she can't deny its beauty.

She runs a finger across the back of a silk brocade slipper chair of the brightest yellow stripes contrasting the softest, first-blush-of-dawn pink, and she crosses to their dressing rooms. Diana slides off her heels and feels the pleasure of her feet flattening and expanding upon the wood floor. Her toes are sore from the long day. From two weeks of long days. Funny how she hasn't noticed the pain and pressure until now—once she's made it to the end.

It is truly going to be a once-in-a-lifetime show. One so meaningful it may launch her to Richard's job. Perhaps not the Tate's directorship. Richard is still fairly young and well respected, but Pullman at the National Gallery is nearing retirement and Stanholp at the Royal Academy has gone sideways with his board. Or the new British Museum, the crowning glory of them all, as the papers recently reported, is due to open in only a few short months. Yes, maybe a directorship there. After all, this exhibition will put her name on everyone's lips—her worth proven, her bona fides assured, her promotion, at any top institution, a foregone conclusion.

Diana pulls off her ruined silk stockings and drops them into the bin. She then unlatches her gold belt and slides her Halston dress over her head. The ultra suede feels and looks like silk puddling in her hands. It's a new fabric, only this season making real inroads into fashion, and it is the freshest lilac color. After draping it across the chair in the dressing room's corner, she pulls on a shift dress of such quality Egyptian cotton that it, too, feels like silk. Leaving her feet bare, she pulls the pins from her chignon and ambles out of her bedroom back towards the stairs.

She ascends each step slowly. Is this truly the direction she wants to go? After six steps, well before the turn halfway, Wagner's dark, pounding notes fall upon her. She can't discern which opera has captured Heinrich's mood this evening, and she doesn't care. She turns and descends once more, heading towards the kitchen for her cheese, apples, and perhaps a glass of Château Margaux. She is in no mood to have her buoyancy dampened by Wagner, or by her husband, who only listens to the composer's most overdramatic operas when in such a state himself.

Warm and comfortable in the kitchen once more, with the glow of that singular candle, Diana opens that bottle of Château Margaux she craves.

"May I have a glass?"

She spins towards the kitchen door, hand to her heart. "You surprised me."

Though Heinrich is over thirty years her senior, Diana still marvels at his ability to move with catlike dexterity. Only the slight sloping of his shoulders reveals the march of time, but that is only noticeable when he's not painting. And Heinrich is always painting.

"Did you not know I was home?" He overarticulates each word, imbuing them with a seemingly innocent curiosity.

Diana twists back to the cupboard to retrieve another glass. Heinrich will know by her eyes if ever she offers a lie. "I wasn't sure. I hadn't gone up yet and was going to search the house after I poured this."

She turns back and watches his gaze travel from her bare feet to the collar of her white shift dress. "Yes," is all he says.

"Opening day is tomorrow." Diana pours him a glass, slides it towards him, then drinks deeply from her own. "It's a triumph, Heinrich. After all my work, all these years . . ."

She pops another cheese cube into her mouth and purses her lips. The contrast and interplay is unexpected; the wine brings out flavors she didn't notice in her first several bites. A very different experience than with the apple. "It's going to be perfect, and it's mine . . . Everything I've ever wanted." She lifts her glass towards the kitchen door into the darkened house beyond. "I was even thinking I might take up painting again after this. It's been on my mind and I've gotten so far in my career. Perhaps—"

She stops as Heinrich tilts his head. The motion, the expression, and the quick sharpening then widening of his eyes tells her he has other plans, or at least that hers do not please him. *Will he tell me?*

Diana steps towards her husband. "You're thinking something." She pitches her voice light and playful, knowing those are the tones he responds to best. "What is it, darling?"

"Nothing." He continues to hold her gaze. He smiles, but it's small and tight, barely reaching the corners of his mouth, and it misses his eyes completely. "I'm simply happy for you. Let's not take on tomorrow until it comes."

CHAPTER 3

Lily

We did it!

It's an exclamation moment, a bright moment—that rare moment when everything you've wanted has happened and everything you want to happen is so close you can almost touch it. It's wonder and giddy excitement, tempered by a startling satisfaction that it's not so unbelievable after all. We've worked for this. I've worked for this.

I reach for my tote bag, resting beside my desk, and dig out the new Salvatore Ferragamo shoes within. A pair of the "kitten heels" splashed across *Vogue* this spring, with that iconic Ferragamo bow to give them an extra dash of class. I saved them for today, only trying them on and crossing my room on the carpeted floor to avoid scuffing the soles.

I shouldn't have splurged on them. I shouldn't have splurged on the dress either—a demure beige-on-cream Thea Porter knock-off, but still expensive—especially as I didn't even wear it. Yet despite the change in dress, the shoes are still perfection.

My dress, however, worries me a bit. Diana requested neutral colors, a dress that would highlight rather than conflict with Picasso's strong use of color. The dress I had to wear today, made from a copy of Emilio Pucci's crazy and chaotic patterned fabrics, is about as far from that as possible. On any other day, I'd love it. I adore color and how bold tones play against my pale skin and cinnamon-colored hair. But Diana was clear about today. Pale, demure, and subtle.

I stand, smooth a few wrinkles down the dress's skirt, roll back my shoulders, and accept there's no turning back. It's time.

I stride from my office down the corridor. Rather than take the side passageway that leads directly to the row of small galleries along the north wall, I pivot and take the slightly longer route through the public spaces, specifically through the Tate Gallery's rotunda—my favorite spot in the world.

The exhibition opened minutes ago, so I have only the briefest moment to glance up, absorb, and savor the bright sunshine through the rotunda's glass ceiling. I catch that magical scent of paint, art, paper, must, wood, and history before I race on, which proves challenging in tiny heels and slick leather soles on the polished marble.

Before I turn into the room, I hear the room. Inhalations of wonder, the clinking of crystal, the soft laughter that accompanies art and aristocracy all tell me it is proceeding just as we planned. Diana charged me with being her set of loyal ears at the opening today, listening and unobtrusive. After all, she wants to know what everyone says, what they think, and what benefits she may accrue from the exhibit's success. We both do.

Her voice drifts above the melodic thrum. I hear her lilting cadence, her posh accent, the thread of pride and delight dancing in her words. My smile broadens. Again—*we did it!*

I step inside and swipe a flute of champagne from Dillon's tray. His eyes widen and his lips part in surprise. On any other day I'd concede my behavior is shocking. Not today. This exhibit is as much my triumph as it is Diana's. We did this together. We pulled off the impossible: a highly personal, highly curated farewell to the twentieth century's greatest and most famous artist—within a fortnight of his death.

I throw Dillon a smile, and rather than explain anything to him, I walk on as I lift the crystal flute and let the bubbles tickle my nose. It's not that I haven't sipped champagne before; it's just that I haven't sipped it often. People who pull the corks on bottles all the time feel no wonder in it. They don't stop and watch the bubbles rise. They don't savor their first sip and let their eyes drift closed as they concentrate on the sensation and the flavors. They walk, they talk, and they throw back mini gulps as if it's nothing more than fizz from a Coca-Cola tantalizing their senses.

Not me. I relish the experience and let the sharp, dry taste spread across my tongue before I swallow it. Circling the room's perimeter, I note each guest in attendance. Everyone accepted Diana's invitation. And by their expressions, we have wowed them. Lady Alexandra Bessing, last living daughter of Sir Jonathan Brookings, glows. I'm glad because that wasn't the case last week when I informed her we could *not* accept her proffered Picasso. Diana felt her 1923 work was not important enough within Picasso's oeuvre nor personal enough to his life and journey to feature within this commemoration. Even though the rejection was delivered with compliments and concessions, Lady Alexandra kicked up a mighty fuss.

Mr. Edward Davies, a scion of British manufacturing, laughs loudly just to my right, as well he should. Diana, despite feeling much the same about his offered work, was overruled. I gather he hopes to sell his Picasso and Richard promised to exhibit it here to drum up publicity. Davies's *Woman Laughing* hangs on the east wall.

I glance to Director Browning. Richard is laughing and looks well chuffed. I feel a sigh, long held, release within me. Though he gave his permission, tempted by the glory of this show's success, he withheld his full approval by pronouncing that such haste could be deemed poor taste. Yet his full laugh and the backslap he delivers to Mr. Davies reveals he isn't above taking credit for this "intimate moment," this exclusive farewell from Picasso's adoring elite and friends.

With my first circle of the room complete, I start again. It's time to take in the art. Since we first devised this exhibition, I've thought of nothing but these seventeen paintings. I've worked with museums across the world organizing their transport, I've sent cables and telexes to secure insurance coverage, and I've organized the printer, the caterer, the rental company, the invitations, the . . . everything. Yes, I've worked twelve-hour-long days overseeing every minute detail for this morning, and I've anticipated taking in the installation as it's meant to be viewed.

I catch Diana's eye as I start my second tour of the room. Something flickers within her glance, and I know it's my dress. It certainly defies her call for demure delicacy, and I make a mental note to explain—and apologize—later.

For now I take another sip of my champagne and begin at the beginning . . .

PABLO PICASSO
25 October 1881–8 April 1973
The Old Guitarist, 1903
Oil on Panel
On loan, courtesy of the Art Institute of Chicago

While Diana eschewed Picasso's most famous works, the ones made into the posters and prints that grace every office and schoolroom, she wanted this one to open our show. It's the iconic work of his Blue Period, but also a very personal work. Picasso painted it just as he emerged from a year of poverty and pain, still struggling to make ends meet and wrestling with the death of his close friend Carles Casagemas. *The Old Guitarist* embodies Picasso's trials as the man arches over and strums his large guitar with almost skeletal fingers. There's an intimacy to the work, as if Picasso himself invites the viewer into his heart. His trials become ours.

The Old Guitarist is also one of the great artist's only works that so clearly pays homage to another—in this case, the famous Greek painter El Greco. That, in and of itself, is a peek into Picasso's heart. Yes, it is truly a masterpiece and, at thirty-two by forty-eight inches, one of the largest paintings in our show.

Next to the huge and iconic *The Old Guitarist*, Diana instructed the installation team to hang a series of sketches. It
was a brilliant decision. After such an impressive beginning, the
exhibition instantly turns more personal. It's almost as if the
viewer can discern Picasso's choices, witness his process, and
share in his emotions.

I take in each sketch and step into Picasso's love life, for
each is a drawing of a woman in varying states of dishabille.
Knowing Picasso, and I feel I do now, I sense what he felt for
each as a lover or what he felt for the woman he hoped would
soon become one.

As I walk on, some of the works feel like old friends. Some I
am truly meeting for the first time. My pulse quickens with one
here, slows with another there. My gaze sweeps to the painting
Edward Davies and Director Browning bullied Diana into accepting for the exhibit just two days ago. *Woman Laughing*, 1930.

Diana was furious, but I'm not sure why. The painting fits in
size, structure, and subject matter. I pause. Is this woman Dora
Maar or Olga Khokhlova? Picasso loved both in 1930. And this
woman is interesting, she's dynamic, she's . . .

I tilt my head to study her better. In form, *Woman Laughing* is
a perfect execution of Picasso's surrealist period. But something
feels off. I take a sip of my champagne and move on. The next
offering, *Bullfight*, 1934, is also stun—

I gulp and choke, straining to control the spasms in my
throat. Champagne sticks to my tongue and cloys. Sticky and
sweet. Warm and wrong. I cough again and turn.

A few steps back and I again examine *Woman in an Armchair*, 1929. Diana instructed the installation team to hang
this one right before *Woman Laughing*. It's the shocking two-
dimensional portrayal of Picasso's wife, Olga Khokhlova, just
as their relationship was warping, disintegrating, and ending.
That means the more peaceful *Woman Laughing* can't be Olga.
His emotions towards her had already soured.

I step forward and study *Woman Laughing* again, painted just
a year later. I see the development of Picasso's style, his comfort in

the midst of the grotesque and frenzied, and yet . . . I look beyond it to *Bullfight*, painted a few years after that.

I clamp my hand over my mouth, shocked at the obvious truth before me as I center myself before *Woman Laughing* once more. I can't pull my eyes from it. My mind reels. Then, unable to think, hold back, or move forward, I call out, "That's a forgery."

The world around me stops.

CHAPTER 4

Time froze. Nothing moved. No breath. No air. Then a singular whisper struck me. *"Get out. You're finished."*

Director Browning's tight words from an hour ago fill my head once more, and my stomach drops as I wait in Diana's office. How many times can I feel this sensation anew? This flopping despair at the bottom of me? In my years working here, I have never seen Richard—Director Browning—turn such a color.

Forget the quick flush of carmine that accompanies any face suffused with blood and anger. He has sported that hue on plenty of occasions—when the installation team let Claes Oldenburg's sculpture *Soft Drainpipe-Blue* drop in a crumpled heap of fabric onto the cement floor just after the Gallery purchased it for an obscene amount a couple years ago. Or better yet, when my friend Sara in Donor Relations seated Ian Campbell, the eleventh Duke of Argyll, beside his ex-wife, Margaret Whigham, last year at a donor luncheon. Sara didn't know about the scandalous 1963 divorce, nor did she check her guest list with anyone in the Gallery. The pop of the first champagne cork released more than bubbly that noon.

No, as bad as all that was, this morning I pushed Richard's florid face past the entire red spectrum as if I'd personally added drops of violet or Prussian blue to his very veins. He was going to either unleash his fury, with lords and ladies looking on, or burst a blood vessel trying to keep it locked tight.

I didn't wait to find out. At his *"Get out,"* I was already fleeing. His *"You're finished"* figuratively kicked me from behind.

Unfortunately, the magnitude of what I'd done hit the instant *after* I'd done it. After Richard and Mr. Davies, standing close by, overheard me. After *The Times* reporter, chatting with them, widened his eyes with interest. After everything grew so still I could actually hear those tiny bubbles pop within my champagne.

Diana grabbed my arm as I flew by. So hard, in fact, the force of her grip swung me around and my shoulder hit the doorframe while my slick leather soles slid from beneath me. These stupid heels almost brought us both crashing down.

She stood her ground, however, in a pair of heels twice the height of mine. She righted me and, in a whisper much softer than Richard's but equally commanding, said, "Go to my office. Do. Not. Leave."

I drop my head into my hands, wishing I was home, burrowed under my covers, rather than sitting in Diana's office. A sharp sting shifts my focus to my index finger. I've shredded another cuticle, and this one now bleeds. I glance around in search of a tissue.

I truly do love this room's refinement and luxury, and I find comfort in it. It's how I'd decorate my ideal space if I could. But I can't. While I hoped such a room could someday be mine, today's outburst is an apt reminder why it can't.

This room is unique; it's an extension of the woman herself, from the desk to the five small Renoir sketches on the wall to the left, to the Miro, Chagall, and three prints from Picasso's *Vollard Suite* she loves so much, hanging to the right. It's perfection—perfection born of generational taste and experience, born of education and acumen, born of knowing what to say and knowing how to keep your mouth shut when required.

Oh my . . . I messed up. Irrevocably. Again.

"What were you thinking?"

I startle and spin towards the door. My mind goes blank. Diana stands stiff and pale, almost as if she's materialized from cloud and shadow rather than walked through the door like a normal person. Absent the flickering muscle along her jawline just below her gold drop earring, one might place her in the South Gallery along with the rest of the marble women.

She doesn't speak or move as several thoughts race through my head. I open my mouth to offer an explanation along with my apology, but no words emerge. I close my mouth and open it again with the realization of what I can't admit: I wasn't thinking. Basking in the best morning of my life and the extraordinary feat we'd accomplished, I simply noted something that marred that perfection. Something that didn't belong. And I blurted it out.

I can't tell Diana this because then I'd have to tell her what truly led to my soaring buoyancy this morning. I'd have to confess that I don't belong in her world, and that I try each and every day not to mess up and reveal all I don't know and don't understand. Then I'd have to confess that this morning, for one brief, shining moment, I believed I'd actually earned my spot in that room, that I'd arrived and could be an equal, her equal. I'd have to admit that because I'd taken charge of so many aspects of this exhibition, it became my own and I grew so excited, so sure of myself, and so hopeful of what it could mean for me that I no longer worried about not belonging or messing up.

So that's exactly what I did.

I forgot everything. I forgot my place. I forgot my reality. I am not a guest at the party. I observe the party. I take notes. I make lists. I get the job done. I do not take sips of swiped champagne. I don't make plans; I execute my boss's plans. And I certainly never blurt my opinions.

"Lily." Diana snaps her fingers in front of my nose. I pull back at the flick of displaced air. The glow from the window frames her golden hair in a fierce goddess-like halo. She steps to the side and the halo disappears. She turns mortal once more.

"I just saw it. I saw— I don't know what I saw," I stammer and drop my gaze. I feel small, ashamed, like a child caught in a lie. I feel unsure and lost. I lift my head. I'm not a child and I am not lost. With a deep breath, I try to articulate what happened. If I can get it out, say it clearly, perhaps she'll understand. Perhaps *I'll* understand.

"I just looked at the painting and it struck me." My hands

reach out in a plaintive gesture like I'm begging. It doesn't look or feel professional. I drop them and try again, in a lower tone this time. "You must have noticed it too, right? You're an expert in all the modernist painters."

Her face clouds and I realize that including her in my madness is just that, madness. Diana is keeper of the Tate's Modern Collections and I am her assistant—I do not tell her what she *must* have noticed. "I'm sorry. I just saw it and blurted it out. I truly am very sor—"

"You just *saw* it? You're *sorry*?" She cuts me off with clipped words and sharp gestures, and her patronizing tone coats each word in incredulous exasperation. I again feel stupid and young. She keeps talking as she circles her desk to her chair.

"You *saw* a forged Picasso in a second's examination? A forgery a top dealer in Paris missed, then sold? And you announced it? With *The Times* there to report the whole thing?" She stands in front of her seat, palms pressed flat to her desk. "You called Mr. Davies a fraud. You implied I'm a fraud. It's my show. I'm finished."

I cringe at her ominous "finished" and hold up my hand in panic. "That reporter can't write about it. I didn't mean to say it. I didn't think—"

"No, you didn't, and of course he's going to write about it. You just handed him a front-page scandal. Didn't you see the article when Davies purchased that piece? He bought it the day after Picasso's death for an extraordinary sum. It garnered unprecedented attention, and now you've given the press a follow-up."

Diana drops into her desk chair, a wood-and-leather midcentury accountant's chair that bounces a touch as she sits. Her usually sky-blue eyes are stormy and I feel their chill. As I suspect she's waiting for me to say more, I open my mouth to apologize again, but she cuts me off as soon as I draw breath.

"You ruined my show, Lily."

Her show. I wilt further, if that's even possible. It is hers. It was never ours. And it was certainly never mine.

"You humiliated Mr. Davies and the Tate, and you denigrated Picasso's memory. This was to be a world-class tribute, not the launch of a kind of scandal that destroys artists and wrecks careers."

She raises her hand to stop me from speaking. "Everything I've spent my life working towards is gone. With funds tight across the arts community, who will feel their support is safe here in my hands?"

I try to pay attention to the litany of troubles I created for her but don't hear much after she said the ensuing scandal could destroy an artist. "Could what I said really destroy Picasso?"

"A lesser artist would be ruined, yes." Her eyes slide closed. "Picasso will survive. I may not."

"I didn't mean to do it," I whisper.

Her eyes open and they've taken on a sheen of vulnerability I've rarely seen within her. Without thinking, I lean forward as she touches the back of her hand beneath her nose as if unshed tears are pricking it as well.

Andrew, the head of the installation team, calls Diana the "White Witch" after that character from Lewis's Narnia. He says she's stone-cold and ruthless. While I laugh with him, because it's best not to make enemies around here, I don't agree. I've never found Diana cold and certainly never ruthless. She's simply restrained, determined, and passionate about a job well done. She's needed those attributes to rise as high as she has, and I respect that. Vulnerability and fear are not emotional states I associate with her. Yet she now pulsates with them. I've brought them to her.

"You humiliated me, Lily. Did you see what happened in there? Did you hear them?"

Diana wants a directorship, and why shouldn't she? There's never been a woman at the helm. Not here, not anywhere in England or across Europe, and she has a shot. She *had* a shot—especially with the donors she's brought in lately.

Unless they all leave. Because of me.

I frantically cast for anything I can say or do to fix this, but every thought ends with the futile reality that nothing can be done. I have truly and irrevocably messed up. Tears sting my eyes and I command them not to fall. "I'm sorry. I should've—"

"Stop. If you've got nothing better than another tepid apology to offer, stop." Her eyes slide shut once more and her hand, gold bracelets clattering down the tight sleeve of her beige silk dress, raises towards me with its palm facing out. "It is a Picasso, Lily. That makes the stakes high. The highest."

Her voice sounds drained of all life and my name thuds on the downbeat as if a lily is a very pedestrian flower, making me a very pedestrian girl. I smooth my hand down my dress's skirt, flattening the wrinkles in my lap. I try to straighten my spine, willing myself to believe that if given a chance, I can make things right somehow. I shrink under the weight that I can't.

Diana opens her eyes and all vulnerability is gone. They spark more ice than storm, and her complexion pales a degree closer to ash. "You set off a bomb in there."

She blinks and I flinch. After last month's IRA bombing at the Old Bailey, such words cannot be used carelessly. She clears her throat to reset our attention. "We have to end this somehow, Lily. *Woman Laughing* is a genuine Picasso. It is not a forgery."

She glares at me. Her head rests on splayed fingertips gripping her temples, elbows on her desk. I notice the small lines in her forehead, the crease in the center of her brow, and the tight purse of her lips. Unlike before when trying to calm her temper, I sense she's now trying to rewind the clock or divine a solution. By her expression I gather she can't find a way out either.

"Regardless of its authenticity, however, we have the issue that your comment will live in the collective memory. Art is not a fixed commodity. Some of its value is and always will be sentimental. That makes it mercurial. You indelibly stained *Woman Laughing*. Then there's Director Browning."

My stomach lurches up towards my heart this time and my throat constricts. I now suspect his "*You're finished*" did not merely refer to my presence at the show's opening.

Diana stares at me so long I shift in my seat. My lower thigh sticks and pulls on the leather. The hem on this dress is too short. I yank at the skirt. I stop. I swipe my hand across my neck. Despite the coolness of the room, I'm damp, overheated, and sticky. I finally can't take her stare or the silence any longer. "What do you mean?"

"He wants you to empty your desk and leave."

"I'm fired? No— He can't—" I stretch forward and reach a hand towards the edge of Diana's desk. Her eyes track it. I drop my hand into my lap and start pulling at my dress's hem again. "I'll apologize to him and to Mr. Davies right now. I'll explain that I didn't know what I was saying. No one should listen to me. I—"

"Stop, Lily." The same word. The same raised hand. This time it's her right hand and the large ring she wears on her middle finger has twisted to her palm. The gold double-sided face of Janus snags my attention. The god of passages, transitions, duality, and doorways. The god of beginnings. And unfortunately for me, the god of endings.

As Diana drops her hand, her thumb reflexively twists the ring to its proper position. "Richard rushed Mr. Davies into his office as I came here. I assume they'll call Scotland Yard."

"There's no need." The words come out too fast, too panicked. I see everything I've worked for slip away.

"Forgery is fraud, Lily. A crime. What about this do you not understand?" Her voice rises a notch and I duck lower.

"Can't I just take it back?" The words are out of my mouth without thought, and they hit me so hard I almost heave up this morning's tea and toast. I said those same words once long ago, yet it feels like yesterday. And no, whatever one says or does cannot be taken back. Some things can never be taken back.

My eyes flood with tears, and I can no longer keep them from spilling over. Not because of this morning, the painting, or getting fired. I swipe at them and, sitting here in my Emilio Pucci knock-off dress, I am no longer twenty-seven. I am five and I am a silly little girl playing dress-up—a silly little girl who thought she could join a party she wasn't invited to. A silly little girl who lashed out and messed up so badly, life could never be the same again. A silly little girl who asked her older sister if she could just "take it back" and the silly little girl who shrank deep within herself when told she never could, not in a million lifetimes.

I'm still that girl and now, twenty-two years later, I have ruined everything again.

"Lily?"

I look up to find Diana's chair empty. It takes me a second to shift my perspective and locate her. She has come from behind her desk and stands beside me. My eyes hit her waist. She's wearing another of those lovely Halston gold chain-link belts I so admire. This one is thinner and more delicate than yesterday's.

"Go home."

I shake my head and push the words out in a whisper. I don't have enough air for more. "Please. I can't. I'm sorry."

"You need to leave before Mr. Davies and Richard come out of his office. Don't clear your desk. Just go." She steps back and opens her door.

"Don't clear my desk?" My head and hopes lift.

"We'll talk about your job later. For now, just leave."

With a single nod and no words, I obey. I flee her office as fast as I fled the exhibition. Upon reaching the corridor, I glance to the left and find Director Browning's office door still shut. I turn right and walk as quickly and quietly as my stupid heels tapping on the wood floor will allow.

At the end of the corridor, I push open my office door and grab my handbag from next to my desk. I wrench off the ridiculous shoes and slide into my everyday steady loafers. I look across my desk. There's a picture of my nieces sitting on one corner and a ceramic mug I made in Year One next to it. There's also a copy of today's lovely exhibition catalogue and the card of Picasso's *Child with a Dove*, from that bonkers bird-launching birthday party, propped against my desk lamp. I open my bag and reach for the card first, then pull back just as my fingers brush its edge. Diana said to leave everything behind.

I'm coming back. I must come back.

I step quietly outside my office, intending to take the nearby door to the basement, when a shout stops me.

"You!"

I slowly spin to meet a red-faced, stocky man standing wide-stance and arms crossed only two meters away. I have never spoken directly to Mr. Davies, but I've seen him in the Gallery. His steel-grey hair, combed back and smooth, reminds me of the steel factories and manufacturing for which he's famous. I've heard his voice too. It's strong and commanding. My first impression was that this man was determined, blustery, and aggressive. Today I find him terrifying.

He strides forward, full steam, and stops a mere whisper from my face. I work hard not to flinch, so sure he's about to crash into me.

"How dare you!"

"I'm sorry— I—" I lift a supplicating hand in the tight space between us.

His voice drops low, heat emanating from him. "You called me a chancer in there. A cheat. A liar. Your stunt will be splashed across the papers tomorrow and will follow *Woman Laughing* forever. It will follow me forever."

"I'm sor—"

"You cost me the half million pounds I'd have made on the sale of that painting. Not to mention the loss of the almost half million pounds I paid for it. I'll not pay in flesh or pounds for what you did in there. You will." He stares down at me, and the thin skin beneath his left eye quivers. "The Tate will."

"It wasn't the Tate's fault. No one . . ." I run out of words. I run out of thought. I take a step back.

Just as I do, Mr. Davies shifts as well. He looks down to my stumbling feet and a startle passes through his gaze, quick as lightning. It feels as if he sees the incongruity of this moment— why should the lion even bother to confront the mouse?

He jerks his head, chin thrusting forward, as if to say, "Be gone."

Again, I obey.

I open the door from the stairwell into the basement and stall as my eyes adjust to the dim light. Accounting, Development, Services and Maintenance, along with a few other offices, are housed here. No one needs to see those departments. In fact, it's better if no one does—art and its display are to appear effortless and ephemeral. No one wants to shine a light on the nuts and bolts required to run this place. But in reality, the nuts and bolts matter most.

It's quiet and cool, and my breath releases. I peek into the offices as I pass, and a few colleagues glance up and acknowledge me with either a nod or a smile. As there are no wide eyes or pitying looks, I suspect the gossip hasn't reached here yet, and I pray I can push through the service entrance door at the back of the Gallery before it does.

"Lily?"

I turn at Becca's call and poke my head through her cracked doorway. "Hallo." I pitch my voice high. "I can't talk right now. I just dropped down to grab something."

My friend smiles. "Is it beautiful? I'm going to walk through before I head home. Will you give me a guided tour?"

"Wish I could." I wave a hand as if that's all I have time for. "Diana has me off running an errand. They're headed into the luncheon soon."

I hate lying to Becca. I hate how easily I do it. But I don't trust myself right now with the truth—a truth I want to change if I can. And I have to get out of here. I flap my hand again. "See you tomorrow?"

Without waiting for her reply, I duck from her doorway and push at the service entrance door—and I stop.

Shaking my head at the stupidity of this impulsive idea, I turn left and head down the corridor to another set of stairs. A glance at my watch confirms the guests have, in fact, moved into the next room and should be seated at the luncheon. Diana even requested that the doors be shut in order to give the party greater intimacy.

That means no one will be in the Picasso exhibition right now. That means no one will see me in it either.

I can sneak into the room and see *Woman Laughing* once more and suss out what I saw—what I *thought* I saw—and then I can explain it better. I can fix this.

The stairs bring me into the rotunda and my steps slow only long enough to soothe my soul a tiny bit. I cross to the row of rooms beyond, my low-heeled loafers making their familiar deep strikes against the marble as I head to the small gallery housing the Picasso commemoration. Rather than merely empty, however, the room is closed with a gate and a guard.

"Why are you here? Are the guests in the luncheon?" I ask Archie, who shifts his weight from one stationary foot to the other.

"The luncheon was canceled. They've all gone 'ome."

"Gone? Why?"

He stares at me. "Everyone fled, Lily. It looked like someone yelled *fire* or like that time back when I worked at the Natural History Museum and someone cracked open the vents to the decaying bug room. That stench cleared the museum in five minutes flat." He dips his head at me. "This clearing was a mite bit faster."

"But it was only a comment. How could everyone leave?"

"Words are powerful things." The sharp aspect of concentration in Archie's eyes is replaced by the softer shape of affection and pity. "You're in a heap of trouble. I've never seen the likes of Mr. Browning a li'l while ago. He hauled me out of the lobby and told me not to leave this post 'til closing."

"But your back—" I take in how Archie is standing, stiff and leaning forward ever so slightly. I note the tight press of his mouth and the pronounced line in the center of his forehead. "You must hate me. Your back already hurts, doesn't it?"

Archie is in his late sixties with a back wounded in the last war. He's earned his comfortable chair at the lobby front desk, glancing into overstuffed bags and placing wet brollies into a bucket.

"Get on with you." His tight smile transforms into a genuine grin. "Don't you be worrying about my back." He looks above and beyond me as if searching for threats. "And don't be getting caught 'round here either."

"Can I sneak in? Just for a moment?"

Archie's eyes widen and his whole forehead wrinkles with surprise and alarm, and I'm instantly ashamed I requested such a thing. I pull back, trying to distance myself from the words still floating between us. "I didn't ask that. I'm leaving." My hand drops upon his arm. It's an apology, another one, and I can tell by his soft smile and long, slow blink that he understands.

I make my way to the Gallery's side entrance. Although it's a public one, it's also the closest to me right now. Archie is correct. I can't be caught 'round here a moment more.

I scan the program posters and exhibition announcements in the entryway just outside the cloakroom, searching for the one that launched my high-flying fortnight straight into the stratosphere.

BRITISH EMERGING ARTISTS EXHIBITION
Tate Gallery—Serpentine Gallery,
Kensington Gardens
1–29 June 1973

I close my eyes. It's amazing how something I believed impossible became possible and so tantalizingly within my reach within two short weeks and by one simple comment.

One comment that sent me soaring.

Soaring so high, a crash was the only way down.

CHAPTER 5

I'm going to be sick.

I step out into the cool morning, surprised after all that has happened it is still morning, albeit close to noon, and lean against the Gallery's massive stone sidewall. My head is spinning. My heart is beating out of my chest.

Blue sky. Stone buildings. Black cabs. Red telephone boxes. Buses. More buses. The world feels colorful, tumultuous, and surreal. Like Picasso's *Three Musicians* rather than his *Three Women at the Spring*. Both were painted the same year, yet they offer diametrically opposed realities. Like two such diverse offerings in his single year, I have fractured all I've worked for in a single day.

I rub my eyes to help them adjust to the sunshine and take off at a fast clip. The cool damp, lingering after a long night of rain, sticks to my skin and along my hairline. It's bracing. Cleansing. I feel myself calm. On any other day I might say this air feels, and even tastes, hopeful.

I race across the street at the last blinkings of the crosswalk light to the Pimlico Underground Station, and after racing down the stairs, I board a train that seems to be waiting just for me. The carriage isn't crowded at this hour, so I drop into a seat and simply let my eyes trail the signs and tiles at each stop heading north to Oxford Circus. The cadence of the train slows me down. It lulls away my rapid-fire recriminations, and it feels good not to think, even better not to feel.

A quick change at Oxford Circus from the Victoria Line down to the deepest Central Line and I sit again, letting the rail work a modicum of magic until Notting Hill Gate. I exit the carriage, climb the stairs, and emerge on the south side of the street. A few blocks farther south into Kensington and the Hill Gate neighborhood, with its charming two-story flats and homes, and I'll be at my front door. The thought stops me cold, but I force myself to walk on, focusing on the past, my surroundings, and anything and everything except what's ahead of me.

Dad landed our flat in this wonderful neighborhood a few years ago. We could never afford this posh post code. But about a hundred years ago, the government built five massive and attached housing units as part of a workers' residency scheme. Back then I guess workers were needed in the neighborhood to maintain one of the most exclusive parts of London. Considering the government still subsidizes the rent in those buildings, workers must still be necessary.

Our flat is in the second of those five buildings along tiny one-way Peel Street. And because of Mum, we were granted a ground-floor unit with direct access to the building's central garden. Mum loves the light and that she can easily get outside to bask in it. Dad loves that she is happy there, and he likes his short walk to the Underground. He can get to almost any job site across London "cheap and easy" now. It's much better for him than taking the train into town and switching to the Underground as he did from our former home out in Hounslow.

I love the ease of my commute too. And I'll admit living in Kensington hasn't harmed me either. In a society where one is pigeonholed pretty tightly and advancement beyond one's societal rung is virtually impossible, my address has opened doors I didn't know existed prior to being able to peek through them. It's a funny thing, that. You work hard, you do your job, and yet it's something so random, so superfluous really, that gives you a boost. It's also something so random, so superfluous really, that can cast you back down.

Two blocks down Campden Hill Road I falter again. I can't bring this failure home. I can't make my mum worry. She won't expect me to walk through our front door this early, and there will be endless questions and concerns the instant I do. I look behind me. It's so tempting—a short ride back to Oxford Circus, a quick switch to the Bakerloo Line, and within a half hour I could be at St. Martin's School, staring at a blank canvas and endless permutations of color with which I can try to understand what's happened. That's the only place and the only way I can get close to finding a way out too.

I can't do it. I can't go to the school. I can't walk through the park. I can't hop on one of those new tourist buses that circle the city and sit until the day ends. I can't do any of the countless things I could dream up to fill the next few hours. I can't because then Mum would needlessly be alone this afternoon. I can't because far too many people have paid for my mistakes.

Especially Mum.

My face set, complete with what I hope to be a stiff but passable smile, I round the final corner onto Peel Street and, at Building No. 2, I swing open the heavy glass and wood door to stare at the worn, slightly warped door to the first flat to the right. I'm so ready to get this initial moment over that when my key sticks in the lock, I almost come undone. Tension, frustration, and fear spill over as I finally push open the door and wrench the key free. My momentum tumbles me into our small foyer.

"Mum?" I call out and peer into the living room, then into the dining room pass-through to the kitchen. She is not in sight.

I hear a rustle from the kitchen. "Is that you, luv? We're in the garden."

"Dad? What are you—?" I then remember he's only working a bare-bones construction schedule during union negotiations. I'd forgotten that. But with so many unions striking, it's good he is still working at all.

He pokes his head into the dining room, and he's lit up with one of his rare smiles that reaches all the way into his eyes. His eyes are clearer with those smiles, and I know he's seeing me rather than seeing through me. My breath catches and my mouth tips into my first small but genuine smile in hours. It feels light across my face.

We're going to be okay.

"Come along, slowpoke. Daisy's here with a surprise."

"She is?" I drop my handbag onto the dining room table and follow him through the kitchen and out into the building's communal garden. It isn't a surprise my older sister has come by, just that she's still here. Daisy often arrives after Dad and I leave for work and helps Mum in the morning, after her own girls are off to school. But she's always gone again by midmorning to do her own work, cooking for an elderly home-care concern.

I walk out into the patch of sunshine. It warms the top of my head, like treacle slowly spreading. Mum and Daisy are sitting at the garden's central table, and Daisy's hair, a few shades darker than mine, looks thick, lush, almost black rather than what I've always called dark chocolate. Both of us have long, wavy hair, not the straight hair that's in style right now, and most days I work Mum's clothes iron to achieve that neat, straight look. But not Daisy. She loves her curls, and today her hair looks glorious. Has she found some new shampoo or conditioner?

I shift my gaze to Mum, an older iteration of both her daughters with the beginnings of silver threading her dark hair. She has her favorite navy shawl draped around her shoulders. The one that sets off her eyes—the only true blue in the family—and the one Daisy knitted for her last Christmas. They don't see me advance. Daisy's chair is pushed back to make room for Mum, and there's a chair for Dad. I slow. There is no place for me to sit.

Daisy pauses mid-laugh as I step into her line of sight. Mum's focus follows hers.

"What are you doing home?" My older sister's voice arcs. Mum's expression doesn't change from one of open delight, so maybe I'm imagining Daisy's bite.

I go straight to the heart of the matter. It's already choking me. "I messed up today. Richard may have f—"

"Daisy's pregnant." Mum's exclamation cuts me off, and her words bounce around us with the pop of a Christmas cracker. She waves her hands, fizzing with excitement.

"Pregnant?" I stare at Mum, then look to my sister. "Another baby?"

"Don't go on about it. I'd hate for you to get too chuffed."

I don't imagine Daisy's tone this time, nor have I fabricated the slight flutter within her left cheek. Either she feels it or she catches the direction of my gaze because she reaches up and presses a hand to her cheek. Dad startles me with a hand at my elbow. He directs me to sit in his chair. I lower myself into it as he pulls up another beside me.

"You could be happy for me." Daisy's words carry a melodic cadence, but something tense and tight in her eyes defies their light delivery. A flicker runs through them as well. A flicker an artist might achieve by dappling a touch of white to the outer edge to soften the lines and create an image of vulnerability. It's a look Mum misses as she cuts me a slice of her crumble cake. It's a glower Dad doesn't catch while he situates his chair, metal scratching against stone, onto the garden's paved patio.

"I didn't say I wasn't." My nose scrunches, and I try to erase what I suspect is an equally evident flicker of fear in my own eyes.

Daisy's glare sharpens.

My sister is ten years older than I am, and we always seem to scrape against each other rather than slide along. She makes me feel juvenile, silly, and frivolous. She says I make her feel clumsy, irrelevant, and useless.

Mum absently hands me a slice of cake as she chats with Daisy about all the joys ahead. I want to participate. I want to feel happy. I want to regard this as joy. But I cannot. Just like Dad, who sits staring quietly into the middle distance, I lean back and say nothing, lost in my own thoughts. And soon Mum and Daisy are so engrossed with plans and prams, needlework and nappies, Dad and I sit forgotten—which suits both of us just fine. Dad because he exists most comfortably in that space. Me because all I can see is trouble ahead.

"Lily? Earth to Lily?"

I blink myself into the present. "Did you say something?"

Mum smiles at me. "I said your sister is leaving." I look up to find Daisy standing near the door rather than still tucked beside me. "Walk her out, will you, luv?"

Missing nothing, ever, Mum clearly noticed the tension between us. This is her way of giving us a moment alone, a moment for me to make amends with my sister. I begin as we cross through the dining room, out of earshot of both our parents. "I'm sorry about earlier. Truly."

"You never make it easy on me. Never once do you even try." Daisy grabs her coat off a dining room chair and opens our front door.

I spill out into the lobby, then onto the sidewalk after her. "I said I was sorry."

"I'm thirty-eight next month, Lily. Much older than when Mum had you. In fact, exactly her age when . . ." Daisy's voice drifts away as her eyes take on the glaze of memories from long ago yet never out of reach.

"Don't," I whisper.

Daisy turns and strides away. I watch her for a few seconds, then look up and beyond her towards Holland Park, as if I can see her flat only a couple miles beyond, see her husband, Sean, preparing to head to work, see their two daughters in their schoolrooms only a few blocks beyond that. I envision Daisy's family, her life, and it's good. I race to catch up and walk with her towards the Underground.

She stops me with a hand on my arm. "Did it occur to you I might be scared?"

"Surprises aren't all bad." I pretend to misunderstand her, and my voice emerges with false brightness. But I can't follow her into the deeper waters of fear and failure she's inching towards.

Her face crumples and I know I've let her down. I swapped one fear for another. To Daisy, all surprises are bad and they always have been. Dad going to war. Being sent away. Oliver. Me. Mum's accident. If pressed, I can't imagine Daisy wouldn't choose to avoid every single one. And as bad as all that is, that was the lesser fear I chose to chase.

But that's what Daisy doesn't understand and never has. While surprises aren't my favorite things either, there are other things I fear much more. I want to blame her for not catching on, but I haven't been open with her. I've never shared what I truly fear—I'm not even sure how to articulate all that scares me. So, as trite as it is, I merely apologize again.

How many more times in one day will I need to repeat these same words?

Daisy glances away and I sense the barrier between us solidify, conjured from memories, misunderstandings, miscommunication, and so much more. A great deal of which is my own fault.

"Are you going to paint tonight?" she asks softly. She knows that much, I concede. She knows I paint to work out life, and maybe even tamp down all those fears I won't discuss.

"No. I'll stay home this evening."

"Then talk to Dad, if you can. Mum mentioned he got cut from a job, and with the union about to strike, he might not get a position for a while."

I close my eyes. We need Dad's income, as meager as it is right now, alongside my salary, if we're going to make it. Another reason I can't let Richard fire me—we're sunk if I lose my position.

As I fall into the abyss, Daisy digs the hole deeper. "If these strikes go on, it'll all get worse. And who's going to hire construction workers in this economy anyway? Who can build?"

Her words don't help, but they do broaden my perspective from the personal to the universal. Strikes, inflation, fuel shortages, uncertainty and everything that comes with it—all have slid people, certainly our family, from comfortably moving along day-to-day to teetering on the edge of a very slippery and precarious slope. Richard and Diana must know how hard it is these days. They'll understand. Perhaps Richard will reconsider . . .

A movement draws me from my thoughts. Daisy has stepped in front of me, and her eyes flash. I sense she believes I wasn't paying attention to her rather than paying attention to her so closely I got lost in her words. She stalks away in a huff and I let her. As I stand stock-still, one thought fills my mind.

We are not going to be okay.

CHAPTER 6

I lean against the door to our flat and let out the longest, loudest sigh and, for the first time today, truly lose hope. The flopping despair that bounced off the bottom of me earlier has fallen right through. I almost gaze down, wondering what it might look like puddled on our scuffed wood floor. How would an artist render such a forlorn reality?

"What's wrong?" Mum, her wheelchair still in motion, sits only a meter away.

"How did you roll in here so silently?"

"Dad greased my wheels yesterday afternoon. I'm rather stealthy now."

I push off the door and turn into the living room, heading to the one step beyond, which leads to my bedroom, a small closet we use for storage, and a half bath.

"That's not fair." Mum rolls forward and side-taps me with her wheelchair, cutting off my one-step escape. "Come chat with me."

I stare at her. I can't talk to her. I can't make her worry. I can't tell her the truth. Goodness, I can't even tell her about the world of words and hurt between Daisy and me that stretches back years. We live with our lies because we must.

Mum's eyes narrow, then widen. What does she see within me? "I'm not asking, Lily. I am telling you. Come."

I deflate. I concede. I follow her as she pushes at the wheels of her chair. I flop into the frayed floral upholstered chair I situated against our living room's back wall. When Mum positions herself across from the small table next to it, it creates the tableau of two healthy, happy friends sitting together. It's charming and elegant, and another little lie we tell ourselves.

She sits silent and expectant and the words "*I got fired today*" teeter on the tip of my tongue. It surprises me that I know they are true, despite how hard I've been trying to reinterpret them. Richard fired me. And though Diana told me not to pack my belongings, my clanger put her job and reputation in jeopardy. She might have gifted me with a day or two of reprieve, but she has no incentive to fight for me—and she might not even be able to.

"*I was let go.*" I run another iteration of it through my brain, and the words are so close to escaping I have to press my lips shut to force them back. I can't say them. I can't tell Mum that almost two-thirds our annual income is gone. I can't tell her that next week's bills will be hard to pay, much less next month's, or the month after that. So I lie.

"I was just surprised by Daisy's news." The words feel as lame as they sound.

"But you love surprises. It's your sister who loathes them."

"Her pregnancies are hard, Mum. She struggled with Hyacinth and . . ." I stop.

"She almost died with Posy." Mum reaches out and lays a hand on my knee. "You can't worry about that. She lives near Queen Charlotte's and Chelsea Hospital now. She has access to the best care. And—"

"You've considered this too." I cut her off. "Why didn't you say something earlier?"

"That's not how it works, Lily. You don't wallow in fear and you don't worry about things that may never happen." Her hand slides from my knee. "I'm much stronger now too. I can help far more than I could when either Hy or Posy were young."

"Mum." I sink lower into the comfy sagging cushion of the armchair.

"Don't 'Mum' me." Her words fire out sharp and clipped, but her eyes reveal hurt more than anger. "You seem to forget I am capable. I can help."

"I don't. I just—" I scrub my hand across my face.

"Need to have it all under control." Mum speaks softly and with such sweet understanding that it doesn't feel like criticism; it feels like love. I don't know how she does it, but without many words, or perhaps with just the right ones, she plumbs to the depth of me and touches upon the secrets I thought I buried so well.

Mum sighs. "I'm beginning to question if you really like surprises after all. They are unpredictable things, surprises."

"Maybe not this kind."

"That's too bad, darling, because a baby is the best kind. Don't let your worries and our circumstances lead you to doubt that. You're forgetting what fun life is. You're also forgetting how resourceful we are." She leans forward and lays a hand on my leg again, just at the hem of my dress. "Was it wonderful? Did you look as good as all those rich ladies?"

I close my eyes. The Dress. After Diana went on and on about an "appropriate" dress last week, I found a lovely cream one at a Knightsbridge consignment shop—only to come home and find my mum, who makes all my dresses, jubilant at surprising me with her homage to Emilio Pucci for the occasion. Yes, I'm not sure I really do like surprises.

I was a fraud when she presented me with the dress. I faked a huge smile and told her it was perfect. And I'm a fraud now, worse than *Woman Laughing*.

"Yes. It fit in beautifully with all those ladies." I look down at it. Bright. Bold. And I can't sit in it a moment longer. I can't pretend all went well. I can't pretend I still have a job. "I should go change so I don't ruin it."

I stand just as Dad enters the room. Mum waves him over. "Come see. You weren't home before. This is the dress I made for Lily's opening today."

My opening. I plaster another smile on my face and hope they can't recognize the counterfeit.

"You look pretty as a picture." Dad's smile is softer this time. It doesn't quite reach his eyes, but I can tell he means what he says.

"Thanks, Dad." I hug him tight and his arms wrap around me in response.

Dad, like me, loves the arts. He was a painter once too. As well as a musician, a photographer, and lots of other things, at least according to Mum. I never experienced any of it, but she shares stories from their days of courting and early marriage when he's not around. Daisy remembers too. Those happy times. Those golden years. Life before the war. Daisy was five when it happened—1939—the year Dad was sent to France and she and Oliver were shipped to the countryside in the government's effort to keep them safe. She and Mum talk about those "times before" with eyes peering into the distance and voices full of longing and regret. Dad and Oliver don't. Well, Dad doesn't. Oliver, of course, can't.

All I know are their stories of Dad. Mum's and Daisy's recollections of the paints, the brushes, the canvases, the piano, the piccolo, the camera, the jam sessions with Dad's friends at their first flat in what's now Richmond, and his afternoons in the Putney School of Art's darkroom with Daisy and Oliver perched on stools behind him. Daisy still laughs at how she and Oliver were mesmerized by the alchemy that made images suddenly appear upon glossy blank paper under the gentle light of a red bulb.

They both glow when talking about those years. Daisy says Dad was smiley and bright, and his laugh came deep like a bellow. Mum remembers how he picked up both Daisy and Oliver at the same time, each child tucked under an arm, and carried them to the corner shop every Sunday for a lolly. He told stories. He built forts. He stayed up all night when they were sick just to be near them.

I've only come close to seeing that kind of joy and spark in him a few times—a couple late-night chats about art, the night I announced that the Modern Collections' keeper at the Tate Gallery hired me to be her secretary, and the most glorious night of all, when I told him Diana promoted me from secretary to assistant keeper. It was—and still is—an unheard-of promotion, and another reason I can't lose my job. No one will *ever* take such a risk for me again.

Dad surprised me that night as he recounted details about the Tate even I didn't know. For instance, he knew Richard Browning had personally built a scaled model of a room for Rothko in '68 to secure the artist's masterpiece *Black on Maroon*, along with his other works. He knew Willem de Kooning's exhibition in the winter of '68–'69 and recalled it with such fine detail it felt as if I were walking the Gallery with him. He then told an astounding story of his own uncle who'd worked on the salvage crew after the Thames flooded in 1928 and the trouble he got into wringing out William Turner drawings like dishrags.

Dad laughed so hard at my incredulity he started crying. "Didn't damage a one, not completely, but oh, what a right mess they landed in."

Mum was beside herself that night as well—enjoying both my news and the brief shining moment her husband was "back." We opened a bottle of sparkling wine and emptied it. Later, after Dad had gone to bed, Mum confided her hope to me that perhaps it was the start of something new and that after twenty-eight long years, Dad might finally return from someplace dreary, dark, and dangerous. Somewhere in France—not far from a beach. Someplace in Yorkshire—on the edge of a moor. After all, the doctors had repeatedly said that shell shock, or battle fatigue, as some called it, wasn't necessarily a life sentence.

It didn't last, however. Dad drifted away once again as the stress of daily life crept back. That said, he loved—still loves—hearing about my work and the goings-on at the Tate. And if today had gone differently, I would have sat with him this evening and shared every moment, taste, and texture of the Picasso Commemorative Exhibition. I would have recounted the bubbles touching my nose before taking that first sip of champagne. I would have told him the bubbles were so much smaller than our sparkling wine and that there were thousands of them, enough to make an effervescent cloud as I lifted the crystal flute. I would have told him how extraordinary it was to stand so close to a masterpiece.

How, at inches away, I saw more into Picasso than I could have imagined possible.

I would have even laughed with him at the "off day" the great master must have had when painting *Woman Laughing.* I would have told him that something struck me as odd about that painting, something I couldn't put my finger on. And I would have been able to do all that because in *that* world, I would've kept my mouth shut at work and only shared my crazy musings at home, just with him.

Dad releases me from his good, solid hug and pushes me back. He takes in the dress again. "This may be your best work yet, Gladys."

I nod my agreement and twirl. The dress flares above the knees with the spin. Tulip petals opening in the sun. Unbidden, my smile broadens and my fake version of the day, and even the pain of the real one, evaporates in the beauty of this very real moment with Mum and Dad. My smile becomes real.

"Perfect." Mum gushes and twirls her hand, asking me to spin again. I do and it's as delightful as the first. After two more, I face her. She presses her hands together as if making a happy prayer.

I bend to hug her and we both laugh as her wheelchair rolls back.

"I'm so proud of you," she whispers into my hair.

My smile fades and tears prick my eyes. "Thanks, Mum."

CHAPTER 7

Diana

How did I get here?

Diana ponders the question for the umpteenth time and stares at her black lacquered front door with a sense of dread, foreboding, and an unfamiliar tinge of disappointment. She doesn't want to be home. She doesn't want to face him. She walked the two miles in the cold, wet, and dark, simply to postpone the inevitable. But her Burberry overcoat is soaked. She is chilled to the bone, and she is hungry. Furthermore, she admits to herself, she—they—have been heading to this place, this moment, for years. It was written in their stars and there is no denying the stars.

Her key slides smoothly, unlocking the massive door without friction or noise. Branford maintains their home beautifully, keeps everything well-oiled and running, the rooms pristine, the fridge stocked—silently and unobtrusively attending to any and all of their needs, often before she or Heinrich recognize what they are. Has she grown too used to such ease? Has she lost her hunger? Her edge?

She slips her heels off as she climbs the stairs. The blister on her right heel that started last evening has burst and now bleeds. At first she believed she deserved the pain, but it's crossed towards unbearable, and no one, she reminds herself, deserves that.

She strides directly to her dressing room, slides off her silk stockings, which pull and stick at the heel, and dabs the wound with a cloth. She glances through the open doorway to her tub and decides against a soak. Now is not the time to rest.

As soon as the bleeding stops, she presses a plaster to her heel before she pulls off her new Dior dress and throws it aside. It's a lovely dress, but it's ruined. Ruined by the day and by dashed expectations. Ruined by the rain. She will never wear it again.

She pulls on a pair of soft velour trousers and a matching jumper and stands with arms crossed, hands pulling her shoulders in. She cannot put off the inevitable any longer. She must find Heinrich.

Six steps up, the dramatic notes of Vivaldi's "Winter" surround her. And just like the previous night, she closes her eyes under the music's weight. Of Vivaldi's *The Four Seasons*, Heinrich only turns to "Winter" when he feels stymied or frustrated in his work. Diana hesitates, vacillates, but unlike last night, she continues to climb.

There is no turning back this evening.

She knocks on the doorjamb of their home's top-floor studio simply to signal her arrival rather than ask permission to enter, though her husband can't possibly hear her light rap over his music. As she steps into the room, she notes a bottle of 1942 Château Margaux standing sentinel on the Louis XIV chest just inside. No glass sits beside it waiting for her as was once Heinrich's habit.

She takes in her favorite space within their house—what was once her favorite space. While each room is unique and dramatic, this floor is only theirs. Outside of the two of them, no one knows it exists. Not even Branford. Sometimes when Heinrich is out of town or at his club, Diana still comes and sits up here on her own. She likes who she is in this room. Or at least who she was in it long ago.

It is Heinrich's now. The slow march of time and steady pull of acquisition have made it his. Only he paints. Nevertheless, the studio room still holds her past, her present, and, she hopes—someday, if she can free herself from so many entanglements—her future.

They created the room themselves, wielding sledgehammers and knocking down walls to fashion a warren of servants' quarters into an open, airy studio. And after painting all the walls a bright clean white, they made love in it. She had found the starkness of the space in that primal moment exciting, almost dangerous. Nothing could hide. Everything was exposed. It was then she felt that she and Heinrich truly knew each other, almost for the first time, or again for the first time.

Thinking back on it now as she watches Heinrich paint, his back to her, she recalls how exciting her husband and their lives felt that long-ago night. Yet if pressed, she feels certain Heinrich would point to these later years as the more satisfying. He would never relinquish them. In them he is a success, and with each sale, he craves more. He would never turn back, even for merely a night of reminiscing and romance. This truth has worried Diana for years. After all, his relentless pursuits led to this moment—just as she had been certain they would.

She reaches for the record player's needle. A screech accosts her ears as she lifts it away.

"Ahh . . ." Heinrich slowly straightens on his stool, as if rising from a dream. He does not turn to her or even look away from the large canvas only a handbreadth from his face. He does, however, reach up to shift his readers down his nose and leans back to regard the canvas in its entirety.

"You didn't hear me come in."

He waves a hand at her, eyes still fixed upon his work. "What do you think?"

Diana steps closer, her bare feet silent on the wood flooring. "It's provocative. It reminds me of Campendonk. His expressionist works of the late teens."

"Good. Good. That's just it. I've had trouble capturing it. It's eluded me, but you see it?" Heinrich remains fixated on the canvas before him. "We said I should slow down, but I've felt compelled to press on. It's good to keep working, even if the muse isn't always with you." He turns and his face falls at something he catches within hers. "You don't like it? What is wrong with it? I knew I hadn't captured it."

He glances between her and the painting. His slippered foot taps at a presto pace, revealing his deep anxiety. His grey hair sticks out at odd angles, and she suspects he hasn't brushed it since two nights ago when he'd been forced to bathe and shave prior to a late dinner with friends at his club. Such has been his obsession with this latest work.

"It's not the painting," Diana says after a prolonged pause, chastising herself for enjoying his obvious discomfort. She reaches for the glass of wine he set on the small paint-spattered table beside him and takes a long drink. She crosses back to the chest of drawers and fills the glass again. Returning to her husband, she takes another sip before holding it out to him.

He waves it away. "Diana? You've always been honest in your opinions. What's wrong with it?"

"I said it's not about the painting." She takes a deep breath. "This morning Lily Summers declared a Picasso in my commemorative exhibition a forgery. She said it out loud. Everyone at the opening heard her, including a reporter from *The Times*." Diana drinks again. "She declared *Woman Laughing* a forgery."

"*Woman Laughing*? Wasn't that sale in the papers recently?" Heinrich twists on his stool to face her. He reaches up and rubs the back of his neck. "Little Lily, your assistant, said this? How is that possible?"

Diana shrugs.

"*Woman Laughing*." Heinrich repeats the painting's name with a note of wonder as his mouth lifts in a half smile. "That girl must be a liar, a lunatic, a savant, or a forger herself, I think."

Diana notes his expression and frowns. He is not taking her or the situation seriously. Considering the glint in his eye and the curl to his lips, Diana knows her husband senses a game, a challenge, or a conundrum, but not a problem.

"She's none of that, and she's certainly not a painter or a forger." Diana's words cut sharp, and her husband's gaze finally meets hers. Eyes locked on his, she takes another long drink. "Richard lost his mind and basically fired her on the spot. And Edward Davies—"

"*The* Edward Davies? The industrialist?" Heinrich stares at her. "I'd forgotten he was the one who purchased it."

Diana remains silent, watching. When the moment stretches

past comfortable, she speaks again. "Well, he did, right after Picasso's death, and now he wants to sell it. Picasso's valuations have skyrocketed and Edward sees a windfall. I had no choice; Richard demanded I add it to the exhibition to drum up publicity."

"Richard heard your Lily say this preposterous thing too?"

"Everyone heard her, Heinrich. *The Times* reporter questioned me, Richard, and Davies on the spot, and once reported in the morning paper, it'll spread across the world. He blames us."

"Who blames you?"

"Edward Davies." Diana huffs before reining in her emotions. She needs her husband's support, not his antagonism. "He says we allowed this to happen. He says we 'perpetrated a crime.' I don't know . . . He wants the Tate's head on a platter. He specifically wants my head."

Diana stares at her husband, waiting for him to speak, but he doesn't notice. He has already turned away and is adding a drop of green to what looks like a man's large hook-shaped nose. "Heinrich?"

After another long pause, during which she bites her lip so as not to speak again, he finally replies. "What made Lily say it?"

Diana blinks. In the morning's tumult she hadn't pinned down that particular answer. Lily hadn't offered it, not really. It had to have been more than just a "feeling" as she implied. "She didn't, or couldn't, say."

Heinrich twists, leans forward, and lifts the wineglass from Diana's fingers. He drains it in a single gulp. "I suggest you find out." He pushes off the stool and stalks across the room to refill the glass with the last of the bottle, only catching Diana's expression on his way back.

Again, a small smile wrinkles the corner of his mouth. "It'll be fine, Diana. You mustn't worry so much." He stops in front of her and runs a firm finger down the center of her forehead. This is his cue, and has been for years, to encourage her to stop dwelling on the foibles of the past and chase the fortunes of the future.

"Not worry?" she whispers. "How can you say that? I put

together the exhibition. I accepted that painting. It's my career, my reputation on the line. It's—"

"And there is nothing you can do about any of that now. What's done is done." He taps the tip of her nose. "Yes?"

Diana flinches, distancing herself from the sense of childishness and inferiority that particular gesture always evokes in her.

Heinrich chuckles softly—he knows exactly what he's done and how she feels about it. The futility of her reaction seems to amuse him. He sets the glass on the table once more. "As you do, you are worrying over much. Simply let it play out. You'll see. It'll come out fine in the end. Tickety-boo, as they say."

"But what—?"

Heinrich cuts off her words by pulling her towards him and tucking her close. With a gentle hand he nestles her head beneath his chin. Almost against her will, Diana's eyes slide closed. She breathes in her husband, a familiar and seductive mixture of bourbon, red wine, paint thinner, paint, and the faintest whiff of cedar and cigar. That final note means he was at his club earlier in the day. Shadows enter into the periphery of the moment, but she snuggles closer in an attempt to push them away.

"No one wants forgeries found," he coos, rubbing small circles across her back. "It's bad for business. But they have existed since time immemorial and now, with Nazi-looted art returning to the market, they are more common, and the gaps in provenances are often so wide we can park Bentleys in them. We talk about this. See it through and don't let it upset you."

Heinrich sets her inches away, just far enough to press a kiss upon her forehead. The pressure and reassurance of it tip her into him again, but rather than fully kiss her, as once he used to, he turns away and gestures to the canvas. "I have more work to do tonight. Come sit with me. You really don't see anything wrong with it?"

She shakes her head once more, sets her stool beside him, and lifts the glass of wine from the table. He glances from her face to the glass and waves his palette knife across the room. "I opened another Margaux. A '53 that will be more to your liking. Go fill a glass for yourself."

Diana hands him his glass and looks to the far window, partially open to the cool evening air. There she finds the bottle sitting deep in the window well. Heinrich's "natural icebox," as he calls it. She also finds a clean glass. Diana smiles. Perhaps he remembered her after all.

Glass full, she joins her husband once more and watches as he paints in silence for several minutes. But rather than feel the warm reassurance and love that often envelops her while watching him work, Diana senses the room's atmosphere sharpen. The air takes on an electric charge that soon crackles. As her gaze trails from the depths of her ruby-red glass to the painting to her husband's eyes in search of the source of the disquiet, her toes curl against the wood floor.

"While I wouldn't worry, my dear . . ." Heinrich stares at her, stormy-toned grey eyes capturing her lighter blue ones, and lets his preamble rest between them long enough to make her anxious for what is to come.

His intense and unblinking eyes narrow, but still he does not speak. And just as she can't stand the suspense any longer and opens her mouth to prompt him, he continues. "I suggest you keep your young protégé close. She is your assistant keeper, your hire, and your responsibility. Do what you must, but do not let Richard fire her. Not yet."

CHAPTER 8

Lily

Early the next morning before anyone, even the sun, is awake, I quietly dress, have a quick cuppa, and sneak out the front door. Sneaking is necessary because I can't answer any questions this morning, and considering I barely slept all night, my face would invite an endless litany of them.

So, with catlike dexterity, I avoid all the land mines that will wake Mum and Dad. I touch my right foot lightly on the side of the one step from my room, stay close to the wall through the dining room towards the kitchen, missing the few squeaky floorboards at the kitchen's entrance, and I do not open the icebox. As much as I would have liked a drop of milk in my tea this morning, the door squeals when you pull it and grates metal-against-metal when you push it shut.

Tea black, I'm out the door within fifteen silent minutes, throat properly scalded and mind racing. And despite the fact that my parents' room directly connects to the kitchen, I successfully accomplished it all without so much as a peep or bed frame creak from their room. Neither of them even rolled over.

I can't lose my job. That's the beginning of the end of my reality and the reason I'm off to work early today. I need it for more reasons than simply a paycheck, though that's more than enough. And I shouldn't lose my job, right? It was one silly mistake and it can be explained. I can explain it away, can't I? I mean, I do good work. Diana can rely upon me. My colleagues and friends can too. I pull my weight. I help out across all departments. I pay attention to details and I don't make mistakes.

Oh . . . bugger. None of that matters. I am so going to lose my job. Without question I will be let go. What does it matter that Diana can rely upon me until the moment she can't? And who is going to take my friends' opinions into account? Sara can't save my job by saying I work well across departments. And what's Becca going to add? That I often deliver bad financial news to Diana so she doesn't look like a plonker when Diana pushes back and scares her?

Who cares if I pay attention to details? Yippee that I file papers well and can tell the difference between a Miro and a Monet, and the need for a full stop over a comma. I certainly missed the teeny-weeny detail that Richard, Mr. Davies, and a *Times* reporter stood mere inches from me when I blurted, "*That's a forgery*," yesterday.

What if Diana loses her position too? She could. I humiliated her, as she said herself, and worse yet, I exposed her to scandal, exposed the Gallery to scandal. What if the one and only woman keeper in all the UK gets sacked because I blundered?

I'm going to be sick . . . again.

I step onto the Underground train and the world blues at the edges. There's no air in here. It's hot, stifling. I can't breathe. I grab on to a pole by the door with both hands high and search for an open seat. There are none. I grip tighter and drop my head between my arms. "Just breathe." I literally say the words aloud. The man next to me hears and steps away. Let him think I'm daft. Fainting is not an option.

A young man dressed in a forest-green corduroy suit taps my shoulder and gestures to his seat. I offer a weak thanks and drop into it, slumping against the carriage's sidewall as the train races me from Oxford Circus to Pimlico.

The hopes of what I want to keep fade as I recall the hopes I have thoroughly dashed. I wasn't supposed to be begging for my job today. I wasn't supposed to be praying all could be made well.

Today, after the high of Diana's spectacularly successful opening, I was supposed to drum up the courage to show her the Polaroids I made last week of some of my work. I was supposed to ask her to view my portfolio. I was supposed to ask her for one of those coveted spots in her upcoming British Emerging Artists Exhibition.

Because while I haven't come up the traditional way, I am an artist. No, I'm not enrolled in school at St. Martin's, but I used to work there. I know what it takes to be one, a real one, and my paintings are comparable to those of many of the students there. Yes, there's a lot lacking in my work and in my portfolio, I understand that too. But isn't that what her Emerging Artists Exhibition is all about? It's not meant to feature artists who have made it, but artists who might, ones who need a boost of confidence, a crack in the doorway, and a chance that may never come again.

I hoped, after seeing my potential as her assistant, she'd see the potential in my art. Perhaps give me that chance, just one spot in the exhibition's lineup. That was the hope at least. That was the grand dream.

Yesterday's grand dream.

———

Everything leading to yesterday started—and ended—with Paddy O'Brien.

Someone encouraging you, believing in you, all while knowing your hopes and dreams, faults and fears, can be a very surreal thing. That's the perfect word, too, because the optimism it invokes is quite distorting and unreal. I should have known better . . .

I first met Paddy while wandering around St. Martin's School back when I was fifteen years old. My friends and I were headed to Covent Garden one weekend for the open-air concerts and street performances. But I wasn't into music as much as they were and they weren't into art as much as I was. When we hopped off the Underground at Charing Cross Station and passed the school like we always did, some instinct, unspoken desire, or epiphany struck me, and while they walked on I walked in.

No one was minding the door. No one stopped me. Only Padraig O'Brien, a burly middle-aged Irishman, even noticed me. He looked up from scrubbing a stubborn stain off the white-and-black-checkered linoleum with a long-handled mop, nodded, and resumed scrubbing. No words spoken. No questions asked. He simply caught my eye and I felt he saw me as clearly as I saw him. I'm not exaggerating.

That day I wandered in and out of the empty classrooms, the half-full studios with stressed students deep into their term-end assignments, and I fell in love. It wasn't just being near art, like one can be when standing in a museum or a gallery; it was being close to the energy of its creation. The messiness, the intimacy, the grandeur, and the soul involved in making art. I sensed both the acumen and ability of those students as surely as I understood their vulnerability and desperation, their rawness and even their heartbreak. They were living Picassos—their souls splayed two-dimensionally across what they strove to create.

That Saturday turned into two, and soon Paddy and I began talking, him often leaning against the second windowsill on the third floor and me perched on the abandoned desk that still rests outside the watercolor studio. Another few Saturdays after that he introduced me to the headmaster, who happened to be in his office that weekend to prepare for a seminar.

Paddy announced with no preamble, "This is Lily Summers. She needs a part-time job here, and I can vouch for her."

I do? His words shocked me as much as they surprised the headmaster. I still had two years of secondary school before possibly heading to secretarial college as my mum hoped. But after being awarded the job, then and there, to clean two evenings a week and work in the administrative office five hours each Saturday, I discovered Paddy was right.

That job filled a hole within me I didn't know existed. A longing. An ache. At first I thought it was about the money. It certainly helped out at home. Then, maybe, I thought it was the opportunity to see artists create and grow. Because while I cleaned floors, washed paintbrushes and sponges, sorted paint tubes, and wrapped molding clay tight in plastic wrap to keep it from drying, I watched them. I studied what each student created, I listened and absorbed every word the professors said, and each evening after work, as Paddy and I made the rounds to close down and lock up the school, I shared with him what I learned and what I'd do if ever I was the creator.

It was Paddy's idea to create a workspace for me in the back of a utility closet, and again, Headmaster MacKenzie gave his permission. Within a day I realized that bringing home extra money, learning from students and professors, and witnessing the creation of art had all started to fill the hole, but none could finish the job. It was the actual creating itself that made me whole, or at least led me to feel that way.

It was only the back half of a utility closet with a window, but it was the most wonderful space I'd ever seen and the most thoughtful, extravagant gift I'd ever received. Paddy stocked it with paint tubes that students had thrown away yet still held a few drops, brushes whose bristles only needed to be trimmed and oiled to get a little more life coaxed from them, and canvases that had been tossed but could easily be painted over and used for a second, third, fourth, or even fifth time.

Then when I was eighteen and wanted to join him full-time working at the school, he stepped in again, in an equally dramatic way.

"You've got a right solid brain and you can get a better job, even here, with a proper secretarial degree. Headmaster MacKenzie won't hire secretaries without advanced training, and he's not alone in that. Most places won't any longer because they don't need to . . . Your family may always need help, Lily. Grow your skills because some jobs pay better than others."

When I pushed back, saying my sister hadn't gone on to secretarial college and did just fine, he marched me into Headmaster MacKenzie's office and told him of Queen's Secretarial College. The headmaster was delighted and, right on the spot, moved me into more office work and raised my pay. Paddy slid me a sideways grin and we never spoke of it again.

And it was Paddy, near graduation time from uni, who showed me the advertisement for the Tate Gallery position. I'm not sure between the two of us who was more pleased when Diana hired me. I'm also not sure who was more pleased when, after I'd studied hard and worked even harder, she promoted me in an unprecedented move to her assistant keeper.

Then a couple weeks ago, I showed Paddy Diana's advertisement for artists to submit work for her British Emerging Artists Exhibition.

"It's time." He grinned.

"I'm not sure. I'm still working on the masters. My technical skills aren't up to scratch yet."

"It's time." His words were short, clipped, defined, and dogmatic. I believed him, and I promised him, if accepted on potential, I'd strive to create something new, something truly mine, for the exhibition.

"Good." He laughed, but it wasn't light and easy. There were notes beneath that signaled a forthcoming lecture. "You're hiding here in your painting. You've copied others long enough. Freedom takes courage."

Freedom takes courage. It was that dictum, that hope—the bright audacity of it—and his belief in me that caused the trouble yesterday. Because in addition to all I'd done to make the Picasso show possible, it was the sparkling hope that I could be featured in the British Emerging Artists show that sent me from standing straight to soaring sky-high.

I didn't take the Underground yesterday morning—I was flying too high to go underground. I walked the almost three kilometers to the Gallery and watched the sun come up in the parks. I smiled at birds, grinned at opening daffodils, and laughed at puffy passing clouds skittering away as the temperature rose. And all during my walk I rehearsed what I was going to say so nerves didn't upend me. I mentally catalogued all the masters I'd studied and copied over the last dozen years and thought of ways to reassure Diana that my work for the exhibition would be original. I was ready for that leap.

Wasn't I?

That's where I faltered yesterday. My steps slowed and I doubted. But she would understand that too, I tried to reassure myself. She loved unfinished works, saying that sometimes they were the most real and the most raw because they touched something so deep in the artist that he had to step away. And she wouldn't be upset I hadn't told her before that I painted because that was part of the same thread. Sometimes an artist needs to begin in secret because, just like those unfinished works she loves, true expression can be daunting, paralyzing, and even terrifying. It's a solitary, often painful venture and it's almost impossible to share such vulnerability with others. Until a chance comes along and breaks you free . . .

I'm embarrassed to admit—even to myself now as the train slows—that the welcoming and all-too-fictional scenarios I created in my head carried me all the way to the British Emerging Artists Exhibition's opening in June. Like a kid on Christmas morning, I envisioned the gift so completely it was as if I'd already unwrapped it. I felt the applause and heard the small gasps of wonder at my submitted work. The prickling bubbles of our raised glasses of celebratory champagne tickled my nose. And after handling all the last-minute details yesterday morning, it was that dream that compelled me to swipe the champagne flute off Dillon's silver tray. I had arrived.

Then I opened my mouth . . .

For what? And why? After a long sleepless night, I still don't know. Was it an impression? A sense? Something in the woman's eyes? Or was it the brushstrokes? Without seeing the painting again, I can't recall. I only know I looked at it, tilted my head to see it from a new angle, looked to the right, looked to the left, and . . .

Bam! A forgery!

CHAPTER 9

The Pimlico stop is announced over a scratchy intercom. I press a hand against my mouth to stave off the jumble that rises from my gut as I, along with several passengers around me, straighten and sit ready to disembark. As the carriage stops, I make my way to the door and exit with the quiet throng making this same trek daily. Climbing the stairs, I catch sight of a newspaper blowing across the stairway's opening onto Bessborough Road.

The Times.

I'd forgotten about the impending press. My breath quickens and I race up the last stairs. Huge white clouds chase each other across a cerulean sky. They convey a sense of movement, a rushing, almost as if something is on its way and about to arrive, whether I want it to or not. The blue hints at a promise. But rather than a promise, I sense a foreboding, a shadow growing within me—like when Daisy would trick me as a child and hold out both hands promising a surprise. I'd tap one, then the other, only to find the taffy was in neither but already in her mouth.

I walk the few blocks to the Tate. This early in the morning only one of the main entrance's glass-paneled doors will be unlocked. It actually opens before the employee and service entrances do, as it is where the night guard is stationed.

Rounding the final corner at Grosvenor Street, I find the source of the smell that's been growing over the past couple blocks. The wind blows from the southeast and is kicking up the scents of fish, oil, and even a touch of briny salt from the Thames. While the wind is certainly pulling in ocean waters, I suspect the massive power plant sitting just opposite is adding to this morning's pungency as well.

I turn to face the Gallery and, once more and always, stand awed by it. It's quite something really—the building itself. It started as Millbank Penitentiary and was converted in 1897 to a gallery named the National Gallery for British Art, funded anonymously by Sir Henry Tate, who also funded its first expansion over the following two years. The gallery wasn't actually called the Tate Gallery until 1932—after my favorite story about the flood and the William Turner drawings had already occurred.

This morning, the wind makes the heavy glass-and-metal door almost impossible to open. I use both hands and even then have to squeeze through the small opening I've made, then tumble in before the door closes upon my backside. I flash my badge to the guard, doubting that with only a single desk lamp lit at this hour he can see it. But that matters little as he doesn't glance up from his magazine and merely grunts as I pass. I count myself lucky. Anonymity works in my favor today.

Though every artificial light is still off, the large open space beyond the lobby is awash in gold as the sun breaks across a corner of the glass rotunda. At dead center I pull my breath through my nose to inhale my favorite scent—the Gallery's unique olfactory signature that is art. It calms me instantly. Everything can be going wrong, and one look up at the rotunda's glass ceiling and one whiff of this world and I'm okay.

While tempted to head straight to the basement and find Lucy in Archives or Sara in Donor Relations to unburden myself upon, I pass through the Central Gallery, the British Collections openings to my left and the Modern Collections on my right, and head to my office. Indulging in gossip with Lucy or Sara is the last thing I should do this morning. The less noise I make, the less chatter I start, and the fewer colleagues I see, the better. Maybe I can be so small and so quiet, no one will notice me at all and Richard won't remember he fired me.

My office door clicks shut, and I see a note sitting in the center of my desk.

come see me first thing this morning

I pick up the stiff card stock. The flowing script, clearly made by Diana's hand using her Montblanc fountain pen, is unmistakable, as is her use of only lowercase letters and no punctuation. So much for small and quiet.

I drop my handbag behind my desk, slip off my coat, and smooth down my hair and my new dress, as I decided to wear that cream jersey I'd bought in Knightsbridge. Then—without so much caution and quiet—I head a couple doors down the corridor. I rap a knuckle on Diana's office door and wait to be invited in. Usually I knock and enter with barely a pause between, but I'm not making any assumptions today.

A curt reply reaches me, and upon opening the door, she glowers at my new dress. It feels like I'm slapping her across the face, wearing the exact dress I should have worn yesterday. Yesterday, when I, too, should have been quiet, demure, and beige. She must believe of me what Mr. Davies said of himself yesterday—only now I'm the "chancer" and the "cheat."

I lower myself into the somewhat uncomfortable chair across from Diana's desk and recognize that, despite working hand in hand for the past five years, she hardly knows me. She knows my work ethic and my address. But she doesn't know that my building is part of a government-subsidized housing scheme. She doesn't know my mum makes my dresses, which are often remade hand-me-downs from my older sister, and that this dress is the first I've purchased from a store in years. She doesn't know I never take cabs or that I haven't gone to a restaurant in months because I can't afford such luxuries. She has no idea how desperately I need this job and how terrified I am that she'll fire me.

Sitting with my legs crossed and the cream jersey spilling gracefully over my knees, I feel frivolous and privileged, which is a lie. In this moment I need Diana to believe me and to believe in me.

"I didn't think you'd listen and stay home." Her lips twist in a sardonic smile. "Tell me, Lily. What did you see yesterday? What *exactly* did you see?"

It's her "exactly" or possibly her slow overpronunciation of it that sends a prickle down my spine. Something whispers to me, and it's so soft and featherlight I almost miss it and believe I imagine it. But rather than launch as I usually do, I wait. I buy time, settling deeper into the chair, as a certainty beyond my understanding grips me. I cannot tell Diana the truth. I cannot take her back to the beginning and share all the parts of my story I've either purposely or inadvertently hidden from her. I can't because something deep and dark dancing in her eyes tells me she no longer trusts me.

The realization throws me off-balance like the first time I saw Raoul Dufy's *Baigneuses en pleine mer et coquilles*. That painting is dark and mysterious, and it was a complete surprise from my go-to artist when I needed a shot of joy and whimsy. Dufy excels at sailboats-on-a-bright-sea kind of stuff. But upon seeing that painting, I wondered if I'd misjudged him, if I'd made assumptions about his inner world based on what I needed in mine. A crack opened within me, and I began to suspect that joy was a mere illusion in art as I already believed it to be in life. Seeing that painting was like losing a layer of my hope and naiveté. I lose another layer now.

I shake my head, first short and frantic, almost as if I am searching, then long and slow as I come to grips with how I must answer. "I simply looked at *Woman Laughing* and thought Picasso couldn't have painted it." I glance to the door and feel her eyes shift with mine. "Positioned between *Woman in an Armchair* and *Bullfight*, with *Woman with Arms Leves* just beyond, it felt wrong. Jarring."

"I laid out the exhibition in an order you didn't like?"

"Maybe?"

Her eyes widen, but she says nothing. I see our years working together. I see the times we sat laughing in this very office over something absurd that happened in the Gallery or something outrageous one of the donors requested. I see the times she shared with me how hard it was to move up in the arts as a woman. I see the afternoon she told me of her relief, even surprise, at securing the keeper of the Modern Collections position.

The fact that I have jeopardized any of that, on a whim as I've just implied, is shocking. For us both. I backpedal just a touch, because it's as close to the truth as I can articulate. "Nothing about the installation surprised me. I mean, the painting was right on the wall, but it was wrong for the man. I'm saying Picasso couldn't have painted those works in that order."

I swipe my hand back and forth as if cleaning a chalkboard, erasing yesterday. "But it doesn't matter. I shouldn't have said anything. I spoke out of turn."

Her eyebrows rise in agreement with my last comment, but still she says nothing. Her brows lower and furrow, and I suspect she is sifting through all I've said.

"I went back to the room yesterday afternoon and studied the painting. What do you mean Picasso couldn't have painted them in that order? He couldn't have painted *Woman Laughing* in 1930?"

Her voice isn't challenging or angry. Her first question drips with condescension, and I sink deeper into the chair. But her second lifts in curiosity.

"I don't know." I hate sounding young, silly, and incapable—a problem rather than a solution—but I have nothing to offer. I'm confused myself. I just want this to go away. My head drops and I see I'm twisting my fingers in my lap and attacking that poor cuticle I destroyed yesterday.

When I look up I catch a flash of triumph in Diana's steel-blue gaze. A split second later it's gone. I ask a simple question. "How can I make this right?"

She leans back and oddly I sense she's more relaxed now. "Since you're unsure of everything it seems, there's nothing you can do. And perhaps that's best. You won't add to the problem." She gestures to the paper sitting at the edge of her desk. "*The Times* had a field day with it, of course, so Richard is meeting with Mr. Davies again to smooth things over." She draws a long, slow breath into her nose and exhales through flattened lips. "We simply need to wait and see how this plays out."

She closes her eyes for a moment and she looks older somehow. Not somewhere in her midforties, but ancient, worn, and weary. Her hair is pulled back in her usual chignon, but it's tighter than usual too. She's wearing a thin black wool turtleneck and matching skirt. There is no color to her—not her outfit, not her face, not her lips. She has transformed from goddess to ghost. She opens her eyes and waves her hand. There are no gold bracelets to tinkle and ting with the motion. "You can go now."

I lean forward, wanting to restore our connection and our friendship. I truly want to help. "Diana?"

She lifts her chin to the door. "Go."

I stand and walk to the door.

"Lily?" She calls me back. "You're not fired, not yet, but you must stay away from Richard. Keep your head down, your office door shut, and do your job."

"Thank you." Just as I'm about to close the door, I look back. "Diana? I'm sorry to ask, but do you . . . ?"

"Do I what?" She swipes a hand across her forehead as if weary or in pain.

"You said you studied the painting yesterday. What did you think? Is *Woman Laughing* a forgery?"

She stares at me and her eyes narrow at their edges. "Absolutely not."

CHAPTER 10

W*hat exactly did you see?"* Diana's question haunts me. It rolled through my mind all day yesterday, and today, like one of Mum's old records, crooning soft and low like Vera Lynn or Jimmy Young, with just a hint of painful mystery, it plays on. Something about Diana's face or tone in that question sits uneasily within me, but I can't slow down the memory enough to hear and see it, to dissect it, and to understand what it means.

And last night, unable to sleep again, I stupidly played the Beatles' *Help* album. It seemed fitting as I need help, but the actual lyrics of that song and those of "Yesterday" did nothing but fill me with more self-loathing and regret.

"I thought you were painting at St. Martin's tonight." Daisy startles me as she steps into the kitchen.

I place the bowls I've just dried into the cupboard and lean against the counter. "There's stuff to do here."

She glances around and senses the quiet in the apartment. "Mum and Dad are still at her therapy appointment?"

I nod.

"I thought they'd be home by now."

"I rescheduled them for a bit later because you don't usually stop by on Thursdays."

Daisy chuffs, small and almost disillusioned, as she turns to leave. "You think of everything, as usual."

"Wait," I call after her, but once she turns back, I have nothing to say. I think I want her help. But it's foreign and hard and I can't get the words out, as I've never asked for her help and wonder if she'd even give it.

My sister understands nothing about my predicament. How can she help me? Yet she also has more grit and common sense than anyone I know. Paddy would call it courage. Daisy has it in spades and I fear I have none. I feel myself retreat without moving a muscle and offer the first inane thought that comes to mind. "How are you doing, with the pregnancy? When are you due?"

Her eyes flicker and something in them dims. "Is that really what you wanted to ask?"

Rather than answer, I move into our parents' bedroom to both strip the sheets from their bed and collect their laundry. Daisy follows me and moves to the head of the bed to pull up the bottom sheet. She yanks at it, tugging it from my hands, and even this simple task becomes a battle between us.

"I asked you a question." She rolls the sheet into a ball within her arms. "And I'm due in August."

I strip the cover off one pillow. "Four months. That's soon. You should be resting."

Daisy straightens and stares at me. Her expression hardens and she snatches the pillow cover dangling from my hand. Without another word she strides from the room to the hall bath to gather up towels. This time, I'm the one following.

"Stop. Let me do that."

"Don't tell me what to do." She spins on me and her words aren't harsh or loud. They're quiet, barely above a whisper. But it's not the words that snag my attention; it's Daisy's expression. It no longer radiates anger, but worry and a wariness.

I blink. In this one look at my sister, all my questions about Diana and our talk yesterday, and why I couldn't tell her the truth, are suddenly answered. But I push that thought away for the moment to focus on my sister, still standing frozen in front of me.

She shrugs and turns away, dropping all the laundry in her hands mid-turn. "Tell Mum and Dad I dropped by and I'll ring tomorrow."

I grab at her hand. "Daisy?"

She dodges me and swipes at her eyes. They glisten with unshed tears. "It's nothing. Hormones."

"Go home and rest."

A flash of anger and resentment shoots through her eyes before she shrugs again and strides from the flat. I chase after her, and once outside, I reach for the one thing, the one place, Daisy and I have in common. Kensington Gardens. She used to take me there from our home in Hounslow on weekends. We never went after . . . Well, it's still one of my best memories with her.

"Do you want to go for a walk?"

She tilts her head towards the park, acquiescing, and I wonder if she's remembering those days as well. Watching the swans on the pond, the sweets vendors lining the thoroughfares, the ducks nibbling at breadcrumbs, the kites soaring through the sky, the carefree joy of it all.

Not much is said as we walk the short distance along Kensington Church Street to reach Notting Hill Gate, then the few blocks right to the park's entrance. It's evening and the grey calms me. It also works its magic on the silence between us. The quiet no longer feels fraught and charged but almost comfortable.

As we step through the gate and onto the park's gravel path, I find my courage and my words. "I'm sorry again about Tuesday. I said all the wrong things."

"Just now too. I have to stop expecting so much."

"What do you mean?"

"I mean you don't see me, Lily. If I, or any of us, don't act according to your expectations, you don't see us. You see what you want rather than what is real."

"Malarkey."

"I didn't come by to fight." She grips my forearm. "I came to talk to Mum and Dad, but I'll start with you. We all spin around you regardless."

My mouth drops. Again, I feel I've been unjustifiably hit, but before I can protest, she continues.

"We're moving at summer's end and I want Mum and Dad to come with us."

I stop walking and we stand staring at each other. Daisy waits for my reaction, but I'm gobsmacked and unable to move.

"Mum is lonely during the days, and it's not safe for her to be alone. Then there's the baby. She could help out and she'd love that, and Posy and Hy would adore having her and Dad near. It's the right thing to do, for them, for all of us, but we'll still need help from you, at least for a little while." She looks into the gloaming. "But you'll be free. Find a guy, settle down . . ." She offers a sly smile.

"You think trilling Cat Stevens will make this better?"

She snickers, and like earlier it doesn't come out light and happy. Yet this time, I expect she intended it to. "It seemed appropriate. You can't live with Mum and Dad and manage their lives forever, as much as you think you should or deserve to."

Something in me shrinks, darkens, grows small and sad. "Where are you moving?"

"Richmond."

Richmond. Where they lived before. Before the war. Before me.

"That's so far," I sputter.

"Not by train, and there are plans to extend the Overground there." Daisy's words are quick, clipped, and I suspect she's thought this through from every angle and probably rehearsed this conversation several times too. "There's a pub there. The owner wants to retire and sell it to Sean. He's reasonable too; he won't gouge us."

"Sean's after his own pub then." My voice lifts, but it's not a question. My brother-in-law has dreamed of running his own pub as long as I've known him. While he's plotted, planned, and saved, he's also always shrugged away the possibility it could ever become reality. I understand that feeling, as well as the tantalizing hope that one's most treasured dream could actually come to fruition.

For me, maybe not. For Sean, it should. He's a natural at pouring a good pint and making every single man—because the patrons are all men—feel welcome and at home within a step of the bar. People flock to him like the pigeons to tourists holding grain in Trafalgar Square. It's the luck, the gift, or the gab of the Irish, he'd say.

"There's a full kitchen too," Daisy adds with excitement.

While Sean has always wanted to own a pub, Daisy takes care of people through food. Her own kitchen, a proper business, would be a dream come true for her as well.

"You'll be busy. You won't have time for Mum and Dad."

"And you do?" she retorts, then reaches for me as I step away. "I shouldn't have said that. But this is happening, Lily. My family needs this to happen. With the baby coming we need more space and we need to move forward. London's too expensive, for Mum and Dad too. Everything Mum needs costs more. It's making her life smaller, not larger."

My first instinct is to fight back, but I can't. Deep in my heart, a whisper concedes to Daisy's point. Ordering the special cabs for Mum is a luxury we cut months ago. Most of the city is cut off from her now, as buses are only just beginning to convert to accommodate wheelchairs. And if that wasn't bad enough, even our neighborhood shops are out of reach. She used to enjoy rolling to the butcher on Kensington Church Street or the cheese shop on High Street by herself, but they've grown too expensive. Rising prices have forced Daisy and me to handle most of our weekly shop a few Underground stops farther out from city center.

"It's got a garden too."

Daisy's sentence drags my mind back to the present. "What's got a garden?"

"The house we found. It's a proper house for two-thirds our current rent and almost three times the space. We won't be on top of each other, and it has a real garden for the girls."

I nod. If I try to do anything more, tears will come and I don't know why. I should be happy for her. Because as much as she says her girls need a garden, Daisy needs one more. Mum does too.

The girls in our family have been named after flowers for

generations, but Daisy is the first born with a green thumb. My sister is never happier than when in a garden, coaxing beauty from dark, seemingly dead ground. And Mum always says a growing garden is the closest she'll get to heaven on earth.

I shift my focus from my sister's expectant face. I sense what she wants from me, but I can't give it to her. Looking into the distance feels safer. It allows me to pretend life is what it was only a few minutes ago—not that it was all that good. But at least I understood it. Now it's spinning out of control.

I reach for solid ground. "I need to get back and finish the washing."

Daisy pushes out a short, harsh breath. "Go then." As I step away, she calls to me. "Motherhood teaches you a lot, Lily. You'll see someday."

I turn back, unsure where she's going with her random statement and annoyed she might be venturing towards Cat Stevens again and my clearly lackluster love life.

She closes the distance between us. "If the accident happened to me, with either Hyacinth or Posy in the car, I'd never blame them, no matter how we got into that car. And don't forget my grabbing you put you there just as much as your barging in on me . . . But I wouldn't love them less, that's my point. And I'd do everything in my power to help them let it go and move on."

"Have you?"

"To a degree, yes. To the degree you'll let me."

"So it's my fault. Like always."

"Only because you see it that way. You hold on to an instant that happened almost twenty-three years ago so tightly it's suffocating us and you refuse to see it."

I shrug away. Her hand drops from my arm. "I have to go."

This time she doesn't stop me—and it breaks my heart.

———

The past floods me with each step towards home.

It wasn't that day, at ten years old, when I started a kitchen fire trying to make Dad his morning fry-up. Or the time I was seven and I added too many flakes to the washer and flooded our building's washroom. Daisy was referring to that moment when I was five—an afternoon we never speak of but constantly relive nonetheless.

I put on my best dress and invited Daisy to a tea party, but she refused to come. She and her best friend Milly were sitting on her bedroom floor playing jacks. At each swipe at the jacks, they dared each other to do something crazy or share a secret or something. I don't quite remember, but I do remember they were whispering and laughing and I wanted to be a part of it. I wanted to be a part of anything Daisy did back then.

So when she bounced the red rubber ball super high to clear the floor of all the jacks, I barged in and swiped the ball. Jacks flew everywhere. Milly screamed and scrambled away from the flying arms and legs as I slid across the floor and Daisy lunged for me.

Here the memory grows technicolor vivid, but maybe that's because I've replayed it in my head so many times I've created it rather than actually recall it. Yet that's art—perception and reality merging in a new form.

Daisy dove for me. Jacks flew. One scratched the back of my leg. I felt the pressure of the ball tightly gripped in my right hand. It was hot, sweaty, and sticky. Daisy had my left arm gripped so firmly, I wondered if it might break and what Mum would say. My right hand rose and the red ball came towards me. Then it was gone. Not swallowed, just held against the roof of my mouth. Pride swelled within me. I had won. I had defeated Daisy.

My euphoria lasted only a heartbeat, however, as Daisy wrenched my left arm so hard she lifted me off the floor. I cried out and the ball slipped past my tongue and lodged in my throat. The world turned spotty at the edges and I sucked in air. Nothing came.

I heard screaming. I felt the floorboards shake with pounding steps. The loud high-pitched tones of true panic filled the space around me. The scene then takes on the distorted dark tones of one of Picasso's late surrealist paintings—that's probably my imagination rather than true memory—but the world swirled like Picasso's Blue Period crashing into his surrealist masterpiece *Guernica.*

Mum threw me into the back of our car. The rear was tiny and, even at five years old, my knees hit the back of her seat. I remember believing that if I could press my knees into her hard enough, feel her back against my legs, I'd be fine. My mum was invincible, all-powerful, and she would let nothing bad happen to me as long as I stayed close.

Then all was darkness and my real or imagined memories ended there.

What happened next remains a stark reality. I woke up in hospital later that day with a terribly sore throat and a broken arm encased in plaster from my neck to my fingertips. Mum didn't wake for days and, only then, after three surgeries. A lorry ran a traffic light and broadsided our car blocks from the hospital, breaking my arm and shattering Mum's lower back.

My arm healed. Her back did not.

So yes, Daisy can call it an accident. Or she can blame the lorry driver who was paging through his *A to Z* while driving. Or she can blame me—the instigator of the entire affair. After all, it's the first drop of paint on a canvas that determines every aspect of the completed piece that will follow. I pushed in on Daisy. I taunted my sister by lunging for the ball. I shoved it into my mouth. Our mum can't walk because of me.

That was the only time, before Tuesday, I'd said the words, "Can't I just take it back?" And while Daisy shot back that I couldn't "in a million lifetimes," her eyes weren't angry; they were filled with fear.

And that's what I remembered today—about Diana yesterday when she said, *"What exactly did you see?"* It wasn't the question she asked; it was her look when she asked it.

Like Daisy long ago, Diana's expression carried the expected mix of anger and disappointment, but it was overlaid with a thread of fear, worry, and wariness. Her look told me very clearly that I had done something that impacted her profoundly and personally, and it was of such importance that the ramifications hadn't fully played out. But most of all, I scared her. More than a job. More than a scandal. I had somehow threatened Diana at her very core. And that made me a problem.

A problem she needed to manage.

CHAPTER 11

Daisy's news hit hard in a light-bulb moment at 1:00 a.m. and cost me another night's sleep. I realized not only do I need to help her with money to support our parents, but I'll also need to find a flat for myself—and that one won't be subsidized. So this morning I head to work early once more, this time with a plan to fix my blunder and ease Diana's fears—and hopefully save my job.

The new security guard—I still haven't learned his name, but neither has he bothered to learn mine—nods me in and, moments later, without a glimmer of surprise, nods me back out. I came to the office for only one thing this early—Mr. Edward Davies's home address.

Back on Grosvenor Street, I pull out my *A to Z*. I've certainly heard of his address, as it's widely considered one of the most notorious in London, but I've never been there and am shocked to find it only three streets away from where I presently stand.

While most of my stories about Dolphin Square come from Sara, as she's been there lots of times to meet with patrons and donors, it's constantly in the newspapers as well. Dozens of lords, ladies, and members of Parliament live there . . .

John Profumo, secretary of state for war, had an affair with a nineteen-year-old model while he called it home. And if that wasn't enough, the model Christine Keeler was simultaneously sleeping with a Soviet naval attaché, making the resulting scandal explosive enough to bring down Prime Minister Macmillan's whole government about a decade ago.

Soviet spy John Vassall lived at Dolphin Square as well—and was arrested there too.

Diana Mitford Mosley also resided in a lovely flat in one of the buildings for a time, Fascist Hitler-loving socialite that she was. She was also Clementine Churchill's first cousin—I can't imagine the Sunday-dinner family dynamics of that one.

And speaking of Churchill family dynamics, the former prime minister's own daughter Sarah called the square home as well—until she got evicted for throwing gin bottles out her flat window.

Yes, it's notorious and somehow it doesn't surprise me that someone like the blustery Mr. Edward Davies lives there too.

I round the corner, and though I've approached the square from the side, I'm shocked at its sheer size once I grasp its totality from the front. Rather than a normal London square, perhaps like Bloomsbury, Eaton, or countless others built within the city of equal or greater renown, Dolphin Square is massive. Beyond massive.

I count . . . one . . . two . . . three . . . thirteen attached buildings, and each appears ten stories tall. There must be well over one thousand flats here. It's a city unto itself. I walk through one of the three front central arches of the building facing the Thames. It opens into the square's central courtyard, which isn't a square at all but a rectangle the length of a couple football pitches. It takes me several minutes to cross it, and I read the names engraved in stone above each building's front door as I proceed. *Grenville. Drake. Raleigh. Hawkins* . . . I recognize *Drake*, assuming it refers to Admiral Francis Drake, and wonder if the other names come from the admiralty as well.

I glance to my scrap of paper and discover I've already passed Mr. Davies's building, Hawkins, and turn back. It sits on the "square's" southeast border, and I imagine the top flats boast extraordinary views of the river.

Twenty minutes later, I pull together my courage and press the buzzer outside his front door—one on the top floor, of course. I realize I've held the button overly long only after a man in a starched white shirt and black tie and coat opens the door, stares at me, then pointedly glares at my finger still pressing the button.

"I'm so sorry." I pull my hand back. "Mr. Davies?"

"May I say who's calling?" His voice drones, level and bored. "At this early hour."

I glance to my watch. It's eight o'clock. Early, yes, but I wanted to make sure I arrived before Mr. Davies left for work. "I'm Lily Summers from the Tate Gallery."

"The Tate?" A bellow comes from somewhere deep behind this man who could've—should've—been cast in that old *Addams Family* television series. "Who the devil are you?"

The man widens his eyes briefly as if frustrated that his job has been usurped. He steps aside, implying I may enter, but he makes no move to lead me to the voice.

I pass him and stand in the central foyer. It's a commanding, masculine space. The walls are painted the most vibrant royal blue and, to the right, three small crystal chandeliers light the length of a corridor. Light dances everywhere, including off a small Duchamp and an O'Keeffe. I pause at the O'Keeffe. This painting is from her *Sky Above Clouds* series, which she only began a few years ago. I've always admired—rather adored—her work, but I have never seen an original. Her color, movement, and perspective; her confidence, freedom, and originality. I clasp my hands together to keep from reaching out and touching it.

"Well . . . get in here!"

I spin towards the sound and see a yellow thread of lamplight spill halfway down the corridor across the dark wood floor. As I step into the wood-paneled room, my eye first catches upon a massive nineteenth-century partner's desk. Although it's clearly an antique and of high quality, it has been lacquered a deep bloodred. At first I decry the destruction of such a beautiful piece of furniture. Then I recognize a new beauty in it—one that's both startling and remarkable. Behind it sits exactly who I expect. But by his expression, I sense he was not expecting me.

"You." His one word, mirroring the same exclamation he made Tuesday, is filled with shock and disgust. "What the blazes do *you* want?" He leans back in his chair rather than make any move to stand, and I notice a cat, a small tabby sitting on the desk just to his right. It's so still, despite the bellowing mere inches from its ear, that I think it's a statue until its tail slowly lifts and curls.

"Mr. Davies?"

"Come to finish me off?"

"I came to apologize, to say I was wrong." I take a deep breath to launch into my version of what Dickens once wrote for Ebenezer Scrooge, *"There's more of gravy than of grave about you, whatever you are!"*—or in my case, *"There's more black tea, boiled egg, champagne, and adrenaline than forgery about what I saw."* But he stands so quickly, I lose all thought.

"Blast, girl, I don't care if you were wrong."

"You don't?"

"The damage is done. What the painting is or is not is irrelevant."

"But it's . . . it's all that matters. It's a Picasso." I blink, I stutter, I'm lost.

"My reputation meant a bloody spot more than some paint Picasso splattered on a canvas. The money I'd gain in selling it meant more, but that's lost no matter the final verdict. That painting carries the odor of scandal now, making truth irrelevant. Didn't you read *The Times*?"

I close my eyes. Like Diana says, art is mercurial. Its value turns on sentiment, and that changes faster than a hiccup. And *The Times* certainly made sure sentiment was very against Mr. Davies. That reporter penned an atrocious article—vicious enough to command a full column on the front page—that actually implied Mr. Davies had tried to "hoodwink" the Tate and wider art community for profit.

"I thought if you and the Tate worked together, *The Times* would be forced to print a retraction. Diana Gilden often authenticates paintings for insurance companies and sales, and her reputation is impeccable. She's considered one of the top modernist art experts in the world. Her word, with your confidence in her, can settle this whole thing."

Mr. Davies drops into his seat again. His eyes never leave mine, nor does he ask me to sit. His hand reaches and swipes down his tabby from head to tail. The cat pads closer to him across the desk. "Did she send you?"

"She doesn't know I'm here."

"In this little scenario of yours, does the fact that Diana authenticated the painting when I purchased it help or hurt? How does her word, simply corroborating her word, 'settle this' as you say? Don't we both look culpable? Don't we both look like we're trying to cover something up? And what are you doing blathering to me about this? She has the provenance and the painting. If she wanted to examine either and make a definitive statement, why hasn't she? She can call *The Times* as well as anyone. She got them there in the first place."

My brow furrows. "Then could you hire someone else? But let Diana help too?" My voice rises. I clear my throat in an effort to bring it back down. "Her authority will carry weight. I know you've spoken to Director Browning, but—"

"I commend your loyalty or your sense of self-preservation." He waves a hand at me. "But get out. I don't have time for this. I'll not throw Diana Gilden a bone to save her job or yours when she's done nothing to help me. My insurance company and Scotland Yard will handle this."

"But the Tate needs— There's no need to call in the authorities." My knees turn a bit jelly-ish and I drop into the seat across from him, despite not being invited to sit.

In an instant the cat shoots from the desk to my lap. Mr. Davies lifts out of his chair and reaches to me. "She bites. No, don't—"

I startle but nothing happens. Or at least nothing bad happens. The cat curls onto my lap and stares straight up at me. I glance to Mr. Davies. His eyes are wide, possibly wider than mine. He gestures to the cat, then to the door. "Still, get out. I don't bloody care what the Tate needs."

While I waited in Diana's office Tuesday, my heart felt like it couldn't beat. It was constricted, frozen. Now it feels like it's grown too large. It beats so fast I can't draw breath around it. I physically hurt. I pop up to leave and the cat slides with a whine from my lap.

"Wait . . . *your* insurance company?" It takes three tries to get air past the lump in my chest and continue. I realize that in all the rush of planning the exhibition, Diana didn't add *Woman Laughing* to the Tate's insurance policy. "You insured *Woman Laughing*?"

"I insure everything with Lloyd's, Miss Summers. Another lesson I've learned the hard way."

A new thought sneaks into me. Perhaps I was right. Perhaps *Woman Laughing* is a forgery after all. And perhaps Mr. Davies knows it. Because while a private collector insuring a painting is not unheard of, it is still fairly rare. In all the years I've been mailing updates to our insurance company, adding pieces as they enter the Gallery for an exhibition, then subsequently removing them when an exhibition closes, I have only come across a handful of privately owned pieces covered on personal policies.

It comes down to a classification, really. Art is not defined in its own insurance category but rather still categorized as "marine cargo," as it has been for the last two hundred years. This leads most people to misunderstand the nature of insurance and drop their policies once the art hangs on their walls. After all, a painting on the wall is no longer "cargo."

But Mr. Davies saw past this all-too-common misconception. He kept his policy on *Woman Laughing*. He'll be paid—not at some devalued price because of this scandal, but the full price for which he insured the painting.

He continues talking, unaware my mind has drifted far beyond our conversation, and it takes me a moment to catch up. ". . . a full investigation is the only way my name will be restored."

"People will forget. Something new will hit the front page."

Mr. Davies smiles something small, almost sad. "You're young and naive, and you're wrong, Miss Summers. In some cases people do forget, when it's convenient. But I don't have generations of trust built into my name, with every assumption tilting in my favor because I'm a member of the club. The toffs in that room Tuesday morning wanted to hear what you said and they want to believe that reporter's vitriol about me. They want to believe because it keeps everything nice and tidy."

He flicks his hand at the wrist as if shooing a pesky and imaginary fly. "The Tate will certainly survive this and Diana will too. She's one of them. Not from here I gather, but their lot knows no borders." He looks me up and down as if taking in every color block of my Mary Quant knock-off dress. "You may survive it too. But not me. I'm the one who will fall because if you somehow manage to rise in this society, they'd like to see you sent right back down." He looks above my head. "Monks, please show Miss Summers to the door. I need to proceed with my day."

There is no sound or movement behind me, but there doesn't need to be. Monks is already standing close. He pulls my chair away even though I'm no longer sitting in it. It's a clear directive to follow him.

As I trudge to the front door, I peek into the wide opening to the living room. My eye travels past the antiques to the view, a sweep of the Thames and the land all the way to Big Ben, now aglow in full sunshine. I stall, ignoring Monks's soft cough, and canvass the room with more intention. Everything is fresh. The furniture is modern, and I recognize pieces by Finn Juhl and Børge Mogensen—only because Diana had me page through the New York Metropolitan Museum's recent Scandinavian Design Exhibition catalogue. I recognize Miro, Mondrian, Klee, and more. This flat is an art gallery. A new gallery. An expensive gallery.

Monks's subtle cough escalates to throat clearing, and I follow him to the door with the certainty that *Woman Laughing* is a forgery, and for all Mr. Davies's talk about reputation, I sense that's a misdirect. Money isn't inconsequential to this man. It means a lot to him, and he needs a lot of it. He reminds me of those men at Sean's pub he's always on about, the ones who have a scheme going, a plan for a quick score, and who don't mind crossing a few lines in the process. And today, in the art world, those avenues are growing wider and those lines fuzzier.

What better way to make a fast quid than to get paid for a forgery and then, as with so much of the Nazi-looted art coming back into the market, sell the original on the sly? Or never have an original at all and just make the whole thing up? We talk about it all the time at work, as it's getting to be a real problem. And even better, insure your whole scam with a company famous for insuring everything and then paying on even the dodgiest of claims.

"Everything" for Lloyd's has gone so far as to include insuring American actress Bette Davis's waist in the 1930s, actress Betty Grable's legs during World War II, the *Titanic* back in 1912, space exploration today, and even some killer whale named Namu that scientists were trying to transport from British Columbia to America last year.

That reputation for "always paying" is what has given them worldwide fame, and in Lloyd's case, I actually believe reputation means quite a lot. They certainly paid—promptly and in full—when American actor James Dean took out a life insurance policy with them a mere week before his not-so-clear-what-actually-happened death about twenty years ago.

With that guarantee bolstering him, Mr. Davies might be willing to risk a great deal. Now I just have to prove he isn't relying upon Lloyd's—he's defrauding them.

CHAPTER 12

Diana

Diana shifts in her favorite reading chair, but she cannot get comfortable. There is a "pea" somewhere in her bed, her chair, her life that keeps her from resting. It has poked at her incessantly since Tuesday, and her nerves near their breaking point. No, it started poking long before Tuesday.

Giving up on reading, just as she has given up on sleeping, she draws her book out of her lap and sets it on the small French table beside her chair. It's a little antique she and Heinrich found on their last trip to Paris together, over six years ago. Since then, she's gone to Paris alone.

She runs her finger over the kidney-shaped table's marble top, then trips it along its gilt metal gallery. It is a precious little detail, the bronze scalloped edging, and she'd fallen in love with it upon first sight. Heinrich purchased it at once without even asking the price. He insisted they celebrate the tiny drawing she'd just sold to a top Parisian dealer, and no cost was too high. It was her first sale of Heinrich's work to that particular dealer, and he was sure the relationship with the gallery would prove fruitful, and the table would always remind them of that.

Of course, Heinrich hadn't met the dealer. Diana handled all of that. He had just held the check and listened, eager and enrapt, as she conveyed the man's praise and compliments over their long lunch and accompanying bottle of chilled Viognier.

Diana raises her focus from the table to the garden outside the window. The daffodils have burst forth overnight and begun opening to the sun, and the cherry blossoms, lining the back garden wall, have just reached full bloom. Spring is well on its way. A new beginning.

New beginnings . . . She sighs long and deep, remembering her own. Some less successful than others.

"*Go.*" When she was nine, her mother had shaken her awake in the middle of the night with clothes in her hand, a sack resting at her feet. Rumors had reached her that the Gestapo was coming for her husband, a newspaper reporter who had written against the regime. She explained as much to her young daughter in whispered words and truncated sentences.

Before pushing her into the dark night, her mother held her tight only for a heartbeat, and Annika never said goodbye to her father. Even now, she wasn't certain he hadn't already been arrested and her mama was too afraid to share the truth.

Diana. Another new beginning.

"*You have fight in you, Annika. Like the goddess of the hunt. Diana.*" Heinrich had looked deep into her eyes within days of meeting her and christened her anew. He guided her, mentored her, praised her, and months later took her for his own, declaring they didn't need to study any longer—he, a visiting arts tutor at her local school, and she, a grant recipient. He didn't give the school notice; he just fled with his young protégé into the night. They could make it together, he told her, and within the exciting world he created, she soon came to believe him.

She loved who she was from his perspective. She loved how he looked at her, touched her, made her feel safe yet alive. He became that set-aside space, free from the pain of war, deprivation, and desperation. It was under his loving guidance she finally shed that scared, always hungry, always searching young girl and became who he said she was, who she had always been. Diana. Huntress. Goddess of the night and moon.

It was so easy to believe back then. So easy to slip into the luxurious fantasy and get lost, primarily because she wanted to get lost within it. But in moments like this, when struggling with rest and silence, she recognizes the lie.

Lie or not, they'd made it, just as he promised. She is surrounded by prestige, security, position, and power. How then is it
possible she still feels like that young girl? Still scared, running,
and struggling with every breath, transforming every shaky smile
with dogged determination into something confident and easy,
consciously smoothing out each word that threatens to crack.

Every day she struggles to master the woman her husband
has carefully set before her and fashioned down to the minutest
detail—the long hairstyle, always pulled back; the sparse yet bold
jewelry, only gold; the best dresses, silk stockings, latest heels—
and yet she is slipping. She feels the ground wet and slick beneath
her, sliding always back, never gaining traction to move forward.
There is no solid ground any longer, and she begins to doubt it
ever existed.

Diana closes her eyes to shut out spring, to banish new beginnings. She is tired. So very worn. Has there ever been a day, a true
full day of rest, since that early morning in 1939 when her mother
jostled her awake? A stillness comes over her as she accepts there
has not. That means thirty-four years of utter exhaustion.

"You are up early."

Diana turns her head at his soft question, a biting answer on
the tip of her tongue. For her husband isn't making a comment; he
is asking myriad questions in his four simple words—why did last
night not keep her in bed next to him? Why hadn't she wrapped
herself around him as she used to? What is she thinking and not
sharing? What . . . ? Why . . . ? When . . . ? Or maybe she is wrong
and it is a simple statement because he no longer cares enough to
wonder and ask. She presses her lips together against any reply
and faces the window once more.

Heinrich steps into the room. She can hear the soft pad of
his bare feet on the polished wood floor. The silk tie of his dressing gown catches her peripheral vision. It is loosely looped over
the silk-cashmere pajamas she'd impulsively purchased for an
outrageous sum at Turnbull & Asser last month.

He steps from beside her to behind her and gently gathers her
long blonde hair, twists it, and lays it over her left shoulder. Both

his hands then circle the nape of her neck and press upon the all-too-apparent knots within. She flinches at the quick shot of pain that travels down her spine.

"Did you sleep at all?" Heinrich whispers. He continues, with both the massage and the questions, before she can reply. "Do you remember after we met? All the trips we took? All we saw? Ate? Drank? Experienced?"

She snickers, failing to make a sound of light incredulity. These were not the roads her mind was traveling. Yet she is surprised at her laugh's derision, worn notes, and breathy delivery. She rushes to speak and direct his attention away from her tone. "Are we so old you need to ask?"

Heinrich chuckles softly, with all the high-dancing notes her voice lacked. Yet he doesn't speak. In the golden morning light growing outside the window, under the pressure of her husband's hands, Diana lets herself be led to where he wants her to go.

She again feels the firm, warm pressure of his hand engulfing her own as they legged it out of school, boarded the train from Liverpool to London, and another from London to Dover. She again tastes the tang of salt as they stood on the bow of the ferry crossing to Calais, feels the wood boards digging into her back as they huddled in the rear bay of a lorry and hitched a ride to Paris. Day in and day out they traveled, using her unspent tuition money along with his savings to fund their adventures. They scrimped and saved in all respects but one—they splurged on food and wine. They indulged in the experience of dining. He taught her the names of dishes, how to pull snails from their shells, calling the buttery dish escargot, how to properly sip an Irish oyster, enjoy a German Riesling, and how to choose the best cheeses to pair with it and the best wines to pair with everything else.

They didn't need to splurge on art. The great museums were free—the Prado and Reina Sofia in Madrid, the Louvre and Musée d'Orsay in Paris, the Rijksmuseum in Amsterdam, the Azulejo in Portugal, the Uffizi Galleries in Florence, and, of course, all of Rome.

And at night, woven together on broken, sagging mattresses in the least expensive inns and hostels they could find, they'd parse through every bite, every sip, every painting, artist, and brushstroke, until she wove herself into his dream. "You can learn them, breathe them, become them, Diana. Just as I have."

It was in Giverny, Monet's beautiful town in southern France, where she finally took that last step. They'd spent the day at the newly opened garden and home exhibition, reading Monet's diaries and letters, peeking into closets at the very clothes he wore, pulling into their nostrils the scent of the land he loved, relishing the colors, birdsong, sunshine, and balmy breeze, until Heinrich set down his travel easel and simply said, "It's time."

Diana watched, silent and stunned, as he created a Monet. Not one she had ever seen, but a Monet nonetheless. Heinrich's painting carried Monet's movement of light, his tripping colors, bleeding one into another at a distance but remaining unique up close. Chiaroscuro at its finest. Her lover had mastered the master.

Then she understood. Heinrich believed she could become someone new because he could become someone new. And he did, time and time again. He stepped within another's soul and existed within that artist on an entirely different plane. While working in Monet's gardens, a soft smile danced upon his lips, and his eyes took on the cloudy focus of a middle-distant memory—two aspects in his visage she'd never noticed before nor believed naturally existed. Not in Heinrich. Not in the man she loved. That was Monet's look. Heinrich *was* Monet.

Jealousy gripped her that day, yellow and green, grasping and forlorn. She remembers that as well. How she would love to do that, escape like that, live in that liminal space between beauty and reality. How she would love to feel, just once, such peace and pleasure smooth her facial muscles and release her ever-tense jaw.

But Heinrich had other plans.

A few days later, after they'd left Giverny and journeyed on to Paris, he pulled another painting out of his luggage and handed it to her. It was the tiny Renoir she'd seen on his desk back at school. At first her heart leapt with the gift. She studied it, loved it, and imagined where in their new home—for he promised they'd always be together—she would display it. But when she finally looked up, she realized it was not a gift. At least not one without strings.

"It's your turn. You will sell it."

She shook her head, sure she had heard him wrong. "You can't sell a Renoir. It's a treasure. We'll find another way." Her heart fluttered with panic, but she needn't have worried.

"It's alright. It's *my* Renoir."

A year later, after the money from the Renoir and a couple more works ran dry, they returned to London. They found a cheap flat in Islington, and Heinrich took a job with a potter in Ealing. At night they'd go together to the old potter's kiln room to use the spare kiln he hadn't fixed, heating it only to two hundred degrees Celsius, well below the danger point for even a cracked oven, and "bake" the canvases Heinrich had created throughout their year traversing Europe. Two Monets, a Campendonk, a Chagall, two Miros, one Renoir charcoal sketch, and three small Cassatts. Each baked just long enough, and not an instant beyond, to achieve aged perfection. They then spent their Saturdays searching for old frames amongst the market stalls along Portobello Road, haggling down the prices, as the art within held no value for them.

And while Heinrich painted in their tiny studio apartment, warm and greasy over a chippy, Diana donned her new persona each morning, in much the same manner as she slid one of the several Christian Dior dresses Heinrich had purchased for her at a consignment shop in Paris over her body, and looked for work.

Gone was the scrappy young Annika, barely twenty-three, with paint under her nails and clothes scavenged from Oxfam. "Diana" knew her worth. Diana knew art. She knew wine. She knew fashion, food, comportment, and presence. Heinrich had also created a backstory for his "Diana" and a résumé worthy of this new creation and the career she was embarking upon.

The famous John Mayor of London's Mayor Gallery ate it up. A year later the National Gallery. After that, the Dulwich Picture Gallery. Finally, with a glowing résumé even she believed, Diana Gilden walked up the broad stone steps to the imperious Tate Gallery and applied for the keeper position for its Modern Collections. Director Richard Browning fell in love with her style, acumen, instinct, and energy and hired her during their second interview—after, of course, publicly canvassing her name amongst the Tate's board and privately among the members of his club.

That's where the plan changed.

Diana wasn't supposed to fall in love—not with anything other than Heinrich. She was *his* masterpiece. Yet she loved her work, she loved the Tate, and she loved what she began to accomplish there. With determination, creativity, and effort, she believed she could make the Gallery's Modern Collections the talk of London and a luminary across Europe and the world.

Another flash of pain brings Diana back to the present. As usual, her husband knows exactly where she holds tension in her neck.

"Talk to me?" Heinrich whispers. He lightly runs his fingers across her neck as if in apology for purposely pressing too hard. "You feel far away."

Unbidden, the corner of her mouth curls at the crack of insecurity in his usually inscrutable facade. She resets her lips in a straight line. "I could lose everything."

"You won't and what you do lose, if anything at all, will be nothing of consequence."

"My career? The Tate? Those are not 'nothing' to me." She twists around to face him. "I have loved my years there. I built that collection."

"On knowledge and acumen we grew together."

"Don't do that." She pulls away. "Not now."

"Shh . . ." He settles her back, nestling her into the chair, and again places his hands on her neck. "I am not belittling your work. You are brilliant at it. But what we do? What we create together? That is what matters."

"Edward Davies's insurance company is flying over an expert from New York to investigate Lily's forgery claim."

"Yes."

Diana twists again. "You knew? How?"

"The club is abuzz, but not to worry. Those roles are often filled by police who know nothing about art or by artists who know nothing about police work. Davies is making a show. He must bluster and blow so as not to appear the lummox he is. Once his claim is paid and his feathers are soothed, he'll settle again nicely."

"How do you know about Davies?"

"Everyone knows about Davies, my dear. His Nazi ties, his failed businesses, his three wives, the last of which absconded with quite a sum to France without having the decency to divorce him. His attempts at reinvention are greatly talked about. This latest fracas is interesting, as is your role in it, my dear, but it's no more than another chapter in his sordid story."

"My role?" Diana presses her lips shut and waits. It chafes that there is another world, a world in which things are known and get done. A world beyond her reach. No matter how hard she works or how well she does her job, she will never have access to that world—the world of men's clubs. Those exclusive smoke-filled rooms where favors are asked and granted, positions secured, some careers made and others destroyed. What bothers her more than not being a part of that world is being a subject of gossip within it.

"As keeper of the Modern Collections at the Tate Gallery, your taste guides his. It's no secret you've helped him procure an astounding collection over the last couple years. You needn't get ruffled. Though some members do feel you could have sent a few pennies their way."

Ah, Diana muses, that is the source of their gossip and malice. Heinrich's club, like all clubs, is centered around a strata of work and life. His revolves around the arts. One must swim in those waters with a high degree of expertise to belong to Goddard's. And there are certainly a few artists within its membership she could have advised Davies to purchase, but she did not. Davies likes household names, artists with world renown so as to mitigate risk. He isn't daring in his tastes, despite wanting to appear so. He isn't daring at all, now that she thinks about it, and yet he'd been quite daring prior to and during the war.

She shakes her head at the incongruence, an issue she has no time to dwell on. Their game began long ago, and they are deep into the moves now.

Heinrich continues, "I wonder what Davies will do. A man doesn't spend millions to reinvent himself and let someone else destroy his efforts casually."

"And?" Diana prompts.

"It's curious how he found *Woman Laughing*."

She shrugs away from his hand. "It's natural he'd inquire in Paris for a Picasso."

"True. But as Picasso's work sells for twice the Continent's prices in New York, whoever sold the painting to that gallery in Paris behaved foolishly. He, or she, should have gone to New York, don't you think, and gotten more money from a dealer there? So the question isn't why Davies went to Paris, but why *Woman Laughing* was in Paris for him to find."

"Let's not talk about this." Diana launches out of the chair and across the room. "I need to dress for work."

"I'll sniff around the club and glean what more I can about this insurance investigator," he calls after her. A touch of laughter laces his voice, but she does not turn.

A mere half hour later, dressed in a dusky-pink Chanel suit paired with a black blouse and matching heels, Diana descends the stairs, and rather than encounter her husband again, she simply grabs her handbag from the entry and lets their heavy front door thud shut behind her.

She hails a cab and, within the hour, withdraws the gold key from her coin purse, unlocks her desk drawers, and drops the key into the crystal dish beside her. She is determined not to let the past nor her husband's baiting derail her. She earned this position, and if hard work can accomplish it, she will keep it.

She pulls out several files and begins sorting through the messages Lily has already left upon her desk. *Yes*, she thinks as she draws a deep breath, *this will work.*

Lily taps on her door and peeks in before Diana can reply. The girl's presumption bothers her, but today is not the day to address it. She fixes a smile to her face.

"The front desk just rang. Someone named Conor Walsh is here for you. Shall I go collect him?"

"No." Diana spreads her hands wide, noting her perfectly lacquered nails. She applied a warm coffee color, just a few shades darker than her suit, before leaving the sanctuary of her dressing room this morning. It, too, calmed her. Like a soldier dressing in his best regimentals for battle. She is ready. "I'll gather him myself."

She walks across the Gallery floor, wood turning to marble turning to tile as she approaches the front desk. Someone tracked in moisture from the outside rain and her heels slip. She rights herself, sets her expression, and approaches the man talking to the security guard.

"Conor Walsh?" Diana calls his name from several feet away, infusing her voice with both volume and confidence.

He turns. He is young. Too young for much knowledge. Too young for adequate experience. The tightness in her chest releases and her shoulders relax. Heinrich was right, as usual, and she should have listened. She should have trusted him. All will be well.

"Yes, ma'am." The young man, dressed in an off-the-rack grey suit, shakes her hand with a firm grip before he bends down to pick up his briefcase.

Facing her once more, he stands staring silently until she realizes she needs to lead; she needs to control the moment. Diana gestures across the rotunda into the Gallery, then steps ahead of him to escort him back to her office.

Feeling almost buoyant, she tosses an opening comment over her shoulder. "The call from Keller Insurance was unexpected. Few insurance companies employ art investigators."

"The field is growing. I expect you'll see more of us soon."

"Really?"

"Art is changing. The market is changing. We're in a tight spot financially in the US right now, but economies shift, and when the money comes back, my bet is art will take off. Money always needs a place to go. The insurance companies certainly expect that. And money in a market leads to misdeeds and the necessity for people trained to investigate them."

"How interesting." Diana glances back as she turns the final corner to her office. "What has prepared you for such work?"

"A love of art, I guess." The man shrugs and seems even younger as a lock of dark hair flops onto his forehead. "My mother used to take us to the Met in New York every Saturday growing up. I blame her."

Diana laughs. *This is going to be easy.*

Conor continues. "But every man in my family is a cop, three generations back, so there was no getting out of going to the police academy. Then when a painting was stolen at the Met and I happened to be there, I found the culprit and saved the museum's insurance company a million dollars. It landed me a new career."

Diana's buoyancy vanishes. There is more to this young man than anticipated. She gestures for him to precede her into her office. "You're a trained police officer? But you have no formal education in art?"

"Oh no, I have that too. I earned a degree in art history at NYU, but like I said, with three generations of cops in the family, my path was always certain."

After crossing to her desk, Diana drops into her chair and

watches as Conor settles into the bucket chair across from her and pulls a pen and a pad of paper from his briefcase.

This is not going to be easy. Her worst nightmare sits staring straight at her with sharp, expectant amber eyes, pen poised on paper, and says in a clear pragmatic voice, "I just have a few questions for you."

CHAPTER 13

Lily

Minutes or hours after telling Diana about Conor Walsh—I'm not sure, as I forgot my watch today and no natural light reaches my office—I lift my head at a soft tap. Diana pushes my door fully open.

"How are you?" I jump up, toppling and scrambling to catch my desk chair behind me. "You should have called me. I would've come to you."

"It's more private at this end of the corridor, despite so few people here today. I also wasn't sure you were still here." She glances back towards her office and the gallery rooms beyond. "It's almost as if everyone knows and is keeping away."

I catch the forlorn note of weariness in Diana's tone and, once again, feel guilty for placing it there. She's wearing a pink suit, almost the color of a sunset through smoke, with a black blouse and heels. Despite wearing jewelry and a little makeup today, she still looks severe, folded in on herself.

She leans against the doorjamb and crosses her ankles and her arms to complete the picture. Her hands grip her elbows so tight, the skin around her coffee-varnished nails blanches with the pressure. Her gold ring glints in my office's lamplight. It's the only bright spot in the room.

"Richard won't be in today. He has another meeting with Mr. Davies this morning, then the quarterly meeting of directors at the National Gallery later this afternoon."

My lips stay pressed tight as I pray Mr. Davies doesn't tell Richard of my visit to his home earlier.

"There is to be an investigation. It's already begun." Diana lifts one finger to gesture towards her office. "Conor Walsh? He's an insurance company's investigator."

I feign shock and surprise, when really I want to shake my head and say, "I know," and start another litany of apologies. An investigation makes this whole debacle formal, public, and truly the scandal Diana predicted. The one article in *The Times* will be nothing now. There will be a series of articles and endless insinuations, conjectures—anything and everything to tantalize, scandalize, and sell more papers.

Her self-protective posture seems fitting, and my own arms cross in anticipation of what's to come. It took months, lots of invitations to the press for impromptu events, and a few forward-looking exhibitions Diana put together before the fiasco created by Picasso's birthday party a few years ago faded away. Who knew such a nice gesture—launching ninety birds in the air to honor Picasso's *Child with a Dove*—could set off a firestorm of criticism? Yet it did. Within days of the event, newspapers, magazines, and artists from around the world slammed the Tate for pandering to the old and the established while neglecting new and emerging talent. The police were even called in when bad press turned to vandalism.

Diana continues as my mind whirls. "As we don't work with Davies's insurance company directly, we'll be lucky to be kept informed." She lifts a shoulder and lets it drop. "I suppose, as things have worked out, it was a shrewd move. Our carrier probably wouldn't have given *Woman Laughing* such a high valuation."

Her comment strikes a chord with my suspicions about Mr. Davies and the insurance question, but I say nothing. It's too soon to share my thoughts with Diana—I've said enough already. I search for something innocuous to say and land on an old Audrey Hepburn film. "Outside of *How to Steal a Million*, I didn't think such art investigators really existed."

"Conor Walsh may not be as charming as Peter O'Toole, but he's real." Her voice holds a touch of disdain at my sophomoric comment. "He'll want to talk to you. Perhaps today. He's up in the exhibition space right now." She looks out into the corridor again. "Please make sure you aren't overheard. The walls around here have ears and I want to minimize gossip."

"Maybe this is good. As an official investigator, he'll give his stamp that all is well and this will blow over, or he'll find Edward Davies was behind some nefarious doings all along." I offer a teaser of my thoughts, hoping Diana will catch on.

Her answering laugh sounds disillusioned and almost cruel. "This won't 'blow over,' Lily. While forgeries are everywhere, no one wants to know about them and certainly no one talks about them. So when the quiet part is said aloud, it's deafening. No matter the outcome, even if, as you wish, Edward Davies's true character is made public, this will plague us for years."

I almost ask what she means, but she pivots towards the door, ending our conversation. She spins on one heel to face me again. "The exhibit won't reopen, by the way. Five owners want their paintings back. They don't feel they can trust us. The Prado even cabled a request for security schematics and ordered we ship back the ones we borrowed immediately."

"You're joking."

"Like I said. Deafening. Just because no one's talking to us doesn't mean they're not talking." Diana lifts a brow.

I drop my face into my hands. I don't expect any kind words or consolation, but I am a little taken aback when I lift my head moments later and find my office empty. Diana has left as quietly as she came.

———

It's remarkable how slowly time passes when you're waiting for something—good or bad. The promotion to be announced. The baby to arrive. The kiss to touch your lips. The surgery to end. The boy to notice you. The shoe to drop.

Late afternoon, after several colleagues have passed my office on their way home, I jump out of my skin when my telephone finally rings. We don't all have those new touch-tone phones that carry a softer chime, and my black dial telephone is particularly old and fantastically accosting.

"Tate Gallery Modern Collections, Lily Summers speaking."

"Conor Walsh." I open my mouth to reply but am cut off before a word escapes. "I need to speak with you about *Woman Laughing*. Are you available now? I'm at the front desk." I hear him whisper to the attendant, "Can you direct me to Lily Summers?"

"No," I call over the line. "I'll come meet you."

"Fine . . ." The word drags long, and the subsequent pause feels weighted, as if he's deciding whether or not that's acceptable. "Let's meet in the Picasso Commemorative Exhibit. I'll see you in a moment, Miss Summers."

The line goes dead. I gather my handbag, put all my papers away, and lock the drawer with today's post and the donor contribution checks I forgot to deliver to Becca in Accounting. My plan, which I've thought through countless times, is to try to lead him out of the Gallery. Talk outside to minimize gossip inside.

I race through the corridor, and rather than take it all the way to the back side of the collections, I push through the hidden doorway right at the rotunda. It's the quickest way to the Picasso gallery space.

Archie still stands sentinel outside the gate. This time without question he slides it open for me. He doesn't meet my eyes. I wonder at that and at what he's heard. I've kept my head so low I'm not fully aware of the "gossip" Diana mentioned. Is it a problem here in the Gallery? I toss Archie a quick "Good day," get only a nod in reply, and head straight into the small room. I'm determined, in talking with this Mr. Walsh, to start making things right, not merely apologize for what's gone wrong.

My gaze scans the room from corner to corner and two things strike me. One, Conor Walsh is young. I can tell by the way he stands and the fluidity in his subtle shift from one foot to the other. I also sense it in the way his shoulders fill out his suit coat and how they move. He's young and he's an athlete.

Two, *Woman Laughing* is gone. My step falters and the hope

I'd been carrying throughout the day, thin as it was, dissipates. I imagined the insurance investigator and I might examine the painting together, he'd point to tiny indicators of a true Picasso, I'd shrug and say I was a fool, and it would be over. But that can't happen now. There is a gap in the center of the room's deep-orange east wall that looks like a sailor with a missing front tooth. Only the painting's white informational placard remains.

PABLO PICASSO
25 October 1881–8 April 1973
Woman Laughing, 1930
Oil on Canvas
Courtesy loan from the private collection of
Mr. Edward Davies

Mr. Walsh turns as I cross towards him. "Miss Summers?"

I blink. I sensed the man was young, but not so near my own age. If he's five years older than I am, that's a stretch. I've studied faces long enough to know when the crinkles gather at the corners of the eyes, the skin at the neck loosens a smidge, and the eyes lose the innocent gleam of first experiences. If this man has celebrated his thirtieth birthday, it was only within the past year or so.

"Conor Walsh. Keller Insurance."

"I thought you were from Lloyd's." It's a dumb comment, but I'm thrown off-balance. I need him to be from Lloyd's.

He stretches out his hand. "Lloyd's is an insurance collective, a marketplace rather than a company. Keller is a member of that collective and it will pay on the loss to Mr. Davies if required."

"So Mr. Davies insured *Woman Laughing* through Lloyd's and landed with your firm?"

Mr. Walsh considers me. "You could put it that way."

His handshake is firm but perfunctory, his hand slipping from mine as he turns back to the blank wall. "Tell me what you saw."

I glance to him. His accent is flat American like in the films, but there's a lyricism beneath, something tripping and melodic I can't quite place. I also catch a hint of something sharp in the air between us, almost like rosemary. It feels incongruent in the Gallery, but fresh and interesting. "Where is it?"

"I took it down this morning."

I stare at him, expecting a fuller explanation, but none is offered. The pause stretches overly long and pulls at my nerves. But as he turns to me once more, I realize it isn't working the same on him. Whether he meant to create it or not, he is comfortable within the silence. He is using it.

"How am I supposed to tell you what I saw if I can't see?"

He appears amused by my question, as if he's learned something interesting about me. He tilts his head to the wall. "That's a bit of my point. I don't want you to tell me what you see. I want you to step back in time and tell me what you saw. The painting would only confuse matters."

I face the wall, not quite understanding his logic but agreeing to his request, as perception changes everything, even reality.

"Miss Summers?"

I glance to him. "Sorry. Yes." I step towards the gap and attempt to focus my thoughts. "Can I ask where it's gone?"

"I sent it to a laboratory. Its days of a Morellian analysis are over. Every aspect of *Woman Laughing* needs to be scrutinized."

I close my eyes. That's another thing my little fantasy entailed, a Morellian analysis, which is when an "expert" examines a painting, bringing all their knowledge into the moment, and makes a determination. It does not require, though it can, of course, paintings to be removed from walls or sent away.

Mr. Walsh clears his throat, prompting me to get to business.

I open my eyes and let the deep orange carry me back to Tuesday. Diana chose the paint color for the life and vitality it evoked. She wanted her guests, at a subconscious level, to remember Picasso—who loved this particular color—at the height of his powers and associate that feeling with the Tate. It was another reason she wanted us both to wear neutral colors to the opening.

Studying the orange now, I feel my fingers prickle with the energy and effervescence I carried within me that morning. Rather than push it away, as I've done over the last few days in a brew of embarrassment and shame, I let myself relive it.

Almost as if in the present and not in memory, a visual re-creation of the morning emerges and I see myself swipe the champagne from Dillon's tray. I smile at his wide eyes as I do it. I nod to Diana across the room chatting with Lady Alexandra Bessing. I circle the room. My smile broadens to a ridiculous width and my eyes widen with wonder at Picasso's genius. My heart swells with the delicious idea that I, too, may soon have paintings gracing the Gallery's walls as part of the British Emerging Artists Exhibition. I take another sip of my champagne. I walk the exhibition in the desired clockwise direction and study each work in turn.

This first is iconic. The second an intimate collection hung tightly together to create a singular emotional image. The installation is perfection. The order of work and how each is displayed invites Picasso's nearest friends closer to savor a last memory with him. I pause to glance back at Diana, awed by her skill in creating such sentiment, and feel proud that I work for her, can learn from her, and call her my friend and mentor.

I again hear in my imaginings her delight at my portfolio. It is this bouncy-happy thought that carries me on as I tip my champagne for another sip and return my attention to the paintings.

Straddling that fine line between past and present, I shift my attention towards *Woman in an Armchair*. It's a breathtaking work. Not because it's lovely. It's not. It's cutting. It's dramatic. It's surrealism at its finest, as if the room, the chair, the woman, and her soul are vivisected and spread before us, distorted in their flat two-dimensional presentation. Even the window in this painting shows no world beyond. Our entire universe is the woman, and she, emotionally flayed, is almost monsterlike in her base reality.

That was Picasso's intention, I believe, to expose our base reality as much as the woman's—at least that was where my mind took me Tuesday. It was the first time I'd ever drawn so close to the painting outside a book or folio.

My heart softens now, as it did on Tuesday, almost to the point of puddling. Because while I'd never seen the original, I did know it is a portrayal—one of his many—of Olga Khokhlova, the ballerina Picasso met and married while she was dancing with the Ballets Russes in Paris. Many other paintings of her are far more flattering because Picasso was besotted with her, and he always painted what he felt, not merely what he saw. Olga is astoundingly beautiful in works prior to 1923. But by 1929, when he sat down and envisioned this large red armchair and his viewless window, his love for Olga had twisted under time, pressure, and his infatuation with Marie-Thérèse Walter, among other things.

Looking at the painting, I surmise it was the last nail in the coffin of their marriage, despite the fact they never divorced. Olga died in 1935 still married to Picasso.

I press closer and take in the colors, the brushwork, the scene. I focus on a single inch, examining the aspects of Picasso's style I spent a year mimicking but could never get this close to truly appreciate. I could certainly never replicate them. They are exactly what I expect—brilliant and effortless. Pure genius. I can tell by the way the paint lies on the canvas that he swept it on with short, swift strokes, without thought, his mind racing ahead of his hand. My nose inches from the canvas, I am too entranced to breathe.

Coming up for air, I remember where I am and with whom. My face flushes with embarrassment at what Mr. Walsh must think of me. And why didn't he stop me from almost diving right into one of the world's most famous paintings? A peek in his direction reveals he watches me intently. There is no emotion in his unblinking amber eyes. They're an arresting color, I think, not truly brown nor gold, but more butter-rich toffee. Deep-set and they fit well within his square face. His jaw firms as if he's clenching his teeth. It adds definition to his jaw, a firm and attractive line. It's— *Enough!* I stop myself.

Stepping to the right, I shift my attention across the wall's gaping wound and examine the next work still present, Picasso's

1934 *Bullfight*, with a little less intensity. It's an insane painting. And after studying the great artist for a full year, I sense this was where he felt most at ease—in the midst of experience, tense and frenzied, unable to lift his head from the tumult. He thrived on the precipice. The bull. The picador. The frenetic crowd. All life, death, culture, fanfare, and pageantry folded into an inverted singular and luminous instant.

I look beyond *Bullfight* to *Woman with Arms Leves* from 1936, to fully grasp all I saw and felt on Tuesday, but I find I'm less assured today. Less entranced. I can't submerge myself into another, lose myself in pursuit of passion or memory. I cannot, as I've often tried while painting Picasso, pretend to be Picasso. I've heard some artists can do that. They can almost fully become the master—and, in doing so, become a master themselves.

I shake my head with discomfort. Something has shifted over the last few days and that endeavor, that desire, somehow feels wrong. A person, as well as a painting, can be counterfeit, and this sense of chasing another and copying is also a form of forgery and deception. The duplicity of it plays on the outskirts of my subconscious, leaving me tight, constrained, almost claustrophobic with some unnamed pressure.

Dora Maar's head bothers me too and I look away. Picasso has divided her soul with his focus upon one eye in blue, and I realize one cannot play two sides of a coin without losing oneself. Oddly, I'm reminded of Diana's gold ring. I once asked her who it was, for the face on the ring doesn't face forward but is split looking opposite directions simultaneously. She told me it is a depiction of Janus, the Roman god of beginnings and endings, duality and doorways. This is one such doorway, one such moment, and oddly I know what I must do.

I peek to Mr. Walsh, then return to poor Olga Khokhlova in *Armchair*. "Picasso was a genius."

"Yes." He chuckles softly behind me. "He was."

"That's it," I say, still facing the art rather than the man. "That's what I saw."

He steps towards me. He's close, too close, and I fight the

urge to sidestep and create space between us. I look to him again, noting new aspects of his features and demeanor. He's about six inches taller than I am in my low-heeled loafers. His hair is darker than mine. The threads of auburn in my brown are nonexistent in his almost-black short hair. Short, with just a little length he brushes back from his brow. He doesn't sport today's longer style, especially popular in my world. Artists love their nonconformity.

His jaw loses that tense aspect and his face softens. He no longer looks at me but at the paintings. He loves art like I do.

My gaze follows his, which has remained upon Olga, and as my eyes leave off studying him, I feel his focus shift and center on me. A second peek in his direction reveals those amber eyes beneath full brows rife with questions, but he does not speak.

Again, the silence starts me talking. "The genius-ness of him. It wasn't in *Woman Laughing*."

The clarity that struck me moments ago settles into confidence. I did not merely blurt without understanding. I did not make a mistake. If Mr. Davies is trying to perpetrate a crime, then I've found him out, and I can help Diana by pressing on. I try to let myself stretch, grow taller, and accept I must venture out onto this limb.

"Picasso was all passion. His emotions permeated every fiber of his being and his work. His paintings, drawings, sculpture—thousands of pieces attest to that. Thank goodness he had talent or he would have been deemed mad. But it was that passion that rolled over him and through him, that kept him moving forward. He was never static. His creations were vital extensions of every move he made, woman he slept with or broke up with, or desired and lost, and every feeling he had in all those circumstances. He pushed himself to extremes, covering five movements across the twentieth century; he created movements within movements. Yet *Woman Laughing* held none of that frenzied life. It looked like a Picasso. It was technically perfect. But it didn't feel like a Picasso. There was a uniformity to the color application, a staidness, an absorbed calm rather than a frenetic chase. Every Picasso is a chase. Within any piece he didn't know where he'd end up. Who-ever painted *Woman Laughing* did."

Mr. Walsh's focus returns to the wall. His face remains impassive.

I almost ask if I've made any sense or simply sound mad myself when he turns to me. "If you'll excuse me, I have some further questions for your boss."

Without another word I am left standing in the gallery alone.

CHAPTER 14

*B*ugger.

I shift my weight from one foot to another. I stare at the blank wall. Despite being alone in the small gallery space, the air takes on a charge and a warm rush of blood shoots straight from my heart to my face. I feel myself redden in full-blown panic. He has returned to Diana. Returned to her with questions about an answer I did not give her. I will pay for this. Despite believing my answer helps her, she will be angry she didn't hear it from me first. I've always known Diana is good to me because I am loyal to her.

Archie's movement, as he shuts the gate behind Mr. Walsh, catches in my eye. His expression tells me he heard us talking. My gaze travels past him, across the closed gate, and three separate clusters of people stand peeking in at me. I shouldn't be shocked—the most popular show at any museum is the one closed and off-limits. But they may have heard me as well. I sigh. I've messed up again. Diana requested—demanded—I minimize gossip.

I pull my bag close to my shoulder and motion to Archie to open the gate again as I approach. He looks at me with wide eyes.

"That was bad, wasn't it?"

"Your boss isn't going to like it, that's for sure. She was in here with him earlier and said you knew nothing about the painting but simply drank too much champagne."

I look towards the administrative corridor. I look towards the Gallery's side entrance. Diana will want to see me. Diana will be furious. I pull my bag tighter and walk towards the exit. I'm running away, yes, but I need time to suss out what to say to her. I'm also giving my boss time to cool down before she certainly yells at me, then sacks me.

Head low, I walk straight through the Gallery's exhibition hall, through the rotunda, and out the main entrance without breaking stride, looking back, or acknowledging the few colleagues I pass along the way. I'll apologize to Becca for my rudeness later.

Once outside I turn north and walk on. I don't think. I don't stop. I simply walk. I walk at such a pace that what usually takes me about forty minutes only takes a bit over twenty. I walk so fast my mind blurs and my breath, fast and shallow, is all I can focus upon. I push open the front door of St. Martin's School on Charing Cross Road and step inside.

The door shuts behind me, and I stand frozen in the wash of the end-of-day bustle. The last classes ended mere minutes ago, and almost every student in the entire school is gathered in the broad stairwells, jostling around each other, calling out plans and discussing projects, or complaining about the part-time jobs they hold to make working on those projects possible. Wading into the melee, I cross the lobby to the receptionist's desk and tap it to gain Veronica's attention. She lifts her head from *The Guardian*'s front page.

"It's good to see you." She smiles at me over a pair of bright red cat-eye glasses dangling from a gold chain.

I try to smile, but as it wavers on the edge of tears, I stop. "You too."

Veronica senses something because rather than say anything more, she waves her nub of an artist pencil—no eraser atop— towards the stairs. "Get on with you then."

I take the stairs rather than the ancient lift to the third floor, and I stop outside the door to my closet. My heart is beating so fast I feel faint and my fingers tingle as if the blood no longer reaches that far. I push open the door.

My home. My sanctuary.

It's still just a utility closet with huge shelving units lined four deep, and bottles of cleaning supplies, tarps, pottery tools, blocks of clay, and detritus stacked high upon each shelf. But it's mine. And while it looks messy and chaotic, it is actually quite organized. Paddy and I keep it so. The room lies semidark with only a bare yellow-tinged bulb for light, and the air inside carries a faint whiff of paint thinner riding alongside the more pungent odor of industrial vinegar.

I breathe it in as I walk deeper into the room, past the shelving units, past the buckets, brooms, and mops, to its far end and its only window. I lift the shade and watch as the late afternoon's more blue-toned daylight pours in, bringing in hues of pink and purple that both drown the light bulb's harsh yellow cast and illuminate the room's dust, dancing as if in a diamond shower. I turn to face the painting on my easel, a postcard-size print of a Chagall, my artist of the moment, pinned to its corner. I reach for a palette and a knife, then search in my basket for a tube of scarlet paint.

A couple hours later, and only about an inch of paint completed, I stop. It didn't work. I never reached that place. I never found myself or felt safe. Again those questions of forgery and deception press down upon me, and my painting no longer feels authentic, real, or even how I want to express myself anymore. Instead I feel like I am trying to write someone else's diary entry. Not only that, but the surety I had when talking to Mr. Walsh is gone too, and I'm left empty and unmoored. I wash my palette, clean my brushes, and lope from the third floor down to the first, wondering if Paddy is around for a chin-wag.

I find Conor Walsh instead.

Just as I turn away, hoping to escape unnoticed, Headmaster MacKenzie spots me. "Lily. Come. I have someone you should meet."

I turn back.

"Miss Summers?" Mr. Walsh stares at me. "What are you doing here?"

Headmaster MacKenzie steps forward. "You know Lily?" He

glances between us. "Of course, the Tate. Lily has worked here, been with us . . . how long?"

"Over a decade, sir."

"Well, she doesn't work here anymore, not really. She's more a part of the St. Martin's family. She's got a little studio on the third floor. Not that I know anything about that." He smiles and taps the side of his nose as if it's all a big secret. "You should go see. You'd appreciate it, Conor. Padraig, our head janitor, raves about her talent."

"I'd be pleased." Mr. Walsh sweeps his arm back towards the stairs. "Miss Summers?"

I look between them. Headmaster MacKenzie smiles with a proud paternalism that would be oddly endearing if offered in other circumstances, and Mr. Walsh's eyes issue a challenge. I lead him up the stairs.

"Mr. Walsh, how do you—?"

"Conor." His mouth lifts in a wry smile. "Miss Summers, I have a feeling you're going to play an integral role in this investigation. Dropping formalities makes the process smoother, don't you think?"

"Lily." I touch the hollow at the base of my throat. I glance back. "How do you know Headmaster MacKenzie?"

We turn the corner and start up the next flight of stairs.

"I consulted him on a case a few years ago. He's an invaluable resource."

Conor—it's awkward to think of him on a first-name basis—studies me as we climb the last of the stairs to the third floor.

"He likes you," he says simply.

"He's been good to me. I started working here when I was about fifteen, filing, cleaning, and such stuff."

"But your studio?"

"About that." I pause outside the door. "It's not a proper studio. It's a storage closet they let me use while I worked here and never took away once I left. I didn't realize the headmaster even remembered it anymore, and I don't have talent. I mean,

I . . ." Unsure how to finish my sentence, I leave off as dread seizes me.

"Lily." Conor cuts into my thoughts and nods to the door.

I push it open and almost laugh as I take in the space as it must appear to him. It's a utility closet, complete with all the chaos a hundred years in a building brings. Without turning on the room's one light, I stride to my easel, knowing exactly where it is, and swipe my attempt at the Chagall from it. I then lift the shade. The colors outside the window have changed yet again to the more dusty and dusky tones of evening, but there is still enough light for him to see by.

Nevertheless, he flips the switch before following me farther into the room. I can't bring myself to look at him, so I focus on anything and everything in the small space rather than the tall man standing in the very center of it.

"Each year, at a professor's suggestion, I choose one or two masters and spend several months on each. I read everything I can find in the library here or in the Tate's archives, and then I try to copy their brushstrokes, their perspectives, their colors and blending, their . . . Everything, really. I try to become them, as trite and imperfect as the results may be. The professors tell their students that's how to grow your technical skills." I bite my lip. It's time to stop blithering.

"Mondrian." Conor gestures to the wood rack under the window. "Who else have you studied?"

I look over to find my first Piet Mondrian painting fully visible in the rack behind me. Rather than answer, I work the latch open to show him. It feels more comfortable to do something rather than to say something. My fingers feel thick and clumsy. I stop, straighten, flex my hands, and will my nerves to calm. I bend again, open the rack, and pull out a few paintings. No one has ever seen these. Headmaster MacKenzie knows about this place, but he doesn't bother to come up here, despite hearing about my "talent." No one but Paddy does, and that's not to look at what I paint; it's simply to chat while I paint.

"Why the masters?" Conor's question is so quiet and calm

that I think he's asking something different, which feels odd as I just answered it. Nevertheless, I find myself chatting on.

"Professor Duncan tells his students that by copying the masters, they can build a strong foundation to serve as a launch-pad for flight. I overheard that tip and took it to heart."

Conor lowers the painting I handed him. "I don't mean why an artist copies the masters; I mean, why do you? What makes you take this route?" He waves a single finger to the wood rack again. "I'd like to see your Picassos as well, if you don't mind."

I follow his gesture and, sure enough, a corner of the *The Embrace* peeks out from halfway back in the rack. I'm impressed he recognizes it as a Picasso from its few visible inches. I pull the canvas out as I try to explain, which is difficult as I've never articulated the what, the whys, the whatnots, or the wherefores of my painting.

"It started when I was young. I don't remember a time I didn't scribble or draw or paint. It's how I think and breathe, and if I could do one thing in my life, it'd be this." I set *The Embrace* on the easel before us and touch my fingers to my lips, unsure if I'm going to throw up or if I feel more free. Maybe both feel the same.

Conor leaves off examining the *The Embrace* and steps to the wood rack himself. He taps the top, asking my permission to pull another work from within. I nod, as I don't sense refusing is an option, and he withdraws each of my four remaining studies of Picasso and studies them one by one. In the end, all five of my Picassos are propped against a shelving unit simultaneously visible.

He steps to the first, then glances back to me. "This is the order in which they rested in your rack. Is this the order in which you painted them?"

I nod.

"Postimpressionism. *The Embrace*." He steps to the next. "Cubism. *Still Life with Lemons*. I saw the original at the Met years ago. It's actually one of my all-time favorite works."

As he sounds as though he's talking to himself rather than

to me, I don't reply. But I like him better now; I feel I know him better somehow. He is speaking a language I understand, and by the lilt of his voice, I know my earlier instinct was correct. He does love art as much as I do. I can hear it in his voice, see it in his eyes. And *Sill Life with Lemons*, as trite and uninteresting as critics often call still lifes, is one of my absolute favorites as well—so there's that too. Picasso captured something clean, bold, and hopeful in that tableau, and the lemon is rendered with such brightness you purse your lips at its tartness.

"Neoclassicism." Conor moves to the next painting. "You covered all the movements. This is *Bathers*?"

"Yes." I can barely breathe.

"Your lines and proportions are excellent." He moves on. "Surrealism. But I'm not familiar with this one."

"*The Dance*."

"Ambitious but well executed." He steps to the last, stares, looks back to the first, and stares some more. "*The Brutal Embrace*. Also from 1900. But an expressionist view of that same moment." He looks to me, his eyes full of questions.

"Art is about love on many levels, I suppose."

"True. You should look up Gustav Klimt's embrace or, earlier, one by Francesco Hayez, though both are called *The Kiss* rather than *Embrace*."

I say nothing. I've seen them both—and Conor is right. In terms of an evocative moment of passion, both those works elicit far more emotion and draw far more need and desire from the viewer than do either of these Picassos.

My voice cracks and I clear my throat to start again. "How do you know so much about Picasso? About art?"

Rather than answer, he points to *The Dance*. "Surrealism is the latest movement here . . . What, 1923? '25?"

"Yes, 1925."

He faces me and the light catches his jawline, putting it in sharp relief against the shadow it creates upon his neck. "Your last examination of Picasso is 1925, making *Woman Laughing*, dated 1930, a natural next step for you."

My lips part.

"Conversely, have you really the acumen to say Picasso couldn't have painted it?"

His question is equal parts challenging and curious. Rather than set me back, it oddly compels me forward.

"*Woman Laughing* has some of the hallmarks, Picasso's touch-points one might call them, of *The Dance*. Maybe that's what struck me. If he was here in 1925, he wouldn't still be here in 1930."

I wave my hand at *The Dance*. "He painted along an internal creative trajectory. To go back would be like walking through his own footsteps. By 1930 he'd left behind some of the whimsy you see in *The Dance* and was moving towards *Guernica*. The early to mid-thirties weren't peaceful in Spain, not to mention his turbulent love life. *Woman Laughing* has peace in her eyes. That's incongruent at best."

Conor doesn't pull his focus from *The Dance*. "According to the dealer and its provenance, *Woman Laughing* was gifted by Picasso to a friend after its creation. It passed hands only a few times, but the last dealer to handle it"—I note how careful he is not to reveal a name—"believes it may be of the man's wife and probably not a commissioned piece as there is no early trans-action data. The painting was hidden in Paris until 1938, then in Germany until it was walked into a Paris gallery two days before Picasso's death and purchased by Mr. Davies the day after. Prior to this exhibition, the work has never been seen in public."

Diana and I talk about this kind of stuff. Germany. Stolen art. Hidden art. Nazi-looted art. What it all means for the art world and the ever-present yet damaging nature of the forgery market. Paddy and I talk about this kind of stuff too. We hear the students and professors engage in highfalutin intellectual debates on art, ownership, and theft, then we tamp it down to a much more practical level—it's a crime. Yet it's top-of-mind for all of us, as works confiscated by the Nazis throughout the 1930s and 1940s have just begun to hit dealers and the public in unprecedented volume.

"Is the timing suspect? I mean, what are the chances?"

Conor shrugs. "Good, actually. Once word got out that the great artist was seriously ill, valuations started rising. Davies wanting to sell isn't curious either, as valuations are through the roof right now but are unlikely to stay so inflated."

I press on, trying to sort through how, why, and when Davies might have devised his plan. "Could it be a stolen work then? Not a forgery at all?"

It's not consistent with what I saw—what I *think* I saw—but it solves a lot of problems for me as I can't quite work out Mr. Davies's motivation for exhibiting *Woman Laughing* if he knew it was fake.

"I'm not drawing any conclusions yet." Conor raises a brow, and I get the impression he suspects I'm trying to obfuscate the matter. "There are too many open questions."

He looks to me and the evening light, now full of purples morphing to grey, hits the small lines at the corners of his eyes. He's used to smiling, I think. He laughs easily.

Conor continues. "In the chaos of our present market, it bears consideration that anyone with skill, high-level skill, can study the brushstrokes, perspective, oeuvres, and psychology of an artist, then create and claim they've found an unseen work." He turns back, sweeps his gaze across my paintings, then fixes his dark eyes on me. "For instance." He pauses. "You could."

"I did not—"

Conor lifts a hand as if telling me to calm down, that he's only joking, but his eyes belie the gesture. "It's something to consider."

I step close in an attempt to get around him without brushing against him. I lift each of my paintings one by one. It's time to put them away. "Maybe someone more talented could. Maybe. My brushwork and blending look crass in comparison with his. But considering Picasso is the most famous artist ever, how many would even have the nerve to attempt a forgery?"

Conor clucks his tongue. "Plenty. Picasso has been dead a little over two weeks and he's already the world's most forged artist."

"He is?"

"I think partly because of how prolific he was and all the movements he canvassed. Forgers have favorites, themes, and styles to which they gravitate. When a single artist spans five movements, he's bound to attract a few copycats."

"Are you going to tell Diana about this room?" I slide *The Embrace* back into the wood rack. My hand spreads across the base of my neck. I recognize the vulnerability in the motion and drop my hand.

"*Woman Laughing* may not actually be a forgery, Lily, despite your certainty. If that's the case, this"—he gestures to the wood rack—"remains your story to tell. However, if it is found to be a fake, I make no promises." He steps towards me. "But why haven't you? Is this some big secret?"

"Yes. No. It wasn't meant to be." My fingers again fumble with the rusted metal latch on the rack. "It just happened. I didn't tell her at first because I don't talk about this. It's like a diary, I guess. It's personal. But over the years, I've realized I want it to be more. I was trying to muster the courage to tell her and ask for a spot in an exhibit she's creating, but I couldn't find the right time and now it's gone and I feel like I've lied to her."

"Haven't you?" He lifts one brow. "You told her you had no idea why you called *Woman Laughing* a forgery. You stated it was simply a 'feeling.'" His finger-quote motion makes me feel as though what I told Diana is now "on the record."

"That's why you went to see her after we talked." My chest constricts.

"It was an inconsistency I wanted to understand."

"This is just a hobby." I whisper the words I've told myself for years, as they make hope less threatening. But after all that has happened this week, I truly believe them.

Conor steps towards me and I sidestep him, unsure of what's about to happen. But he doesn't reach for me; he reaches for the rack. "May I?"

My single nod invites him to reopen the latch I just closed.

He draws out the front panel of wood, which allows him to sift through the unframed canvases with greater ease. "Kandinsky, Mondrian, Klee, Dalí, Dufy, Picasso . . . This appears to be more than a passing hobby, Lily."

The room shrinks. The air grows warm, charged, and cloying. I step between him and the rack and, without speaking, start to reassemble its front panel. I sense rather than see him back away.

"I'll go now. Thank you."

I hear footsteps. By the time I glance up, I have missed him walk all the way to the door and only catch it closing behind him.

My eye catches Lise Tréhot from Renoir's *In Summer*. Before seeing that painting for the first time several years ago, I erroneously believed Renoir to be the master of the benign, almost vacant female expression. But Lise's eyes stare straight at the viewer with stark candor and reveal regret, secrets, maybe even pain and fear. The deep cut of her blouse, the right strap of her bodice falling off her shoulder, adds to her all-too-apparent vulnerability. There is nothing bland about that young woman, nothing vacant. She is fully, achingly aware that her position in the world is precarious.

As now am I.

———

I grab a repainted and now-blank canvas from against the wall and pin a piece of sketch paper to it. Lise Tréhot's eyes fill my imagination. I understand her and I start to draw. Not her, per se, but the emotions she conveys and those I feel. I let my hand work and my mind settle as a sense of control returns, even if that control extends no farther than this small square of paper.

Soon my mind drifts from Lise to Dufy and his *Baigneuses en pleine mer et coquilles*. Darkness. Chaos. That was the moment I started to doubt my perceptions in the fictional world of art as in the real one around me. Is love merely a covering for despair? A plaster that doesn't quite cover the edges of the wound? Does darkness always creep around the corners of joy and press upon it? Shrink it?

But it's not *Baigneuses*. No, that wasn't the first time I doubted. I draw on. His painting is a forgery, a stand-in for the original. I look closely at the eyes I've sketched and they are not Lise's, nor are they mine. They are Daisy's. The original is Daisy and it always has been. So long ago and yet I can feel her shift me off my axis. That look. That day. I draw on, trying to get back to before . . .

Before the "accident." Before I started wanting more or at least something safe for me. Before I believed Mr. Biggins, my art teacher, who praised my talent. Before I came here and saw what real talent was. Before I heard professors say that even a modicum of it could be refined, grown, and developed. Before I clung to that hope like a lifeline—that I could hone what little I was into more.

I drew when Daisy ignored me. I drew when guilt assailed me as I watched Mum struggle with simple tasks she would have accomplished with ease and little thought months and years before. I drew after catching Dad sitting at his desk late at night, head in hand, over bills he could not pay. I drew when tiny comments from Daisy or Mum or Dad, never intending to cause pain but doing so nonetheless, revealed it was the accident that formed the mountain of debt weighing us down. I drew because, with pencil, brush, pastel, or charcoal in hand, I didn't feel guilty, bruised, and desperately sorry.

Glancing back at the tightly packed wood rack behind me, I'm swamped with relief that I didn't show Diana my "portfolio." What portfolio? There isn't an original piece within it. How did I ever believe I could create something unique for the British Emerging Artists Exhibition? It's almost laughable. As laughable as seeing myself through Conor's eyes moments ago . . . Kandinsky, Mondrian, Klee, Dalí, Dufy, Picasso . . . I may not be a forger. I've never signed their signatures to any of my studies, but I am a forgery.

Yes, a person as well as a painting can be counterfeit.

I draw on and only when the light dims to a darker grey and I can barely see what's in front of me do I come back to myself and study what I've created. Dark hair, thick and long, with a single strand that dips below the shoulder, a curl separating from the locks and opening her face. Round, wide eyes. Long lashes. Serious. If I added color, those eyes would be deep grey. Not the Thames, even under cloud cover. No, these eyes are like the slate-brown ocean off Dover before a storm. I saw it once.

I lift my hand, noticing what's yet needed. I add a charcoal mark to represent the flick of gold at the outside of the left iris. Sun breaking through the storm. I reach for an eraser to correct an errant curl of hair on her temple, but I pull my hand away. No editing. I don't want to think, correct, amend, or go back. I'm so tired of struggling, striving, fixing, finding. I'm tired of being stuck. I'm knackered. I'm so terribly exhausted.

Light gone, I don't think; I draw. A petite nose, straight yet not quite. My hand recalls a bump on the bridge. It's sharp, just off the midline, as if a tiny piece of cartilage rests there. Did it happen in a fall? In Yorkshire? I've never asked. I move on to the jaw, the chin, the lips that bow just a touch when at rest.

My mind drifts to *The Embrace*. *The Brutal Embrace*. Klimt. Hayez. Yes, art is love. All kinds of love. Erotic love. Friendship love. Sibling love. God love. I didn't tell Conor; I couldn't. He's not a friend and he suspects me. But I have a small postcard of Klimt's *The Kiss* in a box at home. I couldn't tell him because it's just for me. Again, like a diary.

My small closet takes on a dim yet harsh yellow glow, and I realize that only the bulb lights my work now. Outside my window London is dark. Usually lights from the buildings across the alley illuminate my room as well, but with rising fuel costs and inflation, people and businesses are more frugal now. Leaving on one's lights is no longer a show of prosperity and strength, but one of profligacy and waste.

A shadow darkens the space in front of me as something comes between me and my one bulb. I pull my focus from the easel to above and beyond. Paddy stands next to the last shelving unit staring at me. "Are you all right, luv?"

I smile at his endearment yet find myself wanting to cry as

well. My parents occasionally call me that. Paddy only started using it after his wife did.

"Lost in work, are you?" He lifts his chin back to the door. "You're lucky I switched the lights out from the far end tonight or I'd never have seen yours under the doorway. You mighta been locked in till morning."

"You're locking up?" I blink. "What time is it?" I take in my surroundings, roll my shoulders, and find them aching. I raise my arms above my head and my back makes a crunching sound as vertebrae unlock.

"Going on ten o'clock."

"No . . . No . . . It can't be that late." My hand hits my basket of paint tubes. Colors fly across the room.

"Slow down, child." Paddy steps towards me and bends down to start picking up the tubes. I scurry to beat him to them. "What are you still doing here?"

I stand, drop tubes into the basket, and reach for a sheet to cover my easel before Paddy can see, but it's too late. He stares at my drawing as he drops tubes into my basket. He slides two more from his pocket. "These were in Professor Milburn's studio bin tonight. They've each got a good dollop in them."

"Thank you." Embarrassed, I pick up the tubes and examine them, needing to focus on anything but Paddy as he regards my drawing. He's right. The vermilion has at least a quarter left, and it's from a high-end shop in Mayfair. The other is a carob. If I take Daisy's portrait from a drawing to a painting, it'll be perfect for her dark hair.

I look back to Paddy to thank him again, but his eyes remain fixed on my drawing. "I've always wanted to meet your sister."

"Yes."

Paddy faces me. "What is it, child?"

"An insurance investigator came here. To this room. He was at the Tate and then saw me while he was talking to Headmaster MacKenzie. He saw my work. He . . ."

I tell Paddy everything. Though I outline only the facts of what has happened, I sense by his expression that he catches all the emotions and questions behind it. Brushes cleaned and canvas covered, I'm still talking as we leave my closet studio to finish locking up the school. We walk out the side door together and Paddy locks it with one of the dozen keys he holds on his ring. We then walk side by side through the alley to Charing Cross Road.

"Tell Patrice it's my fault you're home late tonight."

"I will, and then I'll tell her about that fake Picasso you pointed out. She'll be proud of you. You did the right thing."

"But how I did it wasn't right. It's all over the papers. I could be fired. There's an investigation. People are getting hurt and Diana—"

"Slow down." Paddy steps in front of me. "All this is vapor. It blows away."

"My position?"

"You come work here until you find better."

I smile at his practical generosity, no matter how unbelievable it feels to me. I'm about to turn west, as he will walk east, when he puts a soft but firm hand on my arm. "What I want to know is . . ." He stops and stares at me, so deep I suspect he sees all the way through me. "Were you right?"

I take a deep breath. "Yes, it's a forgery." I say the same three words again and realize at a deep level they are true, and somehow that matters above all the mistakes I've made over the past few days.

"There you go." Paddy nods as if everything is suddenly clear. There is right and wrong. There is black and white. And those colors do not create a game or a conundrum or a puzzle; they bring clarity and surety and strength.

"Then you have to see this through." He nods again. "No matter who gets hurt."

CHAPTER 15

Diana

Diana pushes open the front door. The house is dark once again. She is tired of the dark, tired of coming home late. Tired of uncertainty, of this feeling of aloneness. The front hall light flicks on above her.

"Where have you been?"

She straightens and faces her husband. Her hand travels up to smooth a few stray strands of blonde hair back into her chignon. She isn't ready for this conversation. Although she's spent all day imagining the different directions it might take and formulating answers for each permutation, she still feels ill prepared. Young. Naive. All the command and weight she wielded throughout the day—calming Richard, easing donors' worries, advising Davies, and answering the investigator's questions, twice—evaporate when faced with the one man who knows her best, knows the work best.

As well he should. Both are his creations.

At least that's what he'd say. It's what he did say. And he wasn't wrong. In a patriarchal and patrician society where status and benefits are conferred in the men's clubs, by men, it was Heinrich who had assured her promotions all the way to the keeper at the Tate, with quiet comments here, favors granted there.

She is as much his masterpiece as is *Woman Laughing*.

And though *Diana Gilden* is a work she has displayed for years now and wears almost as if it is her own, it isn't. Hers is not a history that claims familial ties to the Hohenbergs, with parents in the upper echelon who valiantly held out against Hitler until forced into the gas chambers at Auschwitz. A young girl who hid in a neighboring estate's wine cellar before making her way across the Wachau Valley. That history is as much a fabrication as Therese de Sales's Jewish roots and her father's silent partnership with the famous Parisian art broker Paul Rosenberg, and as much a lie as Elizabeth Barrow's industrial wealth and American grit.

Part of Diana chafes at how it was all done. Yet another part concedes she has utilized that knowledge and insight to press her own ideas with great success. She's pushed for more innovative exhibitions and acquisitions by planting subtle seeds in Heinrich's mind, knowing he'd unwittingly carry them to his club. And there those seeds found fertile soil in Richard and traveled full circle back to her at the Tate.

Yes, she plays the game well. For through those subtle seeds and her own hard work, she has elevated the Tate's national and international reputation, brought in more funds, installed dynamic exhibitions, and created the team to expand the Gallery.

Granted, the economy's downturn has stalled that expansion for now, but the economy will turn—these things always do—and she is certain the designs approved in 1969 will soon proceed. In the not-so-distant future, the Tate will more than double in size. All because of her. And not only that, but she pulled off a blockbuster Picasso show within days of his death—if only for a few minutes.

"I thought you'd be in the studio." Diana drops her Hermès bag onto the kitchen's small dining table and glances back at her husband. "Where do you think I've been? As you can imagine, it's a little busy at the Gallery just now. Why? Where have you been?"

She stalls on her way to the counter and closes her eyes briefly, willing herself to calm. The impatient notes within her voice will not win Heinrich's confidence. He'd rather lie than feel he is capitulating to any demands leveled by her. He has to be wooed into listening to her, into confiding in her, into following her guidance.

"The club was abuzz this afternoon." An incongruent note of teasing amidst the tension dances within his words. "It seems you have a forgery on your hands."

"You heard that?" His words strike with the force of a punch. "How? The lab hasn't officially released the results."

"My dear, if you want to know anything about the art world, I keep telling you Goddard's is the place. The owner of the lab is a club member." Again, the tone, the words, spill out of her husband as if nothing more than a morsel of tasty gossip was chewed and savored at his club that afternoon.

"And what revelations did you share in return for this news?"

"I never talk." Heinrich's brows arch. "I would never put my art in jeopardy."

"*Your* art?" Diana's voice rises to a shriek she only hears when Heinrich winces. "It's not your art, is it? It's Picasso's. It's Mattise's. It's Ernst's. It's Miro's. What are you working on now? Yes, it's Campendonk's."

"You surprise me, Dyeu."

Dyeu. The proto-European root of her new name—the name he gave her—meaning "to give light." It was his nickname for her, nickname upon name, all beginning their first day together. The hour that turned to days, months, and now years. She is light, he claims. His light.

The nickname, not used in years, rests between them, softening the anger of the moment as it summons memories as clear as pictures. So soft, warm, and ephemeral, she wants to reach out and snatch them back. Dinners with courses selected not for their taste but for the education they provided. Yet the tastes were new and the education intoxicating. Wines chosen in the same manner. Yet rich and delicious. She learned the years, the vintages, the appellations—and she savored each. Every experience was more sensual than the last. A yearlong tour through Florence, Rome, Venice, Paris, Vienna, Lisbon, Madrid . . .

She once laughed that she was Eliza Doolittle and he her Henry Higgins. But it wasn't an apt comparison and Heinrich hadn't known the *My Fair Lady* reference regardless. In *Pygmalion*, professor and student stay primarily in his study and his original intention is to free Eliza for a better life. Heinrich didn't hide his Diana away; he traipsed her across Europe just as the war ended and the world was waking up again. New ideas, inventions, and innovations were born. People rose from scarcity, fear, and hiding to stretch in the sun and celebrate. And she rose, fully refashioned, completely new, to take on the world. Yet above all, she was created and remained only for him.

The glow of memory fades as she watches her husband with the dawning realization that she is only light if she carries it to him.

"I'm scared." The fight leaves her, along with all her energy. Her hands curl atop the countertop. There is no way out of their predicament. As Blake once wrote, there is only through.

"Don't be. I'm trying to assure you, if you'd only listen. All will be well."

"How?" Diana straightens. "How will this be fine? Best I'll be fired. Worst is jail. For both of us."

"It will never come to that, darling. You'll be fired; that's a foregone conclusion, so why worry about it or be frightened by it?" At her expression he smiles and continues. "Richard is not expendable; you are."

"This was the topic over scotch and cigars today?" Diana's head drops, chin to chest. "Did you defend me at least? Remind the powers that be of all I've done at the Tate?"

"What good would that have done? A husband defending his wife is too trite to consider."

She looks up. "You still should have done it." Only as her husband's gaze trails from her face to her hands atop the counter does she realize they are no longer gently curled but clenched into tight fists.

His focus returns to her face. "Let me get you something to eat. There's one of Branford's scrumptious steak-and-kidney pies warming in the oven for you. I was peckish after my long day, so I've already eaten."

The room is filled with a delicious aroma, soothing and comforting. How did she miss it before? She ponders the inability of a person to take in all the information—the sights, scents, sounds, and textures—when one feels in jeopardy. How silly to worry now. Her path was set the moment Heinrich seized her hand over twenty years ago, when she was merely twenty-three. She'd been in jeopardy from that point onward. It was only a matter of time until they reached this moment. This wasn't new worry, rather the mere recognition of worry—over twenty years too late.

Heinrich runs his hand across her back as he crosses the kitchen to the oven. He swipes a towel from the countertop and pulls the pie from the bright red Aga stove centered on the kitchen's back wall. It bubbles in a ceramic dish of a matching red.

"I'm not hungry." Diana slips off one shoe, then the other, and holds them by the heels. "I'm going to bathe."

Heinrich sets the dish atop the stove, throws the towel towards the sink, and reaches for a bottle of wine resting on the counter. "Here." He pours a glass and lifts it towards her. "I'll join you."

"You needn't."

His eyes widen in surprise and he draws the glass back minutely before she pulls it from his hands. She opens her mouth to apologize for her curt reply, but when words do not escape, she closes it.

He stares at her a moment. "I am sorry. I was insensitive. You have loved that job."

"I did." She blinks. "I do. I've worked hard for it, and despite how I got it, I'm good at it. I earned the right to call it my own and to keep it."

"You earned nothing. Not in comparison with—"

"It's not about the money." She presses her lips together. She did not mean to grind her words with such intensity.

"Are you sure?" Heinrich brushes close and reaches into the cupboard behind her for another glass. She can smell wine, smoke, and the musk of his cologne. "You targeted Edward Davies for *his* money. You wanted to take what he valued most and I suspect for how he earned it."

"He earned it by profiting from both sides of the war. He supplied the Nazis with the guns to kill my father, for speaking the truth, then sold bombs to the Allies to destroy my city." Diana presses her fingertips to her mouth, startled by her outburst.

Her husband laughs. His fingers dance in midair as if teasing answers from her. "No need to defend yourself, my dear. I thought it very Robin Hood of you. But *you* put us at risk."

His dropped tone and drawn-out attention upon a single word form a dividing line between them. While she tried to do the same herself upon arriving home, she failed. Her lines never held fast. His never faded away.

"I saw the results too, Heinrich. Davies sent a telex right before I left work, and it wasn't my mistake that landed us here. You used a paint with a compound Picasso had no access to, that was incredibly rare in 1930." She steps towards him. "You never do that. You mix your paints yourself for that very reason. Why? Why did you rush? We don't need the money. How could you be so careless?"

"The tube did not list titanium dioxide in its ingredients."

"That's not my fault, is it? I did not 'put us at risk.'" She mimics him and watches his eyes narrow. But too angry to back down, she sets her glass down on the counter so hard wine sloshes over the rim. "We have a timeline for these things. A process. We don't violate it for too many reasons to count, yet you did."

"We?"

Her neck pulls back. "It's always been 'we.' You can't go to market without me. There'd be none of this without me. I make *you* possible."

"And yet the market you chose was not New York as *we* agreed. You, who are so adamant that we stick to our timelines and processes. We made a decision that an ocean between my work and my person is a good thing, and, conveniently, art sells at a premium in America right now. Yet you took *Woman Laughing*, for less money and more risk, to Paris. All for Mr. Edward Davies."

Heinrich retrieves the cloth from beside the sink and wipes the wine from the counter. The white towel absorbs the deep red, almost like a pool of blood spreading.

"I don't blame you," her husband continues, soft and crooning. "Art is emotional. Money is emotional. You had a score you wanted to settle, if only for yourself. But don't grow cross with me when you fly too close to the sun and your wax wings melt."

"Yes." She rubs her forehead. "I made a mistake."

As much as she wants to blame Heinrich for his careless use of a commercial paint, she can't deny she also put them at risk. A couple years ago, after Davies had first come to her office for a consultation on several modern art pieces he wished to purchase, Diana had asked Sara in the Tate's Donor Relations department to do a full workup on him. The young woman traced Davies's companies back to the interwar years and the companies' boon during the latest world war. She found gossip columns from the late 1930s and early 1940s that insinuated Davies and his companies sold munitions to both sides. He and his partner had Nazi sympathies, everyone knew. He was seen at their dinners. He traveled with them to the Continent. His wealth quadrupled overnight—before England declared war. Then, after all was said and done, he received a Kings Cross Medal for contributions to the war effort and walked away an extraordinarily rich man.

He infuriated her, sent her into a rage beyond anything she thought possible. So she educated the man, she spent his money, and every piece of art she recommended he snatched up. He wanted the old names, the "true" art. Oh, the irony, she thought—a liar seeking truth and legitimacy in his possessions.

She hadn't even led him to the Picasso. She simply noted his collection lacked one. And when his Paris broker called him with a rare Picasso find, Davies paid the obscene amount of almost half a million pounds for a painting he didn't even bother to lay eyes on. It didn't matter that little of the money went to her or to Heinrich, as she'd sold the work to Galerie Louise Leiris for less than half that amount. It simply mattered that Davies paid for it and that he had a fake, a forgery, a deceit hanging on his wall— and she was the only person in the world to know it.

Only now the world knows it too.

Diana presses her palms into her eyes. If she presses hard enough, could she push all the way through? When it doesn't work, she drops her hands. Stars shoot across her vision and the kitchen becomes a sea of racing black and red dots. Hot tears run down her cheeks despite the fact she feels too angry to cry. "What do I do?"

Her husband steps toward her. "So what that it's a forgery? They happen all the time. This is art in a post-Nazi-looting world. We simply need to make sure it doesn't come back to us."

She swipes at her tears. "It won't."

"You trust your provenance so completely?"

"It is impeccable." Finished with her face, Diana picks up her wineglass and takes a deep sip. "We included a photograph, remember? We set the room for Austria, 1938, right at the Anschluss. I even laid that paper we found in Vienna on the table. No one will question it."

"Therese de Sales sold it, yes?" He refers to one of the aliases she employs when selling Heinrich's paintings.

For Europe she uses Therese de Sales. It is a name taken from two saints, both of whom wrote, just as she writes the provenances for Heinrich's work. Yet her Therese is no saint. She is the daughter of a Jewish art broker, the famous dealer Paul Rosenberg's silent partner. Conveniently, no one remembers anymore if Rosenberg actually had a silent partner prior to the war, and it's too impolite to stringently question a Jewish woman, now the sole heir to much of that collection, haunted by loss, pain, and memories.

What everyone does remember, however, is that Rosenberg secreted away much of his collection before his arrest and eventual death, and to see some of those legendary works come back to the market is too tempting to turn away. Dealers across Europe eagerly court Therese, but she doesn't even allow them any means to contact her, so great is her pain. No, she will visit them when need forces her to sell another piece from her father and Rosenberg's beloved collection. It is devastating to pull apart their very hearts, but how else is she to live?

In New York Diana employs a different alias: Elizabeth Barrow. One taken not from saints, but from sinners. The story of Bonnie Elizabeth Parker and Clyde Chestnut Barrow appealed to her the first time she heard it. It resonated with romance—and they, too, always had a predetermined end. It was that shared inevitability that drew her to combine their names. Unlike Therese, who inherited her art, Elizabeth is an independently wealthy American who adores travel. During her trips to France, Italy, and even Germany, she constantly comes across families in reduced circumstances who need money for food on their tables more than they need old art on their walls. She merely helps them, and since she doesn't need so much on her own walls, she often sells their pieces to reputable brokers in hopes of shipping funds back to those struggling families. New York dealers adore being part of such noblesse oblige and pay accordingly.

"I do love Therese best." Heinrich's words draw her back to their kitchen. "Such a good family story, such pain, and she has such a way of inciting guilt. And your trip to Paris?"

"Flawless." Diana casts her mind back to only three weeks prior. She can still feel each detail, as she can from every time she steps into either Therese or Elizabeth. Her ticket, purchased with cash. The cigarette smoke clouding the plane and saturating her clothes and hair. How, upon landing, only her silk Hermès scarf still carried the faintest hint of her favorite Creed scent, White Amber. It was one of the oldest Creed scents, one that, within the fiction, Therese's father gifted to her decades ago before the war. For Therese, only a few drops remain in the cherished bottle.

"I didn't carry checks, only cash, and Therese's papers are impeccable."

"I assume you went to Philip Neroli to broker the deal?"

Diana pauses. She knows Heinrich has read the papers. Yet she also knows this is part of his game. She takes a long, slow breath, then answers in a rush. "Galerie Louise Leiris. She is heavily influenced by her stepfather, and Daniel-Henry Kahnweiler is still the best dealer for Picasso bar none, and Davies was going to go to her no matter what. He has to be seen with the best."

"It was a foolish risk." Heinrich scoffs. "Kahnweiler knew Picasso better than Pablo knew himself. You could have been caught right then. You deserve all that happens to you."

"But I wasn't. Kahnweiler isn't active anymore and Louise

didn't suspect a thing. I didn't do this. Lily didn't look at the provenance. She looked at the painting."

Heinrich drains his wineglass and pours another. "It's fine. *Woman Laughing* made it past Louise, so there is nothing she can add to their investigation that will hurt us, and she'd never make a fuss that could damage her gallery. To be so famous for Picasso and let a forgery pass through your hands is a humiliation, especially right now. We are at no risk from her, but you are lucky there."

Without asking if she'd changed her mind, he scoops a large serving of pie into a deep blue-and-white Anysley dish. Diana raises a hand to refuse, but her stomach betrays her. Heinrich chuckles, and despite her best efforts, she fails to stop a small answering smile.

His grin in return is warm, indulgent, almost patronizing. "You truly believed you could control all the details, didn't you? Such boldness."

"I was angry. It had built up for years." Her words come out strong, but she feels the emptiness behind them, the niggling sense she is more like Davies than she's brave enough to admit.

The scratch of wood against wood draws her back to the present. Heinrich moves behind her chair and gestures for her to sit. She obeys.

He scoots her chair closer to the table and continues. "There are things we can do to help our situation. You must send a few red herrings across Europe, but not to New York. There is no reason to have anyone looking at our recent sales there, and we have future sales to protect. But for now, Europe is lost to us. Let's burn it down. Send cables to all your contacts warning, one keeper to another, about what has happened at the Tate and imply it's part of a larger ring. Maybe call a few clients you've advised and question their private acquisitions. You must create as much chaos as possible. Flood the labs with paintings, flood insurance companies with claims, inundate Scotland Yard with suspicions, and the institutions with nervous collectors, donors, and patrons. Set flame to the very thing no one wants ignited."

"To what gain?"

"Chaos, of course. This will fall behind us as all Europe looks to its walls. And if more forgeries are found, and there will be, it'll blow into such an inferno it'll take years to sweep up the ash."

"And what if one or two of those forgeries found are yours?"

"Let us hope there are at least two. If dozens are discovered, all the better. Therese has already disappeared and there is no trail from her to us. They'll never find her and this investigator of yours will be left in the cold. Let the world chase our ghosts and stir up other specters while they do."

Heinrich sits down and, stretching across the table, pulls her gently forward with a finger beneath her chin. He kisses her. "Either way, we will be fine . . . Now, eat your pie." He leans back. "After you're finished, come to the studio with me. I'm ready to put the finishing varnish on my Campendonk."

CHAPTER 16

Lily

MONDAY

This morning didn't start well. The trains ran late. My stockings ran straight up the back of my leg. The *L* key on my typewriter stuck. Diana sequestered herself in her office and scowled when I knocked and entered. I did neither again. And there was also no word from Conor. Not that I expected one, except I had. *Woman Laughing* consumed me. All I told him consumed me. His questions, doubts, and suspicions consumed me.

I push out the Gallery's front door this afternoon thoroughly depressed. Rather than give me any work, Diana requested I leave early. The writing's on the wall—I've lost her trust. Tomorrow, she'll most likely let me go. Art is subjective rather than objective, and I cannot point to a number or a letter or any concrete justification as to why she should keep me around. I am only as valuable as she perceives my value—and without trust, I am worthless to her.

The day has turned cloudy and looks as though it should be cold and blustery, but it's unexpectedly warm with an almost balmy feel to it. I walk again to St. Martin's School rather than take the Underground. The forty minutes wear me out just enough that my mind stops spinning.

I push through the door, almost feeling like myself once more, and stall at the unexpected blast of warmth. At the beginning of the week, with the boilers off all weekend, the school is usually an icebox, and by the end of the week, if Paddy hasn't guessed the weather just right, it's a furnace. My guess is the warm weather didn't allow the school to cool over the weekend and the furnace kicked on this morning at its winter setting. I shrug off my coat and moan at the clothes beneath.

I couldn't summon the energy and excitement for a decent outfit this morning either. I usually enjoy selecting the right dress, the right skirt, the right look, adding a scarf one day or a splash of color the next—fashion is a form of art too. Wearable art. Sean often teases me about my "new posh ways." And Mum was right when she mentioned the glamorous world of the Tate—it is glamorous and Diana expects me to reflect that. But this morning I needed comfort and safety, so I pulled on an old brown wool skirt and paired it with a red jumper Daisy passed on to me years ago. In the light of day, and here where everyone dresses more than groovy, I look worn and shabby with run stockings and a pilled hand-me-down jumper.

It doesn't matter. No one will see me. I simply want to paint. I flip on the light in my closet, pull open the window shade, pull my sketchbook out of my bag, and prop myself on a stool to look over my weekend scribblings. The book is half full. I need to slow down. Buying one with the proper paper weight of at least 110 gsm is expensive. It's not something I can afford right now, especially not after those indulgent Ferragamo heels I can't bring myself to look at anymore.

I open to the weekend's work and sit shocked by what confronts me—I thought *Woman Laughing* consumed me. I thought Daisy, my life, my mistakes, and Diana consumed me. It's apparently all that and Conor Walsh too. I hadn't realized that or how much I'd sketched over the weekend. I simply sat propped in bed each night as sleep eluded me and drew.

My first drawing of him is rough, just the outline of a face, the shadow of a single eye. But the second is more detailed. I refined his square jawline and even shadowed the cleft in his chin. It's his deep-set eyes in this one, however, that are arresting. Even drawn in charcoal, I can almost see their caramel tones in the way I've shaded them. They are intense, intelligent, and direct, and there's an honest expression I've captured that appeals to me. One that scares me as well. I almost envy it, his look of certainty and knowing. At least I would envy it if it wasn't directed straight at me.

I turn the page. The next drawing leaves me more unsettled as I suspect it reveals more about me than it does about him. Again, I've drawn his face with quick passes of the pencil and created greater detail within his expression. But in this picture his eyes are tight, assessing, and more suspicious. I did not put that look there. I saw that look. Without recognizing it, this is what has bothered me all weekend, and I remember the exact moment I saw it. He had just commented that I could be a forger, then lifted his hand to signal a joke.

He wasn't joking.

Without paging on, as I instinctively know there are at least three more sketches of Conor, I shut the sketchbook and toss it to the table next to me. Yet trying to place distance between it and me is futile in this tight room, just as it's futile to try to distance myself from the mess I've created. I shift on the stool, pretending that turning my back on it will make it disappear, and I am faced with my drawing of Daisy still resting upon my easel. She's changing. We're changing. Things can't stay as they are. I swipe her from my easel and prop her against the wall, facing it rather than me. Again, a futile attempt at distance.

I grab my latest study of Chagall and set it before me. I sort through my paint basket and grab several tubes to ready a yellow that's kind of a cross between a lemon and a pineapple for the goat's nose. I poise my brush inches from the canvas and stop.

I can't do this. I can't be where I am. I say things are changing, but one look at this painting and I'm trying to go back. Am I even gaining skills anymore? Or am I simply executing a sophisticated paint-by-numbers because I'm incapable of more? I'm certainly not capturing the whimsy of Chagall's surrealist masterpiece *The Wedding Candles* as surely as *Woman Laughing* didn't convey Picasso's passion. When does growth end and mere copying, forging, and even dying begin?

I push off my stool and walk to the small sink at the front of the utility closet. I scrub clean my palette and my brush. I put them away, switch off the light, and leave. After three flights of stairs, I step out onto the sidewalk and determine to walk through the parks on my way home. It's no longer that I need space to think or breathe; I simply need to be somewhere else. I can't be where I've been, I don't like where I'm going, and getting lost for a moment feels vastly appealing. I shrug on my coat as the pedestrians bustle around me, and a somewhat familiar voice cuts through the din.

"Lily, wait up . . . Miss Summers." Prickles run up my spine as Conor catches up to me. "I assume you heard—"

He breaks off as we both hear my name called from a distance. I turn towards the street and watch an old friend rush across. He points to the theater behind him and calls out, "Told you I'd come back."

I laugh. When Pierce left St. Martin's to pursue theater rather than art last year, he said he'd be back. We both knew he meant as a collector rather than as an artist.

"Your acting brings in enough money to buy a few studio projects, huh?"

"Not nearly. Not yet." He laughs, blue eyes dancing. "But I've got a lead role and there's a scene in this play you'll love. Imagine a moving Mondrian. It's pure art." He glances between Conor and me.

I wave my hand between them. "Pierce, Conor Walsh. Conor, Pierce Brosnan."

Conor holds out his hand. "A moving Mondrian?" He looks over Pierce's shoulder to the theater's marquee. *The Art Charade* is written in bold letters with Pierce Brosnan's name, equally bright, beneath.

Pierce grins from ear to ear and his blue eyes ignite. "It's brilliant. Ten actors dressed alike in block colors moving in a grid across the stage like a human shell game. The audience can't track the villain. It's right at the play's climax, and it took work, but the scene's in perfect balance."

134   KATHERINE REAY

"Just like a Mondrian." I smile.

Mondrian paintings appear simple, until you notice that perfect balance. I know this because he was one of the first artists I attempted to "copy" almost a decade ago, so sure I had enough skill to tackle basic straight lines and block colors. But it's the balance that gets you. It's within the balance one finds Mondrian's genius.

I take in Pierce's thousand-watt smile and make a calculated guess. "You designed it, didn't you?" I glance at the marquee again. "And the villain is the star?"

He winks confirmation and toggles his bright blue eyes between Conor and me again. "I'll set tickets aside for you. Two, right?"

"Oh no . . . Just—"

Conor cuts across me. "That'd be grand. Thanks."

Pierce nods slowly as if he's just learned something good and waves goodbye before dashing through traffic across the street again.

"What was that?" I turn to Conor.

He looks down at me. "Why make it awkward? He generously offered you tickets. I'm sure you can find a date."

I don't reply to that. I simply start walking.

He catches up in a few strides. "You can't find a date?" His voice holds a note of teasing within it, but not flirtatious teasing. Rather more like a lighthearted, exploratory kind of teasing.

"Is that why you were looking for me?" I counter. "To ask about my love life?"

"No, but now I'm curious." He gestures to the Charing Cross Station opening to our right.

I sweep my hand ahead. "I'm walking home."

Conor says nothing. He simply starts walking again. It takes me four steps to catch up with him. I don't know why he's asking. I can't suss out what he thinks or suspects, but I accept he's been on my mind all weekend and I don't want him to walk away. I want answers too.

"Fine. I dated a guy for about a year. I've dated a couple guys for about a year."

"The same year?"

"No." I balk. "Different years. But after about a year things end every time. I suppose that's the point where a relationship moves forward or it doesn't. Apparently I'm 'inaccessible' and it takes them a year to grasp that." I flap my fingers at *inaccessible*, but it doesn't make the criticism feel any lighter or easier to accept than when it was leveled at me last winter.

"Me too."

"You find me inaccessible?"

"No." He stares ahead, but a smile curls his lips. "That's just about what my girlfriend said before she left me for a band or a kibbutz. I'm still a little confused as to which appealed to her more than I did."

"Joshua did that."

"Joined Rebecca at a kibbutz?"

"Followed a band." I double-step again to keep pace with him. "He managed a club in Soho for a couple years, then went on the road to crew for Deep Purple. It's the rock band that started—"

"I know Deep Purple."

"You've heard of them?"

"Pioneers of heavy metal, which still hasn't reached its peak, I say. I saw them open for The Kinks in New York."

"There you go. He probably made the right choice then."

We walk in silence. At Marble Arch, where Oxford Street turns into Bayswater, rather than go straight, the most direct route, I follow the park path across the top of Hyde Park towards Kensington Gardens.

"What about Pierce?" Conor waves a hand behind us as if the meeting and theater are merely a moment and a couple blocks past.

"Nah . . . he's a good friend." I look back too. "Pierce is a shooting star. He'll do something amazing someday, probably light up the silver screen. Far bigger than anything I can do or be. I'll stay here, placing one foot in front of the other like always. But I'm happy."

I shove my hands in my pockets. What I do and how I live have never bothered me before. But in articulating my reality, I feel how small it is. I may be fired. I may need to start again. Alone this time as Daisy wants Mum and Dad to go with her family. Where does that leave me? Has nothing I've done mattered?

The smallness is apparent in my art as well. It mirrors my life. I say art is love, but it's also risk. I don't see love in my work, and I definitely don't see any risk. I can't take risks. Financially or otherwise. Needs always outweigh wants. I need to make sure we have enough money to get to next month, next week, tomorrow. I need to make sure we can handle whatever comes next. Anything more, wanting more, is too much of a risk.

I become so lost in my own thoughts it takes a black cab honking as we cross Kensington Church Street to draw me back. "I just realized you're walking me all the way home. Did you mean to do that?"

Conor shrugs and gestures for me to continue. "I have nothing better to do tonight. Dinner alone at my hotel can wait." He looks up at the sky. "Besides, it's early and it's nice out."

"Where are you staying?"

"Dukes hotel in St. James."

"Blimey. They set you up right. Have you had a drink in the bar yet?" At his head shake I rush on. "You must. It's where Ian Fleming created the Vesper for *Casino Royale*. It was the first James Bond book, but not the first film. You've seen the film, right?"

"I've seen all eight. *Live and Let Die* releases in a couple months. If I'm home, my brothers and I will go opening night."

"Well, that bar is where Fleming concocted Bond's signature drink. It's wonderful."

"A favorite of yours then?" Conor casts me a quick look.

"I've never been. I've never had one. I only imagine they're wonderful." My confession leaves me feeling smaller, if that's even possible, and I pick up my pace.

Halfway up the slight hill on Peel Street, a cry of "Lilypad" brings me to a sudden halt.

I groan. "You can go now."

"Not quite." Conor laughs. "I should make sure you get home safely."

We take the last few steps and draw to a stop in front of my brother-in-law, who is smoking a cigarette and leaning against a light pole. He looks very James Dean in a black jacket and white shirt underneath—except his shirt is collared. I suspect he's either coming from work or heading there later. Also the fact that he's a stocky Irishman with dark blond hair doesn't quite jibe with the lean James Dean comparison.

"Who's your friend, Lilypad?"

"No one. I mean, he's not my friend. He's—"

"You flatter me." Conor cuts me off with a chuff and reaches a hand out to Sean. "Conor Walsh."

I glance to Sean and briefly wonder what will happen next. Sean's an informal guy. He's more likely to grip your shoulder, offer you a cigarette, a pint, or a good story than to shake hands. He actually hates what he considers fake formality. I should know. Alongside teasing me about my clothes, he's gotten after me about my behavior plenty of times. It seems art is conducive to faking formality in all forms.

His eyes sweep Conor top to toe as he sticks his hand out. "Sean Murphy. What part of Ireland are you from?"

"That was fast."

I look between them as the light bulb clicks on. That's what I was picking up, without picking up on it. The rounded tones of Ireland.

Although Conor chuckles, I catch a note of wariness in his tone.

Sean raises his hands in a gesture of supplication. "Only curious and I heard you two talking before you noticed me. I can't place it, though."

"That's not surprising. My parents crossed to New York when I was about three. I don't hold any memories of Ireland. But the accent stays strong in my neighborhood. Generations deep. My family comes from County Wicklow, but as most of my friends are from the north, no doubt you'll catch a little of that too."

"Derry." Sean taps his chest. "I left in the middle of the night when a couple brothers tried to rope me into the Troubles."

Both men stall, and despite the fact that Conor hails from New York, I sense he understands the gravity of Sean's statement no matter how flippantly he delivered it.

"That's hard. My neighborhood's seen a good influx from Ulster's northern counties over the past few years. I was warned to keep my accent hidden on this trip."

"It wasn't bad advice." Sean blows out a thin trail of smoke and taps his cigarette out against the lamppost. "The past month's been rough, and it's only going to get worse. Two of their lot started a hunger strike that'll not end well. And an accent, along with that last name of yours, could land you in a spot of bother right now."

My brow furrows, then I remember hearing that two of the IRA members responsible for the Old Bailey bombing last month, a couple of sisters, started a hunger strike in prison. I also remember another is named Walsh. It's been all over the newspapers.

Sean continues. "But on the whole, things are better than I expected and could be they'll sort themselves out and settle down soon enough, sure they will." Sean's voice lifts in what I know to be fake optimism. He looks back to Conor. "Another couple brothers thought it'd be better in America than here. I don't hear from them often. How'd they be faring?"

Conor looks down the street, as if taking in all of London. "Pretty well, I expect, but it's not easy there either. Accents lead people to make assumptions and the economy is slow and, like here, inflation is high. Such times put everyone on edge."

Sean nods, flashes me a look, and grabs Conor's arm. "Come in for dinner, not-friend-of-Lily, and we'll talk more. My wife, Daisy, made a meal so fine it'll bring tears to your eyes. Someday soon that woman's gettin' a real kitchen. A proper establishment."

That's my brother-in-law—always making a friend. He refers to the pub, and despite hating change and not wanting any of it to happen, I'm happy for him, for both of them. He practically thrums with excitement at the mere, and oblique, mention of it. I'm so deep in that thought it takes me a heartbeat to realize I'm the last one standing on the sidewalk.

Sean stands in the building's doorway with the hall light spilling out into the deepening grey around him. "Are you coming, Lilypad?" I step into the doorway, and as I pass, he whispers, "This is a bit of craic."

I open my mouth to chide him that this is, in fact, not fun at all, but words don't come out as Sean has already grabbed my arm to yank me into our building's lobby, all while pushing Conor in front of us both.

"Not to worry. We'll be gentle." He thrusts us both through the door.

CHAPTER 17

A heavy sense of dread swamps me as Conor steps into our flat. I look around, trying to see it with new eyes and imagine how it and we must appear to him. Our flat is utilitarian, full of brown furniture we've picked up at secondhand shops and jumble sales. Sturdy stuff that can be knocked into by a wheelchair and not fall down or break apart. We don't have any carpets. They snag Mum's wheels. The art is just as bland too, mostly cheap landscapes we've picked up on Portobello Road. And it's messy. Not dirty, but cluttered as I never have time to put things away and keep everything sorted.

That's not true. It's not about time. We're just cluttery. Crockery bowls and art projects my nieces have made over the years cover almost every horizontal surface. None of it has ever bothered me before—except now it does.

At the door's opening, my two nieces, Posy and Hyacinth, launch themselves from the dining room and crash into their "da," adding to the chaos of the moment. Another thing—we're loud.

As Sean hugs his girls, I speak over their heads. "You're a menace."

His grin grows wide and one might think it's joy at seeing his daughters, but the spice in it lets me know it's all for me. Sean relishes my discomfort. "Too posh by half," he always says to me.

I look up from their happy greeting to find Daisy standing in the kitchen doorway, drying her hands on a dishcloth, with an open-lipped, incredulous expression on her face.

"What?" The question comes out sharp and tense.

Daisy catches it, glares at me, and closes her mouth. Hyacinth and Posy start pelting questions at Conor as if they've never seen a man before, at least not one standing next to me. Truth is, they haven't. I haven't once, not a single time ever, brought a boyfriend home, and it's clear that's what they think he is. That tiny detail was also noted in my "inaccessible" talk last winter.

"Is someone going to introduce our guest?" Daisy calls over the girls' chatter. No one listens. She calls again, exasperated this time. "Sean, stop mucking about. Who's your friend?"

"Not me, luv." Sean crosses the room and soundly kisses his wife. He turns back to me with his arm looped around her shoulders. There's a look of prideful glee on his face. "This is Lily's fella."

"No. He's not" and "We just met" burst out of me and Conor simultaneously.

Conor continues. "Lily and I met Friday at the Tate Gallery. I'm in town from New York for work." He glances to me, but I'm unsure what he's trying to tell me.

"He's investigating something at the Tate."

"What's going on at the Tate?" and "Was something stolen?" come from them simultaneously.

"Nothing like that." Conor's cool, almost dismissive tone stops their questions, and I get the distinct impression that I said exactly what I wasn't supposed to say—again.

I gesture to the living room and rush in, trying to cover my gaff. "Come meet my parents."

The chatter stops as Conor and I cross the few steps from the dining room into the living room and find both my parents sitting and waiting. They've seen and heard everything, of course.

Conor step towards my mum and extends his hand. "Conor Walsh. It's wonderful to meet you and I am sorry to intrude. Sean invited me in, but I don't want to interrupt your evening."

My mum's smile is so genuine and light it makes my breath catch. It's full of peace and vitality, transparent delight and warmth. She holds his hand in both her own. "Please stay."

He nods to her and looks to me. Our eyes meet in quick conversation. His ask, *Is this okay with you?* I reply, trying to convey in a look, *You're fine*, but as his brow furrows for a brief moment before he turns back to my mum, I'm not sure that's what he read from me at all.

"Quiet. You'd think you lot had never seen a guest before." Daisy's yell from the dining room stops our conversation. She strides into the living room with the dishcloth now slung over her shoulder and darts a glance at me. "Or a man, for that matter."

She faces her girls. "Hyacinth, set another place at the table. Posy, clear that puzzle away and help your sister." Daisy turns away, then spins back. "Hyacinth? I asked you to set another place at the table."

"Oh yes." Hy drags her gaze from Conor and follows Daisy back towards the dining room and kitchen with Posy in tow.

I step away from Conor, as he's still talking to my mum, and follow my sister.

"What's this, Lily?"

"It's your husband's fault. Conor was just walking me home. He's an investigator at the Tate."

Daisy pulls a pan from the oven. "He played it off as no big deal, but what's he investigating?"

I wave my hand to dismiss her question, but don't do it as well as Conor did because she pinches my arm. "Ouch."

"I asked you a question."

I can't answer her because only one answer comes to mind: *Me.* Instead I search for a distraction. "What can I do to help?" I look to the oven. "Should that be on so high?"

"Get out." Daisy's voice grounds out low.

I look to her. "What? I'm trying to help."

"You're doing what you always do. Keepin' your counsel yet still managing everyone else. Go talk with Mum and Dad and your investigator. You clearly don't want to talk to me."

She turns away and I'm left staring at her back. After a few seconds I give up and do what she says; I return to the living room.

Minutes later she calls everyone to dinner, shooting me a pointed glare, and we sit. Mum at one end of the table, Dad at the other, Daisy and Sean across from each other near Mum, their girls on either side of Dad, and Conor and me on chairs pulled from the living room and tucked in the middle.

Dishes are passed around, and almost as if I'm a guest myself, I watch the dynamics. We aren't a family versed in small talk. Mum loves company and carries a conversation well, but Dad rarely talks at all. Daisy and Sean talk too, but they're far more likely to ask the deep and inappropriately probing questions than stick to the nothings polite circles blather on about. So tonight, rather than weather and royals, the talk swirls with inflation, debt, trying times, strikes, and the IRA. Seriously, we hit upon every volatile topic imaginable, but I have to give Conor credit, as he keeps up with each and doesn't seem offended by any of Sean's outlandish exclamations.

Then the talk turns directly to Conor . . .

"How'd you get into art investigating? You're like a detective, right?"

Conor glances to me before answering Daisy, and I sense he's uncomfortable talking about work, perhaps because I'm involved. Heat rises to my face as I wonder what he'll say.

He finally speaks. "I am. Just like a detective. It started as a second job for me. I'd just joined the New York Police Department, but with a passel of younger siblings who needed a little support, off-shift security work at the Metropolitan Museum of Art brought me steady hours and extra income.

"Second year in," he continues, "a painting was stolen and I solved the crime. The thief was posing as an art student. You stand so long and still as a guard that you notice people, how they behave and what they do, yet they stop noticing you. This particular 'student' had the necessary paints and easel, but he focused on the rooms rather than the painting in front of him. One thing led to another, and I was soon working freelance for various insurance companies. I finally quit the force when the work got so busy Keller Insurance brought me in-house."

"You must be very smart," Hyacinth comments with wonder in her voice.

Conor laughs. It's indulgent and kind. "I've got three generations of cops in my family and grew up on their stories and watched how they did things. My skills probably stem less from smarts and more from training at birth."

"But that doesn't explain how you know so much about art," I say, recalling how he went through the Picassos in my workroom, calling out each by name, not to mention all the other artists and paintings he recognized.

Conor's eyes soften. "That was me mam." His voice takes on an Irish air and the soft tone of memory. "She hauled us to the Met every Saturday. It was free, still is, and we grew up around all that beauty. That's why when she passed and we needed money, I went there for work. It felt like home. I went to college and studied art too, but it didn't start there."

The conversation continues on and there are smiles, laughter, and the amazing smells of Daisy's warming sticky toffee pudding. I sit listening, watching, and forgotten. Conor is forgotten too—or rather he is folded in.

As the table quiets I stand to clear it and motion for my nieces to stay seated. They're entranced with our guest and their interest in him has given me a little breathing room. I haven't felt him studying me in the last hour. Am I still Suspect Number One? When Daisy comes into the kitchen with a platter, I reach for her arm. "I'm sorry I was a git earlier. I wasn't trying to manage you. I was just nervous."

"I get that. But you coming in here to manage wasn't the problem. You being nervous wasn't the problem. Not even you being a git. It's that you don't let anyone share your troubles; that's the problem. Always has been."

"I don't mean to do that."

"Yet you do, and despite me giving you lots of chances to change, you never so much as try."

Daisy's family soon leaves, and I finish the dishes alone. Only when I finally emerge from the kitchen do I remember Conor. He still sits in the living room with my parents.

"Oh my goodness . . . I'm sorry. You didn't need to stay. Here, let me get your coat."

I'm speaking too fast. I'm moving too quickly. But I can't help myself. I need him gone. I need this night to be over. I need to parse through the charge Daisy laid on me. I need— I have no idea what I *need* anymore.

Outside I turn to him, hoping the darkness can hide my face. "I'm sorry Sean dragged you in. I'm sorry I was—"

"Nervous?" He cuts me off with a low chuckle.

I look up. "Yes."

Conor looks over my head at the building behind me. "Families are complicated, Lily. You can love them and hurt them, want them to draw close while shoving them away. Those two states—the pull and the push—can be true simultaneously." He tilts his head and drops his focus to mine. "Daisy reminds me of my sister Siobin. It took me years to learn how to relate to her."

"I haven't learned yet."

"You will. There's an old saying about a will and a way and all that." He chuckles again, and I somehow feel lighter. "Besides, I wasn't your responsibility so there was no need to be nervous. Those facts are both true too. Thank Sean for me. I enjoyed myself and I like your family. Is there more to be said?"

"No," I acknowledge gratefully.

He looks at me and, even in the dark, I can both see and sense a shift within him. "I got distracted tonight, but I came to find you at St. Martin's for a purpose." He pauses. "The lab results came back."

"I was right, wasn't I?" I tilt forward as the question rushes out on equal parts surety and dread. "Oh no." I clamp my hand over my mouth. I wanted to be right and, deep down, I knew I was. But the consequences will be dire for Diana, Richard, the Tate, me, my family . . .

"You were." His eyes stay fixed upon mine. "I need to ask. Did you forge it, Lily?"

"What?" Like a pendulum, forward one moment, back the next, I lean away and have to step back to keep my balance. "How can you even think that?"

"I'm not sure I do." Conor tilts his head. "You're good, but as a copyist, and that's not what a true forger is. They achieve more than strokes on canvas. A truly great one becomes the artist. And this one is outstanding. Whoever this is, the forgery is the goal rather than the by-product. I sense you use the masters as a means to another end, and if you could, you'd move on . . ."

His voice trails off. Not as if he's forgotten a word, but as if he's choosing to be polite and not state the obvious—that I'm stuck, paralyzed, stymied, or whatever other words fit this trap I've bound myself within.

He talks on. "There's also the fact that you called it out. If you're to blame, I can't discern your motives for that one, but I suspect this whole story is more complex than a single individual."

"I'm not involved, I promise. In any part of this."

"Except you're at its very center too." He breaks off from staring at me. "I suppose I should believe you about *Woman Laughing,* though. Your nose didn't scrunch up." His dark eyes capture mine once more and a smile curls the edge of his mouth.

"How—?"

He laughs. "Your niece shared that insight with me while you were doing the dishes. But she needn't have. I'd already caught on."

"Daisy told them a few years ago. It's a family game to catch me in a lie now." I roll my eyes, not that Conor can see the motion with my face turned away. "It keeps me honest, I'll say that much. But when did I lie to you?" I race through our few conversations and wonder what I've lied about and how damaging it might be.

"When you said painting was just a hobby and, again, when you said you were happy."

"Oh." As I have no real answer for either of those statements, I step away and begin a slow walk up Peel Street to Campden Hill Road. Conor catches up and at the corner we turn right. I assume he's heading for the Notting Hill Gate Underground Station, then wonder if he knows where that is or if I'm leading him. If so, that's where we're going.

"What happens next?" I ask.

"I have the painting. Now I need the original provenance to see if I can find further insights there. When a person makes things up, they're often not as random as real life presents things. A fake provenance leaves clues."

"Like dates?"

"Dates that hold significance to them. Names that don't quite fit the time, the date, the location. Erasure marks, rewrites. I visited the dealer in Paris this weekend and, as usual, she gave the original to Davies upon sale. He says he gave it to Diana. But Diana doesn't recall it."

"Doesn't Keller Insurance have a copy?"

"Xerox copies don't have enough resolution to catch subtle changes. The original was examined when Keller issued the policy, but it clearly warrants closer scrutiny now."

"Well, Mr. Davies and Diana are correct. Usually we'd have it. We always keep the original for any painting on display; our insurance company requires it. But maybe that didn't apply to *Woman Laughing* as Mr. Davies kept it insured with your company?" I lift my voice beyond a mere question in hopes Conor will give something away. He must see it too. The insurance question is an intriguing one.

"Perhaps." Conor faces forward, and I can almost hear gears turning in his head, but he says nothing more. We walk in silence until the corner at Notting Hill Gate. "Thanks for walking me. Good night, Lily Summers, and please thank your family for dinner."

"Will your company pay Mr. Davies?" I probe again.

"As soon as we are assured he's not taking advantage of the situation."

"Do you think he is? Because I suspect—" I stop at Conor's raised hand.

"That's not something I'm willing to discuss, and you should probably keep any further thoughts you have about *Woman*

Laughing to yourself. This is a crime, Lily, not a game." With that he walks away.

No, I think as I walk home, it's a crime and a scandal that are going to harm the Tate, ruin Diana, and get me fired. But to someone, this is definitely a game. After all, that's what art is as well—a form of self-expression. And to manipulate that, to twist and turn it, to hide behind another's genius and work for fame, gratification, power, wealth, or any number of reasons . . .

That is most definitely a game.

CHAPTER 18

Diana

L uncheon, ma'am?"
        Offering no words to Branford, only a single affirmative nod, Diana drops her bag at the front door, sweeps up the stairs to her dressing room, shuts the door, and sobs. By the time she comes out an hour later, she's calmed herself, dried her eyes, and changed from her black jumper and matching capris into a loose cashmere lounge suit.

She finds Heinrich sitting at the dining table waiting for her. The table is laid with a sumptuous repast, and her stomach revolts at the idea of food and the prospect of a quiet hour sitting across from her husband.

While, in theory, a wife should be able to turn to her husband in a crisis such as this, she will not. Nor will she let him see her cry. Her weakness gives him power. It took years to learn that lesson, but she learned it and is not willing to falter now.

Diana sits and slowly drags her gaze about their dining room. It is resplendent with the sunshine streaming through the floor-to-ceiling windows. She also likes the warm glow the candelabra creates deep in its center. Lime-green velvet curtains hang from huge gold-capped bars mounted all the way at the ceiling and puddle onto the wood flooring. They contrast with the lacquered walls, painted a few shades darker green, in a jarring yet oddly harmonious way. But it is the bloodred mohair rug, stretching almost edge to edge, clearly covering a polished and intricate parquet floor, that gives such dramatic richness to the room.

This contrast between the drapery, the walls, and the rug sets the perfect backdrop for Matisse's *The Red Room*. And at five feet by seven feet, the large masterpiece is truly the room's focal point. Always a favorite of Diana's, and also known as *The Dessert: Harmony in Red*, it is the one and only thing she requested Heinrich purchase, once he felt his career had taken off to the degree he could look beyond necessity and indulge in opulence.

That's what life should be—peaceful and tranquil, yet always busy, contributing, and caring. Matisse's woman is at the center, both of the massive painting and the universe he created within it—and she is at peace. While the 1908 work was fashioned in Matisse's Paris studio, he included a glimpse of a green garden through the open window, much like his studio's window that opened onto a nearby monastery's garden. It was that detail that drew her in first. Her appreciation of the woman came later. Yes, Matisse understood the need for nature and wide-open spaces, for freedom, light, and peace—even if only glimpsed through a distant window.

"My dear?"

"Hmm?" Diana, lost in thought, lets her gaze travel from the painting to the window and the cherry blossoms beyond. The trees lining their garden wall wave gently in the breeze, and a fair number of blossoms dance loose of the branches. They have passed their peak and now, as spring carries them away, make a new tableau dancing like fairies before touching down upon the lawn in a snow-like covering of pink and white.

"I asked if you are well."

"I am fine." She turns her head to Heinrich. Her words are curt, even to her own ears, but she doesn't want him giving his opinion on this morning's events quite yet. She wants to let both the past week and the past few hours settle within her longer so she can resolve how she feels—before he weighs in on the issues and resolves everything to his satisfaction rather than her own.

"You are taking all of this much too seriously."

"How is that?" She crosses her arms. "Richard fired me." *Too soon*, she chides herself. *Much too soon.*

"I thought he might." Heinrich sighs, then smiles.

"No." She points at him across the mahogany table. "Don't you dare do that. Don't act as if you knew, anticipated, surmised, or fathomed. That was mine and it's gone. I'm done blindly trusting you. I can't—"

"I gave my tube of paint to your little Lily."

Diana drops her accusing finger. "What are you talking about?"

"Did you know your assistant once worked at St. Martin's School of Art?"

"Of course. She worked there throughout uni before I hired her."

Heinrich leans back and folds his napkin into a perfect square, with overdramatic precision. "Did you know she paints in a utility room converted to a small studio?"

Diana widens her eyes, unsure where her husband is headed but wishing he would get on with it.

"St. Martin's Head of School, Bennett MacKenzie, is a member of the club. Lily's name and *Woman Laughing* have been swarming like bees above our heads for days now. He finally chimed in, could hardly help himself. I commend him, holding such a salacious morsel tight for a full week when it's so tempting to be braggadocious."

"And?" Diana leans forward, twisting her napkin in her lap.

"This morning I visited the school and Lily's little closet."

"You fool." Diana throws her napkin on the table. A corner soaks up the dressing from her salad plate. "She paints there? Did you tell MacKenzie you know her? Were you seen? You've created a link between her and us, beyond just me. I didn't even know she had anything to do with the school any longer."

"Tut." Heinrich shakes his head and trails a finger over the gold filigree lining the edge of his water glass. "No one saw me. No one but a janitor, and he was eager to help. I said I was a gallery owner looking for talent. They do it all the time, especially now that St. Martin's sculpture studio is 'the most famous in the world.'"

In any other circumstance, Heinrich's tone and obvious disdain for St. Martin's accolade, born of jealousy, would amuse her. Today, she finds it tedious and beside the point.

"And?" she prompts again.

"When I said I was more interested in oil than clay and bronze, he mentioned Lily by name and showed me her workspace. I couldn't believe my good fortune."

"You've met Lily. He'll tell her, describe you, and she'll remember."

"She won't. First of all, I wore glasses and the brown wig I often wear to openings. Secondly, he's not going to tell her. He said she'd be furious with him for showing me her work, and I solemnly promised that if I approach Lily, I will never betray him." Heinrich presses his hand against his heart. "I am a man of my word. A true gentleman."

His eyes challenge her to defy him. She keeps silent and hopes he'll continue.

He does. "Lucky for us, my dear, the janitor wasn't exaggerating. She is an artist of no mean talent. I picked through her paintings. Technically, she's solid, not creative or inspired, but solid enough for our purposes." Heinrich waves his long fingers. "On her own, she'll never amount to anything, of course, but that helps us as well."

"What do you mean?"

"She has spent years copying the masters, trying to learn from their color, technique, sensibility, and skill, but she cannot become them. She hasn't surrendered herself. She's trying to glean from them the acumen to create for herself. You can see her desire in her work. And if that's her goal, she has not the means to become them, yet she clearly lacks the freedom and courage to become an original."

He lifts his glass, notices it is full of water rather than wine, and sets it down to reach for the proper one.

"She's copied the masters? Which masters?"

"Five Picassos sit in her rack." Her husband smirks. "They are nothing to the expert eye, but to an amateur, to a mere police detective, she'll fit the bill well enough." Heinrich takes another sip of his wine. "We should be grateful she can't find her own style, I suppose."

"How would she? If she could?" Diana blinks at her own questions. They've laid on her heart for years, and yet she's never had the courage to ask. But now, they are about another. Heinrich may not catch their implications for herself and so he may answer. For that was what he had said upon meeting her as well, that she needed to find other ways to engage in the art world because a "personal style" eluded her, would always elude her, and, without that, there is no art.

"Self-acceptance." Her husband pulls his neck back as if surprised that, after so many years together, such an answer isn't obvious to his wife. "She has to accept who she is, what she is, then surrender her pride to the base reality of her flaws." He touches the corner of his mouth with one perfect point of his squared napkin. "Art is the singular soul, the flaws, the vulnerability, and the memory all on display."

"Is that what you do?"

Heinrich's eyes twinkle. "Nonsense. I have no flaws when becoming a master. I embody their flaws. I fully dissolve into them. That is why I am perfect at what I do."

Diana scoffs.

Heinrich's eyes narrow and she steels herself against the launch of an arrow. "You aren't an artist. You can't understand."

She freezes her features, refusing to flinch or acknowledge the accuracy of his dart. But she was one once, like Lily, an aspiring artist fighting with everything in her to find her own way.

No, she wasn't once *like* Lily; she once *was* Lily. For despite Lily's calm demeanor, it is obvious she, too, doesn't come from the world she inhabits at the Tate. For some time now, Diana has suspected as much, but because she has enjoyed training up her little Eliza Doolittle, she hasn't given it much thought. Yet Lily makes sense to her now—as does what Heinrich says about her art. Lily, she suspects, is unconsciously trying to shed what she was, but art and life don't come in the shedding; they come in the accepting. They blossom in community rather than isolation.

But this is new and possibly dangerous information. That Lily knows art and loves it has been obvious since their first interview. But to be a skilled artist? This is an aspect to the game Diana never considered. Her head starts to pound. "So you left your paint tube at St. Martin's?"

"It could not have worked better. Her tiny room is tidy but cluttered, and her basket of paint tubes is absolute chaos. The girl must use whatever gets discarded, because if you don't mix your own paints, and so few young people do these days, you're at least loyal to one brand. It would drive a true artist crazy to adjust for the tint and viscosity differences across brands. It's a nightmare. I can't understand how—"

"Heinrich." Diana calls him back to the conversation. "You left the tube."

"I buried it in her basket."

"But someone has to find it. Quickly."

"That's your job." His face splits into a long, slow smirk. "And you seem to have time for it this afternoon."

At her dark expression he raises a hand. "Too soon for a light jest? Come now. You've lost your job for a moment, but you'll get it back with my help, and you haven't lost your credibility. That investigator can be led. You said he was young, right? He's eager to make a name for himself, eager to get to the bottom of this, and Scotland Yard will undoubtedly seize upon such an easy answer without question. It couldn't be better."

"We send the girl to jail?"

"Would you rather we go?"

Diana closes her eyes and envisions all that has led her here, to framing an innocent. Her mind then drifts to the future. It is either Lily or them. "I will make the call in the morning. How do I say I discovered this information? How do I—?"

Again, Heinrich raises his hand. He doesn't want to hear any more. He bores easily with the details. "I'll leave that to your ingenuity. But I must say, my dear, it's a little surprising that you didn't see this coming. What secretary carries that much knowledge? Didn't you wonder about it when you promoted her to your assistant keeper, or did you assume that's what they're teaching at Queen's Secretarial College these days?" He watches her. "Or were you overly entranced by your influence over her?"

Diana turns her head, as Heinrich will discern the truth in her eyes. "You needn't say more. I'll get it done."

"Excellent." He stands and places his still perfectly folded linen napkin atop the table. "If you're not doing anything this afternoon . . ." He pauses and glances up. "Our house will be empty following luncheon."

Diana catches a trace of the insecurity and vulnerability Heinrich strives to hide from her. He doesn't want her in their bed. Once the house is empty, he wants her beside him in their studio.

"I'll be up as soon as Branford leav—" She stops. She changes her mind. "Not this afternoon. It was a horrible morning and I have a headache. I think I'll rest."

"Of course." Heinrich's lips open as if he's about to say something more. He shuts them and turns away without another word.

Diana rises as well. The dishes will not be cleared until both she and her husband leave the table. By lingering here alone, she is keeping their houseman in attendance and Heinrich from his work. She is keeping herself from an errand as well.

She races up the sweeping staircase once more and, upon reaching her dressing room, changes her clothes again. After shedding the lounge suit, she digs into a bottom drawer and pulls out a pair of jeans and a ribbed blue-and-white-striped jumper she last wore when sifting through the Tate's donor files in the dank, dark basement. Clothes for dirty, dusty work. Clothes for a student's budget. Clothes for a struggling artist.

She checks her reflection in the mirror and, not liking what she sees, pulls apart her low chignon and tosses her long blonde hair into a ponytail. She adds rouge and pink lip gloss and is out the door ten minutes later, looking ten years younger.

After a quick cab ride down Piccadilly, up Shaftesbury Avenue, and then a left onto Charing Cross Road, she stands outside St. Martin's School of Art, the most famous art school in the country and, despite Heinrich's disdain, the most famous sculpture school in the world. She pushes through the front door and feels her past swallow her.

Those first few years out of secondary school had felt so creative and vital. It was the early 1950s, and while she and her friends didn't feel the freedoms or indulge in the drugs that today's students do, they still had fun. They pushed the boundaries, and even though she wore hand-me-downs and attended a little art school outside Liverpool on scholarship rather than one here in the heart of London, Diana had felt like she owned the world.

Drawing herself back to the present and her mission, Diana savors her good fortune. Classes are just letting out and the corridors brim with jostling students. No one is paying attention to anyone they don't already know. She sweeps by the reception desk without the woman in the cat-eye glasses even glancing her direction. Heinrich mentioned the third floor, so rather than get caught and noticed within the lift, she climbs the stairs.

At the third-floor landing she quickly notes which are studio and classroom doors and which are doors to either offices or storage closets. All the classrooms and studios have glass windows set within the door, offices are labeled with the teachers' names, and closet doors are solid and unmarked.

She stops at the first closet and opens the heavy metal door. She doesn't need to flip the switch as light, spilling in from the hallway, tells her it is jammed tight with clay, wheels, wires, and all the accoutrements for clay sculpture. The tiny room also carries clay's signature wet-earth scent. She breathes it in and shuts the door.

She strides to the next unmarked door across the hall, opens it, and, once again, doesn't feel the need to flick the switch. Brooms and mops stand just inside in a metal bucket. Shelving units stacked at least three deep hold cleaning supplies, papers, and more. As Diana pulls the door shut, a flash catches her eye. A line of light in the darkness. She swings the door open again, steps inside, and shuts it behind her. Only once she is alone in the dark does she flip the switch and venture towards the line of light, now vanished in the ceiling's singular weak yellow bulb.

She steps past four rows of shelves into a small opening against the room's back window. She pulls open the shade. Dust dances in an explosion of color. Her jaw drops. Heinrich was right, on both counts. This is a closet studio and her assistant—her lying assistant—possesses more than a modicum of talent.

Diana lets her eyes travel every inch of the studio. That's what it truly is. Not a formal one certainly, not a large one either. But despite all that, this tiny space is more "studio" than any room she's ever entered. While it reminds her of the third floor in her own house or what she initially envisioned that room would be, this one holds more passion. She can feel it. Or is it yearning? Sometimes it's hard to tell the difference.

And while Heinrich's studio is spacious and light, white and pristine, this old, yellowed, and cramped one feels more pure. Rather than artisan pottery being used to hold supplies, stained Mason jars hold paintbrushes, packing crates propped on end stand in as tables, and an old stool with years of paint splattered on it rests in front of a battered second- or even thirdhand easel.

This is art. Scrabbling for art. Making do and sacrificing for the sake of art. There is also a thrum of creativity that the room itself has absorbed and now holds. It is not unlike the thrum of love. A feeling she misses and still craves after so many years.

She clicks open the wood rack beneath the window and slides the unframed canvases out one by one. Miro. Chagall. Mondrian. Picasso . . . Lily is good, very good, but not great. There is something of herself in her copies of the masters she can't banish. Unlike Heinrich, it seems the girl isn't satisfied in copying. She strives for more.

Diana replaces the paintings. She secures the latches and looks around once more. Is Lily good enough to frame for *Woman Laughing*? Can the authorities be convinced? Diana isn't entirely sure that Heinrich hasn't acted upon what he wants to work rather than a feasible solution. And if he's right and this plan does succeed, there is still the risk that such a close spotlight on the girl might catch them hovering near the edges.

No, this won't do. Lily doesn't possess the skill, she determines. Besides, the girl doesn't deserve this. They will find another, a better and more secure, way out of this predicament.

Diana turns her attention to the large basket that holds Lily's paint tubes. It's an old flower basket like the ones used in Covent Garden during the weekend markets. She runs her hands through possibly a hundred partially used tubes until she finally finds Heinrich's. She holds it to the light to confirm the manufacturer and the color, then slides the tube into her back jeans pocket.

She looks to the easel, curious about what her assistant is working on presently. Heinrich mentioned Lily has no style of her own, and secretly Diana hopes it is true—so far it is. Confirming it for herself, however, is partly why she rushed over. It is foreign, uncomfortable, and strange to envy someone she has never questioned her own superiority against. Yet there it is. Something in Heinrich's voice, a glimmer of admiration, piqued her curiosity and her ire.

She draws back the sheet and, breath catching, drops it to the floor.

The work is stunning. Fresh. Original. It is the beginnings of a portrait of a woman, but not Lily. Older than Lily but not unlike her either. This woman has the same heart-shaped face, the same round, wide eyes, but her hair is longer, her lashes too, and there is a note of sadness within her expression. Her deep grey eyes don't carry the naiveté and eagerness Lily's hazel ones often carry. This woman knows who she is and what she is about, even if life hasn't always treated her well.

Diana's face flushes with heat. Heinrich clearly missed this painting. His assessment of Lily would have been different, much less favorable, if he had. He, too, would have been jealous, and Heinrich hides jealousy poorly.

Diana turns away from the painting, unable to look at it any longer, and glances upon a sketchbook sitting atop an overturned milk crate. She opens it and freezes again—will the surprises never end?

Conor Walsh.

The first page is a hasty rough sketch, but even with a few lines and swift strokes, she recognizes the cut of his jaw, the spacing of his eyes. It is definitely the insurance investigator. But Lily said she'd only met him once, that disastrous conversation in the exhibition space.

Diana turns the page and a new wave of heat, fueled by fear, anger, and betrayal, crawls up her neck. Lily lied again. She knows this man well. This second drawing is more detailed, more intuitive, more intimate. She has captured not only Conor's face but his expression—the same intensity Diana felt herself during their interviews. A look that almost dared her to lie. But here it is softened by some mercurial emotion. Lily has captured an interest in the young investigator's eyes. The third drawing is worse. It hints at something warmer between them.

Diana tosses the book back onto the crate, snatches the sheet from the floor, and covers the woman on the easel once more. She looks to the paint basket, the door, and back to the basket again. Better Lily than them. Diana withdraws the tube from her pocket, shoves her hand deep within the basket, and lets the yellow tube go. She spins, grabs the sketchbook, and shoves it into the canvas bag slung over her shoulder.

In the corridor once more, Diana walks towards the stairs and glances into each room upon passing. One professor's office door is open, yet no one is within. She enters and, without pausing for a moment, lifts the handset off the telephone's base and taps the number for Scotland Yard, happy to have remembered it from the previous year when a disgruntled artist tried to break into the Tate and mark its walls with spray paint.

In less than a minute the act is done. The desk sergeant even reassured her that of course he understood how hard it was to make such an accusation against a fellow student, but if she overheard the young woman bragging, it was right to make the call.

He was so understanding, so solicitous, so gullible. He assured her he would pass her message along and they'd look into it. When she grew anxious, he grew conciliatory. Not to worry, she'd done well, he reassured her, and they would follow up, even if it took a day or so. She was not to concern herself about it any longer.

Satisfied, Diana thanks him again and replaces the handset. She then walks out of the office, down the stairs, and out the front door without a backward glance.

No one gives her a second glance either.

CHAPTER 19

Lily

Brush poised over a mixture of black, white, a drop of yellow, and a smidge of purple, I try to work out the morning. After a midmorning meeting in Richard's office, Diana stormed past my open doorway without a word. I checked her diary and found no appointments listed. I even walked down to ask Richard's secretary what had happened but retreated before turning into her office—to be caught gossiping would surely seal my fate. Unsure what had happened, I worked quietly all afternoon and left early as my desk was clear and Diana had never returned.

Painting helps this time. The swirling questions with no answers recede as my brush touches canvas again and again, and I study Daisy's emerging face. It's a good face. Not one I've appreciated—quite like mine in many ways, yet different too. In hers I see a wife, a sister, a daughter, a friend, a mother, a caregiver. I see experience, common sense, vulnerability, strength, a wicked sense of humor, and loyalty.

I stare at what I've rendered, as if seeing it for the first time, and in many ways I am. I didn't process what I painted last weekend; I didn't direct it, amend it, or criticize it as I usually do. I simply painted. Tired as I am, it was actually easier than I thought, and I carry that through today. I simply paint.

There is a sense of flow and life, and an intangible chase, within the resulting effort that surprises and delights me. Part of me wants to believe I put that there—that I have that skill. Another part of me is terrified I put that there—that I have that skill. For what if creating that drawing and this subsequent painting is a unique moment never to return? What if this freedom and movement is inherent within the subject, not the artist, so I can't claim authorship even if I want to? This painting has captured Daisy. But what if I . . . ?

Panic crowds into my chest—the need to understand everything, sort everything, and, as both Mum and Daisy often say, control everything wrestles within me. And as much as I want to, I can't let it go. What do I hold on to without it? I add a pinprick of dark, almost black paint to Daisy's left eye, right at the edge of the pupil, and dab the fine brush into white to soften it. Her iris needs more blue. Searching in my basket, I note new tubes and smile at Paddy's thoughtfulness. I grab one of a royal blue and am smearing a dab of it into the dark grey on my palette when the door opens.

Light from the corridor spills into my little closet and frames a person in silhouette, almost creating a haloed outline. "Paddy, thank—" I stop and blink as the shadow moves forward and the light shifts from the bright hall to the more mellow interior of the room. "Daisy?"

She waves her arm behind her. "I was told you were in here."

The door clicks shut behind her and the room feels dark, shabby, and sad. My sister turns her head side to side to take in all the cleaning products and stock.

"Yes. I—" I stop again, unsure where to go with my next words. "You've never come here before."

"I never felt welcome." Her voice carries that note of bitterness and wariness I've long felt she reserves only for me.

Her gaze trips over the top of my easel to behind me, to the rack holding years of work. Her eyes then scan my paint tube basket, jars full of brushes lining an old shelving unit, overturned crates and bins full of the clips I use to hold canvases. I see it all from her perspective. I see the hours I've spent hiding here, and I feel young, small, and exposed.

"I need to talk to you." She sounds worn. I look at her and see my painting move in real time. My gaze travels across her forehead, eyes, nose, and jaw. The shape of her chin, her hairline, and her small compressed frown. She carries our visage through life over a decade ahead of me. I see me in our same heart-shaped face, same wide eyes, and same nose with the tiny button at the tip that boyfriends, inevitably and annoyingly, tap and call so "cute." It's similar to what I see in the mirror every morning and exactly what I've painted.

With a start I realize I am only able to stare at her so long because she is not staring back at me. She has stepped around my easel and is studying my painting. Heat climbs up my neck, and I reach to cover both the painting and the original drawing clipped to its corner.

"Don't." She grips my forearm. I drop my hand and she lets me go. Her face looks chiseled. Her jawline sharp.

"Daisy?"

"How dare you." She faces the painting, not me. "How dare you act like you know me when you leave me alone. How dare you spend time with this instead of me."

Her lips press in a line with such force they fold in. I wait.

"You never let me in," she whispers almost to herself rather than to me. "Any of us. You move us about like pieces in a game to make yourself feel better. Then you do this. You paint me as if I'm important to you, as if you know what I love, how I think, and who I am."

"I do—" I want to say she is wrong, that I do know her, that I love her, and that I'm not painting merely what I see but what I feel. I want to ask how she can't see that, how she can't understand. But I don't say anything because right alongside all those thoughts comes the uncomfortable weight that she might be right.

She shakes her head as if trying to reclaim her purpose. "I came to tell you we're moving."

"You told me. In a few months."

"Two weeks." She shifts to face me. "Our landlord let us out of our lease. He'll make more money signing a new one, and that works fine for us. We're talking to Mum and Dad tonight. You should be there. I want you to support this. I want you to be excited and convince them to come."

"Why do I need to convince them?"

Daisy sighs. "Can you truly not see it?" She glances around the room. "You have us trapped, Lily. You keep us right where you want us, right where you need us, and it's stifling."

I pull back. "How can you say that? I do everything."

"Do? No, you control everything. We all *do*. According to your dictates. Nothing out of line. Nothing off schedule. You even changed Mum's therapy because you wanted her home when I had time to visit." She holds up her hand to make sure I don't interrupt. "I'm not saying it wasn't thoughtful, but it wasn't my thought, was it? It wasn't something she asked for either."

"How can you complain when you say it's best?" I leap in before she can draw breath and continue.

"I complain because you manage it for your ego, not for us. We never asked for your martyrdom, little sister. And it was fine for a while, but no more. I'm doing what's right for my family, what's right for Mum and Dad, and you are going to come home tonight, and you are going to smile and tell them that moving to Richmond is the best news you've ever heard, for them and for you. Even if it's a lie, you are going to tell them you have tons of friends begging you to join their flats and you have a great place to land anytime you want. And if that nose of yours scrunches even once, I'll bop it so hard it'll never scrunch again."

"But—"

"No buts, Lily. Mum is alone. Dad's got to retire because if he doesn't, he'll get cut. He'll lose his benefits. Everyone is barely hanging on, and if you can't see that, I'm here to force you to." Her gaze snags on a small crate next to the window and the little plant that rests there. She blinks. She stalls. She steps to it and runs her finger over its fuzzy leaves. "How? How is this still alive?"

I look to the plant I've managed to keep green and growing for almost fifteen years, the violet she gave me on my thirteenth birthday. "I love it. It's always been with me."

"A plant," she chides, her laugh laced with disappointment and incredulity. She looks to me and her expression changes, opens, like she's seeing me for the first time. She then shifts her focus to the painting. "You should share this with Mum and Dad. You should let them in. You should let us all in. It's good. Amazing really."

"It's just a hobby." I shrug and say the same words I always say. The ones that diminish what all this means to me, the ones I believe keep me safe.

Daisy sees right through them and probably sees my nose scrunch too, which to be honest I don't often feel anymore.

"Don't say that. Say this means the world to you. Say this is your dream and that you're willing to sacrifice everything for it. Because from where I stand, you have. You let nothing and no one in, and rather than believe that's who you are, I'd like to believe something touches your heart more than a plant." She taps a leaf of the violet. It bounces with the pressure. "It certainly isn't us."

Without another word and without letting me reply, she heads to the door. She calls over her shoulder, "Be home early tonight," and she's gone. The door slams with a metal-on-metal thud behind her, and I am left standing in the dark. Alone.

I look to the plant, back to the painting, and before I can stop myself, I swipe it and send it crashing to the linoleum floor. Wet paint smears as it slides a few inches before hitting the wall. What felt vibrant and life-giving moments ago now feels like a fake, a sham of a life that I'm only now seeing because, as Daisy said, she forced me to. None of this is real. I am alone. There is no community here, no life here. Only a plant.

I look to the Chagall resting against a shelving unit. It's a flat and trite copy of a masterpiece. I see the stiffness in my composition, my failure to create balance, much less whimsy. I hear

Daisy's accusation that nothing touches my heart. She's not as spot-on with that accusation, but feeling something and having the courage and vulnerability to act upon it are very different things.

I pick up the canvas, weighing it in my hands. It's so light. Almost nothing. It is nothing. I crack its wood frame against my stool. The canvas folds in on itself. I smash it again. Pierce's story about his play comes to mind, with all the characters moving in formation and balance, block clothing and lines, and I reach for a Mondrian from my open rack. Pierce's story had life; my copy of Mondrian merely has lines. I tear at the canvas but only end up popping off a few mounting tacks. I smash the painting against my stool, then drop it to the floor atop the Chagall.

I slide the front panel off the rack and reach for a Renoir next. Young Lise Tréhot stares back at me, exposed and unsure. I envy her self-awareness. I crack the frame of *In Summer* so hard it splinters and sends shards of wood flying across the room.

Renoir's *Two Sisters (On the Terrace)* is next. I pause, seeing me in it, standing alongside Daisy. I swipe at my eyes. How did I not recognize it before? Most of the works I've chosen over the years feature two sisters or a mother and daughter. With our age difference, either could reflect Daisy and me, and I have settled for this counterfeit rather than the real thing. But it's not my fault—the protest rises within me. Didn't she shut me out first? Didn't she reject me before I could reject her? Yet on the heels of that, I recognize the times I turned away first, the times I retreated, the times I shut her out, and I hear only one word.

Inaccessible.

I smash the Renoir and I don't stop there. This one I'm able to pull completely away from the thin wood supports. The dried paint cracks, flakes, and falls across the linoleum to smear with the wet paint from Daisy's portrait. Monet's *The Cliff Walk at Pourville*, portraying his wife and child, is next. I moan at my own transparency or self-delusion, as I'm not sure which it is. Again, it's Daisy and me. Always the two of us.

Soon I lose count. Painting after painting. When the rack sits almost empty, I pull her likeness off the floor. I lift it to crack the wood frame against my stool as well, but I stall. It's the most real thing I've ever created. But it's still just a thing. It's mere paint and canvas, and the real sister just walked out the door without me saying a word to stop her.

I smash its wood supports like all the rest and I want to say it's cathartic, but it's not. There is no rage. There is no passion. There is only self-recrimination and a sense of abject futility. Is this what waking up feels like? Waking up and finding you are nothing? Waking up and realizing that whatever this was, it's over because you never fully invested in it anyway? Because you hid all along, just like your sister said you did? And that in your reaching, you were never reaching for the right thing?

"What are you doing?" Paddy stands slack-jawed only a few feet away. His expression carries a touch of the wide-eyed horror one sees at the cinema. I look around at the debris because that's the best you can call the wood shards, paint chips, and twisted canvases scattered around me.

"I'm done." I expect the words to come out strong and clear, with conviction, but they come out full, almost choking, with the pressure of tears behind them. I will not cry. "I can't do this anymore. I don't even know what I'm doing anymore. Who am I, Paddy? What am I? Don't artists have something to say? What am I saying? What's me?"

Paddy's expression changes in response to something he sees in me. It softens. I shake my head. He will not pity me. He cannot console me. I stand with my arms limp, head limp, and heart worn as Paddy steps forward. He's still staring at me. I cross my arms and step back, away from him.

Then the most unexpected thing happens. Paddy's face breaks into a broad smile. It wreathes his eyes, lifts years from his cheeks and jowls. And although his eyes glisten with what I think are tears, he grins on.

"Child. It's grand. You'll be grand."

A sloppy laugh bursts out of me. "This is grand? Look what I did."

"As you say, it was never you anyway."

It's a tiny gesture. He merely reaches out a single hand, but it's all I need. I tuck myself into his embrace. And perhaps for the first time in my life, the floodgates open.

CHAPTER 20

I wake in a tight ball and struggle to straighten stiff legs. Crossing my room, I rub my neck and gently move my head side to side. How will I keep my hurting, heavy head upright all day? My eyes itch and look so swollen that I bend from the lavatory mirror to splash water on them. Determined not to look again, I brush my teeth facing the wall.

I slip on black tights, a black skirt, and a black jumper. My outfit reminds me of one Diana just wore, and somehow that comparison, that likeness, makes me uncomfortable. While Daisy accused me last evening of not letting anyone in, something deep within me whispered in the night that I've let someone in: Diana. I've been so eager for her approval, so thankful for my promotion, that I have given her influence over my life while I shut others out. But letting her in was easy because Diana's approbation was and is transactional. I can win or lose it by what I do and not by who I am.

And it's the *who I am* that's the problem. I rub my eyes again and sense a shift within me. Deep inside I hear a whisper of hope. *Was.* Who I *was* is the problem. At the end of me, deep in the night, I finally understood. It was like seeing through a cracked doorway, and with each millimeter of opening the truth became stronger, clearer, even cleaner.

I have no control. I never did.

Since the age of five I've been grasping for what Paddy calls "vapor," that elusive smoke that slips through your fingers. Yet I thought I held it tight and moved it to my will, and that I could use it to make amends. That somehow holding tight exonerated me from blame. Yet there was no blame. And in the instant I realized that, the desire to seize control vanished. I wanted nothing more than that crack of light to grow.

When it did, grace was there. Grace that had always been there. Love was there, and that had always been there as well. I played my part well last night and told my parents to go to Richmond, but until deep in the night, I didn't believe my own words. Now I do. It became true without me willing it. It simply is true. I want Richmond for them, for Daisy, Posy, Hy, and Sean. I want freedom for them. I want freedom for me—whatever that might mean.

I shrug out of the black jumper and reach for another top. A pink blouse similar to one I saw Diana wear a couple years ago that I found in a consignment store. My hand drops. I look to the small bookshelf next to my bed and note all the books Diana has suggested over the years. I shift my gaze to my walls and recognize in my posters the art she loves. Expressionist and surrealist works. My eye then snags on two books of poetry. Again, Diana. She once said an understanding of British poetry was crucial "for people of our station." Yet poetry unnerves me. Maybe I would like it if I understood it, but most of the time I can't.

I drop to my bed. Everything around me isn't me. Or is it? But if it is, when did it become me? When did I let myself become a copy, a forgery of another?

Searching for something authentic, my thoughts turn inward and my afternoons wandering through the New Realism Exhibition at the Serpentine Gallery come to mind. That's what I'd paint. That's what I would chase—if I had the time, the ability, and the talent. Not expressionism or surrealism. I want to see clearly. I want things to be what they are, people who they are, without subterfuge and distortion. I want truth.

I smile to myself, and the weight I'd never felt before, but which I know existed by its growing absence now, lifts a little more. I pull a dress from the wardrobe, one Mum made me for a Christmas long before I started working at the Tate, and I slip it on. I glance in the mirror and recognize myself again. After running a brush through my wavy brown hair and pulling it back into a ponytail, I use my finger to swipe on lip gloss and call it done.

I enter the Gallery through the front door and walk back to the closed Picasso exhibition. I expect it to be dark and gated and I am surprised to see Andrew, the head of the installation team, inside. I loop my fingers through the grate and call to him.

"What are you doing here so early?"

He walks over and stops a few feet from the gate. His glare sets me back. It's not that Andrew and I have a warm relationship; we don't. Andrew, with a master's in fine arts from Oxford, is only temporarily with Installations while he waits the prerequisite time for that next jump, and he clearly resents that Diana promoted me. Rightfully so, to be honest. Although he'd only been at the Tate about a week when I was promoted, his education, credentials, and pedigree far surpass mine. I'm the thorn in his side.

"I'm shipping off a marquee installation, one that would have looked great in my portfolio, all because someone couldn't keep her mouth shut."

I refuse to apologize to him, so this time, I do keep my mouth pressed shut. I point to two of the Tate's own Picassos, *Bullfight* and *Three Dancers*, propped against the orange wall. "Those were hanging here before. Why did you take them down?"

"Richard wants every Picasso pulled and placed in storage. Out of sight, out of mind, I guess. The rest are going to labs here or in Paris." He digs his hands into his trouser pockets. "And since he wants there to be no question about how we've handled each piece, I get to personally catalogue and crate every single one. Like some shipping lackey." His eyes narrow at me. "I thank you."

His use of "Richard" snags my attention as this is Diana's exhibition, and I should probably be doing this work. But before I can speak, Andrew continues.

"I'll have the destinations and schedule to you later this morning. Since Diana's gone, I suppose you'll be the one to notify the insurance company that each remains on our policy until the results come back."

"Diana's gone? What do you mean *gone*?"

"Richard fired her yesterday morning. What did you think happened before she stormed out of here?"

"She didn't say anything so I didn't ask."

He looks at me like I'm an idiot. "Go ask her now. She's back today full of her usual charm. My guess is she's shoring up support in the two weeks Richard gave her to clear her desk." He lifts a brow. "It's housecleaning time."

"Relax, Andrew. Richard likes you."

"Doesn't matter what he likes." Andrew's voice drips with disdain. "He won't keep me if it's not politically advantageous, and nothing about this is advantageous. Besides, he and the new keeper he hires will have plenty of favors they'll need to dole out before this smooths over."

Now I apologize.

"Too little. Too late." Andrew scoffs. "You should have handled it quietly, privately. Professionally."

I look past him into the room. "You mentioned labs? I thought everyone wanted their paintings back."

"That'd be too easy. Every single owner, except the Louvre and the Prado, wants a fully certified paint and chemical analysis at the Tate's expense. Proven authenticity."

"You're joking." I have only handled such a request once. Well, Diana handled it. It happened soon after I arrived. A Monet was brought under scrutiny and sent for analysis. The cheque was extraordinary. "Richard must be apoplectic."

"Hence Diana getting the boot. This is the art equivalent of a run on the bank, and it's spreading across Europe. You haven't seen *The Times* this morning?"

My stomach drops. "I gotta go."

I dash across the central gallery, but not towards the administrative offices. While Security delivers the morning papers straight to Diana and to Richard, they also deliver one to Sara in

Donor Relations. I push her door open and drop into the chair across from her desk without saying a word.

"About time you showed up." Sara's thick and usually curly red hair is ironed straight and hangs like a gorgeous sheet of flame down her back. Yet other than the hair, she looks devoid of color. Guilt assails me as many—dare I say most?—in the art and museum world come with a degree of independent wealth, but Sara and I do not. If patrons are angry, her job may be on the chopping block as well. Everyone else's seems to be.

She leans back in her chair, the one she grabbed from her boss's office when his new leather one arrived last month, and crosses her arms. "Do you have any idea what you've unleashed?"

"I'm getting an idea."

She taps her telephone with a pencil. It's not one of the fairly new electronic push-button telephones either, but a rotary dial for which she uses that same dented pencil to spin the numbers. "It's been ringing off the hook since everyone read this."

With her other hand, she tosses me her copy of *The Times*. I don't want to touch it but reach for it anyway. A picture of Mr. Davies and a close-up, probably the dealer catalogue picture, of *Woman Laughing* take up half the front page. The half above the fold.

"No . . . No . . . No . . ." I hear the word, almost as if I'm not saying it myself, as I read the article. It's an interview with Mr. Davies and, as expected, he lays full blame for this "outrage" on the Tate.

Without naming me, probably because I'm insignificant, the article states that an unnamed person declared the half-million-pound *Woman Laughing* a forgery and chemical analysis proved the claim. A paint used in the under-paint contained titanium dioxide, not only rare in paints used in 1930, but of a signature and distinctly modern formulation from Stockholm. Scotland Yard is working with the company to obtain purchase records.

The article then goes on to state that Mr. Davies purchased the work merely weeks ago at the suggestion of the Tate Gallery's Diana Gilden, who not only authenticated and appraised the work upon purchase, but accepted the painting for the Tate's recent Picasso Commemorative.

I moan. The article gets worse and worse for Diana as I continue. She is singled out as the keeper of the Modern Collections, an expert on Picasso, the sole organizer of the commemorative exhibit, and the one who has not only advised Davies on all his art purchases over the past couple years, but also provides expert appraisals and authentications for clients and companies across Europe. This thread then sends the reporter in a new direction. He actually implies that anything Diana examined or authenticated should be called into question and insinuates a forgery ring may be operating throughout Europe.

"This is bad. Really bad." I set the paper back on Sara's desk.

"But an effective way to twist the Tate's arm." At my expression she taps her phone again. "It started yesterday. I guess word about this 'forgery ring' hit museums first, but now almost every patron who has donated or lent a painting to us in the last two decades wants it lab certified. They don't want to be 'hoodwinked.'"

"Hoodwinked?"

"Lady Alexandra Bessing got the term from the first *Times* article and is running with it. All over town." Sara pokes her pencil towards her boss's office. "Every museum across the Continent is getting calls. Then they're calling us. We've had donors and board members yelling at us since last Tuesday, pulling their support, but now we're taking calls from colleagues across Europe experiencing the same."

"How is this possible?"

"Someone's stirring the hornet's nest." She ruffles the paper.

"I'd better get upstairs. Diana is back this morning."

Sara sighs. "Good luck."

Upstairs, there is a note on my desk.

see me immediately

I drop the note into a drawer, set my bag down, and head down the corridor. After a quick rap on her door, I wait until she calls me in. Her hand flutters towards the chair opposite her desk and I sit.

She stares at me. "You've heard."

I open my mouth to reply, but as she's hurriedly digging through papers, I stall. Offering what would amount to condolences right now would not be welcome and I suspect another apology less so.

"I need you to take notes. There are things to do."

"Of course." I sit straight with pencil poised. "I'm ready."

She bends to her file cabinet again and draws up a stack of folders. She passes them to me across the desk.

"Here are the documents for each of the paintings to be sent out. Andrew is getting shipping organized, but insurance must be retained."

I glance into the top file. "I'll get it done."

"Make sure you do." She levels her eyes at me. "These two weeks are important. How I leave matters for my next position. My last day is the fifteenth of May. Unless you choose to quit now, consider that your last day as well."

"I'm let go?"

"Your reprieve was never meant to be permanent." She taps a single finger atop the folders as if impatient with me for not understanding my situation sooner. "I need your help to clean up what I can. Can I rely upon you?"

I nod. I may feel differently about Diana today than I did yesterday, but I don't respect her any less—and the undue influence I gave her in my life was my fault, not hers. I will miss her. I will miss this position. But not yet. Two weeks of pay are vital. "Yes. The fifteenth of May is fine."

"Compile a full timeline for the British Emerging Artists Exhibition. Richard may cancel it, but if he doesn't, Andrew will need to step up if a new Modern Collections keeper isn't brought on board quickly." She stretches the file towards me. "Pass this file to Andrew and tell him he has three spots to fill. At this point, it doesn't matter who he selects. The spots simply need to be filled or the space will look sparse."

She passes another short stack of manila folders across the desk. "Go through these and see if there is anything left to close out, and while you're at it, go through my diary and push all my appointments. Don't cancel any, but give me at least a month before the reschedule date. Do not say Richard is letting me go. Give any excuse you want."

Diana rubs her forehead. Her fingers whiten with the pressure, and red-raised streaks mar her brow when her hand drops away. "This is humiliating. Edward Davies wants my head on a platter." She looks at me, and I get the impression she doesn't actually see me, or she sees who I was mere days ago—someone she trusted. But it lasts only a moment. With a quick flash of her eyes and an impatient gesture with her hand, I'm dismissed and leave with the files as quietly as I came.

Within a short time I realize that tasks that should take only a few hours are going to take the whole day, if not more. I'm not distracted by the phone ringing or by Lucy, Becca, or Sara stopping by, but by Diana herself. She drops into my office almost every ten minutes, terse and tense, to give me another task. "Call him," "Type this," or "Let me read that." In my years working for her, I never would have said Diana hovers. This morning, she hovers.

At eleven o'clock she fills my doorway once again. "I can't be here." She points to my pile. "But I want you here. I want that done. Today."

"Yes."

"If Richard needs anything, you are to be here to help him as well." She pushes away from the doorjamb only to swing right back in. "Until day's end. Do not leave a minute early. Do you understand?"

My brows lift before I can school my surprise. Richard never needs my help, and I have never been told to stay "until day's end." She stares at me, waiting for my reply.

"Don't worry. I'll get it all done and I won't leave early."

"Yes. Good." Something flickers across her expression, almost like suspicion, but before I can fully catch it and define it, it's chased away by a tightening of her blue eyes and a flex within her jaw. "Don't disappoint me." The unspoken—yet loud—word *again* hovers between us. She turns away.

My eye catches upon the insurance file and I call her back. "Diana?"

She steps back within my doorway.

"*Woman Laughing*'s provenance. It's not in here, but we had it, didn't we?"

"We don't have the painting, Lily." Diana tilts her head as if she's explaining something that shouldn't need to be explained. "Why would we keep its provenance?"

I don't answer, as the question is clearly rhetorical, nor does she wait for anything else I may say. She is simply gone and I get back to work.

But a little after noon, as Richard passes my office, curiosity gets the best of me. I dash to his secretary and learn he's left for the day, first to see Mr. Davies—she says with a sneer—then to meetings across town.

The statement Diana made has danced at the edge of my imagination for the last few hours. Why does Mr. Davies want Diana's head on a platter? Another question dances alongside it: the question of the provenance. But here and now, I can only deal with the first, and I can deal with that, hopefully, by understanding more about him.

I head to the basement. It's time to see Sara again.

When a prospect first reaches Diana's or Richard's attention, one of them always asks Sara to look into them. It's not meant to be intrusive so much as it's meant to guide the Gallery's approach in creating a relationship. After all, it's a lovely thing if a potential donor enjoys portraiture or impressionism or modernism and he or she receives invitations to those exhibitions. Or if they have a background in construction or design and are invited to see the plans for the new expansion approved a couple years ago. The belief is that the more personal the connection, the more loyal the support.

Sara sits behind her desk eating a tuna-mayonnaise sandwich. Peeking into her boss's office, I note he's out. I sit. "Finish lunch."

"Forget it. I know that look." She lays her sandwich on a square of wax paper. "It's gotten warm anyway."

"May I see Mr. Edward Davies's file?"

She narrows her eyes. Part of me suspects she'd like to say no, but Diana sends me to look at files all the time. It *could* be a legitimate request.

"For you or for Diana?" When I don't answer, which is an answer, she finally sighs. "Only the upstairs file."

"There's a downstairs file?"

"You have no idea." She crosses her office to the little attached anteroom and opens the door.

While never giving us names, Sara often shares stories from the Tate files over lunch. Becca, Lucy, and I eat them up. The slights and scandals she reads about are more riveting than that American horror show *Night Gallery* that just started playing on telly last week.

"So and So," she'll say—and she actually calls them "So and So"—"was caught in flagrante delicto back in 1913, then lost all his money and was institutionalized by his children in 1940." Another So and So faked an injury to avoid serving in the army, murdered his father in 1943, then spent his inheritance on clubs and mistresses. There's even a file on Wallis Simpson—Sara gave us her name—as she attended several exhibitions in the 1930s and was thought to be an ideal prospective donor. That is, until her Nazi sympathies became too public and she absconded to France with our king.

She pulls out Edward Davies's file and hands it to me. "Brian's gone all afternoon so I'm letting you see this." I open my mouth. She holds up a hand. "Don't say anything. Just stay in here, read the file, and come out when you're done."

"Yes, ma'am." I salute her.

She closes the door on me. I lean against the cabinet and start paging through the sheets.

The top sheet lists Mr. Davies's donations, amounts, dates,

and special notes. It seems he has given small amounts to the Gallery since 1953, primarily designated for the British Collections. Then about three years ago, something changed. His giving went up by a factor of fifty, and he started attending events for the Modern Collections. Pages deep there are also citations of meetings with Diana about purchasing art: Chagall, Modigliani, Ernst, Miro. That aligns with the paintings I saw in his flat. They definitely mirror Diana's taste. I run my finger down the page, surprised there were so many meetings between them, none of which I scheduled or knew occurred.

Another page deep I find notes on the day he joined the board of trustees last year. There are the usual scribblings about what was said and to whom and the general tenor of his reception, but nothing out of the ordinary. Nothing to indicate a fallout between Diana and him or why he'd want her ruined.

I turn the page. It's a summary of the newspaper archival search that Brian always asks Sara to complete. Mr. Davies's businesses are in construction and metal fabrication, with companies listed as far back as forty years. Many early ones have the notation *bankrupt* next to them, but then his businesses seem to have turned around near the end of the war and in the booming postwar years.

I learn his birthday is 12 June 1903, and that he's almost seventy years old. He moved from a good address in 1956 to a great one, adding an estate to his real estate holdings in 1965 and a French villa—presumably where his estranged wife lives—in 1968. I also learn he has two children: Frank, forty, and Lyle, thirty-six. Neither one has an address or interests listed, which is curious because Diana always asks me to look into that for her and Brian asks the same of Sara. It's important to remember to ask, "How are Frank and Lyle doing? Are their families well?"

I then learn Mr. Davies's first wife died on 9 November 1941, and something shifts within me. The Blitz. While I'm not certain that's how she died, it's a reasonable guess. I close the file, more curious about Frank and Lyle—which always leads to Daisy and Oliver.

The only pictures of Oliver that still exist are on my mum's nightstand. He is probably about five in my favorite one, holding three-year-old Daisy in his lap. Both have their heads back and they are laughing. I can't tell what color eyes he had or what color his hair was—was it a lighter brown like mine or darker like Daisy's?—and I never ask. I don't ask because I wasn't there, I wasn't born, and I can't trespass. Daisy has taught me never to trespass.

She was five and Oliver was seven when Operation Pied Piper was executed in September 1939. Over a three-day period about three million children were evacuated into the countryside. Most came back. Oliver was not one of them. What happened is unclear, but he and Daisy were sent to a home in Yorkshire, and while I never got the impression the family was abusive, they were certainly negligent. Too old to be watching children and too tired to keep up with them. So two young city children were left to roam the moors on their own. One day Oliver got lost and fell down a chasm. He wasn't found for four days, and by then he had died.

Daisy was shipped home immediately and lived out the remaining months of the Blitz in London, hiding in the dark flat with Mum or spending her nights in their designated bomb shelter. I think those years haunt my sister just as much as those months in Yorkshire.

I wonder which town Frank and Lyle were sent to, if they were sent away. I wonder if their eyes sometimes take on the faraway look of loss and regret that Daisy's do, and how that translates into their present. Do they keep their children close? Do they worry? Do they fear surprises, risks, and change? Or did that time push them to be independent and self-sufficient, knowing they may need such skills in a heartbeat?

I pull myself back to the file resting in my lap and open it once more. The notes paint a picture, but as with a painting's provenance, there are gaps. And one doesn't want gaps. All the interesting bits are in the gaps. I close the file once more and realize that rather than learn anything helpful, I've spent the last twenty minutes merely satisfying my curiosity.

I slide the file away and open the door. Sara is paging through a ledger. "Did you find what you need?"

"You said something about a downstairs?"

"Nope. Not happening. I was specifically told not to leave this telephone today."

I almost laugh as it seems the hovering-protective-boss illness is spreading, but I don't because it's not funny. My boss has lost her job; I've lost my job; and I can't be responsible for the thread of firings to stretch to Sara's boss, then on to her.

"Can I go alone?"

Sara assesses me. "If I let you do this, will you be quick and quit bugging me?"

"Yes, and if I get caught, I'll say I did it on my own."

"You got the key on your own?" She smirks and reaches into her top drawer and pulls out a large antique key—the kind that opens locks and doors from the last century or two. "Do you know where to go?"

"I assume down those stairs at the end of the hall?"

"At the bottom of the stairs, use that key to unlock the door on your left. Go down another flight of stairs, turn right, and you'll find a room with about ten huge wood filing cabinets. That's the room you want. And take this." She stretches a massive metal torch towards me.

My hand drops with its weight. "This is from the last century too."

"Give it a little respect, mind you. I bought that last year with my own money. And if you want to go down there with just a few working bulbs, be my guest. That's the brightest torch I've ever found."

"Nope. This is perfect."

"Good. Take it and stop whinging." Sara narrows her eyes in a mock glare. "Don't you dare get caught."

"I wouldn't dream of it." I raise the torch like a banner, check to make sure the coast is clear outside her office, and take off.

At the end of the basement corridor, I open the door, shut it quietly behind me, and flip the switch. A single light flickers and emits a low hiss, along with little light. I head down the stairs. With each step the air grows damper. Although it shouldn't surprise me, it does. I mean, the Tate is both temperature and humidity controlled, yet only steps below exist the catacombs and chambers of the ancient Millbank Penitentiary on which the Gallery was built—the same passages that flooded in 1928. It's creepy.

The key slides into the lock fairly well, only sticking as I try to pull it out. A few wriggles and I finally wrench it free, then drop it into my dress's square pocket for safekeeping. About a third sticks out, and I hope it won't fall or at least that I'll hear it clank against the stone flooring if it does.

Down another short passageway, peeking into small cell-like rooms as I walk, I find one with several huge wood filing cabinets. Each holds a metal nameplate with a paper insert, but the paper has curled and the writing faded with time and moisture. I can't fully make out which cabinet holds which donors or what years.

I open the first. The wood sticks on wood and I must set down the torch to pull the drawer open fully. The files are organized by name. A quick perusal reveals they go back to the year the Tate, under the name the National Gallery for British Art, opened in 1897.

I shove the drawer shut, as it seems to contain only information pertaining to anyone and everything from *P* to *S*, and I search another cabinet. Moving up the line, assuming they are in alphabetical order, I stop at the first and open the third and bottom drawer. I expect *A* to *E* might be in this cabinet and *D* would be near the bottom.

I find the file for Edward Davies, begun in 1937, and "Oh my goodness" escapes. It makes an odd, echoey, empty sound, and I decide not to speak again.

While Mr. Davies didn't begin to donate or be involved with the Tate until 1953 as I learned upstairs, a notation at the top of the first page reveals his file was created in '37 because he was business partners with Sir John Brookings, a longtime supporter of the arts and the Tate as far back as 1920.

The first page is a scattered list of details I assume someone gleaned either from meeting Mr. Davies back then or from comments made by Sir John. What whiskey Mr. Davies drank. His nicknames, education, upbringing, and address. Details about where his wife shopped and where his kids hoped to attend school. Estimates on his income. Guesses on his interests—a fairly short list, which includes fly-fishing, reading, and pugilism. The last doesn't surprise me. He looks like a boxer.

I skim the file and realize there is much more here than was available in his file upstairs—and I suspect these files, and not the ones in Sara's office, are where she gets all her great stories. But while her stories are fun, they are only fun because they are anonymous. They are just stories. There is something uncomfortable and predatory about these files. I wouldn't want to meet the man who created them. That said, I'm still going to read them.

Mr. Davies's file reveals conclusions as well as facts. Whoever created it seems to fully believe that Mr. Davies was manufacturing munitions for both the British and the Nazis before and during the early days of World War II. There are a few notations about business transactions, but mostly references to dinner parties, travel, and social engagements. Mr. Davies's business partner, Sir John Brookings, is mentioned in each one. It seems there was no Mr. Davies without Sir John, and after 1943, there is no Mr. Davies at all. His file abruptly ends in June 1943 with the notation, *No longer of interest.*

I pull another drawer and extract an even thicker file on Sir John Brookings. I find alongside copious amounts of donor information listed, there are the same parties, colleagues, and events easily cross-referenced with Mr. Davies's information. His file also ends in 1943, but rather than stating he was *no longer of interest,* it cites his death on 17 May 1943.

After a while my stomach growls and I realize I am cold, damp, and learning nothing new. I slide the files away—they stick and crumple with the moisture—and shove the drawers shut.

A few minutes later, I hear Sara on the phone and wait outside her office.

"Yes . . . No . . . Please do not worry . . . We'll soon have this in hand. I'll pass your message on to Director Browning . . . Yes, the Tate Gallery remains fully open . . ."

I round the corner. Her forehead rests on her desk. "Hallo."

Her eyes are worn. "What a day."

"What time is it?" I drop into the chair.

"Past four o'clock. You were down there forever." She reaches for the key and torch. "What did you find?"

"Notations about companies, constant parties with his business partner, Sir John, and someone only referred to as David. Also some notes about Germans. Everything ends in 1943."

"Edward Davies was a Nazi then."

"What?" Sara's tone was too calm to have said what I thought I heard.

"Trust me. MI5 has nothing on those files. If he was hanging out with 'David' and there are notes on Germans, he was a Nazi. It was oddly fashionable back then to be one. Bad, but fashionable."

"Who's David?"

"Our short-reigning King Edward VIII."

"Oh . . ." I lean back. "How do I find out what happened after 1943 when the file ends? The file up here starts in '53."

She shrugs. "I have no idea why the gap. Maybe he went quiet and didn't donate or visit. It was the war. But leave it alone. He sounds like a dark horse, Lily. You should let Diana and Richard tangle with him. This has gotten too big for any of us." She drops the key and torch back into her desk drawer. "Honestly, I don't even use those files anymore. They're horrid. Brian asked Richard if he could haul them out of here for destruction."

"Smart move." I think back to a blackmail story about a security guard finding donor information and extorting money from patrons years ago. I had always thought it was Sara's upstairs files he accessed, as I had no clue about the downstairs. "Where do you find your information?"

"I mostly research the newspaper archives. If that gap is bothering you, go there. But I wouldn't."

I thank her and head back upstairs for my coat and handbag.

Archie, breathing fast and shallow, intercepts me in the corridor. "I thought you were gone."

"I was in the basement." I say nothing more as I don't want to get Sara into trouble.

"Scotland Yard was here looking for you, but I couldn't find you. Miss Gilden is gone too."

I reach for Archie's arm to reassure him it was inevitable Scotland Yard would come here. "She went home early. I expect they'll ring her there or call here again tomorrow. It's probably about *Woman Laughing*."

"But they weren't asking for her. They were after you."

"Me?" My heart skips a couple beats as I catch he said "after" rather than "asking for." I try to reassure myself as well as him. "That was to be expected too, I suppose. Did they leave a number?"

"Didn't need to. Director Browning confirmed your home address."

CHAPTER 21

Diana

"You're happy this afternoon."

Diana shrugs at her husband's comment without replying. She sets down her shears, sweeps the debris into her hand, and muses that she, too, can let silence work between them. She, too, can control a moment.

She drops the flower cuttings into the bin, satisfied they'd done their job. Upon arriving home, she'd felt anxious and tense about *The Times* article, furious that Edward had turned on her, then accepted she would have done the same. She also realized that perhaps it wasn't an unfortunate turn of events as it added to the chaos she desired. The flowers helped her reach these conclusions.

Yes, they had wielded their magic and gifted her with a new perspective—what did it matter that Edward bellowed and huffed? To beat Diana down would only help her rise. Because as soon as the police catch up with Lily, Diana thinks, she will be vindicated. Thought a fool, perhaps, but the embarrassment will be short-lived. And Richard will most likely rehire her, as she understands her assistant and her talents and reach better than anyone. Diana will publicly concede that she was used, blinded for a short time, and then remind everyone how ideally situated she is to navigate Lily's perfidy and set things on the right course once again. Yes, with Diana's calm guidance, everyone will soon forget this uproar ever happened.

Once painting played this role in her life. Merely putting brush to canvas soothed ruffled feathers, calmed her fears, and brought clarity and perspective, but that was years ago. Now refashioning the exquisite flower arrangements throughout her home, trimming them down into small bouquets to coax a few days more from them, gives her almost as much enjoyment. The result is a work of art. A living work of art.

She plans to place this bouquet, created from cuttings gleaned from the dining room table's extravagant centerpiece, beside her this afternoon in the reading nook. Curled up with a cup of tea and the new novel she's secreted away for just this moment, Madeleine L'Engle's *A Wind in the Door*, Diana cannot anticipate a more luxurious way to celebrate success. A secret way, as she'd never admit to anyone—especially Heinrich—that she actually listens when Lily mentions books. *A Wrinkle in Time* had been the girl's teenage favorite and, curious, Diana had purchased a copy at Hatchards on Piccadilly last year.

It had proved a captivating story on a deep and personal level. Something about Meg's search for identity and her dogged determination to fight against fear and to fight for truth spoke to Diana, and something about Meg's courage and conviction inspired her. Now, a decade later, L'Engle had finally penned the next in what looks to become a series.

Diana glances up. Her husband still waits for her reply. "I am happy this afternoon," she confirms, then turns away, refusing to add anything more. She sets the kettle on the Aga and reaches into the cupboard for today's selection, the Fortnum & Mason Royal Blend. She opens the tin and inhales the scent of the loose leaves within. Perfection.

"Well . . ." Heinrich's confidence wavers.

She peeks his direction and notes him shift from foot to foot. He wants more from her. He stands waiting for her to notice him, talk to him, coddle him. She fixes her focus to the tea caddy, the strainer, and her cup. Today she chooses a lovely delicate Halcyon Days floral cup with matching saucer.

"I'm heading to Goddard's for the afternoon."

"Excellent." Diana brightens. "Keep your ears open. I called the police yesterday afternoon, so by now they'll certainly have talked to Conor Walsh and perhaps searched St. Martin's. I made sure Lily stayed at work all day today, so if they go to her directly, she's right where she's supposed to be. Why don't you discreetly find out what Bennett MacKenzie knows?"

"You needn't tell me how to arrange my affairs, my dear."

"Yet I do." Jubilance makes her bold. Success, cheeky. She doesn't feel cowed by Heinrich this noon. She saw something he missed. She knows just how well his ill-conceived idea might work. He believes Lily to be a mere copyist, but that isn't enough for their purposes. *Woman Laughing* is beyond the girl's skill.

Yet Heinrich missed Lily's true talent, and that is where the success of their plan lies. In her painting of the woman who must be her sister, Lily touched upon greatness, and to the untrained eye, greatness was greatness—in a Picasso or in a rendition of one's sister. And just to make sure that becomes clear to the authorities, as well as the girl's compromising relationship with the insurance investigator, Diana swiped her sketchbook and plans to drop it into Lily's desk at the Tate. After all, once Lily is in custody, the police will search her desk and the drawings will further attest to her talent and destroy Conor's investigation.

"What are you up to today?" Heinrich pauses. "Since you'll be home rather than at work."

She doesn't let the barb needle her. It barely scratches the surface. "I'm going to enjoy a cup of tea and reread *Frankenstein*," she lies with a grin. "I so enjoy that story, the twisting of a man from brilliant to monstrous. I haven't read it in years. Not since we met, actually."

Heinrich chuckles, low and measured. Being cowed is not in his repertoire either. "Enjoy this victory. It's ours, and I agree, you should celebrate it in your way as I will relish it in mine. But don't forget we are a team."

He nods to the teakettle, which begins to hiss. He waits as she takes it off the stove and pours water through the strainer into the cup. Tension builds within her. He is waiting for some purpose. She can feel it. His timing always plays to his advantage.

She presses her lips together to keep herself from shouting, *What? What do you want from me?*

Only after she has replaced the kettle onto the stove and turned to him once more does he continue. "You may need to rethink New York for the Campendonk. It seems your little European fires have crossed the Atlantic."

She lifts a shoulder and lets it drop. "I told you they would. The world is becoming increasingly global. I also told you we should wait on the Campendonk."

Heinrich waves away her concerns with a flick of his long fingers. "It's ready and I don't like works lingering in my studio. It affects my process, impinges on the next piece. There is no clarity within when old friends linger about." He taps his temple.

"I'll handle it." She sighs. Part of her wants to simply shove the painting into a back closet and be done with it. But while Heinrich doesn't get involved with the details of selling the paintings, he keeps a keen eye on the funds each one brings in.

"Perfect. I knew I could count on you." He glances to her teacup, sitting and steeping on the counter between them. "I won't keep you any longer. I'm away." He turns and throws a last barb over his shoulder as he crosses into the living room. "Enjoy your little children's tale, my dear. I suspect L'Engle's new offering will be far more delightful than another reading of *Frankenstein*."

Heinrich saunters out the front door.

Diana's afternoon lies in ruins.

CHAPTER 22

Lily

I leave the Tate feeling vaguely unsettled. It's not the work Diana left me. I can easily finish all that first thing in the morning. It's not really what I learned in the basement either. Mr. Davies's file actually bolsters my case against him. I mean, if he's willing to sell munitions to the Nazis, he'd certainly have no problem defrauding his insurance company. It's not even that the Scotland Yard investigator talked to Richard and obtained my home address.

It's none of these things as surely as it's all of them, and without consciously determining it but knowing it's happening the whole time, I find myself walking to St. Martin's School. I'm not going to paint. That's over—and that leaves me feeling jumbly as well—but I do need to clean up. I need to return the storage closet to its original purpose. I need to be done. Then I can move on. To talk to Scotland Yard. To a new job. To a new flat . . .

I trudge up the stairs. Classes are finished for the day and most rooms are empty. There are a couple studios with their doors open, and a radio plays the Grateful Dead down the corridor. I push open the heavy metal door to my utility workroom, flip the switch, and discover it's perfect. Completely clean and completely empty.

I stand shocked that Paddy not only cleaned it for me but also cleared away my paint tubes, brushes, and cloths. He cleared away all signs of me as efficiently and effectively as if I'd never been here at all. I glance to the overturned crates I used as tables, and each now sits properly stacked on the floor. My Mason jars are gone. My easel is set to the side. Even my blank painted-over canvases have been taken away. I glance around the room, searching for something I know to be here, yet it's gone too. Paddy even took my sketchbook.

My mind races with questions and I feel adrift, not certain what I feel or what I want to feel. Those are two very different emotions, I've found. But what's done is done. So with a soft "Goodbye" to the room and all the hopes and dreams the sanctuary once held for me, I pull open the door and leave it for the last time.

Paddy is nowhere to be found. He's not on any floor from three down to one. He's not in the basement utility room. I push open the door to the back alley, and he's not outside smoking a cigar. Turning back into the alley service door, something catches my attention and I freeze.

Daisy's eye.

I walk down the alley a few meters to where the metal rubbish bins line the building. Three have been pulled from the wall and block the alleyway. That's where I find Daisy's eye peeking from the top of a bin. I approach slowly as if something dangerous awaits me, and my stomach churns at what I find.

My paintings are shoved deep into the bins. If you can call them paintings. They are twisted blackened bits of canvas with paints scorched, burned, and melted into a morass. A few muted, disgusting melded colors of greens, dark reds, and browns reach up the sides of the metal bins and an acrid chemical smell accosts me. Foam has been sprayed all over the outside of the bins and dries atop the charred debris. Only that corner of Daisy's painting remains, sticking out at an odd angle, as well as a sliver of Chagall's dancing goat.

Now I really need to find Paddy.

I dash back into the door and head straight for the reception desk. Nothing escapes Veronica. "Where's Paddy?"

She looks at me through her red reading glasses and her eyes appear massive, like the big eyes Margaret Keane painted in the 1960s. She pulls them off her face and her eyes shrink to an almost-normal size.

"It was horrible, Lily. They took him away."

"Who took him away?"

"Bobbies. An inspector. They found him burning paintings in the back alley. I didn't see it, but some students out smoking did. They said he was involved in a forgery, that he was an accomplice or something and that he was trying to destroy evidence. They found all sorts of stuff in one of the utility closets upstairs and marched him straight past me in handcuffs."

"Where is Headmaster MacKenzie?"

"He's gone to the station to find out what's going on." She looks up at me. "You should go there too."

Something in her voice catches my attention. "Why?"

"They were looking for you. You're who they asked for when they came. Four of them. I directed them to Paddy because I knew he could find you. That's when they found him burning the paintings."

My brow furrows as I try to work how Scotland Yard knew to come here, or why, when they have my address, or why Paddy would do something so crazy, or why on earth anyone would put him in handcuffs.

"Where did they take him? Which station?"

She hands me a card. "The inspector gave me this."

I fold it in my palm and thank her. Outside the evening is cool and cloudy. I turn left. I stall, my mind still swirling. All this must be about *Woman Laughing*, but it doesn't make sense. Paddy had nothing to do with what I said. No one at the Tate knows I paint here. My paintings have nothing to do with any of it regardless. Then I envision my empty studio and I remember *The Times* article. The paint. A tube with titanium dioxide, a "modern formulation." My paints are missing. *No*, I think. *My paints were taken*. I rush back inside.

"Veronica, did they take anything from that closet you were talking about?"

"Everything. Paddy had paints, brushes, canvases, and all sorts of stuff. They took away boxes worth."

I turn and push through the door again, vaguely hearing Veronica still talking to me, but it doesn't matter. Paints. Brushes. Canvases. Five Picassos. A sinking feeling swamps me. They don't think I called out a forger; they think I am one, and somehow Paddy got caught in the middle.

I race down the block, only slowing after I bump into an old man and almost knock him to the pavement. I steady him, apologize, lift my eyes, and find Conor Walsh staring at me from the street corner a few meters away.

"Lily." He says my name and nothing more.

"They took Paddy O'Brien away in handcuffs. To Agar Street."

Conor tilts his head down the street. "I'm heading there now." He looks back. "Inspector Gray called me about his bonfire at the school. It doesn't look good for you. Or for him."

"What he did has nothing to do with *Woman Laughing*. They think I forged it, don't they?"

Conor says nothing.

"They took my paints, everything. They'd only do that if they believe I'm guilty."

"Are you going to the station? We can walk together." He skips over my statement, but I read confirmation in his eyes.

I stand still and estimate that I'm just far enough away he can't lunge for me without me having a split second to react. "I was headed there."

"Good." He gestures down the street. I step back. He watches me, but he does not move.

"Will Paddy be okay?" I calculate my options—as if I know what any of them might be.

Conor lifts a brow. One. It gets lost in a lock of hair that's fallen across his forehead. "Eventually, yes. But this kinda thing can go sideways fast. Something's at play here, Lily. Something I can't put my finger on." His eyes narrow. "Can you explain how they found the tube of paint in your basket?"

I take a shuddering breath. "The one from the papers? The one with titanium dioxide?"

He nods.

"My basket holds hundreds of tubes, all of which come from bins throughout the school. Anyone could have put it there, and I bet you'll find countless more in there too." I gesture to the building behind me and step back with the motion.

Conor's focus shifts from my face to my feet, but he does not move. "Not another tube was found in the entire school, and this particular one is very expensive and made by only one manufacturer in Stockholm. I assume you read that in the papers as well?"

"Are you going to take me in?" I look to his hands, ready to bolt if one so much as twitches.

"I'm an insurance investigator from New York. I have no authority here. What Scotland Yard does is their business, and at this point, it's time to turn over my notes. I would, however, advise you to go to the station and answer their questions."

"I don't know how the paint got into my basket. I had nothing to do with the forgery and you know that—you saw my work." I step back and hold a hand up. "I need to find out what's going on because they're going to arrest me, aren't they? That's why they came to the Tate and here, and now . . ." I step back again. "How can I find answers from jail?"

"You let them find the answers, Lily."

I step back again. "Give me a day?"

"What about Paddy?"

My chest constricts. What about Paddy? He doesn't deserve this. He's done nothing wrong. But I can't help him if I'm jailed beside him. "I need a day."

"A day." His tone doesn't offer permission, nor is it questioning. It simply confirms what I said, and in that, I hear an acceptance of terms. Somehow Conor and I have made a bargain.

But just in case I'm wrong—I run.

I dart through the crowds of pedestrians and drop down the stairs of the Leicester Square Underground Station and hop the Northern Line to Tottenham Court Road. After a quick switch to the Central Line, I ride the train past home's Notting Hill Gate stop to Shepherd's Bush. It's growing dark when I finally knock on Daisy's front door. The sun has set behind the row of buildings opposite her door, casting the street in shadow. A sense of being stalked and hunted permeates me, and I feel grateful for the grey. Daisy answers the door and her face morphs from something between questioning and alarm to outright fear.

"What's wrong?" Oddly it doesn't occur to me that Scotland Yard would have come to her home as well. "What have you done?" comes in quick succession.

"Can I come in?" I step forward as she backs away. "Just for a minute," I add.

My nieces catch my voice and rush into the hallway. Both start talking at once, but I can't hear either.

"Oi," Daisy shouts and shuts the door behind me. "Give your aunt some room. Get back to your homework while we talk."

Fifteen-year-old Hyacinth rolls her eyes, but she obeys. Eleven-year-old Posy follows her sister back to their kitchen.

Daisy tilts her head to the left and to her bedroom. "It's the only truly private place here."

"I need help," I whisper. "I need you." The last part comes out unbidden, yet it's true. Truer than anything I've said in a long time. That feeling I had when smashing the paintings, that aloneness, that emptiness, can only be filled with grace, love, forgiveness, hope—and it starts with Daisy. It always has. I need my sister.

She hauls me into her bedroom with a yank on my forearm and shuts the door behind us. "Scotland Yard was here, Lily. *The* Scotland Yard. Looking for you."

"What did you tell them?"

"The truth. That I saw you at St. Martin's School last night in that closet of yours. Then they asked about your painting, how long you'd copied the masters, had you ever given any of your paintings away, sold them, or—"

I put my hand on her arm to silence her rush of words. "It's okay."

She pulls back. "It's not okay, Lily. They were after something. They were after you."

I drop onto the edge of her bed. "I should have told you. I should have told you all."

"Oh no." She drops next to me, her hands over her eyes. "This is about that Picasso from the papers, isn't it? The forgery they found at the Tate. That's why Conor's in town."

"They think I forged it, Daisy."

"Did you?"

I shoot off the bed. "How can you ask that?"

"That's not my world, Lily, and you've got talent. Anyone can see that. Your paintings are extraordinary, good enough for a museum. I wouldn't think you would, but couldn't someone just take one and sell it? You might not even know. You had tons of them in that room."

Oddly, my heart lifts. While there's a lot in her short speech that's bad, there are a few good things too. My sister believes I have talent, enough talent that someone might swipe my painting and try to pass it off for a Picasso. A real Picasso. It's so loyal, so lovely, so laughable—yet Scotland Yard is not laughing.

"Thank you." I drop onto the bed again, closer to her this time. I lean into her and she absorbs my weight.

She twists and throws an arm around me. "Why on earth are you thanking me?"

"You think I'm talented."

"Goodness, girl, that's what you heard?" She pulls me tight and kisses the top of my head.

Tucked against her, I add, "That's not how it works, by the way. Someone doesn't just steal one of my practice paintings and try to pass it off for an original."

"How does it work then?"

"I wish I knew." I look around her bedroom. It's so like my sister. Not fancy or frilly, just simple with everything in its place. Yet beautiful too. She has an old dresser she took from our childhood home that she's polished to a beautiful shine. On top is a dish I made her in pottery class when I was about twelve that holds her jewelry. It sits next to the bottle of Chanel No. 5 Sean gave her for their last wedding anniversary.

I glance to her bedside table. "Susan Cooper? I read something by her." I pick up the book *The Dark Is Rising* and hold it in my hands. This moment and this book suddenly feel more real and grounding to me than anything has in years.

"I'm reading it to the girls. You probably read *Over Sea, Under Stone* when you were a teenager. That one just came out."

"Yes." I look up. "I remember."

"Lily, you're not here to talk about a silly book."

Tears prick my eyes. "I wish we could, though. I wish I'd just come over to read to the girls. I wish you and I were close. I wish . . ." I swallow. "I'm scared, Daisy. Someone is framing me for that forgery."

She crushes me into a hug so tight I can't breathe, which is okay as I don't want to. I grab her back, determined never to let go.

"Those coppers weren't joking around," she whispers.

When we settle apart, I run my arm past my nose to clean up the soppy mess I've created. I've left a damp spot on Daisy's flowered blouse as well and try to swipe at it. It's such a ridiculous gesture we both end up laughing. Not a nice, light laugh but a snuffly one, the kind that only comes out when the pressure is so great the alternative is nothing but tears.

"Do you have a friend I could stay with for tonight and maybe tomorrow?"

"Why not stay here?"

"They'll come back. I can't be here, but I need a little time to figure this out."

She hands me a tissue. "Doesn't hiding make you look guilty?"

"Yes. But someone did this to me. Someone put a tube of paint in my basket at St. Martin's on purpose. The very tube the forger used. Then that janitor you met, Paddy, made it all worse by burning my paintings. I think he was trying to protect me."

"He did what?" Her indignant shout makes me smile.

"I'd already destroyed them." I shrug.

"Why would you do that? They were wonderful." She shifts away from me to look into my eyes.

I drop my focus to the book I still hold in my hands. I think about stories, art, expression, and freedom. I think about love. I've always said art is love, and yet those paintings weren't love. They were hiding from it. "I didn't want to be stuck in them anymore." Tears squeeze out of my tightly closed eyes. "Daisy, I took Mum from you."

"No, you—" She cuts me off, and I cut her off right back. "Wait. Listen."

I continue. "I thought I took Mum from you just as Oliver was taken, and we'd already lost Dad. At least you did, because you knew he'd been different. Then with the baby . . ." She stiffens slightly and I press on. "I got scared because, with Posy, I almost lost you. I never wanted you hurt again, I never wanted to hurt again, so I tried to make everything right and got it all wrong, but if you died, then you'd have never known and I wouldn't stop hurting."

"Known what?" she whispers.

"How much I love you. How sorry I am."

She pulls me into another tight hug. "You are such a git." She laughs into my hair. "Can we be done with all this now?"

I nod into her neck, marveling that her love and forgiveness can be given so easily. I hug her back.

"Now let's get you to Janice's." She sits back and I do the same.

"Who's Janice?"

"A friend who won't ask questions." She pops up and dashes about her room, grabbing things and shoving them into a canvas bag she pulls from her closet. "How have they not found you, by the way?"

"Odd luck, I guess. I was in the subbasement when they came to the Gallery and the security guard thought I'd gone home. Then at St. Martin's they'd come and gone before I arrived. When did they come here?"

"Right before the girls got home." She glances to her bedroom door. "I didn't tell them."

"And Mum and Dad?"

Daisy pauses. "Mum rang. They went there before they came here. She's undone."

I rub the back of my hand against my mouth, my nose—everything seems to be leaking.

"Hey." Daisy crouches in front of me. "She'll be fine. If you're fine, she'll be fine. It's how motherhood works, okay? So let's get you fine."

I nod because I must, not because I believe I will ever be fine.

She stands, leaves the room for a moment, returns, and drops the bag onto my lap. I set her book back on her bedside table.

"Come on. Janice lives a few doors down. She watches the girls for me sometimes and, in return, I watch her cats." Daisy quirks a smile. "Fair warning. She's got at least seven." She yells back towards her kitchen as we open her bedroom door: "Girls, I'll be back in a jiff."

It's almost fully dark outside, and I notice how Daisy turns quickly to the side as she leads the way out her building. I almost quip she's watched too many spy films, then realize someone actually could be watching her flat.

We walk to the left and she knocks on another door at the end of the block. It's an individual home in a row of five tucked together with doors opening onto the street. A tall, almost gaunt woman answers. Her face is angular; her long and iron-grey hair hangs limp to her shoulders. She reminds me of Picasso's Old Guitarist, and I wonder about the life she's led, what she's seen, and, like the Old Guitarist, what weight she carries.

Daisy quietly introduces me and asks if we can come in. Janice picks up on the tension in my sister's voice and ushers us in with no words, quick gestures, and a peek side to side out her front door. That makes me curious as well.

After Daisy's very curtailed and mostly inaccurate version of the past week, Janice merely says, "No worries, luv. I like the company."

I look to Daisy, then back to Janice. She's nothing like Paddy, yet I sense the same kind spirit within her and feel compelled to add, "I didn't forge that painting, but if you're caught helping me, there could be trouble."

"Let's not get caught then." She actually grins like it's a jest. I stand speechless as she says goodbye to Daisy, then leads me to the back of her flat. "You've got your own room here. The loo is down the hall, and if you want to go in and out the back garden, it's probably safer for you that way. There's a gate and the alleyway will lead you to the street."

She leaves the room and returns seconds later, stretching her hands out to me. "Here's a key and some fresh towels."

"Are you sure about this?"

"I wasn't being cavalier. It's obvious you're scared and in danger." Janice's gaze travels beyond me into the room behind me. "I've come to believe, however, you need to help when and where you can. The old 'damn the torpedoes' and all that." She picks up a framed picture of a young boy off the bookshelf. "My Roger got into trouble a few years ago, and your brother Sean was good to him, went out on a limb, several limbs, to get him work and set him straight. And these past couple years since he's been gone, your sister's been good to me too. Anything she asks, I'll do, so don't you fret—you're safe here."

"Thank you." I look around. I'm clearly standing in Roger's room. And while the picture she holds is of a young boy, that young boy clearly grew up. Posters of the Rolling Stones, Led Zeppelin, and The Yardbirds adorn the walls. Copies of *Rage*, *Private Eye*, and other similar and salacious magazines fill an old milk crate by the desk.

Her gaze follows mine. "Them dens in Soho killed him. He couldn't get away from them no matter how hard he tried. Eventually he gave up trying. That was two years ago now, Christmastide."

"I'm sorry."

"Me too. He was a good boy. Just like his father." She presses an arthritic knuckle to her nose as if stopping any emotion from seeping out. "We don't choose what life throws at us, do we?"

"I suppose we don't."

After Janice leaves, I pull open the bag Daisy packed and find a comb, a toothbrush, a nightgown, and a change of clothes. I smile. My sister is a good mum.

I pull out the toothbrush and head towards Janice's lavatory. Her corridor is lined with photographs. Some in the dark sepia tones of the last century with no smiles and stiff poses, but others more recent and lighter in both tone and aspect. There's a large one of a handsome man in uniform and another of him with a young woman laughing at the camera. I see Janice in the young woman's eyes. In the next picture, the two smile at each other over a three-tiered wedding cake. I let my gaze trail down several more pictures as the story of two-lives-in-one unfolds. A story that, as far as I can tell, comes to an end in the last world war.

She's right about Roger too, at least as far as looks go. He sports the same strong chin and close, deep-set eyes as his father. From the outfits and haircuts, I put him at about Daisy's age. In the last photograph his hair is long and greasy, his eyes defiant and angry. He's not looking at the camera; he's glowering at it with a cigarette dangling from his lips, his hand on the way up to pull it from his mouth. There's something artistic about the lighting and the framing that makes me think Roger wasn't so much angry as he was artistic. It reminds me of Joan Didion's famous photographs from the 1960s.

Was Roger sent away like Daisy and Oliver? What did he remember from those months or years, and what role did it play in his struggles?

Janice was right on another point too. We don't get to choose what life throws at us. I suppose we only choose our reactions, our responses to it. What will my response be? I brush my teeth, return to Roger's room, and lie in bed, pondering that question most of the night.

CHAPTER 23

THURSDAY

The next morning I scan Roger's bookshelves as I dress, with one plan in mind—to find out more about Edward Davies—and I stumble upon a second—how to find *Woman Laughing*'s original provenance.

The second plan—admittedly a crazy one—starts to form when a familiar cover on a bottom shelf catches my eye. It's an expensive book on Mondrian written by Italo Tomassoni. St. Martin's resource room holds it, as does Diana's office bookshelves.

The heavy book takes two hands to pull and lift, and after dropping into Roger's desk chair, I page through Mondrian's early periods and styles, finally pausing on the chapter covering his retrospective exhibition at the Stedelijk Museum. That was the moment in which Mondrian began deconstructing the very idea of the line in art and the definition of *art* itself. His innovative thinking on this subject, and his questioning of our very ideas of the use of the line and its value in art through the Renaissance all the way to modernism, is what inspired me to choose him as a subject of study. Besides the fact that I presumed I could draw straight lines and fill in blocks of color with his proficiency. How hard could it be?

It's those works that inspired Pierce's scene in *The Art Charade*. The scene in which . . .

The idea blooms. It's theater. It's art. And it may be the only way I can get some answers—and *Woman Laughing*'s original provenance. As I was pondering Edward Davies last night, I remembered he mentioned he needed it. I also remembered Conor wants it. Diana said she didn't have it. Yet I know she did once. I saw it. A messenger brought it the day before the Picasso opening—and I laid it on her desk. If she didn't return it to Mr. Davies or give it to Conor or keep it in the file for me to find, where is it? And why did she act like she didn't know?

I can only conclude that she still has it, as the others are still searching for it. And if so, Mondrian's art and Pierce's scene have given me a perfect way—at least an interesting and daring way—to get it.

My sister doesn't answer her telephone, and I realize she's probably visiting Mum, as she often does after her girls head to school. Considering it's Mum I'm trying to reach in an oblique fashion, I call home. Daisy answers.

"You want her to do what?"

I slow down and explain again. "Four identical dresses. The bolder the better so you can't mistake them for anything else. Think Mary Quant, but bolder. If you see one, you'd naturally think that's the only one there can be."

"What?" Daisy asks again. "Why on earth—?"

I talk over her. "Please. Just ask her. And tell her I'm sorry I can't share more."

"She won't like this, Lily."

I wave my hand as if Daisy can see it across the telephone lines. My endless apologies are for another day and should probably be given by me personally. "The dresses don't have to be perfect. They just have to look the same from a distance. Four of them. She has dress patterns for me and she can use one of those or tell her she can remake dresses from my closet. Only one needs to be a tiny bit larger, if possible, and maybe one a little longer. No, never mind all that . . . Just four dresses all alike."

"You sound crazy." Daisy huffs. "Do you want to talk to her?"

"No," I bark. "She'll ask questions."

"I've certainly got plenty of them," she quips. There's a pause, but I don't speak into it. My sister finally says, "Don't you think she has the right to ask a few questions, Lily?"

"Yes, but not yet. I don't have answers and that'll frighten her. I think I've found a way to get some, though. And the less she understands about these dresses, the better. Scotland Yard might come back. That goes for you too."

"You've told me nothing."

"Precisely."

Daisy huffs again. "You know she'll do it. I don't know how, but she'll try. When do you need them? And you said all the same size?"

"Tonight." I pause to give my sister time to balk again. But she doesn't. "I need them tonight for first thing tomorrow morning. And basically the same size is fine."

We aren't all the same size, but we'll fit. Sara's will be super short and Lucy's a touch tight and Becca's too big. But for my purposes, it won't matter as long as we can each zip it up, and I am pretty sure we can.

"This will help you figure out who put that paint tube in your workroom?"

"I believe so." I take a deep breath. "I have to try, Daisy. Everything's stacked against me, and if I'm guilty, then Paddy is too. He's a good man—you'd like him. In some ways he reminds me of how you and Mum used to talk about Dad, if you gave Dad Sean's accent."

The sound of a half breath, half laugh carries across the line. "I'll ring you back." She hangs up.

Though it feels like forever, I suspect only a few minutes pass before she rings me. She begins with no preamble. "She's on it. Betty at the Sew and Stitch says she's got plenty of green, red, and blue to make simple block shifts, and she's called in their sewing circle. Mum also said to tell you your whole idea of re-making dresses is bollocks and that if you knew anything about sewing, you'd know they have to be newly made."

I smile. It's been our long-running war—Mum wants to teach me to sew just as much as I don't want to learn.

"You're really not going to tell me what you're up to?" Daisy's voice is exasperated, but not as put out as I am used to hearing.

There is something light, almost indulgent, in her tone that reassures me. "Lily?"

"I'm here."

"You're not alone."

Her words fill me, and for the first time I sense the courage within me to believe them. I feel boneless and slide down Janice's wall. Tears start falling. "Thank you. Is Dad home?"

"Nah, he got put on a job for the week. Only this week, but he needed it. He's been a little quiet. Quieter."

I nod as I noticed it too. "Give Mum a hug for me?" I sniffle, hoping I'll soon get to hug Mum myself. I then say what's really on my mind. "I'm sorry, Daisy."

I can't tell her for what because I hardly know myself. It isn't this mess. It isn't because Scotland Yard came to her house. It isn't because I come at her rather than come beside her most days and have for years. It's none of that and it's all of that—and I sense she understands that too.

"Me too." Her words are soft and they pierce me.

We hang up and I put the next step of this plan into action. I need friends for those three extra dresses—Lucy, Becca, and Sara. I call their flats and reach each of them before they head to work. I ask each if they'll do me a big favor—all say yes with little hesitation—then I ask them to meet me outside a closed millinery store on Bessborough Road, right behind the Gallery, at eight twenty-five, eight thirty-five, and eight forty-five the next morning respectively. I give them the very basic outline of what they are to do and when, but I do not tell them why and I do not tell them about each other. As with Janice, my mum, and Daisy, the less anyone knows the better.

With Plan Two in motion, my mind returns to Plan One—the way to answer my questions about Mr. Davies. Something about him still doesn't fit. If he's trying to defraud his insurance company, it feels that speaking to the press and exploding the scandal into something greater makes little sense. Wouldn't he simply want a quiet investigation to declare him innocent and pay him, assuming he's covered his tracks well enough? Pointing the finger at Diana, churning up gossip, doesn't fit if he's guilty—it only draws attention to him. But if he's truly innocent, then maybe what he's doing holds a certain logic.

I pull on the dress Daisy packed for me. She threw one of my favorite outfits of hers into the bag—a light brown linen shift to layer over a cotton blue-and-brown-striped jumper. She also packed a pair of thin brown tights, which I need as my stockings have runs up each leg and need to be tossed.

Within the half hour I'm on the Underground heading to the newspaper archives in Bloomsbury. A library act passed last year will form the British Library right here in town, and soon that's where the consolidated archives will be located, but it's not scheduled to open for another couple months. So for now, as Sara told me, finding the information I want is a long process of traveling to the various annex buildings to learn what each one holds.

I start with the closest, the Bloomsbury annex.

Bloomsbury tells me the archives of *The Times* and *The Guardian* have recently been moved to the Colindale annex in Barnet, the borough created from Hendon and Finchley, among others, a few years ago. I only know that detail because C. S. Lewis's Pevensie children were from Finchley and when it was folded into a new borough, I felt like we all lost a piece of our childhoods. I take the Northern Line to Edgware rather than to High Barnet, as my *A to Z* positions the Colindale depot between the two, favoring the Edgware Station by a few blocks.

Once seated with newspapers spread across a wide metal desk, I start with papers from January 1944. The 1943 papers, covering the June that three of the Brookings-Davies companies went bankrupt, were destroyed in a fire about a decade ago. But considering the pressures around manufacturing things at a fast and furious pace during wartime, there's got to be prolonged coverage when something goes so terribly wrong. I find a short listing in the 13 January 1944, *Financial Times*.

The beleaguered Brookings and Davies munitions manufacturing company officially closed doors yesterday. Three
of their factories, beset by problems in both raw goods and
subpar workmanship, lost a contract by the Ministry of Defense several months ago, following Sir John Brookings's
death. Mr. Edward Davies, presently the sole proprietor,
could not be reached for comment, but sources confirmed
a soft shipment of lead stopped manufacturing early last
summer and irrevocably harmed much of the manufacturing
machinery. Davies personally shut the doors of the factories
last June and closed the overseeing concern. The losses are
estimated to be . . .

I read on and find that in June 1943, right after Sir John's death,
five of the Brookings-Davies factories failed for various reasons.
Soft lead shut three and ruined all the machinery. Sabotage shut
the Dover plant. And as the Ministry of Defense withdrew support,
decreased demand shuttered the last in Suffolk.

Reading on, I discover that Mr. Davies then divested all his
holdings in anything associated with Brookings-Davies and walked
away. *The Financial Times* called the divestiture "sophomoric and
unwise," not to mention unheard of. He paid the Brookings family
their percentage of the failing business and liquidated everything
left at pennies-on-the-pound prices.

There was also a notation in *The Times* that Sir John's heirs
sued Davies for handling the divestiture and liquidation poorly,
but that was settled quickly and quietly out of court. In that same
article I learn that Davies donated his portion of the company's
proceeds to the Spitfire Fund, a national campaign to purchase
fighting planes, and he single-handedly supplied the RAF with
over 150 planes. Davies then started his own private company
with a single factory and, after a year of producing grade-one
munitions, won another Defense Department contract in late 1944.

I sit back and ponder all I've read. Somehow he no longer
strikes me as a man making munitions for both sides, one enam-
ored with Crown Prince David, Wallis Simpson, and others with

Nazi sympathies and alliances. He sounds like someone who was trying to make something right. But what?

I read on.

———

Three hours and seven years of newspaper articles later, I present myself to a steely-faced Monks at Mr. Davies's front door again. This time, of course, I do not ask if he is Mr. Davies. I simply say, "Is he home?"

Monks lifts a brow and shuts the door on me. I step away, sure I've done something terribly stupid, and consider where to run next. The door opens once again and Monks gestures for me to enter, then sweeps his hand down the corridor.

I walk in and notice Mr. Davies is not standing in the direction to which Monks points but straight in front of me in the center of his living room. There is a collection of fashionable people sitting with him and I realize I have interrupted evening cocktails. Faces turn my direction, but Mr. Davies steps forward and fills the doorway between his guests and me before I can focus on any of them.

I open my mouth to speak, but he shakes his head in the most minute manner, then tilts it towards his office. I feel a hand on my elbow and turn to find Monks gently directing me that way as well.

I step into Mr. Davies's study, and Monks closes the door behind me.

"You're bold coming here." Mr. Davies enters through another door across the room. "Scotland Yard suspects you're my forger." He reaches for his telephone. "You've got three seconds to tell me why you're here before I let them know where to collect you."

"Please don't." I reach out my hand. "I am not your forger."

"It doesn't matter to me one way or the other. I just want this over." He lifts the handset.

"The truth does matter, sir."

"Truth," he scoffs. But there is something questioning in his voice that compels me forward.

"You said it didn't matter for you. That everyone would believe what they wanted to because you weren't in their clubs. I'm not either. The truth is all I've got because someone wants me blamed for this. I thought it was you, but then . . ."

I figuratively lay my cards on the table. Literally I spread my hands across his desk. He watches me but doesn't stop me, nor does he pull his telephone's handset closer to his ear. It rests in his palm suspended in midair. I start with his statements to *The Times*. I explain about the Tate's files, the downstairs files—that gets his two eyebrows shooting skyward—and about the newspaper archives.

"I couldn't figure it out. All the different things I read about you didn't make sense. Then I realized it's like a painting. You have to step back, take it all in, and see the story behind it. After Sir John Brookings died, you sabotaged your own companies, didn't you? He was the one supplying munitions to the Nazis."

"You need to leave." He uses the handset as a pointer and thrusts it towards the door.

"Please. It's what I would've done."

He stills and stares at me. "Would you have?" His question is more curious than challenging and his eyes lose their bluster. He places the handset back into its cradle and uses the same hand to gesture towards the chair across from his desk.

I drop into it though I don't relax, still expecting him to either call Scotland Yard or kick me out at my first wrong word. "You said it yourself. No one would believe you about the painting because you weren't one of them. No one was going to believe you about the munitions either. Ending everything was your only way out." I gesture to his wall. "Because you're the real deal. Real matters to you. Truth matters."

"You understand that from my walls?"

"Art reveals a lot about a person."

He huffs through his nose almost like a sigh. "Sir John had prestige, power, the weight of all society behind him. I only found out what he was up to after he died. Sure, there were the parties, the weekends, the jaunts across Europe, but all that was in vogue at the time. I didn't think he took it further than that. But he was a true devotee, it turned out, and it almost killed me. To expose him would have ruined his family, who I believed to be innocent, and his girls were so young. It would have ruined me too, I don't deny that. I'd have been blamed, arrested, and destroyed. Even dead and gone, Sir John had everyone in his corner and I had no one in mine."

"I have no one in mine." I say the words while simultaneously acknowledging they are no longer true. No, they have never been true. I simply hadn't recognized it. Daisy, Mum, and Dad have always been there, willing to help me, and now Mum's sewing circle and three friends have come alongside them. Suddenly that feels like quite a lot. Overwhelmingly so.

"What do you want from me, Lily Summers?"

"I don't know the way through."

"Let Mr. Walsh and Scotland Yard do their jobs," Mr. Davies softly suggests.

"I got the impression Mr. Walsh is no longer involved?" I lift my voice. Conor said he was handing his notes over to Scotland Yard. Also, I sensed that in letting me go last evening—not that I'd ever tell a soul he did it—Conor crossed a line, even if only in his own mind, and he'll step away now in order not to interfere again.

"He handed his notes to the authorities and plans to leave London tomorrow, but that doesn't mean he won't follow the investigation." Mr. Davies watches me. "Believe me, Keller Insurance wants to recuperate the funds they'll pay me. Finding the true culprit may lessen their loss." He stares at me again. Hard.

I lift a hand to defend myself. "I'm not the culprit and there's definitely no money to be found with me." I lean forward. "Did Diana return *Woman Laughing*'s original provenance to you?"

"Not to me." His voice lifts in surprise. "I'd like it, though. Walsh needs it for the insurance claim and I'd like to get paid." He slides open one of his desk drawers and pulls out a sheaf of papers. "I have a Xerox copy, but it seems this won't do."

"May I?"

He stretches the document towards me. It has sections handwritten, in several different hands, mapping the painting's movement from Picasso to Francis Planchard to Paul Rosenberg to Therese de Sales, and, in a final notation, from her to Galerie Louise Leiris in Paris.

The copy is fuzzy, with marks that look like stains, errant pen swipes, and more. But it's impossible to tell what was part of the original and what is dust or a mistake created by the copy machine itself. Additionally, the resolution isn't strong enough to catch subtle markings, erasures, and other indications that it has been altered. It's why insurance companies often won't accept anything but originals when creating a policy and why Diana requests originals every time the Tate borrows a painting. Not only does our insurance require it, but she wants that personal assurance of authenticity as well. She wants to examine every step each painting has made so as not to be "made a fool of," she says.

I scan the paper again. Something bothers me about Therese de Sales. I reread what she's written about the painting and how she acquired it, but I find nothing odd. Mr. Davies stretches his hand to me once more. "Here's a copy of the photograph that accompanied it."

I turn the photograph over. *Therese de Sales, 1938* is penned on the back. Turning it to face me once more, I stare at the dark-haired woman seated in front of the painting. She is tall, but it's hard to tell how tall while she sits. She wears a dark wool suit. Good quality and cut, but not particularly fine or flashy. She is serious. She doesn't smile, and from what the provenance says, she may have little reason to as she inherited *Woman Laughing* and her entire collection when her father, and the rest of her family, was killed in the final horrific days of a panicked Nazi frenzy.

Something about the woman feels familiar, but I can't place it, and I cast back to my drawing of Daisy and then to my one of Conor. Is it a look, an expression, or the shape of her eyes I find familiar? The harder I try to grasp it, the more elusive the answer becomes.

"It's awfully grainy. Do you have the original photograph?"

"It stays with the provenance." He leans back and, once more, his cat suddenly appears. It jumps from the floor to his lap, then pads across the desk to me. I startle as it settles in my lap. Mr. Davies chuckles. "What is it about you? She hates people. She barely tolerates me."

"She's an excellent judge of character." I can't help but smile as the cat arches her back and purrs against me. "Truly, I'm not your forger, Mr. Davies. Mr. Walsh knows it too. He saw my work and said I lacked the talent to paint *Woman Laughing.*"

Mr. Davies chuckles again, and this time it carries genuine mirth. "While in some respects that's good news, it had to have hurt your ego."

I shrug, as he's right of course. I reach my hand out to pass back the photograph but pull it back as my gaze catches upon it. "Oh my . . ."

"What is it?"

I page through the provenance again, recognizing what bothered me about Therese. It wasn't what she wrote. It was how she wrote it.

"I know who's behind all this." I stand and gather the papers, still holding the photograph. "May I take these? I promise I won't lose them."

"I have more copies." He waves a hand to them. "Are you going to tell me?"

I look to his phone. "Are you going to call Scotland Yard?"

"Yes. I won't jeopardize my position in this to save yours. But I will give you a good ten-minute head start."

"And I'll keep my own counsel for now." I stand. "One more thing. Why were you so accusatory towards Diana in the papers?"

Mr. Davies drops his gaze, almost abashed. "I wanted to rattle her. I got it in my head that she must have known. She came here the day *Woman Laughing* arrived and gave it her seal of approval. If she is the expert we all trust her to be, then she had to have known, right? But I shouldn't have done that. She's been good to me. It was a mistake."

"I wouldn't be too hard on yourself." I hold his gaze just long enough for questions to arise in his, then I shift my focus to his telephone. "Ten minutes?"

He nods.

While I would have liked the grace Conor gave me, I grudgingly respect his position. I look around his study as I step away from the chair and sweep a hand to his walls. "I see her influence in your purchases. How did you start working with her?" I keep my voice light and curious—because I am genuinely curious.

"I got tired of trying to be someone I wasn't. I wanted to see what I liked, who I was, without everyone else weighing in. She helped advise me. I wasn't one of those with generations of landscapes and ancestors in my past, so I stopped looking for those in my art."

"Have you found what you like?"

He smiles, but it's not broad and open this time. "Not entirely."

I can relate, but now is not the time for that discussion, so I merely nod and point back to his wall. "She wouldn't suggest it, but I think you might enjoy Andy Warhol."

"Do you now?"

"Everything in your home is the best, authentic too. It's another reason I came today. You wouldn't willingly put a forgery on your walls or let it tarnish your name, not after what you've been through, so you couldn't be involved in this. Yet Diana shouldn't form your tastes either. You should. I think you'd like Andy Warhol as he's forging new ground. I'm not saying you should buy one, just that he might appeal to you."

He laughs. "You are an interesting young woman, Lily Summers. I actually know a bit about Warhol and asked Diana to find me one. She said he's a fad, used the words *derivative* and *lackluster* to describe him."

"I'm beginning to think she might not be our best guide."

At that, Mr. Davies's brow lifts in question, but I don't elaborate further. For my plan to work, no gossip can reach my boss.

I step towards the door. "She's wrong. Warhol is on the rise.

He's different, innovative, and has something unique to say. Art changes just as music changes just as fashion changes. I bet Pop Art will take off and it'll gain legitimacy too. In fact, you should look at a few other American artists as well, perhaps the Ashcan School, maybe George Bellows or John Sloan."

"I'll consider it." He stands and gestures to a wood-paneled side door rather than the main one I approached. "Leave through here. I'd rather my guests not see you again."

The door opens to a small back corridor and Monks stands waiting. I follow him through the flat's kitchen and out into the vestibule without incident. I even ride the lift down ten floors alone. Only outside do I pass people in the square and on the sidewalk, but no one looks at me at all.

I figure my time is up and Mr. Davies is now calling Scotland Yard, so I leg it down the block. And despite everything, an odd buoyancy hits me, along with a line from last year's hit song by Johnny Nash: "*I can see clearly now . . .*" I almost laugh. I almost sing aloud.

And if everything didn't feel so charged and fraught, I might. Because I do see clearly now. Before, I was standing too close to see the picture. Again, chiaroscuro at its finest. But stepping back . . . the swirls. The eyes.

Diana Gilden forged *Woman Laughing*.

———

There's one more person to see . . .

It's just over a two-kilometer walk from Dolphin Square to Dukes hotel, but it feels like an eternity. I again attribute it to the time-bending properties of dread. It's not that I don't want to see Conor—it's that I do. It took drawing Conor several times for me to admit that it's a far more unsettling state to find a man who might understand you than to be called "inaccessible" by those who never will.

It's not fair, though, me seeking him out. I am putting him in an untenable position. But I need him. Well, I need someone to know what I'm about to do so that if it goes wrong, someone can attest to the attempt. Conor is the most objective person in this game—which isn't a game at all.

I turn left from St. James's Street onto St. James's Place and find a charming-looking hotel before me. It's tucked into an alleyway so small a cabbie might hit his side mirrors entering if he didn't drive true. British flags drape from poles at the entrance, and blooms of red peonies line the window boxes. I step up the three marble and tiled stairs, enter the lobby, and head straight for the massive wood desk in front of me.

"Could you ring Conor Walsh for me, please?" My voice cracks. A nod, a call, and a few minutes later, the man himself stands in front of me. "Can we talk?"

Doubt flashes across his face for an instant before he tilts his head to a door across the lobby. Through the door I find a tiny bar. Ian Fleming's bar.

A bartender, dressed in a white coat, immediately takes our order. As much as I want to relax and order a Vesper, sounding so sophisticated as I do, losing my head—or my heart—is unwise. I order a ginger beer. Conor does the same.

"We're a boring pair." I try to inject levity into the moment.

"What can I do for you?" Levity rejected, Conor looks around the small room despite our being its only occupants. "You're wanted by the police, Lily. I should make that call and turn you in right now."

"I'm innocent. Give me two minutes."

Conor holds up two fingers.

"Don't forget I willingly showed you my paintings."

He smirks. "Most forgers are narcissists, Lily. They draw you in just to prove how brilliant they are."

"That's how you see me?"

He leans forward and stalls as the bartender places two ginger beers, in crystal glasses on white linen napkins, before us. "Here's what I see. You have talent, rare talent, and you had access. You need money. You destroyed evidence. And you're leaving a friend in jail."

His last statement condemns me.

"Is Paddy still in custody?"

"They can hold him for forty-eight hours and they are. Turning yourself in would help him." Conor stares at me and I feel selfish. But I can't help Paddy if I'm in the cell next to him. It's a weak justification, yet I cling to it.

"Why'd you let me go yesterday?"

"Despite all that, I think you're innocent."

"Thank you." The words come out in a whisper as I feel my breath release. "Diana did it."

Conor pulls straight. "Diana painted *Woman Laughing*?"

"No. Maybe. I haven't worked that out yet, but she did paint once, she told me. But actual painter or not, she's involved. She created the provenance." I lean forward. "She lied to you, Conor. She had Davies's original provenance, but she told you and Davies she didn't. She told me she gave it back, but I believe she still has it. And then when I saw a copy at Mr. Davies's flat, I noticed—"

"You went to see Mr. Davies?"

"I figured out he wasn't involved either."

His mouth lifts. "Are you sure you're in the right business?"

I sit straighter, feel lighter. "He showed me a copy of the provenance, and on the fourth page, like when your hand gets tired, there are a couple swirls that I've seen in Diana's notes, and I have those notes in the right-top drawer of my desk at work. You'll see the handwriting matches."

I reach out and lay my hand on his arm. His eyes drop to it and I lift it away. "And the photograph." I pull it from my bag and place it on the table before him. "Look at her eyes. Anyone can change her hair, her clothes, even her face shape with tissues or something tucked in her cheeks, but beneath all that, the eyes never change. Those are Diana's eyes."

"Tell this to Inspector Gray at Scotland Yard."

"It's not enough. They may not even listen to me."

"I shouldn't be listening to you." He lifts his hands in the air, frustrated, exasperated. "I'm leaving tomorrow, Lily. Why are you even here telling me this? I can't help you."

I lean back into the armchair. It's deeper than I anticipate and I pop back up. To settle so far back is for someone who's enjoying a drink and relishing their company and the moment. That's not me, not right now.

Conor looks around the room again. He glances to the door, to the window, and I feel him pull away. My two minutes are up. "You need to go."

"Are you going to ring Scotland Yard?" I hate that I keep having to ask people that question today.

He looks at me and a world of emotions passes through his expression—interest, regret, disappointment, and something more, something I can't name, but it wrenches my heart. He gives me a tiny nod and my chest cinches tighter.

"It'll take me several minutes to get to my room. I'm on the fifth floor. But once there, yes, I will call Inspector Gray."

I pick up the crystal glass in front of me and toss back the last of my ginger beer. It's meant to look like an act of defiance, of confidence and courage, but between the fizz and the spice, I cough, sputter, and almost choke. It's not the image I want to leave him with, but as he stands, I'm left with little choice and pop up as well.

"Thanks for the warning."

Hurt flickers through his expression at my curt delivery.

"That came out wrong, too harsh. I was sincere. I appreciate the warning and your slow walk upstairs." I step from the table. "I'll prove I'm right, Conor."

"I hope you do. And . . ." His voice takes on a soft tone, but rather than finish his sentence, he presses his lips shut.

With nothing more to say, I walk out of the lobby and down the hotel's tiny alleyway at a slow and steady pace.

But once I hit St. James's Street, I run.

Again.

CHAPTER 24

Diana

Diana slams down the telephone. The crash feels loud enough to shake the house, yet Wagner still plays two floors above. It is too early for Wagner, too late for Wagner, too much of Wagner.

She stalks up the stairs and wrenches open the bookcase entry to the third-floor studio door, sending it crashing against the wall. The music skips. She lifts the needle. Her hand trembles and scratches the record again. She flips off the player, picks up the record, and shatters it with a single blow against the table.

"She's gone," Diana rages.

"What are you doing?" Heinrich, leaning over his worktable, bolts upright.

Diana can tell his first instinct is anger over the record. Blood suffuses his face. But before he voices a single thought, he looks from the record to her eyes and remains silent. Possibly because she is ready for a fight, and wants one. She steps forward in anticipation of a doozy.

She notes the instant her husband backs down. His face drains of red as he drops his chin, looking at her over the tops of his black-rimmed reading glasses.

"Who's gone?" His voice comes out calm and steady.

Diana trails her gaze from his eyes to his hands. He's realigning the nails, reattaching the canvas to the frame after baking it. It takes time to settle each nail into its precise hole once again. His left hand remains tightly gripped around a brass mounting nail. His right pushes his glasses up his long, sloping nose. This is one of the last steps within his creative process. His new "Campendonk" is almost complete.

A weight settles over Diana, almost too heavy to bear. She closes her eyes for the briefest moment, trying to absorb it rather than be crushed by it.

"Diana?" Heinrich prompts her.

"Lily Summers," she snaps. "Who do you think? Scotland Yard can't find the blasted girl. They came to the Gallery yesterday afternoon and she was gone, despite my telling her to stay for the entire day. Inspector Gray just telephoned to say they sent officers to St. Martin's School, her home, her sister's flat, and nothing. They even revisited each location today and still nothing. They actually believe her family hasn't seen or heard from her. She is nowhere."

"Do you believe that?"

"What does it matter what I believe?" Diana yells. "I can't visit her family, can I? I can't make enquiries. I can't have the police questioning my interest. I have to sit here and wait. This was supposed to be over and done by now."

"Did someone tip her off? That investigator?"

"Conor Walsh?" Diana recalls the sketchbook and the intimacy of Lily's portrayal of him. It wasn't intimate in the more common sense; it was intimate in the more dangerous sense—her assistant saw Conor, understood the young man, and had captured him fully.

Diana shifts her thoughts to the timeline of the past week. "Impossible. He didn't know. You left the tube of paint. I made the phone call. And I've met with him. The girl may be in love with him, but he's not protecting her. I can read people, Heinrich. He'll do his job. If he had an idea of where she was, she wouldn't still be out there."

Her voice screeches. She hates her tone and her cadence, and the fear behind them. They remind her of her own mother in those last days together in Vienna.

"Are you certain?" Her husband straightens. "You failed to understand your own assistant. She's quite resourceful."

"Talented and resourceful apparently. It seems she was a poor choice for your fall guy." Diana grinds out the words.

Heinrich's expression shifts, concern and irritation sweeping away and leaving behind a look of benign amusement. "It's a mere inconvenience."

A lilting note to Heinrich's voice sets Diana's teeth on edge. "Take this seriously, please. Did you tell someone at your club?"

"I'm not an imbecile."

Diana glowers, unwilling to levy a retort. Yet his expression makes it clear he caught what she refused to say.

"Don't question me."

"Don't you question me." Her tone matches his, dark and foreboding. They stand staring at each other. Diana's glance skitters away first.

"Think." Heinrich's tone softens, now that he's won. "Someone must have warned her."

Diana shakes her head. "No one at the Gallery had any idea. I made the call from St. Martin's and I was not overheard. I checked the corridor. There was no one nearby. And she was at the Tate. Richard's secretary spoke to her. I don't know what happened. She wouldn't have run because talking to her would have been natural. She wouldn't have suspected any problems. No . . . She found out somehow, but not through me."

"Think. There's someone you're not considering."

"What does it matter? We need her caught. We need—"

"Calm down." Heinrich bends over his worktable and taps another nail into place.

"Stop." Each tiny ping stabs Diana. "This is serious."

His focus remains on his work. "It's a mere delay."

"I'm not working on that." She points to the picture.

"Why not?" Heinrich looks up, eyes wide and voice rich with curiosity.

"Are you serious? Enough has gone wrong. We're still embroiled in the Picasso. New York is blown." She steps closer. "What part of this have you not grasped?"

"They will find her. She's a young woman. Alone. Her family has no connections, no power. No one has the ability or the interest to protect her." He lifts his painting off the table.

At thirty-six inches by fifty, it stretches his arms wide. He holds it up, shifting it and twisting at the waist, so Diana can see both the painting and her husband simultaneously. A look of pride and joy suffuses his face. It is an expression Diana once loved and, long ago, thought was reserved for her alone. It has been many years, however, since she was disabused of that notion.

"Come. See how well I've done." He carries the painting across the open room to the corner they use for their photographs and hangs it on one of the hooks he's permanently mounted on the back wall. "I chose 1919 for all the reasons you'll appreciate."

"*I'll* appreciate?" Diana blinks.

"It's quite safe as years go within his oeuvre. Campendonk was incredibly prolific that year, transforming his style from painting to painting, becoming ever more modernist from expressionist. All that movement in an oeuvre creates a window for a work that sits within time but doesn't conform to it. And being one of the most Nazi-confiscated 'degenerates,' we have even greater opportunities with him." Heinrich smiles. "See? I've mitigated risk from several angles. Now it's up to you."

Diana closes her eyes again. Her body sways as if trapped in some warped carnival ride. A tipping sensation overcomes her and she quickly opens her eyes to gain her equilibrium.

"I've even created someone new for you."

"Someone new?" Her voice croaks small and weak. She clears her throat but does not speak again, fully aware that nothing stronger will come out.

For years she's been Therese, Elizabeth, Diana. So many people, so many roles, she wonders who is real, who is fabricated, and how much of any of them are still Heinrich's and not her own. But look what happened when she tried to seize something for herself. That is the quiet condemnation she cannot admit to her husband nor bear to hear swirling in her mind. When she first asked that girl in Donor Relations to research Mr. Edward Davies, she had no idea how the answers would incite her.

Diana needed him to pay for his duplicity. So while it was a risk to plant Heinrich's work so close to home, she willingly did it, hungering for Davies to bite. She wanted the man who craved legitimacy to pay through the nose for something false, hang it on his wall, wave at it with pride, brag about it, adore it, while all the time it was as false as he was.

And to get to that moment, she had cultivated and educated him slowly. As with Lily, her own Eliza Doolittle, his taste began to mirror her own. He bought what she recommended, and when she suggested a Picasso, he believed it was a sign from the gods that the most famous gallery in Paris for the great artist, Galerie Louise Leiris, had just acquired a significant piece only days prior.

The one thing Davies hadn't consulted her on was his plan to immediately turn around and sell the blasted thing—and display it at the Tate! That stunt shocked her and wrested the game from her control.

"We must wait." Diana pulls herself from her reverie. "Leave this and work on something new."

"New York is not fully blown. With a new persona, it's worth the risk."

"Everywhere is blown, Heinrich. Those little fires you had me create all over Europe exploded. It's the chaos you wanted, but it's engulfed the entire art world. That investigator is from New York. He'll already be swamped with cases when he returns. He's not dumb. He'll make connections soon enough."

"That investigator." Heinrich scoffs. "What has he found? Nothing. Seems he's done little more than become infatuated with that brilliant assistant of yours."

Diana freezes. Heinrich had seen the sketchbook and the drawing after all. "She is brilliant, isn't she?" she whispers.

"Shockingly so. It's her brilliance that'll clear the board. This time next week, New York will be just fine. It could not have worked out better." He waves a hand to her. "Come. I have a new dress for you."

Only then does Diana notice the corner of their studio is staged for a photograph. She steps to the table and picks up a copy of a French paper. "1969? Why so recent? Isn't that a little close?"

She also notes how the chair is positioned, the table organized with cheap knickknacks just slightly out-of-date, and, hanging on a hook just outside of focus, Diana finds a dress, grey wool with a small flower pattern. A rough, stained, undyed cotton apron is hanging on the hook beside it. Timeless yet contemporary too.

"What's this?" She runs the wool between her fingers.

"A wonderful idea." Heinrich reaches above her and unhooks the dress's hanger from the wall. He lays it gently in her arms while he spins his tale of a young woman whose family came across the painting and others in a wine cellar in 1947, and only recently, when tourists came to buy cheese, was the painting photographed—and now that she and her family know its value, they want to sell it.

"How many more works are hidden in this fictional cellar?"

"A few." Heinrich shrugs. "The rest, like the Campendonk, are mostly from the Der Blaue Reiter. It plays into the story of Nazi-confiscated art. Taken but not destroyed. Some of those officers weren't brainwashed, destroying everything they got their grubby hands on, or maybe they were secret degenerates too."

Heinrich sneers and Diana catches the notes of his long-running hatred of the Nazis and knows he's envisioning their march into Hungary in 1944. Yet, as Hungary prior to that had been a staunch Axis power, Diana often wonders if Heinrich's hatred is ideological or born of a more personal betrayal. Again, questions she never dares to ask her husband.

But this is beyond dangerous. Her husband is no longer simply emulating an artist; he is now attempting to tackle a whole school. In this case the famous German Blue Rider Group of early twentieth-century modernists.

"It's too much." Diana lifts the dress back to him, but he steps away.

"Not to worry. We'll go slow. This was the only work photographed. It will merely set the stage for the rest. We can wait longer for the next offering."

"They'll want to verify authenticity. We can't expect the chaos we've created not to have consequences. Everyone will take precautions."

"As they should . . . The Bumbaugher estate was taken by the Nazis in 1941 and abandoned in 1945. Bombed and left to ruin."

"And the family?"

"None. That's why it sat empty. To this day it sits empty deep in the forest. No one can prove this woman hasn't squatted there, and no one is going to actually go and question the neighbors. There are no neighbors." He narrows his eyes. "Do you not think I've thought through every detail? I mixed my own paints. I became Campendonk. More than I have in years. He wouldn't know himself that he didn't paint this. Do you doubt me?"

Diana feels rather than hears the tremor within his voice. They near a precipice and she needs to retreat. "The painting is excellent." She nods to it. "But a real house? There must be family somewhere."

"We're going to sell it differently this time. This is not a family story; it is a transaction, almost mercenary. We're going to use a Polaroid as if a tourist took the picture and handed it to her right away. There's a desperation to this story, a greed. I want our chosen dealer to feel they have the upper hand. They must believe they are taking advantage of this woman, can pay her less than market value. The very opposite of noblesse oblige, and we will let them seize that upper hand. Then they'll want to unload the painting quickly so nothing comes back to them."

"You're playing on their pride. To keep them from looking too closely."

Heinrich smiles, something long, slow, menacing. "Pride and greed are powerful vices. Ubiquitous too. Plenty of the disreputable and greedy are in New York. And if, as you believe, the markets are blown, that only means the black markets grow faster."

"I'm still not—"

"*Zeet*." Heinrich hisses a quick flash of tongue behind his teeth.

Diana shuts her mouth. She pressed too far. His chest rises and falls with his breath. She stands silent as he visibly works to calm himself.

"Please dress."

She clutches the dress, crushing the wool and rough cotton in her hands. Then she releases it and obeys.

Once dressed, with her hair tangled and darkened with an umber stain he applied by brush, Heinrich pulls her hair back from her face as she sits on a stool before him. He then tucks a wad of cotton wool into each of her upper cheeks. He dusts dark rouge in the hollow created and applies the thinnest line of coal to her lashes. In the Polaroid, with its poor resolution and weak color differentiation, the rouge and coal create the illusion she is darker toned, darker eyed, tired and worn. Makeup does not look like makeup.

He positions her in the chair, sets the large painting at her feet, then rolls a temporary wall he fabricated into position behind her.

She twists to face him. "Where did you get that wood?"

"I took a drive yesterday afternoon and found a construction site. It creates the perfect background, like an old wine cellar, and the photo will be tightly framed. Never worry." He studies her. "Slump just a little, darling. That's it. Right there. Freeze."

He slides the Polaroid off the table and takes her picture. Then another.

She sits while he waves the photographs, developing them in his hands. After a few minutes, he hands them to her.

She has to concede that they are excellent and the right dealer will eat up her story, using the pictures as the proof needed to support the provenance. They truly look authentic. The lighting is terrible and the woman looks worn yet serious—a woman trying to pretend she can control her world and what happens to the painting, which she clutches so tight and clearly believes constitutes her liberation. Her need and clearly evident greed will match the dealer's own and create the emotional gold standard of authenticity.

Diana changes out of the dress and pulls the dressing gown she's long kept in the studio over her naked body. She shivers in the chill of the room.

If only that painting, any painting, might affect her liberation as well.

CHAPTER 25

Lily

It's almost ten o'clock when Janice's doorbell finally buzzes. I had almost given up. After calls at six o'clock, seven o'clock, then again at eight to ask about the dresses, Daisy stopped answering Mum's telephone and I started wearing out Janice's carpet.

I fly to the door, but Janice beats me to it. Before she opens it, she points around the corner into her bedroom. "Just in case it's not Daisy."

I step aside as she opens the door, then fly out upon hearing my sister's voice. I launch myself at her, and only after noting there is no bag in her hands do I pull away.

"What happened?" I whisper. "Could they not finish them?"

She steps aside. Down the two steps leading to Janice's front door sits my mum with a bag in her lap.

"It's time we had a chat." She speaks firmly, calmly, and quietly. Yet I hear every word as if she's shouted at me.

"I'll leave you two." Daisy backs off the steps and walks towards her building.

I step down. Mum can't come to me, so despite this feeling of exposure on many levels, I step down once more to the last stair and drop in front of her. I sit inches below her and feel like a small child about to be chided—which I fully deserve. "I've made a mess of things."

"What exactly have you done?"

Her question sounds simple, but since it's coming from my mum, it's not. She wants me to go deeper than the surface details, and learn and grow. My mind drifts back to Paddy after he found me smashing all the paintings. His words were simply, *"You'll be grand."*

He, too, wasn't talking about this forgery fiasco. He was going farther back and deeper in. Because the crux of the issue isn't that I called *Woman Laughing* a forgery, not for me at least. In that instance I said the wrong thing at the wrong time in the wrong place and in the wrong way. That was the mistake of a moment.

Mum. Paddy. They're talking about a mistake of a lifetime. The way I reimagined my past, view my present, and approach my future. I think of my years of sketching, painting, hiding, prevaricating, controlling, striving, wanting . . . The list feels endless, and rather than push it all away as I usually do, I sit with the discomfort of trailing back into time and memory. I see Daisy from last night; I feel her pull me close.

"I blamed myself?"

It comes out small and lifts like a question. It feels both humble and arrogant simultaneously, and I recall Conor's words from a few days previously: *"Both can be true."* I look up to find, in the glow of Janice's front light, my mum's eyes glistening with tears.

"I'm sorry, Mum."

"I wondered how long it would take for you to get here." I blink. She smiles. "Do you finally realize the weight of the world was never yours to carry?"

"Oh, that." I swipe at my eyes.

"You must be exhausted."

"I am." I feel myself tip forward for her hug.

"It's hard trying to rule the universe." Her voice holds a note of teasing, but it's supported by steel.

I straighten and an odd noise escapes. It's part question, part grunt, and full of surprise.

Mum smiles at me and lifts my chin with one finger. "You have a lot of arrogance, luv."

"Where do you find arrogance in any of this? I just apologized." My voice is high-pitched, a small child chafing at her dressing-down.

"When did I ask for that? When did you need to apologize for an accident that happened twenty-two years ago? You took that all on yourself. That's pride, my girl, not humility. If you want to apologize for something, say you're sorry for diminishing my life by believing I can do nothing on my own and for making me feel that too."

"What? That's not fair."

"I agree. It wasn't fair of you at all." Her words are harsh. Yet her voice and her expression are soft. She waits and watches me, and just as I feel my indignation settle away, she continues. "Are you ready to see that I am capable? That I am still living? That I have a life I love?"

"Mum, I never—"

"Yes, you did." She leans her upper body forward and tucks a strand of hair behind my ear. She waits until I drag my eyes to meet hers.

"How dare you," she whispers. Tears prick my eyes. "How dare you keep such a large part of yourself hidden from me. From what Daisy says, your painting is far more than a mere hobby. You hid that part of you. You never brought anything home for Dad and me to see or share with you. Do you know how much he would have enjoyed that?"

Guilt assails me. I never shared my painting with him because while art brought a light to his eyes, that light inevitably faded and the aftermath felt more painful, for Mum, for Daisy, even for me. I didn't want him or them to go through that again and again. Yet I didn't protect them. I created isolation. I created pain.

Mum continues, unaware she lost me for a moment. ". . . for money? For my safety? How dare you not follow your dreams because you claimed responsibility for destroying what you thought were mine. But you never asked, did you? How dare you put me in a box so small that you couldn't see me and you never let me see you."

Tears stream now. It's like a tidal wave washes over me until there is little left. But I suspect what remains may be all I need. It's painful and yet I feel scrubbed new.

She wipes away tears, the pads of her thumbs pressing firmly against my cheeks. "What do you know of my dreams, luv? I live a rich, full life and I wouldn't change any of it. Not a moment, even for the chance to walk a single step again. You have no idea how much more I experience, how much more I see of people, within people, all because I sit here. You have no insight into my heart, mind, or perspective because you assumed you held the answers. And it's not just me you shoved into that tiny box. You forced your sister and your father into it too." She lifts my chin again. "And I let you. Today, while making your dresses, I realized that too. I'm not without blame, and for that I am sorry."

"I'm sorry, Mum." I repeat the same words, yet they are not the same at all. I sense she knows it as much as I feel it.

"Hush now." She lifts the tendril of hair she just tucked behind my ear and curls it around her finger lightly before she tucks it away once more. "We've had enough apologies for a lifetime." She pats the bag on her lap. "Here are the dresses. What are you planning to do with these?"

I appreciate the way she asks. She doesn't demand like she sometimes does in order to make me talk to her, a favorite line of hers being, "*I'm not asking, I'm telling you.*" But I see now why she did that. I thought I held all the answers and she didn't deserve them—no, I acted as if she couldn't manage them. It hurts me that I put her in that position, that *box* as she called it, more times over the years than I can count. Or was it the one time and I never let her out?

I take a deep breath and explain to her about *Woman Laughing*, my week at the Tate, my suspicions of Mr. Davies, my change of mind, my thoughts about Diana, my feelings about Conor, and what I plan to do next. She is the one person to whom I confide the entire plan. I also tell her about Paddy, who he has been in my life, what he has done, and where he languishes now.

"If this doesn't work, you must turn yourself in, no matter the consequences. You can't let that poor man stay another night in jail. His wife must be beside herself."

I nod. I, too, have come to the same belief. I have already harmed Paddy more than I can ever make amends for.

Mum lays her hand on the bag, which now rests in my lap. "Your friends agreed to this?"

I scrunch my nose and Mum clucks her tongue. Does everyone know I do that when I'm about to lie? I concede they must and opt for the truth. "They have, but they don't know the risks. I've only told them each their own small role: to put on the dress and walk a predetermined route."

"You should tell them. What happens if they get caught like Paddy?"

"I was honestly trying to protect them." My head drops. "But you're right. It's crazy and dangerous for everyone but me." I look up. "I have nothing to lose, Mum. They're going to arrest me." I clutch the bag tighter. "As Mr. Davies so astutely pointed out this morning, nothing protects me. Not wealth or privilege or support. They have the paint tube and my paintings. If anything was salvaged from those bins, they've got five Picassos. Lots of evidence points to me."

Mum presses her lips together, and I can tell she, too, is trying not to cry. "Daisy says your paintings are extraordinary." She looks towards my sister's flat before continuing. "How do you think I felt when an inspector came to my home and told me my daughter had the ability to forge a Picasso with such artistry that it could actually be sold, in Paris, as an original?"

"I didn't do it."

"I never thought you did. I asked how do you think I felt learning you *could* do it? That's a different question." She waits.

I nod, but I can't lift my eyes to look at her again. "The inspector may have said that, but he never even saw one. That's another problem. As Paddy got to them first, Scotland Yard can't actually see the original brushstrokes. If someone could study those alongside *Woman Laughing*, they'd see they're different. Whoever painted *Woman Laughing* is remarkable, Mum."

"When the inspector came back today, he said something similar about you. They found one of your sketchbooks in your desk at work. You, too, it seems, have great talent."

I blink. *My sketchbook?* My eyes widen. *Conor.* My heart drops as I imagine the inspector calling him in, asking him questions, making demands, all because I drew his picture. Assumptions and insinuations will be made—ones that will get Conor in trouble, maybe fired, maybe worse. But to find it in my desk at work? Once more, I can only think Diana put it there, which means Diana was at St. Martin's and most likely put the paint tube in my basket. I've been so stupid, so blind, thinking Diana was the mere forger without taking that thought to its final conclusion. Diana is the one framing me.

Mum lifts a brow. She's asking where my thoughts have taken me, but I can't tell her. I give her a lesser truth but still a truth. "I should have told you. I should have let you in long ago." At her nod I crumple. "I've made a real mess of things, haven't I?"

"A little." She swipes at her own tears now and I use the sleeve of Daisy's blue-and-brown-striped jumper to scrub at mine.

We share a look and both laugh. It's snuffly, weak, and a little pathetic, but we're definitely in agreement.

This is way beyond a little.

CHAPTER 26

Diana

Diana checks her watch. Right on time. Well, early. Visiting a patron at seven thirty in the morning is inappropriate, but it's also necessary. She needs this conversation done. Searching for ways Lily might have learned about the investigation has robbed her of sleep, and Edward Davies is her last open question. A visit, a little tête-à-tête with him, before heading to work is warranted.

She rings the buzzer and looks down the long swath of corridor running through the building. There is something tantalizing about these apartments, daring and risqué. Dolphin Square has certainly acquired a flavor and a history in its short forty years. A reputation that far surpasses anything the designers intended while creating it. Then again, isn't that art? In any medium it takes on a life of its own.

Monks, as usual, answers the door and Diana briefly wonders if he keeps Edward's secrets as well as his home. Or like Branford, does he not know any of his boss's misdeeds at all? She steps in the foyer and takes a breath to center her emotions, calm the storm building inside, and put the work before all else.

She can't deny that Edward has gotten the best of her. She wanted this man ruined, and taking his money wasn't enough. She wanted to hold one over on his pride. All that is gone now. The tables have turned. Perhaps one day she will try again. But for now, she concedes defeat. She needs to save herself.

Hands outstretched, he meets her at the edge of his living room.

"Good morning, Edward."

He gestures towards his study and she precedes him through the doorway as he talks. "I was surprised to receive your call so early. I certainly could have come to the Gallery this morning."

She takes in the lacquered desk that comprises his study's focal point. It is gorgeous, but a bit of an abomination as well. Who would paint over such a masterpiece? Try to fashion something so valuable into something new, and something inferior? She averts her gaze, feeling discomfited by wayward thoughts that seem to point homeward, and gets to the point. "I thought this conversation is best away from prying ears. Besides, the rest of my day is back-to-back meetings as I tie up loose ends. This is my only available time."

She lets her eyes trail over the works of art she's curated for him. A Miro. An Ernst. A Campendonk drawing. She'd forgotten she suggested that one. All authentic. Originals, of course. One only offers a forgery when the circumstances are ideal. That's where she failed. But only once in all her years had she let her temper get the better of her. All things said and done, she should have sent the Picasso to New York.

Diana's eye snags on something and she pulls back so fast her heel digs into the plush carpeting and almost topples her. A new painting sits propped against the paneled wall. A silk screen of Andy Warhol's latest Pop Art offering, a portrait of Chinese leader Mao Tse-tung.

Momentarily distracted from her mission, she thrusts a finger towards the painting. "Where did that come from?" She hears the notes of betrayal in her voice and hates how easily interactions with this man tear into her nerves.

"John Mayor's Gallery. I got the idea late yesterday afternoon, and he sent it around last night. A bit of an impulse purchase. I believe Warhol only completed it a month or two ago."

"A month ago? Is it still wet?" Diana tries to check her disdain but can't. "Warhol is not an artist I'd recommend. He's crass and commercial. He'll go nowhere. A month ago? Who suggested this?"

"I find it intriguing. I thought the Sunday B. Morning scandal was fascinating, remember? It's like art meets populace, don't you think?"

She watches as Edward regards the painting with fondness and a sense of playfulness. The man, who doesn't have an original creative bone in his body, hasn't answered her question.

"I'm quite pleased with the acquisition, and Mayor certainly didn't offer any discounts." He chortles. "And I find that album cover Warhol did for The Velvet Underground to be a work of genius. Art and music. They change with the times, don't they? We should too, I expect."

Diana cringes. She notes he catches her reflexive movement and it seems to please him. She wants to ask again who advised him but fears it will sound petulant. She draws a breath to speak, but he cuts her off.

"Since you didn't come here to discuss my Warhol, how can I help you?"

Diana circles the chair across from his desk and sits. She crosses her legs at the ankles, one silk stocking–clad leg slipping past the other with ease, and waits for Edward to sit as well. She needs to regain control.

Once he is seated, she begins. "I'm here to ask you to talk with *The Times* again. Come alongside the Tate. We were all deceived, and with another statement, we can put this embarrassment behind us."

"Have they caught the girl yet?"

"Not yet." Diana keeps her focus soft, concerned, and caring. "But she's clearly guilty. I thought if you got ahead of it, it would benefit you even more than the Tate. It would shut down all questions." She lifts her voice just enough to let him know that she, too, cares about his reputation.

"You want her tried in the press rather than in court?"

Diana schools her expression. She didn't expect Edward to

care what happened to the girl as long as he got his money and the status he so clearly craves restored.

"Both will happen regardless. She didn't exactly pick a low-profile crime."

Edward sits back. "It's good of you to think of me or the Gallery, for that matter, now that Richard has fired you."

"I'm not vindictive." Diana's temper flares and she lifts a hand to her neck. The gesture, practiced and perfected over the years, always gives her a moment to calm and offers a visual distraction to whoever is bothering her. "I want the best for Richard and the Tate and would have done the same thing myself in his shoes. I also have not given up hope that, as the scandal settles, he might bring me back on board."

"I wouldn't doubt it. You've done amazing work there."

His compliment surprises her, disarms her. "Thank you."

"May I ask you a question, Diana?" He regards her with a look of curiosity she finds disconcerting. "How did your assistant access my painting? And when? Did I even buy an original Picasso?"

"Of course you did." Diana leans back. She'd launched too fast at his last question. She smiles. She recrosses her legs. She pretends to consider his questions. "Galerie Louise Leiris would sell nothing less. Her stepfather is world-renowned, and I came here and examined it myself. As for when and how Lily became aware of it, I can't give you any answers. I expect we'll discover that during her trial."

She offers a sigh. Even to her own ears, her voice sounds a little pitchy and dramatic. She waves one hand, sending her gold bracelets tinkling, and Edward's focus shifts from her face to her wrist as she intended. "She may have seen a picture in my files from when you purchased the piece?"

"She is quite extraordinary then, to forge a painting from a photograph. In a fortnight? Or is there no true *Woman Laughing*? I ask again, did I purchase a true Picasso?"

Diana schools her surprise. "Yes. I authenticated it. It was an original. Lily must have copied it. Then when you sent it for the exhibition, she was ready to make the exchange."

"That story relies on tight timing and a lot of coincidences, don't you think? Richard mentioned the exhibition only days before its opening."

Richard. Diana considers him for a split second, then rejects the notion. To embroil Richard would take more time, more planning. It isn't out of the question, but as Heinrich reminded her only a few days ago, Richard—unless deeply compromised—is not expendable. She is. She has to keep her wits about her and not tease threads that might fail to pull tight.

"What does it matter?" Diana snaps, then smiles. "We'll get answers when she's in custody."

"Of course we will. And perhaps she'll lead us to the original provenance as well." Edward leans forward and clasps his hands, resting them atop his desk. "I'll call the editor today."

Diana soon walks out of Edward's apartment, out of Dolphin Square, and proceeds the few blocks to work. While she isn't quite content—in fact, there were moments in that short discussion she found alarming—she is content enough. Her imagination is playing tricks on her. There is no way Edward can suspect anything. Just as Heinrich said, it might take time, but all will be well.

CHAPTER 27

Lily

After a night of no sleep and a secret midnight trip to Soho, I answer a knock on Janice's back door barely after dawn. Daisy stands with two mugs of tea in her hands. Without a word she hands me one and steps through the door.

I shut it behind her and rather than ask what she's doing here, I simply say thank you.

"You shouldn't be alone."

"I was about to get dressed. Come see." I lead her into Roger's room. She looks around with a sad expression, and I'm reminded how she and Sean tried to help him, how she's tried to help me. I reach out and touch her arm. Her smile tells me she understands.

Her eyes light up when she sees all four dresses splayed on the bed. "They turned out really well."

"They did." Each dress is white with blocks of red, blue, and green. All created from the same pattern, yet one is longer and one a little larger, just as I'd briefly shared with Daisy. The detail she remembered and the amount of work those ladies put in yesterday astound me. I'm swamped with gratitude.

I lift the hem of one. "If I end up arrested today, will you thank everyone for me?"

"You're not going to get arrested. Well, not until you get what you need to prove your innocence." I smile at her confidence, which makes it falter. "I must believe that," she adds in a small whisper.

"Me too," I whisper back.

I quickly dress and Daisy hands me a large pair of sunglasses from her pocket. She grins at the resulting image. "You look like Audrey Hepburn in that film."

I drop the glasses down my nose in a signature Hepburn move. "*Charade*?" She shakes her head. "*Breakfast at Tiffany's*?"

"Later than those. The one about the art . . . *How to Steal a Million*."

I laugh at the irony.

An hour later, I'm at the south entrance to the Pimlico Underground Station, and minutes after that, I'm tucked in the doorway of the designated and now closed millinery shop. It's 8:25 a.m.

Becca arrives first and right on time. I hand her the dress.

She giggles. "This is so exciting."

I take a long, deep breath. "Please don't get caught. Race away if you have to. A fast walk, not a run. You're not guilty of anything so don't look it, but stay on course. The north side of the Gallery, first floor. If you get stopped, tell the truth. I gave you a dress and you put it on this morning. End of story." I take another deep breath. "I need to tell you, Becca, I'm in trouble, and if you're caught, you could land in trouble too."

"Gossip has been raging for days. Don't fret. I know what this is about."

I pull her into a hug and feel her intake of surprise before her arms squeeze back. I'm not typically one who hugs.

When we pull back, I remind her of a last but vital detail. "Remember, start at nine o'clock only if you see the basement hall light flick on and off twice. If it doesn't, it'll mean Diana is not in the building. This is all for Diana, so if she's not there, there's no walking. Wait a bit, then change back into your normal clothes and act like nothing happened."

"Wait. Isn't this about the Picasso? What's Diana got to do with it?" I shake my head, as does she, mimicking my gesture. "Alrighty then, I didn't ask." She digs into her bag and pulls something out. "I forgot. Look at this."

At first I think it's a cat. Then she holds it up. "It's my hair," I squawk.

She tosses her head and blonde curls bounce across her face. "You didn't think I could ever pass for you, did you? My mum has bunches of wigs from her theater days."

I actually had thought of that but accepted that if Becca was far enough away, maybe Diana would miss that detail. It's why I had Becca walking on the north side of the Gallery.

I lower her hand holding the wig. "You can't wear that. If you get caught, you might be able to claim innocence wearing a dress, but if you're wearing hair that looks like mine, no one will believe you."

"Then I shan't get caught." She grins and I finally step outside my concerns and really look at her. She's buzzing with energy. Always up for a concert or a show—and not because she has the money, but because she has the connections—Becca is more authentically art and theater and show, despite working in accounting, than anyone I know.

She shoves the wig back into her bag and chirps, "I'm off."

I call after her, "Don't forget. Make sure that new security guard looks at you when you walk in the front door."

"Not a bother." She turns and rolls her eyes. "I can't get him to stop looking at me."

"You can't?" The question blurts out just as I note how ludicrous it is to wonder why the new guard never looks at me. I tuck back into the shop's shaded entry. Lucy should arrive soon.

A few minutes later, she does and I hand her the dress.

She looks at it skeptically before she tucks it into the large bag I asked each friend to bring. "Are you going to tell me why I'm doing this?"

"Later. Because if you don't know, you don't have to lie. Afterwards, I promise to tell you everything. But that said, I'm in trouble and helping me could land you in trouble as well."

"You didn't say last night on the telephone, but this has something to do with the police coming to the Gallery Wednesday, doesn't it?" I nod. "Does it have something to do with *Woman*

Laughing?" Lucy raises her brows waiting for an answer. I don't reply. Her voice drops and I get the sense she's deciding which way to go. "Did you forge it like they say?"

"I had nothing to do with it. I promise."

She looks down at the dress again. "But if I'm caught doing this, it'll look like you did and that'll make matters worse."

"Look, Lucy. I'm asking a lot here and you don't owe me anything. If you don't want to do this, just say and I'll come up with another plan." I press my lips together as I don't have another plan, and even if I could think of one, there's no time. I need Lucy. I sense this plan can't work without the confusion four women dressed identically can create. Three of us is too few. "I can't get into any more trouble than I already am in, but you could. That's my concern."

I study Lucy as she vacillates, and for the first time since I devised this plan, I truly doubt its feasibility. I shouldn't have asked her, or anyone, to help me. I should have gone to the police like Conor said.

I reach for the dress in Lucy's hands. While she is fun to chat with over tea and lunch, Lucy isn't like me. She's much more like Diana—the Diana I thought I knew. Lucy is married, steady, smart, polished, and poised, and she feels confident and safe about her place in the world and about her future. And she should—she's the real deal, good and honest too. She's quiet, an introvert, and managing the Tate's archives is her dream job. She should not be involved in this.

She steps back, pulling the dress with her. "I'm in."

"You are?" Incredulity pours out of me.

Lucy grins. "Sure. What's happening to you isn't right and I'm not blind or dumb. Something strange *is* happening. I feel it. But I appreciate you didn't push me." Her voice lifts. "And since you've never asked me for help in the five years I've known you, you must be desperate."

"I am." I quirk a smile back. "Thank you. Remember to stay in the south corridors and don't head upstairs until the basement lights switch on twice. Nine o'clock."

She assures me she's got the plan and she's off.

Sara arrives next. She looks around. "Where are Lucy and Becca?"

"Come and gone." I hand her the dress. Without missing a beat, she shoves it into her canvas bag. That's why she's my best friend.

I grip her shoulder. "When did you get fringe?"

Sara gasps as her hand flies to her forehead. Sara's red hair was always going to be an issue, of course, but I thought if she wet it in the bathroom, then pulled it up and back like I sometimes do, it might look dark enough not to catch Diana's notice, but a full forehead of fringe?

"Yesterday after work. I didn't think." She smooths them off her forehead. "It'll be fine. See? I'll slick them back when I wet my hair."

I gulp. It simply has to work. "The others know the lights will flick on and off, what to do, and how serious it is, but they don't know about each other. I thought if they get caught, it will be better if they only know their roles."

"Such a little mastermind you are," she teases. " Are you robbing banks next?"

"I'm retiring after this." I look towards the Tate. "And finding another job."

Sara squeezes my hand. "On my walk here, I realized you can't see the second-floor window from Bessborough. You'll need to be in the back alleyway."

"I thought of that too. I'll move closer."

"You'll be seen."

I shrug an it's-all-I've-got kind of shrug and Sara gives me an answering one. She pulls me into a quick hug. "See you on the other side," she whispers into my hair.

"I hope so." I push her away. "Remember, if *you* get caught, tell them everything I asked you to do. Say I forced you."

"As if you could force me."

"Don't try to protect me, Sara. Say I tricked you, if you want, say I lied, blackmailed you, anything. Promise me you'll say whatever it takes to get you clear."

"Stop." Her eyes flash with alarm. "Breathe. I'll think of something and I'll be fine. We will all be fine." With another hug, she's off.

While I appreciate her confidence and bravado, a lot can go wrong with my hastily devised plan. First of all, all three of them need to pass that security guard in their regular clothes and get noticed. Then they need to head to three different lavatories to change into their dresses, unseen. But before doing that, Sara has to confirm Diana is in her office. If the door is shut, Sara must knock on it and make some excuse as to why she's bothering a woman she rarely speaks to—perhaps looking for me?—both to make sure Diana is inside and, again, to be noticed by Diana in her normal clothes.

My bet is that Diana will be there. She has been coming in each morning, then leaving around lunch. I have to trust she'll keep that pattern, both to keep an eye on things at the Gallery and to keep an eye and ear out for me. That is, until I'm in custody.

Once Diana's presence is confirmed, Sara needs to race to the second-floor ladies' room to pull the window shade down, then up. She then quickly changes and hides her regular clothes in the cupboard there, wets her hair and now her new fringe, and takes the stairs back down to the basement. There she will flick the lights on and off twice.

At that point all three women, dressed alike, go to their respective areas and start walking. Becca along the main gallery, north wall. Lucy along the south corridors and smaller gallery rooms. And Sara farthest away in the upper gallery, but near the railing so as to come in and out of sight. Each of them is to be seen, but none of them is to be close enough to where Diana could stop them.

As for me . . . the shade is my cue. Once I see that, I do the one part of the plan no one knows about, then circle the Gallery and walk straight in the front door. And unlike Becca, I'll need to make a commotion to make sure that the guard notices me and remembers my crazy block-patterned dress. And while I want him to see me, I can't let him stop me. I'm banking on the hope he'll call Diana first, describe what I'm wearing, and ask her what he should do.

As I watch Sara walk away, the holes in this plan overwhelm me. So much can go wrong. And it's thin even if all goes right. I should have given them more time. Sara only has about five minutes to confirm Diana's there, race to the second floor, change, race down, and then race back up again. It's too quick. I should have spent more time devising a schedule. I should've given them better instructions. I should have synchronized our watches. Don't all good plans begin with synchronized watches?

Pushing my churning thoughts aside, I head towards the back of the Tate and the shipping bay. For the plan to work I need Diana herself to search for whom she assumes to be me. I suspect she will because she'll want to keep control. But that's not good enough. I need no one else to be available to help her. She can't send Security to find me or even a spare guard to track down one "me" while she races after another. Security needs to be occupied elsewhere.

Diana must dash out of her office in a mad race, wildly searching for the girl in a multicolored, block-patterned dress. Alone. And in her haste, she must leave behind her gold key. The one that rests in her crystal dish while she's at work. The one that opens her always-locked desk drawers.

I walk the alleyway pressed along the Gallery's west wall. While I can be seen, the windows don't provide a clear visual from the shipping bay until I come out at the end where the alley meets the driveway entrance. And there just to the left, mere feet from the Gallery's back service entrance, sits a series of metal bins. It feels like a horrible twist of irony that Paddy's actions on Wednesday in St. Martin's alley gave me this idea.

I pull three tubes from my pocket. Last night, on my mission to Soho, I met up with an old friend who handles the pyrotechnics for a couple clubs. He promised me these little tubes will do the trick. *"All flash, no flame."* As none of his clubs have burned down, I trust he knows what he's about. I made that point and he smirked in reply. While his smug reaction was not reassuring, his assumption that I'd be available to pay him back with a story and a pint was.

I reach into my other pocket and pull out the Clipper lighter I found in Roger's room. Holding the lighter near the first tube's rag wick, I pause and pray my friend is right. The shipping door is closed, but a shipment of paintings from the Picasso Commemorative is set to leave this morning. The men are in there—as is some phenomenally expensive art. Burning down the Tate Gallery or getting anyone injured is not my intention. I light the cracker and drop it into one of the metal bins—after checking that it's empty of packing paper.

I close my eyes and take a deep breath. Time is slipping away. Time I do not have. I light the second, drop it, then light the third and do the same. I run as fast as I can around the Gallery to the front entrance. I race up the huge flight of marble steps, willing my breath to calm and my heart to stop pounding. As neither is going to happen, I slip off my coat, pull open the heavy glass door, lower my sunglasses dramatically, and—per Daisy's suggestion—give a performance that would make Audrey Hepburn proud.

"Oh my goodness, it's windy out there. Hallo," I call to the guard. "I don't believe we've ever actually met. I'm Lily Summers. And though there's wind, it's a beautiful morning. Perfect for this dress, don't you think?"

His jaw actually drops. I actually twirl, then throw him another huge smile, adding a wink over dipped sunglasses, and walk on before he gathers his wits.

In my periphery I see him launch out of his chair and head after me. I pick up my pace. Within a few steps I turn my head a touch and see him drop back to the desk. I assume he's calling Diana.

Showtime!

CHAPTER 28

Diana

Her complacency carries her up the Tate's broad steps and encourages her to smile at the new and somewhat lackadaisical security guard, and it walks with her down the administrative office corridor, past Richard's office door. It feels good to be back where she belongs, and she anticipates her return will be made permanent very soon. The complacent feeling brings a sense of satisfied peace—one that vanishes as she opens her office door and finds that pesky insurance investigator, Conor Walsh, sitting inside.

He shoots out of the bucket chair as she slams the door behind her. "What are you doing in here?"

"I'm sorry I startled you. The front guard told me to wait here."

She drops her bag on the ledge of the highboy behind her desk. "I'll need to have a word with him."

"Yes. It's not an ideal security situation."

Diana looks at the young man and her temper cools. After all, he hasn't been the threat she feared upon first meeting him, and he has proven himself, to some degree, beneficially unprofessional with regard to the crime's supposed culprit.

Yet she isn't about to underestimate him either—especially with the girl still at large. No, he may still be working the case. Lily's drawings are indicative of her feelings alone. They don't necessarily signal a mutual interest over a one-sided crush. They don't imply he is helping her. There are reasons to still be wary of him.

"What can I do for you, Mr. Walsh?"

He shifts uncomfortably and she makes certain not to smile. The bucket chair's tall sides prevent him—and everyone else—from relaxing in it, which is why she positioned it across her desk in the first place. It keeps one unsettled within her office without understanding why.

"I'm heading back to New York this afternoon and wanted to check one last time if you'd found the provenance for *Woman Laughing*."

The provenance again, she thinks with alarm. While it was always going to be a problem, it seems to be getting out of hand. She huffs what she hopes sounds like an exasperated breath. "Surely Edward or Louise Leiris had copies."

"Both do, but as you know, we would prefer the original. I believe you still possess it?"

Diana sits back. "Has Keller decided to pay on the policy?"

"I've determined Mr. Davies had nothing to do with the forgery, but the original provenance is still required. My hope, of course, is that reparations will come once the forger is found. If not found, however, that's the game we play, isn't it?"

Keller is going to pay. Diana lets her smile break free, knowing once Edward is paid, he will back down and the scandal will die away. His call to *The Times* will also expedite matters. "That's wonderful. But Lily may have spent or hidden the money."

"That's always a possibility." Mr. Walsh tilts his head to the side as if either the girl's guilt is up for debate or the prospects of recovering the money is. Diana can't tell, but rather than pursue it, she merely shrugs as if to agree they are all waiting for answers.

"The original provenance?" he questions again.

Diana laughs and, even to her own ears, it sounds light and easy. "We're all after the original, Mr. Walsh, and I promise I will reach out if I find it in my files. But I have looked thoroughly. With my feckless, duplicitous assistant on the run, everything around here is in disarray."

"I can imagine." He shifts again as if trying to sit back and get comfortable.

This time she can't stop a smile from blooming.

"This whole experience has been terribly upsetting. I trusted her." Diana reaches behind her and withdraws her coin purse from her Hermès bag. She pulls a small gold key from within and leans down to open a desk drawer. She pulls out a handful of files. "This really has been such an ordeal." She drops the key into the crystal dish on her desk and opens the file. She is out of small talk and it is time for Mr. Walsh to leave.

He catches the hint and stands. "Thank you for your help on this investigation, and I wish you the best."

"Yes." She reaches out her hand, but she does not stand. "Safe travels back to New York."

Just as the door shuts behind him, Diana's telephone rings. The slipshod guard, who allowed that man to sit in her office unattended, announces that Lily Summers, in one of her usual loud dresses, just walked through the Gallery's front door.

"Impossible," Diana yells, then collects herself. "Did you stop her? Did you call the police?"

A clear answer doesn't come as the guard starts to panic over something about a blinking light on his security board from the shipping dock, static, and . . . He hung up on her?

Diana stands, smooths her skirt, and decides that she will find Lily herself and finish this once and for all.

Lily

I hasten through the rotunda, not pausing today, and sneak past the entrance to the administrative offices and into the gallery of marble women beyond. Tucking behind a lovely young lady sans clothing, I wait. Footsteps reverberate off wood and marble all around the Gallery, and I'm certain the crackers have fired.

As the Gallery isn't open yet, I believe Security won't set off the fire alarms until they know what's going on, as that's how they handled a similar situation a couple years back. I peek around the statue and see three guards, as well as Archie at a slow trot behind them, race to the stairs under the rotunda. I then catch Diana stride across the main gallery towards the front desk.

Once she has passed me and turns out of sight, I head down the corridor to her office. The door is shut. I crack it open and peek in to make sure it's empty—as if I didn't just see her heading towards the front desk. I rush in and shut the door behind me.

The gold key rests in the crystal dish.

I open her left bottom file drawer as that's the one she always opens when searching for papers on running exhibitions. Only after an exhibition closes does she move the files to my cabinets where they rest for a year before I send them on to Lucy in Archives.

I page through all the papers for the Picasso Commemorative she didn't pass along to me. There are logistics, guest charts, meeting notes, planning notes. But no documentation of any painting, including *Woman Laughing*.

My breath catches. It's like I'm choking. I was so sure. I page through the entire drawer. Nothing.

I shut it, lock it, and frantically open the one above it. I page through the files there. Nothing. I lock it and move to the right side of the desk. There I find it. It's not filed with any of the other Picassos from the exhibit or even with other paintings held by the Tate. *Woman Laughing*'s original provenance rests in an unmarked file that holds the paperwork for a Monet I don't recognize, a Miro, and notes on a 1919 Campendonk.

I hear something outside and panic. I slide the entire file up my dress and into the waistband of my tights. It's stiff and the papers feel like they'll cut me, but there's no time to readjust them. I lock the drawer, drop the key in the dish, and race towards the door.

I crack it open, sneak out, and turn down the corridor towards my own office. I need Diana's notes—those little missives she constantly leaves on my desk, with no capitals and no punctuation but lots of swirling *q*'s, *p*'s, *f*'s, and *s*'s. I launch across my desk, grab them from the top right drawer, and shoot to the corridor again. I don't peek first. Time is out and it's only a short flight of steps between me and the service entrance at the back of the basement offices. No matter what, I know I can make it now.

I swing right to disappear through the door to the basement but find myself flung left.

Flung by Conor Walsh.

Right into Conor Walsh.

CHAPTER 29

Lily

"Conor?"

His name comes out short, soft, and breathless. I stumble back, but before I fall, I get hauled up by my arm so hard I lose my footing and, within an instant, find myself smooshed into the utility closet right next to my office.

"Wha—?" I yelp and Conor's hand clamps over my mouth. I feel his body pressed to mine, but in the dark I can't see him. I catch a hint of rosemary and something deeper, almost woodsy, and I shake my head, trying to dislodge both the power that scent has on me and his hand clamped over my mouth.

"Don't scream," he whispers.

"Why would I scream? I'm trying not to get caught." My lips move against his palm, but my words make no sense. I bite at his hand.

It jerks back. "What are you doing?"

"Getting your hand off me. I couldn't breathe," I whisper. "Why on earth would I scream?"

"Give me the provenance."

My eyes begin to adjust and I can see his face, only inches from my own. "No." I blink. "How'd you know?"

"It's what you need. It's what we all need. You said she had it. I came this morning to try to force her hand myself."

I lean back, but he pulls me forward. He whispers close, "It doesn't lock. The door could pop open."

"You didn't believe me."

"I never said that. I said you needed to turn yourself in." He takes a breath, blowing it out through his nose as if accepting something he didn't think possible. "I wasn't going to stop looking for answers, Lily, but I don't want you hurt either. Criminals can become desperate and dangerous."

I smile. He smiles. He has a dimple in his left cheek.

"I was just leaving through the main gallery when I caught sight of Sara. She's wearing a dress a lot like the one you wore the day we met. It got me thinking about your friend's Mondrian scene."

"You remembered that?" I squeak. "Did you tell Diana?" My thoughts go straight to my friends. "You're supposed to be at the airport or already on a plane to New York. How'd you find me?" My words come out harsher than I intend, but I can't decide if I'm disgusted with myself or impressed with him.

"Of course I didn't tell her. She dashed out of her office just as I was leaving the cloakroom." He looks over my head as if imagining Diana racing through the Tate. "That's when I saw Sara, and unlike Diana, I had a little foreknowledge of this scenario and a pretty good idea what you were up to and where you'd be."

I clamp down the little glow growing within me. He believed me.

"Give me the provenance," he repeats.

"Not yet." I step back and this time he doesn't stop me. "It's only a theory right now, and a theory doesn't help me much."

"I'll help you."

I shake my head. While I appreciate the offer—beyond appreciate it—too many people are getting hurt. My mind casts to my sketchbook and I realize even Conor can get hurt if I don't clear my name quickly.

"If you misstep, you could lose your job. I drew a picture of you and Diana gave it to the police. Anyone might think . . ." I grow warm and can't explain any further. "Please. I want to take it to the police myself. The less you know, like everyone else at this point, the safer you are."

He leans towards me and I suspect a counterargument is coming. I lift a hand to cover his mouth. Unlike me, he doesn't bite at my palm. "I like that you have integrity, Conor. I like that you're good at your job. I even like that you figured out what I was doing way too fast. After I see if I'm right or wrong about this provenance, I'll go to the police regardless. Trust me." I stall, then jump in. "Like I trust you."

He wriggles my hand away. "Promise?" I nod and he gestures to the door behind me. "Get out of here."

"Thank you." Without thinking I rise on my toes and kiss him. Not a peck. A firm, real, and possibly-too-long kiss. But once I start I don't want to stop, and if I judge correctly, past his first instant of surprise, he kisses me right back. At least, I'm going to believe he does.

I pull back, just far enough to look in his slightly startled eyes, then kiss him once more. "Goodbye." I twist and duck out from beneath his arms, which have somehow slipped around my waist, dash out the door, open the next one, and race down the basement steps.

Within another thirty seconds, I'm outside the Gallery rushing south to duck behind the next row of buildings. And despite all I've done, all I am doing, and all I have yet to do, only one thought fills my mind.

Conor tastes like coffee. How very American of him.

My time is short. There is no way the security guard or Diana hasn't called the police already, if Security didn't after the crackers fired off. I only hope Becca, Lucy, and Sara are back in their original clothes and sitting at their desks as if it's just another boring day.

Sliding the file from my dress, which makes for an awkward moment on the stoop of a paper shop that hasn't yet opened this morning, I realize I need a place to hole up and to finally look at this provenance I've risked so much to obtain—preferably a place with a telephone so I can ring Sara and make sure my friends are okay.

If they are not, if Diana or Security caught any one of them, I'll forget holing up at all and go straight to the police. Enough is enough.

Dolphin Square.

I ring the doorbell and, once again, Monks opens the door. This time he doesn't shut it in my face; he doesn't say a single word; he simply steps back as if he's been expecting me.

I walk straight to Mr. Davies's office.

"I've got a bloody revolving door today," he bellows, but not unkindly.

"Who else has been here?"

"Your boss. Steel beneath velvet, that one. She's got her sights on you, young lady." He flicks his hand at the seat across from his desk, and I sense something has changed. Diana, by coming here, has somehow lowered her status in Mr. Davies's mind and elevated mine. "Seems I'm to give another interview to *The Times* to exonerate the Tate and drive a stake in your heart." He lifts a brow and quirks a small smile. "She wants your reputation ruined before the courts destroy your life."

"And you?" A single butterfly lets loose within my stomach.

"If you were my forger, there wouldn't have been fear in her eyes. I've been duped enough to learn how to read people, Miss Summers, and Diana is hiding something that, if discovered, will cost her dearly."

I hold up the file. "I may have that 'something.' May I make a telephone call first?"

He pushes back from his desk and gestures to his telephone. It's a sleek modern one: black, touch-tone, with a handset that's so light I bounce it in my hand before holding it against my ear. I settle my fingers over the buttons to tap in Sara's number, then realize I can't remember it. My fingers know it on a rotary dial.

I look to Mr. Davies, who laughs at my expression. "Go to the kitchen. It happened to me for a few months too."

I walk through the door I exited only yesterday and find a rotary telephone sitting on the kitchen counter. I dial Sara and find out that not only is she fine, but she, Becca, and Lucy each had

Diana on them at one point or another, but they all kept her at a safe distance. There is no evidence she recognized them and no one stopped them. Not only that, but no one has mentioned anything other than that Security is furious over some kids dropping crackers into the outside rubbish bins. Sara even laughs that the day is so quiet even disgruntled donors haven't begun ringing yet.

I hang up with a sigh of relief and return to Mr. Davies's study. He's poring over the file that, in my haste, I left on his desk. My first instinct is to snatch it away as it's vital to securing my innocence. But before I do, I recognize I could use his help.

A painting catches my eye. "You bought a Warhol."

"I got a good tip." He waves me to him. "We'll talk about that later. Come see this."

I draw closer and he points to a notation on the second page. "Everything in a document matters. If things are true, they're often random, but if not, it's very hard to make them random."

I smile. Conor said the same thing.

"Look at the date here."

"The twelfth of March 1938." I say the date aloud, but it means nothing to me.

"Did they teach you nothing about history in school?" Mr. Davies glances up at me. "It's the date of the Anschluss, the date Germany took over Austria. Your Diana Gilden is Austrian. Seems unlikely one's focus would be on recording the movement of a painting on that day, wouldn't you agree?"

I pull out the papers from my pocket. Diana's notes to me. I smooth them and set them before him. "Here's something more. Look at this."

Turning the provenance to its fourth page, I set a note next to it. The handwriting is identical—undeniably identical. The same *g*, the same sloping script *f*.

"Assume she penned the provenance in order, like a story she's telling. She starts at the beginning, fresh and ready to go, but her hand gets weary, and she grows sloppy or she simply runs out of fake handwriting styles. Here on page 4 and then"—I turn the page—"on page 5."

I tap several letters, pointing first to the provenance, then to the corresponding letter on one of a dozen notes I grabbed. "That's Diana's handwriting."

"So it is." The disbelief—or belief—in Mr. Davies's voice lifts a weight off my chest.

"That's usable, right? That proves she's involved."

"It sure does." His smile broadens to a wide grin. "And it's been 'usable' in court for over a century." He leans back in his chair and I straighten. "You're saying Diana Gilden is my forger?"

"Maybe. I'm not sure." I walk around his desk back to the comfortable chair across from it. I sink in and oddly notice how different it feels than when I sit across from Diana's desk. "Something still doesn't fit. She wrote the provenance, but I can't pin her as the actual forger. When she described painting, she spoke as if she'd lost part of herself when she gave it up. That wouldn't make sense if she still painted."

"I'm calling the inspector." Mr. Davies gathers the papers. "We have her, Lily."

I note his casual use of my first name, and I marvel at how far we've come and, though still in trouble, how jubilant and light I feel. "But what if she's not the actual forger?"

"It doesn't matter. She'll tell the police who is. There is no way Diana Gilden will cover for another. If I'm any judge of character, she'll take a deal so fast her accomplice will be in handcuffs before noon." He looks to me, then gestures to the phone. "Would you like to ring them? You should get the honors."

I close my eyes briefly, trying to let myself truly believe I may be near the end. "Can you? I need to go home and tell my family what's going on. They're worried sick. If you want to tell the inspector I'm there, I'm fine with that. You can tell him I'll come to the station as soon as I've talked to my parents or he can come get me. I won't run."

Mr. Davies nods as if he understands more about my complete exhaustion than I do myself. "You go."

I glance back to the Warhol, then to him. His eyes dance to it, then to me. "Like I said, we'll get to that another time."

I nod, turn, and find silent, stealthy Monks waiting for me at the doorway.

Back on the street, I stand almost listless. The jubilation and lightness lasted mere moments and I'm left feeling disillusioned, exhausted, worn out, and I simply want to cry. I don't have the energy to walk home. I don't have the energy to take the Underground. I simply want to curl up right here on the sidewalk and let the world spin along while I try to . . .

What? Go back and make different choices? Not need validation so much that I chase after it from someone like Diana? Go back to age five and not pick up that bloody red ball? I squeeze my eyes shut. *It's over. Don't go back.*

An image fills my mind. It's Monday night and I'm at family dinner, sitting across from Conor as he shares his story with my family. No one is paying attention to me—and it's wonderful. That's what I see. I see my family, as if for the first time, and they've been there all along. Flawed, generous, horrible at small talk, frank, opinionated, real, and mine. In my mind's eye, I watch each family member in turn and wish I could tell them how much I love them.

I watch Conor and my heart softens in the same direction. I wish I could tell him how much I hope for him, maybe even for us. I want to thank him, kiss him again, tell him I can be accessible—I will try.

I wish to dwell on that thought, on him, but the litany of failures, slights, missteps, and my own blindness that landed me here creep into the edges of my envisioned family dinner. If only I'd shared some part with my family, some part of how I felt or who I wanted to be, none of this could have happened. In isolation I became vulnerable. In isolation I became Diana's patsy.

Something quickens within me and I need to know what's false and fabricated and what's real and true.

Only one person holds those answers.

CHAPTER 30

I flag down a cab and direct the cabbie to take me to Diana's house. I could go back and confront her at work, but I doubt I'd get past that unnamed guard this time, and that assumes he isn't accompanied by all Scotland Yard racing through the Gallery's corridors. No, I need to see her, surprise her, catch her unawares, and make her answer my questions. Besides, if she is the forger, painting takes space. It's messy. She must have a studio at home, and maybe I can catch sight of that too.

I hop from the cab three doors from Diana's Mayfair home. I watch the windows as I approach but don't see any movement within. I ring the bell. I almost laugh at all the care and caution I'm taking, especially as I'm not sure why I'm taking them. Diana is probably not home as she has left the Tate closer to lunch the past few days. But that's okay too; I just need to see inside . . .

A tall man in a dark suit answers the door. He isn't Diana's husband. I met her husband once, and he's much older, thin and almost breakable. He's also creepier. A rapacious look smoldered in her husband's eyes that set me back that time I met him. It wasn't about sex, as those looks often are, even in art. It was about power.

"I'm Lily Summers, Diana's assistant. She asked me to come pick something up for her. I believe she said it was in her desk? Or perhaps her studio? I can't remember now."

His look flickers, but he opens the door wide. "Follow me."

He leads me past the kitchen to a room facing the back of the home. It's a small, neat space, beautifully appointed, with only an armchair and ottoman, a delicate French side table, and a small writing desk and chair. A large Herend bird and gold letter opener sit on the desk beside a beautiful maroon leather blotter with gold detailing. I glance around, searching corners and through open doorways, but see nothing that could be a studio.

The man slides open the desk's single shallow drawer to reveal two fountain pens and a stack of linen stationery. "Here." He looks to me. There's a glint of challenge in his eyes. "Take whatever she requested."

I stall. "Perhaps the papers are in another desk? One upstairs?"

A voice, low and firm, behind me says, "There is no other desk."

I turn to find Diana's husband standing in the open doorway.

"But that's not why you came, is it, Lily?" He steps towards me but looks to the other man. "Branford, you may go for the day. I'll take care of our guest."

A single nod and the man walks away. My hand reaches out, almost as if to stop him from going. He wasn't exactly welcoming, but I sense he's less dangerous than the man who now stands before me.

"I've underestimated you, and my wife certainly has."

My gaze drops to his hands. Color stains the rims of his fingernails. "You painted *Woman Laughing*."

He taps his nose. "Clever girl. Follow me."

I don't move.

He laughs. "Come now. Don't deny you're curious. It's why you came, isn't it?"

I follow him out of the small reading room, through the kitchen, and back into the black-and-white-marbled entryway. We walk up a sweeping flight of stairs. At the next floor I catch glimpses into each of the bedrooms as we circle the landing to walk up once more. They're sumptuous rooms. Rich carpets, full draperies—the colors are mesmerizing. I stall at a bold purple room. A thick wool rug in a dark royal purple covers the floor, while draperies with massive purple blooms on aqua fall all the way from the ceiling.

"Come along." Heinrich stops two steps above me and flaps his hand. "I can't give you all day, my dear."

Again, I follow.

We reach the top of the stairs. It's a small attic landing, and for a moment I feel disappointed and confused. There are merely bookshelves, a reading chair with a light, and a side table stacked with books. Heinrich pushes on a bookcase to my right and it pops open. Light spills into the dark space. I catch a glimpse of openness, white walls, and light. Stepping in, I'm enveloped by color.

It's a massive room and must take up the entire depth and width of the house. Lights are set within the ceiling. Bright, neutral daylight. On the walls hang paintings in various stages of completion and some, I suspect, that will never be completed. They look almost like rough drafts, canvases used to capture an aspect of technique. I'm almost jealous at the cavalier waste of expensive canvas and paint.

Most works on the walls are recognizable too—at least the styles are. None are actual works I've ever seen before. They are all modernist paintings, loosely speaking. There are no stuffy landscapes, pets, or even the more stylized Renaissance works here. I spot a Dalí, a Duchamp, a Miro, two Chagalls . . .

"Come."

I step in farther and follow Heinrich to a corner of the room. It's almost like a room within a room. The flooring is different. There is a short wood wall on wheels, and a chair and table set up as if it's a set on a stage. I feel like I've walked into a fantasy world, a play, a twist on reality.

He picks up a painting from the floor. "What do you think of this?"

I look at the painting. It's clearly one of Heinrich Campendonk's, the early- to mid-nineteenth-century German painter. I tilt my head. Part of me knows it's a forgery, that all these paintings are forgeries, but this one looks perfect. Campendonk has not been one of the artists I've painted, yet I've studied him and spent hours poring over the Tate's catalogue from its Blue Rider Group exhibition—Campendonk's school—offered in the early sixties.

"Yours?" I gesture to the painting.

"Campendonk's." He sets it down. "That's the true art, Lily. Becoming the artist. Stepping outside yourself and reaching into them. It's not mine. It's his. And why not? Why is it not a true Campendonk? Who is to say it's not as valuable? As authentic? The emotions were the same. It's certainly as beautiful."

"But he didn't paint it. You did."

"Semantics."

He lifts a canvas from a rack and I discern, through the charcoal outline and brushstrokes, that an early iteration of *Woman Laughing* rests before me.

"How could you tell? No one ever has before." He sounds curious, light, as if we are talking of nothing more than artistic theory in the abstract, where there are no right answers, just the enjoyment of discussion. He sounds like the pretentious students at the school who have time for such talk and the means to indulge in it. Paddy and I sometimes laugh and mimic them as we lock up late at night.

I think of Paddy. I think of my family. Anger rises within me. People are suffering and this man is playing a game. A game he's been playing for years by the looks of it, indulging in the fantasy that because he can paint like Picasso, Campendonk, Ernst, or Modigliani, then he *is* Picasso, Campendonk, Ernst, or Modigliani. That his work should be equally revered, valued, accepted, and praised—as if genuinely theirs.

"It was easy." I catch a flicker of fury flash through his eyes. "You lack Picasso's passion. Yours is a mere paint by numbers."

At the first flicker of doubt in his eyes, I feel powerful. As his eyes ignite I recognize my precarious position, and once more, the moment *after* the words fly from my mouth, I want to seize them back.

Something dark and primal passes through his expression before he gains control, and the strange benign look he's been wearing the last twenty or so minutes finally returns. I hear a soft rapping from outside the room and use his momentary distraction to inch closer to the door. I don't like this place. I don't like this man. I'm only a few steps from the door when Diana steps into view.

"What are you doing here?" Heinrich calls to his wife. "I am handling this."

"I came home for an early lunch. What—?" she replies to him before noticing me. "Lily." She stares at me, but I can't read her expression. Her face reveals nothing as her gaze toggles between her husband and me.

I speak to her because I want nothing to do with him. "You did this together. You were going to frame me together. He painted *Woman Laughing*, but you wrote the provenance, didn't you?"

She stares at me but still her face reveals nothing.

I talk on. Heinrich's fidgeting from foot to foot and her steady stare unnerve me. "I found it this morning, the original provenance. I gave it to Mr. Davies, and by now he's handed it over to Scotland Yard. It's over." I point my hand around the room at painting after painting. "There's no way you can hide all this."

"You can't be sure, though, can you? I might be able to think of something." She steps towards me. "You couldn't let it alone, could you? I knew that was you at the Gallery, but not only you. There was too much going on. Did you light the crackers? Break into my desk? Who helped you?"

I don't answer.

"You always have to have your finger in everything. You try and try to control all the variables. Yet this is something you cannot manage . . ." Diana surveys the room. "This is my house. I determine what happens here."

"It's over." The words don't come out quite so emphatic this time. I hate that they reflect the growing alarm that fills me.

"No, it's not." It's Heinrich who speaks and his words are quite forceful. There's not a drop of anxiety or alarm in them— and that worries me.

I slowly turn towards him, but I don't see him. All I see is the gun pointed straight at me. It's an old antique gun, not that I've seen many. But the Tate had an exhibition on the Art of War several years ago, and I've thoroughly combed through that cat-alogue too.

"Heinrich, what are you doing?" Diana's voice lifts and she steps between me and her husband. "Put that away. We don't need that."

"She's going to ruin us. That . . . that girl." Spittle flies and gathers at the corners of his mouth. I sense I'm not human to him any longer, if I ever was. I'm an aberrant speck of paint, one that must be blotted out and covered over.

"Put that away. I'll take care of this. I can handle her." Her tone drops.

I look to him to see if her change in approach has effected a change in him, but it hasn't. He still stares at me. The gun re-mains pointed at me and his sneer is terrifying.

Diana takes another step forward, and I can tell by the way she straightens, the way her back uncurls, vertebrae stacking upon each other, that her husband's mania shocks her as well. Although she's stepped forward, her weight shifts back as if she, too, is try-ing to distance herself from what faces us both.

"You are incapable, Diana. You put this into motion and at every step you have messed it up." He waves the gun as if the mere sideways motion will shift Diana to the right and away. I pray it won't.

"I can fix this." She grinds out the words.

Heinrich, however, isn't reassured. His eyes take on a rage, and I suspect he no longer hears his wife. "No. No. It is me. It's always been me. I will take care of this." The words seem to be for him as much as they are from him.

Diana steps towards her husband but glances back to me. She whispers, "Lily, run."

I look to her. I look to him. He heard her. He stiffens his arm and the gun rises another inch in direct aim. I run.

I race down the steps. There is screaming above me, angry screaming, frightened screaming. I hear tone rather than distinct words as I make it to the second floor, to the first, and throw open the front door. In that instant, right after the door slams behind me, a shot rings out from above. I dive back to the door, but it has automatically locked behind me.

"Diana!" I scream her name and pound upon the black door, as if she might poke her head out a third-floor window and tell me she's okay.

That does not happen. I look to each side of the door. The floor-to-ceiling windows are shut tight. I glance down the flight of metal stairs off to the left of the door, down to the garden entrance, and see a window cracked open. I lunge for the wrought iron gate. It, too, is locked.

A hand pulls me from behind. I spin and find Conor.

"Don't."

"He had a gun. He shot her."

"I heard. I'll go." He leaps over the locked gate, landing two steps down. He has the window pried open by the time I clamber over the gate, snagging my dress, and almost fall down the stairs. I throw myself through the window opening behind him and we race upwards. Conor pauses outside the kitchen.

I topple into him and pass him. "This way."

"Lily."

"They're upstairs," I yell, taking the front stairs two at a time, again to the landing, and again to the third floor.

A keening hits me halfway up the final flight, and I stall for an instant. It's an almost animalistic sound, broken, hurt, and in some way dying, yet with such strength I can't believe that's the case. I launch through the open bookshelf with Conor at my heels. Blood is everywhere.

Diana lies curled, half kneeling, half lying, sobbing over Heinrich's body. The gun lies beside him at the edge of the growing pool of blood.

"He's shot," Diana cries to us, then drops back upon her husband.

I can't figure it out. Diana was across the room. Heinrich had the gun. I was gone for hardly a moment before the shot rang out. Diana's call for "help" pulls me out of my shock and stupor.

"Where?" Conor pushes past me and kneels across from her. "Where, Diana? Where is he hit?"

Her body sways back and forth, she's crying and blithering, but I can't understand what she's saying. Conor gives up trying to listen and runs his hands over Heinrich's body. I remember he was a cop and trust he knows what he's doing. He sits back on his knees and casts me an amused look. It's so out of place and inappropriate I jerk back.

"Diana." He gently pushes her shoulder until she sits back enough to look at him. "He fainted. He's not hurt." Conor looks down at Heinrich. "Well, he is hurt, but he'll be fine. When he fired, the gun backfired. It blew through his hand. That's where the blood is coming from."

I look to Heinrich's hand, amidst the pool of blood, and see that it might now be missing a finger or two. My stomach lurches.

"But that's his painting hand. He'll never paint again." Diana continues sobbing.

That brings my focus straight back to Conor. *What?* I widen my eyes, as does he. We can't have heard her correctly. That can't be her primary concern.

"But he'll live. He'll be fine, Diana." Conor looks to me again. "Lily, find a telephone and call the police. We also need an ambulance."

I nod, and as I leave the room to find a telephone, I hear Diana once again crooning over her husband. At least this time, there's a note of hope within her voice.

"Darling. Darling. Wake up. Darling . . . You're going to be fine. All will be well. Just as you said. We'll get through this together. You will paint again and you were right . . . You were right . . . I'm here."

CHAPTER 31

About an hour later, all adrenaline seeps out of me and I drop onto Diana's front stoop. Head in hands, I can't watch any more.

Diana has been put in handcuffs and sits in the back of a police car just a few feet from me on the street. She stares straight ahead and hasn't looked right or left, or made any motion at all, since placed in there about ten minutes ago. Heinrich, loaded onto a stretcher and rolled into an ambulance, is on his way to the hospital. I don't know which one. And I don't care.

Police officers step by me, but no one asks me to move. I scooch closer to the wrought iron railing and lean against it. They've been walking in and out of the house since they arrived, and considering a whole new team pulls up to the curb now, I suspect they'll be here a long time yet.

Catching Conor's voice, I lift my head and watch as he shakes Inspector Gray's hand, then walks my direction. A small smile creeps across my face. I wish it could be more, but I don't have the energy.

Standing in front of me, he pulls off his jumper and motions to my arms. "Arms up?" He says it like a question, and there's something playful in his voice. Unlike before when I thought his amused look was completely inappropriate—I had no idea Heinrich had merely fainted—his tone feels pitch-perfect. It's like a thread of sunshine cutting through clouds, that birdsong you hear the first day of spring. I lift my arms and in a fluid motion, he pops his jumper over my head and arms and pulls it down on me.

"I would have draped it over your shoulders, but you're shivering pretty badly."

I hold up a hand. My nails are blue and, he's right, my hand shakes. "I hadn't noticed."

He drops next to me. "It's super normal and it'll come and go for a while." He shifts the jumper around my neck. It's warm, soft, and smells of wood and rosemary. I sink deeper into it. "Better?"

"Yes. No." I glance at him. "I don't even know what happened here. I don't know how—" There's a warble in my voice.

"Shh . . ." He wraps an arm around me and tucks me close. "You'll go through the whole gamut of emotions in the next few days. Just roll with them." He lifts his gaze from me and looks towards the car in which Diana sits.

I touch the jumper. "I didn't recognize you at first."

That draws a laugh. "I'm not surprised. I was hopping in a cab when Mr. Davies called the hotel and told me everything. I went straight back to the Tate and Richard's secretary told me Diana had gone home. I came here to confront her. It was dumb. I should've called Inspector Gray, but I was angry. Somewhere along the way this case started to feel personal." He looks down at me. "But what on earth were you doing here?"

"I wanted to do the same. Confront her and make her tell me she was the forger, that she was trying to send me to jail for her crime. I wanted to understand how she could do this. I wanted—I wanted not to be right even though I knew I was."

I pull the sleeves of his jumper over my hands and tuck each under my arms to warm them. "I should have listened to you. You said criminals can be desperate and dangerous." His arm slips away and a coolness prickles me. I snuggle deeper into his sweater to counterbalance the loss of his warmth. "Have you seen this kind of thing a lot?"

"A gun backfiring, no. I've never come across that. Criminals rarely use two-hundred-year-old weapons. But a shooting, yes. Several times while I was a cop." He looks to me. "And no, it doesn't get easier. My hope is this will be your one and only."

"Me too."

"You'll need to give a statement, but I asked Inspector Gray if that could be done tomorrow."

"Please tell me he said yes."

"He said yes." Conor smiles warm and broad. "You're in the clear, Lily. He wants to hear everything from your perspective, and today or tomorrow isn't going to change your story, nor will it change this outcome. I doubt he'll even get too worked up about your day on the lam."

"My day on the lam," I repeat. "That doesn't sound good. What about breaking into Diana's desk?"

Conor looks towards a collection of officers. "I don't get the impression he cares much about that either."

"What happens to them?" I shift his attention to the right. The police car holding Diana pulls away from the curb, with lights flashing but no siren.

"Statements. Processing. A trial sometime soon and then jail time for both of them." He looks back to the house. "I expect this place will be sold for restitution, and any assets they have will be seized. It'll be interesting to see how much money they've banked and how much can be recovered. They've been at it for years."

"Forging paintings?"

"It's what he does. He finds holes in an artist's oeuvre and he fills them. It's fascinating, really. The way Diana was describing it, he becomes the artist. He studies everything he can about them, visits where they lived and worked, studies how they talked, and he eats only foods they ate and drinks the drinks they favored while working on their paintings. He even speaks their language and dresses like them. He truly believes he becomes them."

"It doesn't sound normal or healthy."

"It's neither." Conor laughs. It's short and devoid of real humor. "I'm certain there's something diagnosable in all that. But bottom line, he's good at it, really, really good, and they've made millions over the years."

"Will Diana go to jail too?" For all that's happened, something in me hurts at the thought of Diana sitting in a jail cell. I try to remind myself I don't really know Diana at all—that who I envision sitting in that cell isn't a real person; it's a character she made up. My brow furrows. That's too much thinking for how tired I feel.

"She was the one who created the provenances, visited the dealers, sold the works, and even used her position as an expert at the Tate to authenticate them. She's not innocent, Lily."

"I thought I knew her." It feels like a confession rather than a statement. "She was good to me. I let her influence me. How I thought, how I dressed, how I . . ." I can't go on as tears fall.

"Who influences you now?"

Images of my mum, Daisy, Sara, Becca, and Lucy fill my mind. The women who've surrounded me with love even though I didn't recognize it for the most part, nor did I deserve it. But that was part of it too—it wasn't about "deserving." Their love and loyalty were gifts.

I open my mouth to recite their names to Conor, but before I do, they too fade away. I'm left with nothing racing through my brain and an odd calm fills me. "Me. A better me."

His soft chuckle reminds me of Paddy's chuff just the other evening, after I ripped apart all my paintings and smashed their frames.

"Paddy!" I push forward as if I'm about to launch off the steps and chase down Inspector Gray, who is now talking to another cluster of police officers.

Conor tugs at his jumper and draws me back. "He'll be fine. The inspector sent word to release him, and when you give your statement tomorrow, you can explain to Gray what happened."

"Will it be enough?"

One corner of Conor's mouth tips up. It's not a smile born of pleasure but one born of experience and, possibly, disappointment. "It will, but you did Paddy no favors. You didn't trust me to do my job, nor did you trust Inspector Gray."

"I got it in my head that all the evidence was against me, that someone was against me, someone with far more influence and power than I had. I wasn't wrong, but I wasn't right either." I glance to him. He's not looking at me. I only see the side of his jaw and the muscle that flexes beneath when one clenches his teeth.

He's right, of course. I didn't trust him, or Gray, or anyone else, just as I haven't trusted I wasn't responsible for everything that came before. Long before. How many times do people have to tell me, point it out, and sit me down before I finally get it? I watch Conor as I recall all the people I've hurt. All the people who might give me another chance and those who won't. I wonder in which category Conor fits. My head drops to my hands again.

"I'm sticking around for at least another couple weeks."

My head pops up. "You are?"

"Once I got a look at that room upstairs, I called my office in New York from a shop the police commandeered down the street. We're not dealing with one painting. We're dealing with who knows how many across the years. Keller wants me on the ground here for the time being. There will be work on the Continent as well. Diana said she's the one who spread the rumor there's a crime syndicate forging paintings."

"Why on earth would she do that?"

"She hoped to create so much chaos we'd all chase our tails rather than her. It was a good move. If you hadn't gotten involved and gotten that provenance, we might have."

"So I did help." I smile, but it's fake, and thank goodness, I can tell by his expression he sees that too.

"Uh-huh. So helpful. Getting in the way and underfoot at every turn." He mumbles the last as if annoyed, but he isn't. I can tell that too.

Looking down the street, despite the fact the police car holding Diana is long gone, I find my thoughts returning to her. "She probably shouldn't have told them all that."

"My guess is she wanted it off her chest. They couldn't stop her from talking. Her husband's got a hold on her, there's no denying that, but I suspect she was growing uncomfortable with their scheme. She wanted it over."

"She tried to save me. Whether the gun worked or not, he

had it pointed at me and she stepped in front of me. She stepped between us and told me to run." I make a mental note to tell Inspector Gray that in the morning as well.

Conor reaches for my hand and holds it on his lap. He stares straight ahead, as if looking at nothing but seeing everything. I feel the same way. The images of the past couple hours feel as real and present as if happening in front of me this very moment. I look at our hands. Does he even realize he's taken mine?

"That's something," he finally whispers. "She cared for you."

I chuff a short laugh, unable to forget what came before that moment too. "She also tried to send me to jail."

"Two things can be simultaneously true, you know." He covers our entwined hands with his free one.

Yes. I smile to myself. *He realizes.*

CHAPTER 32

SIX MONTHS LATER

Diana's trial is next week. Heinrich's, I gather, is next month. They won't be tried together, as Diana's counsel is pursuing some argument of emotional manipulation or something like that, which simply means she wasn't entirely responsible for her actions.

Part of me understands, but part of me feels that lets her off the hook too easily as well. I guess I feel that because, while she might sidestep some of her responsibility, I've had to accept my own.

First things first, I let Diana define me. I gave her that authority, whether I realized it or not. I let her in those cracks within me that I kept sealed off from everyone else. I fully recognized it the very afternoon she was arrested and the police dropped me off at the Agar Station. I wanted to be there when Paddy walked out. I wanted to be the first face he saw, assuming his wife, Patrice, wasn't hovering beside him, and I wanted mine to be the first voice he heard in apology.

He took one look at me and drew in a huge deep breath. His whole chest rose and fell with the motion and the emotion, and all words fled my brain. I simply walked up to him and hugged him tight. Only then did I whisper my apology.

And after my interview with Inspector Gray the next day, I took Conor to see him too. The three of us broke down the whole affair and it was after that, I think, Paddy started to truly understand and finally relax. Until that point I suspect he thought I was still in danger. It was when the truth finally broke through and his countenance lightened, I decided I wouldn't stop painting.

Diana wasn't going to take that from me; my past wasn't going to take that from me. It simply had to change—just as so much else had to change.

I got rid of all those books I hate, especially the poetry I never understood. I took the posters off my walls of art movements, primarily surrealism and expressionism, that never interested me. I also purged over half my wardrobe, anything and everything I'd ever purchased or asked Mum to sew that emulated Diana's style.

In every way I pared myself down to my essentials and finally felt a little bit free.

Eventually I did have to start replacing some of my wardrobe, after my new boss commented I'd worn the same dress three times in two weeks.

"Do I not pay you enough?" Mr. Davies barked one day.

I set down the files I'd been creating—the man's art collection across his three estates was an absolute mess—and told him why I had so few dresses. I also told him my mum had been asking to make me more and that, only recently, I felt it was time to let her.

"You needed that much penance?" he scoffed.

I shrugged and his gaze softened, and he assured me that he liked my brown linen shift with the light-blue-and-brown-striped jumper beneath just fine. After all he'd gone through with Sir John Brookings, I knew he understood—regardless of whether my self-imposed penance was objectively necessary.

He then nodded to the files in front of me and brusquely told me to hurry up and get the job for which he hired me done.

And I am almost done. His entire collection is researched and catalogued, and all the paintings Diana convinced him to purchase, but which he never liked, have been sold and replaced with paintings that make him smile. For all his bluster, we have found we have much in common.

As for Conor, he stayed in town for a couple weeks after Diana's and Heinrich's arrests to sort through Keller's London and European clients—three of whom held forgeries in their collections. It's still uncertain whether any are Heinrich's, as he refuses to talk. But perhaps we'll get those answers during his trial.

It was a good two weeks, and I saw Conor as often as he was available. Slowly, we became friends. I say *slowly* because, despite the fact I was already half in love with him, I had a lot of *me* to sort through. I needed to find out who I was. I needed to spend time with Daisy and my parents, and in many ways, I needed to take my story with him right back to the beginning. I wanted Conor to know the real me without suspicion or forgeries in any form lingering between us. I also needed to help Daisy and her family move, and help my parents go with them.

Daisy and Sean moved to their Richmond home a week or so after the Forgery Finale, as I've come to call it. Mum is over the moon with the house and is thrilled to be the first face her granddaughters see when they walk in the door after school each day. She's also thrilled to care for the new baby, Lily, who arrived a couple weeks ago, as Daisy and Sean work on their new pub. Mum is invaluable to them—something she always was, yet something I denied her.

We had to have another sit-down over that one. She had to remind me, once more, that it was pride and not humility that made me hold so tight to my guilt. But how is one to know the difference sometimes? She laughed, hugged me tight, and told me to stop trying to control all the answers as well as the world, and to simply enjoy my life.

Dad is home more these days. He left work, which allowed him to keep his benefits, and when Mum telephoned a few weeks ago to tell me he went to a local art store to purchase a small palette of watercolors, I almost cried. We paint together now. I take the train to Richmond, and we head to his local park most Sunday afternoons. He carries our supplies in an old wooden box a student left at St. Martin's, I carry our two second- or thirdhand easels, and we sit and work for hours. We don't talk a lot. We don't need to. It's nice just being together.

Speaking of being together—Sara and I have had a grand time living together these past six months. But it's time for me to go. Her boyfriend has been dropping hints and sly remarks lately and I suspect a proposal is right around the corner. In fact, I fear my presence has delayed it by a few months.

But back to Conor—because pondering Sara's boyfriend and her impending engagement can't help but lead me back to him . . .

As I said, we had two weeks together last May and now we've had over five months of writing letters, as transatlantic phone calls are way too expensive for either of us. But I don't mind. In fact, this is better. There is something so truthful and revelatory about writing to someone. I feel I know the true Conor now and he definitely knows the real me. I can also definitively say I'm not half in love with him; I'm all in, and I believe—again a few dropped hints and sly remarks have led me this direction—he feels the same.

I guess I'll find out next week . . .

I leave for New York Thursday next. At Paddy's encouragement I started creating my portfolio again. I shouldn't say "again" as there is nothing in what I do now that resembles what I did before. There is no copying the masters, no emulating another's style, or brushstrokes, or lighting, or scene . . . Nothing.

I paint what *I* see, what *I* feel, and what matters to *me*.

Once I completed three works to Paddy's satisfaction rather than my own, because a perfectionist is never truly done, I sent off Polaroids and an application to the studio master's program at New York University—a leader in the new realism movement I so adore. I was not only accepted; I won a full scholarship with a living stipend too. Those Americans sure do fund their arts.

So next week I'll find out if I have any talent at all. That's not right. I won't find out if I have talent next week—that's not something I can let anyone else determine. Next week, I'll find out how far I'm willing to stretch, how vulnerable I can make myself, and how much of myself I'm willing to splay onto a canvas. Whether the art world chooses to laud my efforts or eviscerate them is beyond my control.

After all, as Picasso taught me, the act of painting is the vivisection of one's soul, splayed out before the world in a two-dimensional format. And in art, as in life, success lies in holding nothing back. The world can hate it, but I can still have a marvelous time.

After all, both those states can be simultaneously true.

AUTHOR'S NOTE

Very quickly—because you all are wondering—I want to share how Pierce Brosnan got a cameo in *The English Masterpiece*. One of the original inspirations for this story was his 1999 *The Thomas Crown Affair*, rather than the 1968 film by the same name—though the clothing was more accurate in that one for this novel. But the Steve McQueen movie follows a bank heist rather than an art crime. Yet Mr. Brosnan himself, of course, was not going to be referenced—as the movie was a mere inspirational touchpoint. Then, while researching the school in which I wanted Lily to work and paint, St. Martin's School of Art—whose building now holds the famous Foyles bookstore—I learned that Brosnan actually attended St. Martin's School and studied art around the same time I had my fictional Lily working there.

Well, that set off my imagination and I wondered if a moment within this story might not have led to that brilliant scene in his later movie—the scene in *The Thomas Crown Affair* in which he and dozens of identically matched men race around the Met dressed like *The Son of Man* by René Magritte. A perfectly choreographed shell game.

There you go—that is how Pierce Brosnan ended up in this novel. And if he ever reads it, I hope he thoroughly enjoys his brief shining role.

Now on to the rest of the behind-the-scenes . . .

While so much is true about time, place, and art, I definitely allowed some inconsistencies to place facts within the story: The Price sisters, who participated in the Old Bailey bombings, didn't start their hunger strike a month after the actual bombing, but rather after their trial ten months later. And to be honest, I have no idea if the eleventh Duke of Argyll was actually a major contributor to the Tate. I just know he had a scandalous divorce a decade earlier and died within days of Picasso—and that made for a good story.

You're probably also wondering about the inspiration for Diana Gilden and Heinrich—who has no last name. They were inspired by real people, but I very purposely did no research into their lives, motivations, and current undertakings. I was introduced to Wolfgang and Helene Beltracchi's story, read a few articles about them to get the skeletal facts right, and watched their 2014 documentary *Beltracchi: The Art of Forgery*. After that—I did nothing more. I wanted Diana and Heinrich (though I did give my antagonist Campendock's real first name as Campendonk was an artist Beltracchi favors and Beltracchi was caught after using a modern paint formulation) to be fully fictional with no attribution to the real duo. That said, I am sure a deep dive into Wolfgang and Helene would prove fascinating.

Also, you'll notice I flipped around a bit, according to where it fit best, between the imperial and metric systems of measurement. Britain began to transition to metric in 1965, but it wasn't a done deal by 1973. Government memos from the time expressed a desire for the country to be compliant within ten years, and as 1973 falls just short of that mark, I expect people were still thinking in both systems.

And now for a few Easter eggs . . . There was no way when talking about Picasso's *The Embrace* that I couldn't mention Gustav Klimt or Francesco Hayez. I researched both their paintings, each titled *The Kiss*, for *A Portrait of Emily Price*, and they remain two of my favorites. I think I even mentioned Klimt's work in *A Shadow in Moscow*. I also had to briefly mention the power plant across the Thames from the Tate. It's a completely odd reference, but as that plant later became the Tate Modern, it felt appropriate and necessary. And some of you might have recognized the name Goddard's as the school Harriet attends in Jane Austen's *Emma*. I was reading that novel, for the umpteenth time, while writing this one and couldn't help give it a little nod. It's small, but there you go. And last but not least, Dukes hotel. This charming little hotel seems to make it into many of my books when one stops over in London because it's my favorite and it's where I stay when I "stop over." So thanks for taking a little trip there with me as well.

That's it for now. I hope you had a wonderful time in this story, and I truly thank you for spending this moment with me. Let's meet again within the pages of a book soon, and until then, all the best to you!

Katherine

ACKNOWLEDGMENTS

So many people helped create this story—and I want to thank them all—but I will unfortunately and invariable miss a few, as so many people come alongside what is often perceived to be a very singular process. So I will start with a blanket . . .

THANK YOU!!!

But to be more specific, thanks to Mason, who fully committed to an impromptu London research trip and planned not only an amazing adventure but a culinary triumph as well! Also, many thanks to Filippo Guerrini-Maraldi, Chairman of Fine Art & Specie at the Howden Group, for his time, his intricate description of the insurance market and its history, and for an amazing tour of the Lloyd's offices. All the mistakes in describing the insurance industry are my own because even I couldn't write in my notebooks fast enough to absorb all three hundred years of fascinating detail.

I also want to thank Kevan Lyon and the extraordinary team at Harper Muse—Amanda, Becky, Julee, Kerri, Margaret, Taylor, Natalie, Nekasha, Halie, Mallory, Caitlin, and the entire Sales Team—for your dedication to this story! Thank you also to Angela and Ashley for your extraordinary work on this book.

Many thanks—as always—to Elizabeth for her encouragement and for loving this story from the beginning, and Marie and Rachel for a fabulous weekend of brainstorming all the details.

And thank you to all my writer friends, as this is truly a community that supports one another—and, in this world, that is a tender and valuable thing. Bookstores and libraries too!

Thanks for so generously opening your doors to me. I have so much fun sharing my love of books with you all!

And thank you, dear readers, for trusting me with your time and your hearts once more! I hope we meet within the pages of a book again soon.

DISCUSSION QUESTIONS

1. There are several "masterpieces" in this novel. What constitutes a true masterpiece?

2. Lily comments that she and Daisy scrape rather than slide along. Discuss the complexity of family relationships and why or why not they were portrayed well within the story.

3. Perspective versus reality provides a theme throughout the book with many examples of two people seeing the same event differently. Is that an authentic representation of how we often see and experience events? What does that say about true objectivity?

4. What do you think of Daisy's comment that Lily controls rather than "does"? Is her criticism valid and is there a distinction?

5. Heinrich asks why his painting can't be a masterpiece, even Campendonk's masterpiece. What makes a work of art a "masterpiece"? Heinrich claims his work should be a Campendonk as it is just as beautiful—in many ways asserting the beauty in art should transcend the artist and attribution doesn't matter. What are your thoughts on this?

6. What do you think of Gladys's charge to her daughter that she "put her in a box"? Do you think she was harsh

or just right in pressing Lily to recognize how she has treated her family?

7. Lily sheds herself of all that is inauthentic. Can you relate to this and how do we do this in our own lives?

8. What do you think of Gladys's statement to her daughter that arrogance can be a counterfeit humility?

9. Conor and Lily both state "two things can be true simultaneously." Do you agree?

10. What do you think of Diana, who appeared to be growing weary of her life and deception, to then seemingly stand by her husband in their final scene together?

From the Publisher

GREAT BOOKS

ARE EVEN BETTER WHEN THEY'RE SHARED!

Help other readers find this one:

- Post a review at your favorite online bookseller

- Post a picture on a social media account and share why you enjoyed it

- Send a note to a friend who would also love it—or better yet, give them a copy

Thanks for reading!

LOOKING FOR MORE GREAT READS? LOOK NO FURTHER!

Illuminating minds and captivating hearts through story.

Visit us online to learn more:
harpermuse.com

Or scan the below code and sign up to receive email updates on new releases, giveaways, book deals, and more:

@harpermusebooks

Bestselling author Katherine Reay

returns with an unforgettable tale of the Cold War and a CIA
code breaker who risks everything to free her father from an
East German prison.

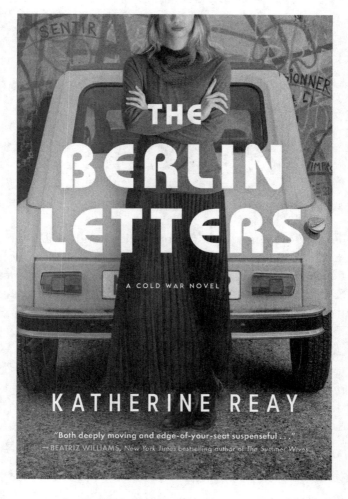

Available in print, e-book, and audio

ABOUT THE AUTHOR

Photo by Elizabeth Reay

Katherine Reay is a national bestselling and award-winning author who has enjoyed a lifelong affair with books. She publishes both fiction and nonfiction, holds a BA and MS from Northwestern University, and currently lives outside Bozeman, Montana, with her husband and three children.

You can meet her online at katherinereay.com
Facebook: @KatherineReayBooks
X: @katherine_reay
Instagram: @katherinereay